Into the Tiger's Mouth

A Novel of the China Trade

Best Wishes

D. T. Crane

DAVID T. DANA III

Into the Tiger's Mouth

A Novel of the China Trade

1857–1863

Based on unpublished letters and reminiscences

ARCHWAY
PUBLISHING

Archway Publishing books may be ordered through booksellers or by contacting:

Archway Publishing
1663 Liberty Drive
Bloomington, IN 47403
www.archwaypublishing.com
1-(888)-242-5904

The views expressed in this work are solely those of the author
and do not necessarily reflect the views of the publisher, and the
publisher hereby disclaims any responsibility for them.

This is a work of historical fiction, using real figures, well-known and not
well- known. All incidents, personal characteristics, and dialogue are products
of the author's imagination and are not to be construed as real. Where
real-life historical or other real figures appear, the situations, incidents,
and dialogues concerning those persons are entirely fictional and are not
intended to change the fictional nature of the work. In all other respects,
any resemblance to persons living or dead is entirely coincidental.

Image credit: Jonathon Spence, & Stanford University Press

Any people depicted in stock imagery provided by Thinkstock are models,
and such images are being used for illustrative purposes only.
Certain stock imagery © Thinkstock.

ISBN: 978-1-4808-0663-4 (sc)
ISBN: 978-1-4808-0665-8 (hc)
ISBN: 978-1-4808-0664-1 (e)

Library of Congress Control Number: 2014905404

Printed in the United States of America

Archway Publishing rev. date: 04/09/14

To Marcie, always at my side

Preface

THIS NOVEL IS based on my great-grandfather Richard Starr Dana's letters and reminiscences about living in Hong Kong, Shanghai, and Hankow (now Wuhan) from 1857 through 1864, during the Taiping Rebellion, the Second Opium War, and the American Civil War, while working for Russell & Co., then the largest American trading firm in China.

"It is the experiences of an American in establishing himself in business in the Far East at a time when it was far indeed," Richard's sons wrote about their father's reminiscences. "The stories that he tells give something of a different picture from the one we get from the books we read. [...] To the end of his life, we always knew him to be able to sleep at any time of day, and be broad awake like a flash at the slightest sound."

This novel is a work of fiction, although real places, events, and people are involved. Incidents and details from the letters and reminiscences are included in it. Fiction fills them out and adds details and stories. One hundred and fifty years have obscured any attempt to give to real names, their words, character, and action other than fictionally. To describe individuals, I imagined appearance, motives, and dialogue. My great-grandfather's stories are embellished fictionally. Some business and personal situations are entirely fictional, although I fancy that these happened to someone, somewhere, in the turmoil that was China at the time.

Place names as Richard Dana used in the 1850s will be recognized today, such as Peking (Beijing) and Canton (Guangzhou). Hankow is now part of Wuchang (Wuhan). Less well-known geographic names or titles are used as he spelled them or as spelled in a source or map, regardless of transliteration system (e.g., Wuchang not Wuhan, Foochow not Fuzhou). Chinese conversation rendered in English omits articles and verb tenses, because Chinese language, which depends much on context, does not use them. Chinese words are from a current tourist phrase book or are gibberish as it might have sounded to Richard.

Dollar amounts for purchases, savings, earnings, or profits are arbitrary. The Chinese used both paper and coin. Many moneys and redeemable notes were used in Asia in the 1850s—English pounds, American dollars, Spanish pesos (also called dollars) and Chinese taels, and the exchange rates among them varied greatly and frequently. US dollar figures may be considered as one US dollar approximately equivalent to twenty US dollars today in purchasing power.

Historical Note

FOREIGNERS, OR *FANQUI*—BARBARIAN devils—for centuries entered China through the Bogue or "The Tiger's Mouth," a narrows in the Pearl River to Canton. There, they did business with regulated "Hong" merchants and brought home teas, silks, and porcelains they had purchased with the silver and gold that the Chinese paid them for opium imported from Turkey and India. By 1850, Americans had built vast fortunes from "the China Trade," lived luxuriously and invested in US railroads, real estate, and mining companies.

In 1839, the Chinese had seized opium ships and tried to prevent *fanqui* from importing the drug. The British and French military forced their way to Canton and soundly defeated the Chinese defense in the "Opium Wars." The Chinese abolished the regulated Hong trading system, ceded Hong Kong Island at the mouth of the Pearl River to the British, and agreed to allow trade in five coastal cities, including Canton, Foochow, and Shanghai. The British and French continued to push diplomatically and militarily to legalize opium trading, allow permanent diplomatic representatives, and open still more ports. The Chinese Imperial government continued to resist.

In the 1850s, the imperial government also had to defend itself from internal rebellions. Originally established by Manchurian invaders two centuries previously, many ethnic Chinese opposed the Ching dynasty, foreign to them. One rebel, Hong Xuiquan, dreamt that he was Jesus's brother and, starting near Canton in the 1840s, began a movement called Heavenly Peace or "Taiping," that grew into a rebellion that spread into and down the Yangtze River valley, lost its religious roots, turned corrupt, grew strong, and burned, killed, and destroyed anything in its path. The Imperial Army, derisively called "Imps," was spread thin; government councils were divided; the Emperor was old and weak, and the local mandarins (imperial officials), governors, and Taotais (city officials) often acted independently and at cross purposes to the Manchu Emperor's government.

Characters

Ahyue: Shanghai comprador.

Apun: Richard Starr's comprador in Hankow.

John Blake: Russell & Co. clerk, Hong Kong.

Herbert Boyd: Russell & Co. tea taster, Shanghai.

Simon Brown: merchant from South Carolina.

David Clark: Russell & Co. partner, Shanghai, 1861.

Chen-Lan: Taotai for diplomacy and trade, Hankow.

Ching-ka: landowner, Hankow.

Constance Cunningham: Mrs. Edward Cunningham.

Edward Cunningham: Russell & Co. head partner, Shanghai.

Dora Delano: daughter of Warren Delano.

Warren Delano Jr.:   head of Russell & Co. China.

Harold Doyle: Russell & Co. clerk, Shanghai.

Percy Dundas: captain of Yangtze steamer *Scotland*.

Lord Elgin: English minister to the Chinese.

Fan Li-gong: Chinese farmer.

Peter S. Forbes:	head of Russell & Co., Hong Kong.
Will Forbes:	son of Peter S. Forbes.
Fookie Tom:	pirate; an English adventurer, and possibly more than one person.
Baron Gros:	French minister emissary to the Chinese.
Townsend Harris:	US consul general for Japan.
Augustus Hayes:	Richard Starr's cousin. Clerk for Olyphant & Co., Shanghai
Hop Tzu:	Richard Starr's houseboy, Shanghai.
Howqua:	Chinese merchant.
Kung Loong:	Shanghai merchant and banker.
Kuo Chi-chi:	Houseboy, Shanghai resident.
La- Li Xuicheng:	Taiping rebel army general.
Frederick Macondray:	San Francisco merchant.
Ma-Wei:	house comprador, Hankow
Sean McShefferty:	crewman on steamer *Scotland*.
Nicholson:	Captain, American man-of-war *Mississippi*.
David Olyphant:	head of American mercantile house, Olyphant & Co., Shanghai.
Boris Sauermann:	Russian lieutenant and spy.
Walter Tanner:	Augustine, Heard & Co. clerk, Shanghai.
Thomas Sloane:	Russell & Co. partner, Foochow and Shanghai.

Henrietta Starr: "Etta," Richard Starr's sister.

Juliette Starr: "Meto," Richard Starr's mother.

Richard Perkins Starr: Richard Starr's father,
                                    an international merchant.

John Powers: British marine. A Canadian.

Samuel Starr: "Uncle Samuel," Richard Perkins Starr's
                                    twin brother, Boston merchant.

William Starr: "Willy," Richard Starr's brother.
                                    US Navy officer.

Sunchong: Russell & Co. comprador, Shanghai.

Tien-Wang: Heavenly King, the Taiping rebel leader,
                                    aka Hung Hsui-chuan.

Frederick Townsend Ward: American soldier of fortune.

John E. Ward: American minister to China.

Webb: Russell & Co. clerk, Hankow.

Wen Chi-chong: Shanghai resident.

Abner Whipple: Baptist missionary, Shanghai.

Harold Wiggins: American consulate translator, Shanghai.

Wuo Sang: tea grower.

Wu Hsu: Shanghai Taotai for law and order.

Wuxi: Chinese farmer's wife.

Yang Fang: aka "Takee,"   Shanghai banker.

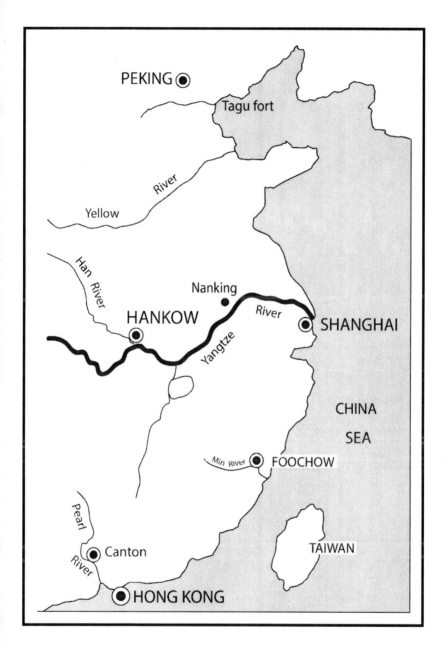

CHINA IN THE 1860s

PART 1

Hong Kong

JULY 1858 TO JULY 1859

Exaltation is the going
Of an inland soul to sea
Emily Dickinson

1

A NOTHER DAY OF closed doors and rejections. His jacket draped over a hooked finger hanging down his sweat-soaked back, Richard Starr turned away from yet another locked business. His day had begun, neat and starched, with the long trek from Fourteenth Street to Wall Street, and now, six hours later, his dark trousers wrinkled, his white shirt unbuttoned and damp, he was bone-tired from walking around block after block, climbing stairs, and getting nowhere. He shuffled back to Wall Street, passing by commercial banking, trading, importing, ship owners' and counting office signs that he had been confronting for months since graduating from Columbia College. "Not hiring," "Do not apply within," "Closed." The city's financial and investment houses were victims of the crisis of 1857, the most devastating financial panic ever to seize the country.

"Four years in mathematics and accounting to prepare for a career that no longer exists. Not hiring even a scribe," he muttered to himself and began the trudge home.

Few pedestrians walked the streets. Only an occasional carriage rolled by, the working horses glowing in the oppressive summer heat. Tops of the bare masts of docked ships poked above shuttered dockside warehouses where Richard had been reduced to seeking even menial work. He crossed an alley, stepped around a pile of offal, ignoring the familiar stable odor, and continued on sidewalks littered with papers and cigar butts. Turning a corner, he saw a crowd of men a block away dressed in the grime and tatters of poverty. They shut off the street and shouted insults at the huge granite columns of the Merchant's Exchange building. Amid the din, he made out the chant, "We. Want. Work! We. Want. Work!" He considered joining them, until he sensed that they would be angry with anyone they thought wealthy. Not thinking about his watch chain, mother of pearl buttons, or loose cravat, he just wanted home, to drink some tea and to put his feet up. "I. Want. Work," he said softly.

Just then, two horses pulling a shiny carriage thundered out of the crowd, knocked down several men, and raced down the street toward him.

"Runaway!" Richard shouted, and jumped aside. The wild-eyed horses turned sharply, flipping the carriage onto its side. A woman in silk skirts, a man in a business suit, and their driver pitched onto the street. Someone shrieked, and the carriage dragged along, dropping splinters, cushions, and a broken step, until the horses stopped. The two men rolled, sat up, dusted themselves, and then reached over to help the woman, who was bleeding from her forehead. Richard ran to them. "Are you hurt?" he asked.

"I think we're okay," the businessman said from his knees. He blotted a scrape on the woman's forehead with a handkerchief. "The crowd tried to rush us. Jumped for the carriage ... Tried to seize the horses ... They panicked."

Two policemen who had been responding to the unruly crowd took charge to help the victims. They seemed unhurt except for scratches and bruises. Richard called out, "I'll get the horses." He ran to the scraping, stomping, crying, animals that struggled in the twisted traces. Unhitching the two frantic geldings from the carriage, he took hold of their bridles, held their heads until they quieted, stroked, spoke softly, and calmed them. He led the horses around several blocks to further quiet them. When he had returned them to the carriage driver, Richard dragged himself away and turned toward home.

He walked on, somewhat numbed as usual after another futile day. The carriage accident was just another unfortunate incident that seemed to happen too often in the troubled city. No work, filthy streets, smoky air, frustrated immigrants attacking people, a worrying tension. Trudging sore-footed for twelve more blocks to his home, his sweaty clothing and limp jacket made him look like what he was—unemployed and without income.

He entered his family home's spacious foyer at 112 Fourteenth Street, relieved from traipsing the streets in the suffocating city heat, entered the parlor, dropped his jacket on a chair, kicked off his shoes, stretched out on the velvet settee, and swung his feet onto a needlepoint pillow.

"Richard, for heaven's sake! Put on your shoes. You are twenty-one. You know better." His mother strode into the room and parked herself in her favorite wingback toile chair. "Sit up and act properly. Tea is about to be served." A dark-haired maid cautiously set on the low table a silver tray set with Chinese Rose Medallion porcelain tea paraphernalia and a dish of sugar cookies.

"Will that be all, mu'm?"

"Thank you, Bridget. Please call the children."

Juliette Starr arranged teacups on their saucers and poured steaming water over tea leaves as Willie and Henrietta, called Etta, soon bustled in. The teenaged young lady pirouetted onto a soft chair and sipped delicately. Young Willie squatted Indian style on the floor, his bare knees jutting into the air beside Richard's stocking feet.

"Why do we have to drink this stuff?" Willie said, reaching for the rock sugar. "It's hot, and I don't like it."

"Behave yourself, Willie." Under their mother's stern eye for proper manners, the two children stirred, blew on the brown "stuff," and sipped in silence. They all missed Richard Starr senior, now at sea somewhere between England, Capetown, Bombay, Singapore, or Hong Kong. The family always waited anxiously for his occasional letters, afraid that he might not return at all. When he had married Juliette, he had already circumnavigated the globe three times, and continued voyaging in international trading ships soon after Richard had been born. The children did not know their father. When he did return for a few months, he seemed to Richard a tall, formal, and somewhat stern visitor from afar to be admired and respected.

Richard reported about his day and the carriage accident he'd seen. He paused then, and, using the affectionate name he gave her since he first tried to say "mother," the discouragement in his voice hard to conceal, said, "Meto, this was the last day I try to find a position in this city. I don't want to wait any longer. I'm going to Boston. Things may be better there."

"You don't have to go away," his mother said. "The financial crisis will pass. We get along well on the money your father sends."

"Yes, but father goes away for years. We have not seen him for three years, nor received a letter in six months. I'm sorry, Mother, but we have always known that he could be lost at sea, sick, or caught in some foreign war in the wrong place at any time." He saw a startle in her eyes, mixed with a disquiet that revealed the fear she long carried. "Meto, for all we know, he could be dead," and immediately wished he could take back his words.

"Richard! Say no such thing."

"I'm sorry. I'm thinking about you, Meto, dear."

Now an adult, he felt the responsibility to become the head of the family. After a pause, he said, "You and he deserve a comfortable life together. I know that father has written about retiring and coming home. Soon I will need to help support the family. My turn to earn for us all is coming."

Her eyes teared, she swallowed and did not respond.

THREE DAYS LATER, Richard sped to Boston at thirty miles-an-hour on the new high-speed train. When he had finished a round of visits to his father's large family, said all the polite greetings and compliments at his grandparents', aunts', and uncles,' he returned to Boston's waterfront to meet with his uncle Samuel, his father's twin brother.

If there was such a thing as an omen, the gray rainy day did not auger good fortune; light rain dampened the clopping of four sad-looking horses drawing a wagon of barrels, and the sailing ships docked at the Long Wharf rocked slightly and rode high in the water, revealing that their hulls were empty of cargo. Dean, Starr & Co.'s office overlooked the wharf from the second floor of a plain brick building. Its musty and wet inner stair led him directly to his uncle's office.

Uncle Samuel, tall, austere, and intimidating, a successful merchant and ship owner, immediately greeted Richard. Samuel smiled over his square jaw, and they shook hands. Richard took off his dripping overcoat and cape, hung them on a rack, and sat on a seat before a broad oak desk as Samuel parked behind it. After commenting on the wet weather, exchanging brief reports on the state of their respective families and the latest letter Samuel had received from his father from Singapore, Richard related his efforts to find work in a financial house.

"Uncle, is there hope for work in Boston?"

"These are difficult times," Uncle Samuel said.

"I know. New York had nothing, so I have come here. By any chance, does your firm have some work for me?"

"What kind of work are you looking for?"

"I feel prepared as much as Columbia College can make me for a starting position in finance. I know that experience is necessary. I want to learn money, banking, trading, accounting. Skills I will need to support our family and then my own one day."

Richard did not expect the positive answer he wanted, but even so, his heart sank when Uncle Samuel said, "I'm very sorry. We have no need for another person here."

"Do you have any suggestions or advice?"

"As far as I know, other houses are not hiring either. Some have closed entirely. Why not wait until the economy improves? Your father does nicely for you all."

"Yes, but we haven't heard from him in six months. She won't admit it, but mother is worried. Have you heard from father?"

"He has not written me for about that long." Samuel frowned and looked out the window at the rain. He stared at the grayness for a few moments. "You may be right not waiting much longer to concern yourself with finding a trade."

Uncle Samuel knew the risks involved in the import-export business, and owned several cargo ships. His insurance business had handled many shipwrecks. Did Uncle Samuel know something about father that he was afraid to reveal? "I mean," said Samuel, "that I have heard that he wants to retire when he returns from this latest voyage."

"Lost or ready to retire," Richard said, "I have to keep up the family income."

Outside, the window, masts and spars, bare of sails, above empty hulls, poked the gray sky. The horse-drawn wagon, now emptied of its barrels, slowly rolled along the wet wharf, no one to splash.

Richard waited while his uncle seemed lost in thought. When the awkward silence had almost prompted Richard to try to change the subject, Samuel explained difficulties the import-export and trading businesses endured in both good and bad times. Richard shifted in his chair. Was his uncle trying to discourage him from seeking to make a living the same way he and Father had? He tried to listen and not interrupt or argue. Finally, Samuel lifted his piercing eyes over wire-rim glasses and asked, "Would you consider working overseas … in China?"

The idea immediately excited him. He had not thought that possible without more experience. Richard quizzed Uncle Samuel about what sort of work might be available in China. Hong Kong, the British colony, would probably be the location, Samuel said, the work strictly clerical to start with. "Beyond that, you must make your own opportunities," Uncle Sam said.

AFTER AN UNSUCCESSFUL week of knocking on doors in Boston and nearby Salem, Richard returned to New York. He wanted to be closer to home, but the idea of a position in China would not go away. He knew much about China already.

"Dig a hole straight down far enough and you will come out in China," Meto had once explained to her oldest son. She had read him stories about Tin-Tin, a mischievous yellow-skinned boy with slits for eyes and a pigtail, who lived on a houseboat called a sampan on a great river called Yangtze, where he caught fish and tended a family of ducks. Picture books and travelers' writings about Chinese emperors and armies, square-bowed boats with eyes on them, and men wearing gowns filled the Starr's library. Jade animals, elaborate jewelry, bronze vases, and polished furniture decorated his home. He ate on brilliant blue-and-white or jade-green porcelain and silver dinnerware that his father had sent home. The family drank tea steeped in ornate silver pots made to order by Chinese artists, all luxuries of his father's work in the Orient.

Father had first gone to sea when he was twenty years old. On his return visits, when he spent a few months with his family, he had told tales about adventures in China, most recently, negotiating with the amazing Howqua, said to be the richest man in the world, and, during the British war over opium trading, he advised the British plenipotentiary, Lord Elgin, on the Chinese character.

"The Chinese can be scoundrels," he had told his family, "but they are honest in their own way. Once they give their word, they will honor it." "Celestials," as he called them, did not like foreigners but were peacefully subservient to them.

The more Richard thought about it, the more excited he got about the possibility of going to China. The idea of living and working in the exotic place among unusual people seized his waking and dreaming thoughts. The adventure of it appealed.

Meto argued persistently against his going. "Richard, do you really know what you're getting into?" She cited the horrors of a heathen land, the strange foods, the dangers of ocean travel, and even the friends and parties and countryside that he would miss. He thought he knew what he would be getting into. He resisted her entreaties for a while and then sat down and wrote Uncle Samuel:

"I have thought about your suggestion that I might work in China. The idea of such an opportunity does interest me. I would be most grateful if you could see what might be available for me there. I will consider it a most interesting adventure and a perfect opportunity to prepare myself to help the family now and when Father retires."

Over the course of the next months, Uncle Samuel helped Richard obtain a clerkship with Russell & Co., the largest American trading house in China. As soon as Sam Starr's clipper ship *Alfred Hill* could be loaded with Maine lumber, Massachusetts hardware, New England furniture, and ship's stores, Richard would sail off to the exotic, ancient, and rich land where he would begin his future.

He would miss "The Pines," the family farm he loved, nestled among the idyllic Berkshire Hills in Massachusetts where he galloped his horses in the woods and helped with the animals. Richard's slight frame belied health and strength developed riding horseback, practicing gymnastics, boxing and rowing on the East River. Certainly he would miss his "dears," as he called all his female friends—the buxom, striking Sarah, funny and smart Mary, and the delightful dancer Dolly, but he would especially miss Annie Wiley, her smiles and laughter, her delightful dancing, and their carriage and horseback rides.

Shortly before he was to leave, he sat with Annie on a bench in a grassy square around which gaslights glowed and fireflies flitted in winter dusk. Annie let her hand slide over to his. "Soon you will be going to China. So far away. You will be gone for so long."

"I'll miss you, my dear."

She stared into the city. "Why do you have to go at all?"

"You know why. My father has been trading in Asia for years. It will be a great adventure. I'll see and bring back fascinating things. Father has supported mother, Etta and Willie and me. Now it's my turn."

"But he's away a lot ..." She stopped, closed her eyes, and dropped her head onto his shoulder.

"I am excited for the adventure of it. Away from home. A frontier, like crossing the Great Lakes and hunting quail in Michigan. New and different sights, people, businesses."

She was silent for a while, then: "Richard, let's get married now."

He shook his head as if to clear it out. The thought of marrying Annie had never occurred to him. Once they had speculated in fun what it might be like together, but they never talked seriously about it. Annie was fun, he liked her company, and her family was first-rate, but ... well, she was just not for him—yet.

He was not ready to make that choice. Besides, he had a business to establish first so he could support a wife. "Not now. I couldn't support you properly."

She sat up. He squeezed her hand as he watched disappointment fall across her cheeks. Her lips fluttered, fighting a tear. "I'm sorry. I should not have said such a thing. I was foolish." He took her hand hoping to ease her embarrassment. Her infectious nervous giggle played with a smile, and they both laughed. "I'll wait for you."

"When I come back, we'll see."

While Uncle Samuel drummed up cargo and passengers for the *Alfred Hill*, Richard read China travelogues and helped on the family farm in Lenox, rowed on Lake Mackinac, hunted small game, and rode and drove his favorite horse, Toodla, as much as he could. When in the city, he rowed the East River, rode horses, and played and danced with his friends. In the days before departing, he walked and talked with Annie, often happily, often sadly, holding hands and embracing when they could get away with it. He had no doubt that he would prosper abroad.

NEARLY A YEAR had passed since his meeting with Uncle Sam the previous summer. Richard had packed clothes for the voyage and, for business, classic and mathematic books to read, and other necessary belongings. In mid-June, aunts and uncles and cousins gathered on Boston's India Wharf to see Richard off. Meto tried to hide tears while she, Willie, and Etta watched him board the steam shuttle to the *Alfred Hill*, bound for China. "Write often," she said, voice cracking, moisture trickling down her white cheeks. After a few moments, she added, "God bless you and help you."

"In a year or two I will return with treasure enough to sustain us all," he promised.

2

S EVEN WEEKS OUT of Boston, having overcome bouts of retch-ing bile and all of his meals overboard, having endured the monotonous and seemingly endless stillness of the doldrums, and having felt the thrill of snapping sails and rushing breezes across the Atlantic, Richard Starr prepared for a hurricane.

Inside the passenger cabin below the first deck, he locked his loose books, toiletries, and clothing into his trunk, secured his bunk, and then ventured to the main deck to watch the darkening sky while the little *Alfred Hill* rocked in the rising sea. Rocking quickly became lurching, lurching became pitching and yawing, and Richard clung to the rail. Below deck, goats and chickens fidgeted, bleated, and clucked, and the cargo began to moan and shift. Deckhands scrambled to batten spare spars, hatches, and lines. Two sailors high in the rigging struggled to set the ship before the coming onslaught. Soon, the roiling sea became re-lentless pounding of uncontrolled, mountainous waves. The sky released a thunderous downpour, stinging like liquid spears driven by explosive blasts and flashes, mixing with salt sprays. The bosun lashed the ship's wheel he could no longer hold. A lightning bolt lit the tumult for an instant, then darkness swallowed all again until the next electric explosion. The ship climbed, seemed to tip backwards, then fell forward and walloped hard, an enormous belly flop. Splash hit Richard full-on. A deckhand bellowed, "Bloody 'ell! Git inside!"

Grabbing at anything he could hold, Richard lurched across the sloping deck toward the gangway that led below. The ship bucked; Richard toppled, bounced off the deck hatch wall, reached for a handle, wobbled back, fought forward again, found a grip, and slipped off. Rigging roared and whistled; the lone topsail trembled and clung to life. Sea tugged at his ankles. He groped for a firm hold somewhere, stretching in vain to reach the closed gangway.

Suddenly, the cry, "Man overboard!"

"Starboard ... it's Rodriguez."

Someone threw a barrel overboard in vain hope that the poor Portuguese could find it. It was impossible to jump into the maelstrom to help him. Deckhands tore at lashings to loose a rescue launch, but the violent lurching forced them off balance. Rodriguez could not be heard.

"He don't swim!" Too rough, too dark, too late for rescue. Rodriguez was gone. The little clipper bucked and yawed for its life. The exhausted crew worked to ride it out.

The hull lifted and dropped with a stomach-churning whomp. Richard, unable to climb to the gangway, unable to open the door against the wind, was swept off his feet and spun across the deck until he slid hard into a corner between bulkhead and bulwark. Pain stabbed his leg and ankle. His elbows locked onto jammed belaying pins. He clutched his knees to his chest. A foam-topped black mound overhead crested over him to pound again.

"God help me."

The ship shuddered, lurched, then settled momentarily to brace for the next thunderous wave to pound the deck. Richard prayed and hoped against hope.

"Meto, Meto, I'll be all right," he said, trying to convince himself.

Eyes closed, Richard hung on.

HOURS LATER, HE removed his soaked clothes and flopped onto his bunk. Shaken deeply, not only by the sea but by the sudden death of the seaman, Richard looked at the overhead, "No good-bye ... just gone." Death at sea happened, he knew that. Meto had reminded him. But he had never been so close to death, himself. Had never seen a person die. Never so suddenly. Never been near death at all. Richard hoped he'd never have to see a dead body.

Richard sat up on the rumpled bedcovers and rubbed his eyes. He stood for a moment, stepped to his sea chest, and dragged it to its proper place in the forward corner. He squared up the chest, then dropped back onto the bunk, his energy spent. Water lapped against the ship, a soothing sound that did not soothe. He closed his eyes and thought of death and home.

He heard his mother as if she was in the cabin. "You do not know what you are getting into," she had said. Reality was, he now knew, that he had not known what he was getting into.

Later Richard, still unsettled by the death, joined the seven other passengers and the crew at a service for the drowned sailor. Fellow passenger Simon Brown, a merchant and Charleston plantation owner's son, stood next to Richard while the crew gathered.

"Why're we goin' to this?" Brown said. "We didn't know him. Y'all can't fret when a field nigger drops dead. Just happens."

Richard had heard such remarks from Brown before and had passed them off as the familiar southern political attitude toward slavery. This time, he was appalled by Brown's casual disregard for human death. He did not respond. He looked sharply at Brown, then averted his eyes.

Captain Nagel addressed his tired sailors. "Mourn poor Rodriguez's death, praise those who tried to help him, and let us pray for his soul. The waters give and they take away. Give thanks to a merciful God who saved the ship."

The crew sang:

"Eternal Father, strong to save,

Whose arm doth bind the restless wave,

O hear us when we cry to thee,

For those in peril on the sea."

"Amen," said the captain, and the crew murmured, "Amen."

The crew went back to work, the passengers returned to cabins, and Richard dug out one of the books that he loved from his classical studies and, for encouragement, read about the seagoing travails of Odysseus.

EVERY DAY THE *Alfred Hill*'s officers shouted orders as Yankees, Scandinavians, Portuguese, and freed slaves scrambled over the wet deck and the rigging to keep the clipper ship sailing as fast as possible. They cleaned and repaired equipment and occasionally roughed each other up. To pass the time, the passengers read, played checkers and backgammon, looked for sharks, whales, albatross, and flying fish. Richard learned about life at sea by observing the sailors, and the ship's carpenter taught him nautical terms, knots, woodworking, and yarns of the sea, albeit with a Swedish accent that made him sound as if he had a hot potato in his mouth. Although Richard shaved weekly, he let his hair grow long, and climbed the rigging to exercise his slight and muscular body, which had been toned on rowing, Indian clubs, and boxing. After the storm, he came to enjoy the relaxed shipboard life and motions of the sea. The *Alfred Hill* rounded the Cape of Good Hope and sailed the Indian Ocean for a month with no land in sight.

Two and one-half months from Boston, the cliffs of Java Head at the entrance to the Java-Sumatra straits glowed in a glorious

red sunset. Passengers came out on deck to view through the
equatorial heat waves the distant volcanic peaks of Poeboewetan,
Krakatoa and Rakatau, which thrust up from rain forests.

"This is the perfection of sailing," Richard remarked to
Brown.

The little clipper came to rest off the sloping hills at Anjer
where a dirty Chinese junk and an English schooner lay anchored.
The crew launched the longboat and hove for shore to collect
fresh water from a stream spilling from the jungle. Soon, darkness
surrounded the weary little clipper.

After a usual dinner on ships' stores, Richard returned to his
cabin, rinsed his wind and sun tanned face, and shook out his
thick black shoulder-length hair. A tan, shaggy stranger looked
back at him from the mirror. Wrinkled clothing made him look
as if he had lost weight. Would anyone at home recognize this
dark, weathered, long-haired stranger now?

As he settled in for the night, something inside tied a knot
in his stomach. His eyes would not shut against reality. Not only
did he have no idea what he was going toward, but he had sailed
nearly half-way around the world to get there. His father had told
tales about China's isolated emperor who thought the world owed
him tribute, about stubborn negotiators, and about resistance to
foreigners and heathen morals. What lay ahead for a young man
from polite New York society and peaceful New England hills?
What would his work be? Where would he find friends? In another month he would reach the exotic land of his imagination.

He got up, opened his trunk, and took out the leather-bound
Bible that Meto had given him as a parting gift. Inside the front
cover his mother had neatly written:

*"My Dearly beloved son Richard, When you leave your home for
a strange land, will you take this precious volume with you—and
when you read, consider it a token of love between us and feel as*

if your mother's hand was on your head, praying for a blessing on her son—with the most tender affection."

The ship rocked softly in this remote anchorage a world away from home. He felt very, very lonely.

3

Farther away, while Richard was crossing the Indian Ocean on his way to Anjer, two imperial junks confronted an anchored British ship near the Tiger's Mouth, the Pearl River's gateway to China near Canton. Soldiers boarded the ship, seized, bound, and carried away its entire crew. The British sailors were never seen again. Soon after, Chinese authorities jailed a French missionary for trespassing, then caged, beheaded, and dismembered him. Local British military commanders were incensed, but the diplomats who were negotiating treaty revisions had prohibited any retaliatory attack on the city. Instead of firing on Canton, a line of four British and French gunships blocked the Pearl River to deny Canton all commercial trade.

The men aboard a small fishing sampan could see the four blockading ships in the distance. "Easy now. Head to port toward that cliff," Fookie Tom ordered his crew in perfect Chinese. Fookie Tom was a pirate, a British adventurer whose criminal money-making adventures ensured a legendary reputation. In a clandestine meeting in Hong Kong, an experienced and tough trader, American Peter S. Forbes, partner in the Russell & Co. trading firm, had hired the heavily bearded adventurer to carry Forbes's cargo around the British and French blockade to sell it in Canton. Forbes knew he was dealing with a crook, but the agreement was simple. Tom would receive a fee to provide men and boat to take Forbes and a clerk and their cargo safely around the blockade. Forbes had paid half the fee, the other half to be paid when they successfully returned. If Fookie Tom and his crew confronted firearms, Tom would receive a bonus. This satisfied Forbes, for there was no other way to get opium into Canton and the prospective profit was worth the cost. Fookie Tom's eyes crinkled at the corners when he fancied he had something up his soiled sleeve.

The evening Fookie Tom turned into the river's islands and swamps for a route around the distant blockade, he had not dressed as foreigners thought a pirate would dress. Instead, he was a fisherman, clean-shaven except for a small pointed chin beard in the Chinese fashion.

His four Chinese rowers left the Pearl River and rowed into the maze of islands that would hide them. Through the dusk, Peter S. Forbes and a Russell & Co. clerk, John Blake, could see the tops of the four distant ships anchored in the river.

On the sampan's deck, a pile of fishnets had been heaped on top of a tarpaulin covering a hatch to keep water from seeping below the deck. Dead and stinking fish folded into the net reinforced the masquerade that this was a dirty fishing boat, while in the hold lay hidden five cartons of opium worth a small fortune.

Facing backward, unable to see where they were going, Tom's men pulled the oars directly toward piled, ragged rocks. Forbes saw nothing but land ahead. "You'd better know what the devil you're doing," he said to Fookie Tom.

"You paid half of my price to get this far," Tom said. "I'll get you to Canton, then you 'better know' enough to pay the total … or I'll leave you in a Chinese jail for importing contraband."

Forbes had agreed that he would pay the second half once the opium had been delivered and they returned safely from Canton. They had to trust each other but did not.

"You'll pay my bonus, too, if I have to fight off any pirates. Mark my words."

Tom directed the rowers through a narrows between small islands that Forbes had not discerned until they entered it. Two other crewmen looked into the night, scanning the waters for other boats and low rocks. The Americans had pistols in their belts, and a shotgun lay nearby. Quietly, the sampan snuck along. The warships' masts could not be seen in the dark. As they pulled parallel to the blockade, Tom whispered sharply and pointed at a sampan approaching from a break in the rocks.

Tom had warned the Americans that if anyone approached, they were to hide, keep quiet, and follow his commands without question. If the Americans were seen, the ruse was lost. "Quickly. Under the nets, and be quiet."

Forbes and Blake lay knees to chests, pistols in hand. They wriggled and shifted for enough comfort to lay still. Stale fish stink pervaded every breath.

Tom inspected the unusually high pile of nets. "Shut up. Don't move."

He raised a small banner with Chinese characters. The sampan continued toward them and pulled alongside. The hidden Americans dared not peek at what was happening. They heard Chinese shouting, Tom's guttural protests in Chinese, and angry squawks from all sides speaking at once. Then Forbes felt the boat suddenly tilt. Someone had jumped aboard. Tom shouted. Something poked at the nets, jabbing into Blake's ribs. Blake involuntarily jerked his legs at the pain. The nets were pulled away.

Forbes stared a dark-skinned, fire-eyed robber in the face. He fired his revolver at the robber holding the tarpaulin, just as Tom's crewman tackled the man.

The shot missed, and the robber fell back onto the deck. Another crewman swung an oar at the next robber, and when he ducked, pushed the oar and shoved him overboard. The tackled robber started to rise. Fookie Tom drew a saber, turned the blade flat, and spanked the tackled boarder in the buttocks, sending him back to his boat. Blake shot at a third man. Blood gushed from the man's neck as he fell overboard to thrash with the other already in the water. The boats drifted apart, and the two men in the water swam to the robber's boat. One pulled himself aboard, the other fell back into his own blood, too weak to swim any more. The robbers rowed away, leaving him struggling in the water.

Forbes and Blake climbed out from under the remaining nets, stretched, and gulped fresh air. Tom and the crew laughed. "You guys stink!" Tom said, grinning, and his eyes brightened with a twinkle.

"Not funny," said Forbes. Blake picked a fish fin off his sleeve.

"Now sit and shut up. Those stupid shots will draw a patrol."

The rowers worked quickly to find a cove or rocks to hide the sampan. Forbes noticed the wounded robber struggling in the bloody water as they moved away. "Stop," he cried. "We have to go back. He needs help."

"He's no good to us now," Tom said. "We need to avoid patrols."

They rowed on, and the robber sank in their wake.

"Now you owe me the bonus for fighting off robbers," Fookie Tom said, his eyes crinkling.

In half an hour, a steam patrol boat flying the Union Jack caught up to them. Tom turned to Forbes. "This is your game now. You get rid of the limey."

This time there was no hope of hiding the presence of white men. A uniformed British officer hailed the boat. "Ahoy, sampan. State your business."

Forbes said, "I am an American. Going to Canton to pick up a load of tea." It was obvious that the Americans were trying to smuggle contraband past the blockade while disguised as a Chinese fishing boat. Two British sailors and an officer boarded the sampan, seized Forbes and Blake, and escorted them back to the pilot boat, where the officer presented them to the captain. Captain William Hughes watched a grinning Tom and his crewman acting as if they were mending a net.

Fookie Tom had brought Hughes another customer. In his cabin, Hughes said to the two Americans, "You want to get to Canton. It's my duty to stop you." Looking most official, he waited. Forbes did not react. After a moment staring at each other, Hughes said, "There must be some way we can get around this sticky wicket. What do you suppose, Mr. Forbes?"

Forbes took the hint. "Do we owe this blockade a fee?"

"A true blockade will not allow a fee. You know that, sir."

"I am prepared to pay a fee of up to one hundred US dollars."

"There is no fee, as I advised. However, if there were one, it would be at least two hundred US dollars."

Forbes drew coins from his pocket and counted them out.

Hughes pocketed the money, then looked straight at Forbes and said, "You may go on to Canton. Bon voyage."

He summoned an officer and slipped him two coins, and the officer ushered the Americans back to Tom's sampan, where he passed the coins to Tom. When the Americans were aboard, and the sampan was moving away, Tom waved to Captain Hughes. The Americans and their opium were on their way to Canton.

When they had unloaded the opium and begun their way back to Hong Kong, Forbes said to Blake, "We had best not say anything to anyone about this sorry affair when we get back to Russell."

"Good God in heaven," Blake said. "What do we say we did for three days? We broke the law, got cheated by a pirate, shot off guns at robbers, and were duped by phony threats. We abandoned a drowning man, lied to an official, paid a bribe, and we end up stinking like old fish. Is that what it takes to make money in this God-forsaken place?"

4

A BRILLIANT SUN ANNOUNCED a clear day in the Java Straits. The distant volcanoes brightened, a cool breeze swept the ship, and the jungle began to warm. Simon Brown joined Richard at the rail. "We're about to enter the South China Sea," Richard said.

Brown's uncut rusty mane tied into a ponytail made him look like an unkempt Thomas Jefferson. The Carolina plantation owner's first son assumed an arrogant smile. "Y'all think we'll be able to whup up some pirates?"

Father had said once that the nearby islands and bays harbored pirates. "Not likely," Richard said.

"Look. Yonder." Brown pointed to a dugout log proa filled with dark-skinned natives. It slid into view from around a point of land. Seated between its upturned bow and sternposts, Malay natives pulled paddles in unison as the proa sliced through the quiet water, right behind it another one appeared. Each stroke heaved the proa forward with a grunt that echoed over the water. As the Malays neared the anchored *Alfred Hill*, buxom women sitting among stacks and baskets of local produce caught the stares of Richard, Brown and the ship's crew.

The clipper's crew rigged lifts and pulleys from the main and forward yards. The proas banged into the clipper's hull, and the paddles clattered onto each other. Rope ladders and cargo nets from the yards dropped over the sides. Hardened seamen whistled and flirted while the bare-breasted women bent over baskets of produce, waved, laughed, and teased them. The passengers watched the proceedings. Bananas, yams, oranges, limes, mangoes, coconuts, chickens, fish, and turtles packed the proas. Soon fruit baskets and chicken-filled cages swung up and onto the deck, forcing those at the rails to make way. Richard stepped back and had to stop staring at the bare breasts.

Dark-skinned men began climbing up and onto the ship. Citrus and fruit fragrances relieved native odors of fish and sweaty bodies. Richard teased his Carolina cabin mate: "Simon, better be careful. They can't resist stealing. Father says it's often better to let them steal what they will."

A savage in a brass-buttoned Portuguese captain's jacket dangling with beads and feathers grabbed the rail and pulled himself onto the deck with a shout.

"Bet he stole that jacket," said Brown.

For the next hour or so more proas came alongside, and more supplies and Malaysian men came aboard. The half-naked rogues soon squeezed among the crowd on deck, their narrow eyes, squinting from cigarette smoke, appeared cunning and treacherous to Richard. These savages could easily turn into pirates if they felt strong enough, he thought. The tease of Simon Brown about thieves might come true.

The Malays shoved fruits and fish at sailors and passengers, shouting, "One dolla', one dolla'," poking and fingering the foreigners the while. Brown cringed when a black finger poked his chest.

"Watch what you're doin', nigger." The redhead's eyes darted about as if he had stumbled into a crowd of slaves. "I'm going below," he said to Richard. "I don't like this." Brown turned his back on a swarthy Malay with black teeth who waved a handful of eels at him, and strutted away. "Too many niggers," he said.

Richard remained on deck, stifling an aversion to dark skin and body odor. He hitched up his shoulders. He had come to learn to trade—it was time to buy something.

The Malay price for everything was a single Mexican peso, a Spanish dollar. He offered two pennies for a bunch of green bananas. A young Malay holding a fruit basket under his arm shook his head; Richard's fingers pointed and counted, and the two men haggled until Richard's first experience in oriental bargaining had yielded twenty small bananas for five cents. Even though Meto had warned that it would not be easy to make money in China, he mentally congratulated himself at having gotten a bargain. If he made more bargains like that, he'd do fine in China, Richard boasted to himself, only half-seriously.

Now that he was closer to China, Richard's thoughts turned more often to imagining what China would be like. The colorful clothes the citizens wore, the unique architecture, and the tranquil country scenes returned to his head again and again. He imagined himself bargaining with businessmen for tea and beautiful porcelains and silks.

By the end of the day, everything edible from the Malays had disappeared into the stores of the *Alfred Hill*'s crew, cook, and passengers. When the natives had quit the anchorage, the captain mustered all hands to get under way. The anchor was raised, the sails filled, and the ship moved through the strait into the Java Sea and up the South China Sea.

ONE HUNDRED AND five days out of Boston, a light breeze blew the *Alfred Hill* into the anchorage on the western side of Hong Kong Island, well sheltered from the sea with access to the Pearl River. A ridge of high, rocky, mountains rose directly from the shore; low clouds hid the summits. Treeless tan cliffs and ragged verdure covered the foothills, an unsettling view to a young man raised among purple rolling hills and maple forests in Massachusetts. Tile roofs and white walls of several small mansions colored the lower foothills. Factories, godowns, and offices lined the flat shore. Union Jacks flapping from poles and eaves proclaimed that this island was a British colony. In the Chinese quarter in the distance, separated from the city by sand and rocks, smoky wisps rose from low wooden structures.

Two extreme clippers, black and sleek, floated at anchor to Richard's right, each unloading cargo onto steam and oared shuttles. Redcoat marines scrambled to the tops of a nearby thirty-gun British man-of-war to his left, and ahead of him a battered British gunship sailed slowly into the bay, its crew cleaning its broadside guns, painting damaged wood, and working high on the yards repairing the rigging. Smoke from a small steam tender made Richard blink as it putted by. In the near distance, a red-sailed junk labored in the soft breeze, and its painted eye surveyed the foreign merchant and military fleets.

The *Alfred Hill*'s cutter left Richard standing next to his personal luggage on the stone-paved wharf clad in shirtsleeves, sweat dripping down his forehead, thick hair bound in the back, hands on hips, taking in his new residence. Set back from the wharf rose a row of white and gray warehouses and office buildings, some with columns, the whole appearing like a London financial district and distinctly not Chinese.

Alfred Hill passengers greeted men who had come to meet them. Along the waterfront a single shirtless Chinese servant wearing a broad flat hat pulled a rickshaw carrying an overweight English merchant puffing a cigar and dropping ash. European men in black suits and top hats talked in front of a warehouse, and a squad of British soldiers marched to a soft rhythmic cadence.

Their red coat uniforms reminded Richard of paintings of British soldiers shooting Boston patriots. No one from Russell & Co. met him.

"Good luck," Richard said to Brown after a missionary had greeted his fellow passenger. "Keep in touch, Simon. I'll be at the firm."

"Good luck to y'all, too," Brown said as he walked away.

Richard had instructed the ship's purser to send his trunks to Russell & Co., and he strode toward an American flag on a featureless colonnaded building several blocks away. He entered to find a slim individual about his age behind a simple table in a small anteroom decorated only with a single print of a clipper ship in full sail. A pile of papers occupied one corner of the table, a top hat another. The fellow stopped his writing, frowned, and looked up. He smiled as if delighted to have an excuse to stop working but effected annoyance at the interruption.

"Where might I find someone from Russell and Company?" Richard asked the seated American.

"I'm someone."

Richard introduced himself and said that he was to work as a clerk and had just arrived.

"Oh, yes. I'm Will Forbes of Boston. Father has been expecting you." He stood up from the table.

Will was six inches taller and looked down at Richard over a thin nose, beneath which were the beginnings of a mustache. He took a black suit jacket from the back of his chair, put it on, and led Richard upstairs to a door labeled "Peter S. Forbes," knocked, and entered.

A high collar ringed with a black cravat propped up Peter S. Forbes's rigid head as he concentrated on papers on the desk before him. A gray mustache drooped from the stiff man's long straight nose, turning his small mouth down with it.

"Finally," he said still looking at his papers. Forbes had been a Russell & Co. partner for over a decade. Uncle Samuel had said that Forbes's extensive experience in the China trade enabled him to rule Russell & Co. with strict discipline and little warmth.

Standing before this person whom he wanted to impress, Richard became blatantly aware that he was unwashed, wrinkled, and shaggy. He endured an awkward silence while Forbes finished his reading. In time, Forbes looked up from the papers, remained seated at his elaborately carved teak desk and, in an impatient tone, said, "You have two days to settle in and will begin work on the third day."

The partner who would be Richard's boss and trainer made no effort at a welcome or a smile. Richard, concerned at the rude manner in which he was being greeted, handed Samuel Starr's letter to Forbes. "Pleased to be here, sir."

Will stood at attention and said nothing. Forbes set the letter aside.

"Show him to his room and work station," the senior Forbes said to Will. He returned to the papers before him.

"Thank you, sir," said Richard.

He turned and left the office. Had living with the British turned this American into a crusty, somber man? Richard understood that the senior partner and supreme head of the house did not need to know a starting clerk personally, nor would he have much to do with his everyday work, but he did expect better welcome after Uncle Samuel's introduction.

Will and Richard set out through the city in a two-horse carriage to tour the firm's facilities. Several sleek bay geldings mounted by redcoat officers trotted past them.

"Cocky bastards," Will said. "Soldiers think they own the road."

They're English; they do, Richard thought.

The carriage pulled up a low hill to a two-story, whitewashed edifice covered with ivy overlooking the harbor. Ionic columns supported its second-floor piazza. A single room on the second floor, furnished only with a bed, an American-made walnut armoire like one at home, washstand, and bathtub made up his future home. He would have to get a table to work on, a chair, and a carpet.

A little Chinese servant, his braided queue falling halfway down his back and over his white housecoat, quietly opened Richard's luggage and began to paw through it.

"The boy will do anything you want, Rich," Will said.

"Please don't call me Rich. I prefer Richard. I'm not rich yet." Will did not react to the pun. Richard asked, "Does the boy understand English?"

"Some do, some don't." Will advised. "You have to use Chinese English." Will turned to the boy. In the voice of a drill sergeant, he ordered: "Boy. No takee clothes." The boy snapped his hand away from the open trunk. "Bringee tea to lounge. Chop-chop." The boy let the trunk lid drop and padded silently away.

The two clerks descended to a finely paneled redwood lounge where brown leather armchairs reserved for the partners created a gentlemanly elegance. Windsor chairs around a small table under a yellow paper lantern hung with red tassels seated Will and Richard.

Richard sipped his tea.

"Don't worry about money, Rich," Will said, slouched in his chair. "The house will pay for almost everything. For anything you want. They advance the money. It makes getting on quite easy."

"Please, my name is Richard. Please do not call me Rich."

"Righto."

Richard's first meal on solid land featured familiar roast beef, roast potatoes, fruits and vegetables of all kinds, fresh breads and biscuits—certainly not the rice and eels that Meto had predicted. It all washed down with appropriate red or white wine for each course until the meal ended with brandy and cigars. Richard tried not to overeat or overdrink on this first meal and failed miserably.

When the clerks had drained the brandy bottle, Richard yawned a bit too much to be considered polite. Rather than follow several clerks into the billiard room for a game, he said, "I'm ready for bed. I'll see you all tomorrow. Thanks, Will, for showing me around."

While Richard, still rocking with the ship's motion on his first night on land, tried to sleep, he relived Peter S. Forbes's rude welcome and Will's cocky attitude. A new employee arriving at an unexpected time had no right to expect cheers and welcome banners. The food and drink certainly satisfied him more than he expected, and the people he had just met were polite, even if their leader was not. He'd do as they expected: work hard to learn, and get to know them all better.

The next day, he purchased a table and chair for his room from an English furniture store, found the Chinese barber who cut and trimmed his shipboard tangles, met Russells, other employees who liked to be interrupted, and in the evening, wrote a letter to Meto to tell her that he had arrived and that all was well. He described his voyage, his room, and the food he had been eating, and even told her his weight. That night he slept an exhausted sleep.

The houseboy woke him at seven and brought tea and toast while he dressed. After a lengthy breakfast allowing choices among fish, potatoes, eggs, and fruit, Richard started to walk to the waterfront office where he planned to meet Will to begin his first assignments.

"Rich. Come here," Will called from a stand of rickshaws lined up outside the house like hansom cabs at a train station. "The partners want us to use the rides. To show our status to the limeys."

Being carried less than a mile by a servant did not impress Richard as a symbol of status. "Thanks. I'd rather walk. See you there."

"Don't let a partner see you."

Richard decided not to argue, climbed into a one-man rickshaw under a sun umbrella behind a thin Chinese boy in dirty white coat who pulled and jiggled him down the hill.

Each day, Richard spent hours as a new clerk, bent over a table, pen in hand, repeatedly dipping in ink, sprinkling and blowing blotting-sand for a boy to sweep up later. For each transaction, he wrote in longhand three copies of bills of lading, invoices, forms, or merchants' notes, checking carefully against originals. As he did so, he read about exports such as tea and silk, imports such as cotton, furniture and iron wares, and their prices and quantities. He questioned specialists and studied the papers as hard as he had studied Latin translations, and in that way steadily learned the firm's business.

Russell & Co. earned its money by finding and arranging exports and imports brokered and sold for the accounts of others, a business model deemed more profitable and less risky for the partners than buying goods to resell. They allowed employees, but not other partners, to speculate on such ventures and take on the currency exchange, markup, and credit risks. Richard earned a monthly salary that did not leave enough to try such speculations.

When Sunday came at the end of his first week of work, Richard attended the Anglican Church service in a staid stone edifice, its interior dimmed by stained glass in its windows, reminding him of the Anglican church in Lenox, a familiar setting.

Christianity in his family had been treated as automatic and natural. His grandfather had often preached at the Methodist church in Boston, giving soaring lectures on the dangers of sin and the torments of hell. That was all overdone, but without worrying much about the torments, Richard did believe that God had defined sin—thou shall not kill, lie, steal, commit adultery, and covet. At church he routinely asked with everyone else for forgiveness for sins he had never committed.

As he left the Anglican church that first day, Richard noticed that only nine ladies had worshipped among over one hundred men.

"Where are all the women?" he asked John Blake, a fellow clerk from Boston with a ready smile and playful nature.

"We bachelors are out of luck looking for an American girl," said Blake. "Or a pretty English wife, for that matter. You can look but not touch every Monday and Thursday when the married society ladies come out on the parade grounds to watch the military band play."

"Not much to look at, from what I saw in church."

"I've gone to Brit society dance parties," Blake said. "More often than not the single men dance with each other. If you want, you could dance with somebody's wife, at least."

Richard already missed Annie and her great grin, her giggles, and her good cheer. He recalled a shy fifteen-year-old boy who had sat along a wall in Miss Southerd's school for dance whispering rude jokes to his pimple-faced neighbors about the lineup of timid girls on the opposite wall. The grey-haired matron took the boy's hand and marched him across the dance floor to introduce him to a frightened Annie Wiley. After this "proper" introduction, Richard had found that he loved girls' company, albeit chaperoned by a critical and suspicious adult. Annie, Mary, Sarah, and Elizabeth became "dear" friends as a result. Meto had warned that in China he would miss his "dears" and the New York cotillions. She was right. He wanted to dance to a sprightly tune alongside bright smiles, sparkling eyes, and approving looks, especially Annie's.

"There is always the Chinese quarter," Blake said with a teasing smile.

Richard had just arrived at the British island and not entered the fabulous China, not seen a Chinese person other than those working as servants to the Europeans. Chinese women would appeal even less than British matrons. A relationship with one was beyond his imagination. No jokes, no teases, no way to know her. Blake's remark about the Chinese quarter implied a visit to a lady of the night, or was he just teasing? "I've got a girl at home," Richard had told him. The idea of dancing with a married woman did not appeal to him either, but he figured that he would see what he thought about the society dances when he got a chance.

One day a few weeks later, Will Forbes pushed a large stack of copy work over to Richard and, having finished his own short stack quickly, left the office and did not return until dinnertime. Will Forbes's habit of shirking work and leaving Richard to complete it became increasingly frequent. Will's excuse of seniority to supervise Richard and his continually arrogant remarks began to gnaw at Richard. So did the suspicion that Will received a larger salary. Richard had drawn on the company for necessities such as a tailored suit, two chairs for his room, a haircut, and small gifts for his family, not on entertainment and trifles that amused many of the other young men. His work had not been evaluated in over a month when senior partner P. S. Forbes called for him.

"Sit down," Forbes said, waving his hand without looking up. "Disagreeable" was one of the kindest adjectives the young clerks used to describe the head of the house. Richard thought that the collar probably prevented looking up.

"Mr. Starr, your work is satisfactory," he puffed through his mustache. "The partners are content."

Richard relaxed a little. The intimidating man was still stiff but did look up at Richard, fixing on his eyes. "Your salary for the year will increase to fifty Hong Kong dollars a month."

Richard leaned forward. "Sir, I have been doing ..." then decided to be quiet. I've been doing the work for two, he wanted to say. Better not to complain right away to the partner who controlled his welfare nor say that he was unhappy with a heavy workload when working with the man's son.

Forbes shot him a look. "Yes ...?"

"Nothing, sir. Thank you." Remembering the desperate searching in New York, he should be happy to have work at all.

"You have drawn fifty-five dollars and twenty-eight cents," Forbes announced, sounding as if he was passing statistics to an accountant, which, in a way, he was, and Richard knew well what he owed. "With interest the total will be sixty-one dollars at the end of this month." He hadn't expected to pay so much interest. "This sum will be deducted from your salary."

He would have liked to argue for a higher salary, or to request Forbes waive the debt, but he blinked and stifled the urge. The debt was of his own making. He would have to cut his minimal advance draws even more. Any speculative investments of his own now seemed even further away.

Despite what he considered economical living on the way to making his fortune, Richard was now in serious debt.

THE *STAG HOUND*, a magnificent clipper from New York, anchored in the harbor with another senior partner to join P. S. Forbes. The added partner, Warren Delano, a former head of Russell's Canton house, was also well known for austere and demanding work habits. Clipped, brief, speech dared any listener to disagree with him. Delano knew what it took to make money in China.

The day after Delano introduced himself to the Russells, another cutter from the *Stag Hound* carried four passengers to the dock, each sitting under sun-protecting umbrellas. The four-man crew tied up parallel to the dock so they could help four women one by one up onto the dock.

"For heaven's sake, young man, hold steady," the older woman said. One sailor took her arm; a sailor braced against the dock to hold the boat steady, a third pushed from behind, and they lifted her safely onto the dock's solid footing. She flapped her fan vigorously, harrumphed, and, chin forward, strutted out of the way for the three other girls to disembark as they might.

"Good day to you, Mrs. Delano," said a crewman.

The next, a young woman, stepped with pride onto the gunwale and, leaning on a firm male hand, alighted on the dock. "Oh, Mother," she said, "Don't be such a sissy," and strode after her.

The other two young passengers tucked up their skirts and stepped up while the sailors waited for a stumble so they could grasp a tiny waist. The two bounced up and out with youthful agility and trotted along, chattering and looking around like tourists.

"Louise. Dora. Come along. Stop dawdling," said Mrs. Delano.

They all soon boarded a four-horse carriage that took them to a house high on the foothill. The sailors followed the girls with their eyes until the cab door closed, then looked at one another. "Those young beauties will have a time of their lives when the bachelors find them," said one of the sailors.

"Aye, if that mother ever lets 'em out of the house."

WARREN DELANO INVITED all the Americans in Hong Kong to celebrate the Fourth of July on the American steamship *Hankow* for the evening. His daughters had persuaded him that Americans ought not to celebrate their independence while in a British colony, and he arranged to celebrate on a ship in international waters far from Britain's military presence and their socially superior attitude that hung over the colony.

Richard joined the other Russells to shuttle out to the *Hankow*. His family genes carried a firm American patriotism. Just over eighty years ago Richard's great-grandfather had furnished clothing and uniforms to George Washington's troops. British attacks in 1812 had ruined his grandfather's rum importing business, and other uncles and cousins had fought and died for American freedom. Richard was in the mood to celebrate America's independence.

Two Russell steam shuttles carried Americans from all ships and business firms to the *Hankow*, at anchor in the harbor. The ship shined in a red sunset, patriotic bunting lined her rigging and ringed her hull, and red, white, and blue flags topped every mast and spar. When all the celebrants had boarded, the big steamship cruised six miles away from the Hong Kong harbor, cut her engines, and dropped anchor. They were free of the British. The night settled in, and a nearly full moon rose. Richard would drink and eat and laugh that night.

He joined John Blake, William Hemsley and Will Forbes for the all-American dinner. Simon Brown, whom Richard had last seen on the dock, joined them for feasting on Virginia ham, Boston cod and baked beans, New York steak, and New England fruit pies, all washed with French wines and American whiskeys. To cheers, jokes, and a little drunken heckling, P. S. Forbes, Warren Delano, the *Hankow*'s captain, and others gave patriotic speeches and toasts. A rowdy "Yankee Doodle" roused laughter and applause.

Blake suddenly pointed and said, "Girls! Across the way."

The young men turned. The three Delano sisters chatted gaily and greeted a succession of ships' officers and trading firm partners.

Will, as usual, boasted. "I've already met them. Quiet girls. Mother, father and I called on them yesterday."

Richard's gaze settled on the youngest looking girl, a beauty that struck him immediately. He knew he had to meet her. *Bet she dances well*, he thought, and announced, "I'll have the first dance with the one in the blue dress."

"I'll take the older one; she's got the right look for me," said Blake.

"I met them first," Will said.

Their squabbles minutely analyzed every rare and lovely feature. The girls grew more beautiful the more the bachelors analyzed from their distant table. When revelers stopped to watch fireworks, the girls disappeared into the crowd.

Sparkling colors, showers of red, white and blue rockets, booms and bangs, shot into the sky to "Oooos" and "Ahhhhs." After an explosive finale, a volunteer twelve-piece band struck up the music, and dancing started. The *Hankow* rocked through polkas, schottisches, and vigorous square and round dances.

Will Forbes quickly swept up Dora Delano, preempting Richard's plan to dance with her quickly. In a few minutes, Richard spotted an auspicious moment to cut in when a tall, handsome officer took Dora's hand from Will. Richard decided that the party, the occasion, and the dance protocol allowed him to dance as much as he wanted with Dora and eased aside the officer and cut in for a slow dance.

"What a relief you are from that drunk," she said.

"Hello, I'm Richard … Richard Starr."

"I am Dora Delano. I hope you are enjoying the Fourth." Her voice was pure and musical, her clean brown hair tucked into a bob which, as they swung in rhythm to the dance steps, revealed her slim white neck. A row of clean white teeth lit her broad smile. She looked about sixteen.

"Weren't the fireworks magnificent?" he said.

"Yes, quite spectacular." His eyes met hers. A cheerful spirit shone from the pure blue. She looked away as if waiting for the next man to cut in.

"It's wonderful to be under the American flag," said Richard quickly, spinning her around. "I hope we can dance awhile." They twirled right and left as if on a cloud.

"I do too."

"May I call next week?"

A uniformed ship's officer whisked her away before she could respond to his question. Thereafter, she returned to her social duty, was available, charming, polite, dancing with clumsy older men one after another. Someone sang a bawdy "Derry Down Dell" to peals of laughter.

Richard continued watching Dora and her sister Louise among the swirling dancers, hoping for a chance to dance again. In time he realized that the girls were bound by their social duties to entertain every celebrant, especially the ones their mother and father favored. He danced a square dance with his friend Blake, a short fox-trot with Louise, a waltz with another merchant's wife, and managed a short turn with Dora.

"Do call," she said.

At midnight, the *Hankow* raised anchor and slowly steamed back to Hong Kong, firing rockets the entire way.

Dora had the same appealing vitality that had so entranced Richard about Annie. One day soon after the Fourth of July party, Richard climbed the hill to the Delano home at the proper ten o'clock hour for formally calling on ladies according to the proper custom in English Hong Kong, as in New York. He rang the bell and told the Chinese houseboy that he wished to call upon Miss Dora. The boy motioned him to wait in the foyer and disappeared. The room was elegantly furnished with Chinese dark red wood chairs and cabinets, and was large but not imposing, like the federal architecture popular in Boston's better houses. Presently a fair, round-faced lady of about forty came to greet him.

She was as polite as the occasion required and no more. "Hello. I am Mrs. Delano. And you are ...?" Richard told her, and said that he had met Dora on the Fourth. He would like to call on her.

"Dora is not available now." She said that she intended to invite some clerks to dinner on Sundays, and he could see her then. He left his card and walked slowly back down the hill.

5

Mrs. Delano was good to her word, and every other Sunday she invited the young American bachelors of the island for dinner. Rather a formal way, Richard thought, to teach and show off her daughters' hostess talents, conversation, and music. While the houseboy cleared dishes after his third Sunday dinner, Richard asked Dora if she would like to play a duet on the piano with him.

"Certainly. But we have had no practice."

He lowered his voice. "Would your mother let us practice a bit while others have after-dinner drinks?"

"A good reason to get a few moments out from under her. I'll persuade her."

They sat side by side on the piano bench and decided to play a melody by Chopin that they both knew. Their first few bars clashed in dissonance and Dora broke out in giggles, which set Richard into laughter too. They tried again, got further into the piece, and after a few more rounds of play and smiles they decided to try it in front of the guests.

"That'll be fun. We'll have to do it more."

Over the next days, they managed to play together unchaperoned, learning a number of pieces, always accompanied by some laughter. Once, when they both hit the same keys, Dora let her hand rest on his and gave it a squeeze as she nudged his hand over.

He felt a tingle in his groin. Dora told her mother that these practices were necessary each time they planned to play at a dinner.

They often made time to chat between tunes. "My father says he knows your father," Dora said one day.

"I think so. Do you mind if I ask … Is your father always as strict as he seems to be?"

"He's always been formal and serious with us. Growing up we never really saw him very much. He was always away in China or some other place."

"So was my father. He's very serious, too. You were raised by your mother then?"

"Yes. And a nanny. We had to follow the rules or risk a spanking." Dora laughed and began playing.

He picked up the tune, and they swayed together with the music. They decided to practice a slow, melodic song that could very well put an audience to sleep, but it allowed them to let their thoughts wander.

"Why are you working in China?" Dora asked.

"When I graduated from Columbia there was a financial crisis in business. I couldn't get a job. My uncle helped me get a position with Russell."

"How do you like it?"

"China? I've not seen China at all. I've only been here a few months. I hope Russell doesn't turn me into a formal and serious person like our fathers."

"Don't change, for heaven's sake. Go home before that happens."

"I want to make enough to go home for good in two or three years," he said. "How do you like China?"

"I don't. Mother keeps us under wraps. She thinks it's dangerous in the streets. What would she do in China proper? Lock us in her trunk?"

"She certainly hasn't stifled your spirit, though."

"We do get out to ride the ponies."

She laughed again, and he grinned and chuckled, happy to be with a pretty girl. "I ride too, when I can. I frequently help Hawkins at the stable. Let's try to meet there soon."

"Yes. Another riding companion will be welcome," she said and quickly hit a short trill as her mother looked in on them.

As the days went by, at every opportunity, he opened doors for Dora, respected her mother, obeyed the rules of etiquette, and rarely drank too much wine. On occasion, he helped her in and out of sedan chairs and carriages. He did everything Meto had taught him to do to please a lady.

Richard attended a Saturday gala that Mr. and Mrs. Olyphant held to which the Delanos, Forbeses, and several Russell clerks had also been invited. He promptly found Dora seated across the room, not mixing gaily as usual at such affairs. He noticed pallor in her skin, and her cheeks were unnaturally red. She was clearly not well. She moved slowly and did not want to talk. "You are not your usual cheerful self," he said.

"I'm not, I guess. I do not feel well."

He touched her red cheek. "You are feverish. We must get you home as soon as possible." He left her sitting on the chaise lounge. "I'll tell your mother that you have to go home."

He left to call a nearby cab, then approached Mrs. Delano.

"Oh, she'll get over it. All right, Mr. Starr, you may take her home. I trust you to see her into the house and that our Irish maid is with her. Do not leave her with Chinese helpers. And you come back and tell me she is home."

When he had delivered her into Maggie's arms, Dora said, "Thank you, Richard."

"Bless ye, young man, "Maggie said. "She needs rest."

Periodic letters had gone off to Meto to tell her that he was well, to ask about Willie and Etta, and to confirm that he missed them all. This time he added a brief report about the Delano girls' arrival. "Dora is a very pretty girl," he wrote. "If I could fall in love with anyone it would be with Dora Delano. I think that I never saw such a pretty girl at home, and I like her very much. She is very bright and intelligent." The next morning the mail ship took the letter.

During the days when clippers were loading, Richard's desk filled with papers, but when the initial rush of buying and selling activity passed, his work with the accountants and shippers slipped into routine. This also gave him a chance to write home to ask Meto to send some boots and kid gloves and to respond to her news of his friends. He was content to devote himself to business and see what turned up.

The partners had all the contacts with clients, customers, and middlemen, and the British dominated every business otherwise. Richard had seen no opportunities to find personal business. As he wrote Meto, he now felt as poor as Job's turkey.

He had been in Hong Kong for over three months when he and John Blake walked some papers to the waterfront for delivery to a ship.

"You've been here a while," Richard said. "Have you made any personal trades of your own?"

Blake hesitated. "I did ... once. In my three years here. It's hard to do."

"I'd like to find something. How did you find that opportunity?"

"You'd probably have to work with a Chinaman ... or someone who speaks both English and Chinese well."

"There's not much opportunity for a clerk to do that on this British island."

"The only way is to work with someone who already has the contacts."

Neither Forbes nor Delano had given the impression that they ever wanted to include clerks financially in some speculation. "Who did you work with?" Richard said.

Blake said nothing. Why was he hesitating? Richard was about to speak again, when Blake said, "I guess telling won't matter ... since I'm leaving soon ... I went with Old P. S. Forbes."

So partners might be amenable to taking clerks along. "Where did you go?"

"Let's just say that we left Hong Kong."

"Did a Chinaman help you?"

"Yes." Blake looked thoughtful, then said, "Sort of ... No we didn't." He still seemed reluctant to talk about it. "It also helps to understand Chinese methods of doing business. That takes time." A moment later he added, "And experience."

"That sounds impossible right now. I haven't seen anything of Chinese business methods myself—just what's in the firm's papers and talk with others."

Richard asked about the Chinese methods, and Blake's answers became more evasive, until he said with inpatient exasperation, "Please, Richard. Forbes made me swear not to talk about it. If I broke my word, if Forbes finds out, I'll never get another job in finance. Here or at home."

"You can't tell me anything about what you did? Or what the Chinese do?"

"No more. Please."

Richard understood that financial matters required keeping information confidential, especially clients' personal matters as well as company internal information. He would do the same himself. Blake's insistence had to be respected. "I'm sorry. I'll not press any more."

ALL THE BACHELOR clerks were enamored with the Delano girls. When Dora was close by, Will often dominated conversation by telling stories about his prospects as a businessman and his acquaintances with well-known people. Blake liked Louise. Other young men hung around the girls at parties, trying to get their attention. At the racetrack, some of the men rode with them and the girls became adept at fending off advances, often using their mother as a foil or excuse.

At dinner one Sunday, Dora stepped out onto the veranda. Richard tried to be playful as he came up behind her. "*Ni Hao*, Dora." His garbled pronunciation of the Chinese greeting sounded like "knee hail," which made no sense, especially on a veranda at night. "I'm glad that you are feeling better. We kind of fumbled the first tune, didn't we?" he ventured.

"Yes," she said. "You did." He chuckled.

The harbor lay far below them. Ships' lanterns shimmered on the water like tiny fireflies in the clear air. A million stars in an especially brilliant Milky Way shone on them.

She pointed her fan skyward. "Look. A shooting star."

He looked up. "I ... I missed it."

She continued looking up toward the glorious sky. He scanned the sky with her. "We've had such good ..."

"Hush." She still had not looked at him. "I have to make a wish."

He had to wait while she finished. *I wish she would pay attention to me now.* Far down hill, the bobbing lights on the harbor seemed to dance to the Mozart interlude someone was playing in the house. As he stood there looking at Dora's beautiful face gazing skyward in concentration, a bead of perspiration slid down his back. Was it the hot night or something else?

Presently, she turned to him with a coquettish smile. She said, "Goodness! Wish upon a star ... I could make a wish every time I see you!"

He blushed.

"Mother told me," she said, "that to make a wish come true you have to seal it with a kiss."

She leaned over, put her hand on his shoulder, rose to her tip-toes, and kissed him on the cheek. Then she hitched up her dress and trotted back into the house, slowed, and majestically entered the parlor. Tunes tinkled away while Richard stood motionless with his hand on the fiery spot on his cheek.

TWO DAYS LATER, Richard stole away from work and went to the racetrack to saddle up for a ride. As he tightened the girth, he saw Dora on the other side of the stable climb onto her white pony. Quickly jumping into his saddle, he trotted out to meet her. She greeted him with a smile and wave.

"Come ride with me out the west road," he said.

"Let's." She turned, looked behind her, and called. "Mother, Richard Starr asked to ride with us."

As they had done often in the past, the three rode together down the packed dirt road out of the city. The August day was brilliant and hot.

When the three had gone about two miles, Mrs. Delano let the two go on ahead. The only sound was the soft clopping of their horses' hooves. Richard looked around and pulled over to ride close beside Dora. Up ahead the road turned sharply. They trotted quickly, rounded the corner, and rode out of her mother's sight.

"Dora, I need to ask you something."

"Certainly."

"I don't know how to say this exactly ... At your house the other day ..." He reined to a halt and took a deep breath. The sun was straight overhead. "What did you mean when you kissed me?" He exhaled. His fists tightened on the reins.

Dora halted beside him. She looked at him directly. "To make my wish come true."

Richard filled the silence quietly, "I mean ... more than that. I mean ... I enjoy your company. Very much."

His borrowed thoroughbred shook his head, stamped a hoof.

"Good." Her coquettish sparkle teased. He could still feel her lips burning his cheek.

He heard hooves trotting behind them and knew Dora's mother was coming. They had not been alone for long. He was concentrating on Dora and did not look behind. A horse's head came up on her other side.

"Hello, Will. Good to see you," Dora said.

Will Forbes had ridden up even with them. Richard's frustration with his office partner erupted to the surface with this latest annoyance. "What do you think you are doing? Dora and I were together. We didn't ask you here."

"Bugger off, Rich. It's my turn now."

"You bugger off. Go back and do some work for a change."

Startled, Dora reined back to move out from between them.

"I do believe you both are jealous." She turned her mount around and trotted back to her mother.

The men argued until Will swung at Richard, who easily ducked away. Richard stood in his stirrups, grabbed Will's extended arm, and pulled him off balance. His horse stepped apart, out of Richard's reach, nearly bucking Will onto the dirt. Richard moved closer, and their words grew more and more angry.

"Mother," Dora said, a closed-lip smile on her face, "did men ever fight over you?"

6

"BRITAIN'S MILITARY HAS stifled our business while the diplomats pressure the Emperor to allow more foreign trading," P. S. Forbes said to Warren Delano. Canton, the central trading port for many years, had been virtually closed since it had been blockaded in the squabbles over opium. The relatively new ports such as Shanghai and Foochow were gaining business as a result. "Since the British and Chinese began provoking each other seriously we lost our Canton factory and way too much business with it."

The partners discussed whether to reduce the number of employees. In Forbes's view, this was a necessity becoming clearer by the week. "John Blake has been here for three years. He is going home on the next voyage. Will, Hemsley, and the two others all have too much free time. The new man, Starr, has recently begun. I don't know his capabilities yet, but we promised his uncle Samuel that we would give him work for at least a year."

Before making harsh decisions, Warren Delano wanted to know more. "As you know, I'm going to Canton soon to see what might be involved in rebuilding the factory. I can discuss business prospects with Howqua," Delano said. "He will have a sense of the business prospects."

"Take Starr and Hemsley with you. Get them away from my idiot son. Get to know them. Will can do their work for a few days."

On an early September morning a week later, Richard responded to Delano's summons. Even though he had been doing the bulk of Will's work as well as his own, he had sensed the slowdown of business at the firm and spent much leisure time in sport and play. As the newest clerk, he feared what the slowdown might mean for him.

Without preamble in the manner Richard expected from a partner, Delano said, "I am going to Canton next week. I want to examine our factory's damage and review business with Howqua." Richard took a deep breath. He suspected that this meant Delano was assessing the firm's plans for the future, including his. "I want you to come with me." Richard relaxed a little. "This will give you some experience beyond a clerk's desk."

Father had told Richard about the first Howqua and his son, the current Howqua, who Richard will meet. The Howqua family had been trusted agents for American traders in China, easing transactions past authorities and brokers, and two generations of Russell partners had been Howqua's American agents, who made investments for him in American growth. One shipment of tea had made Howqua money at each trading step as farmer, packer, broker, and shipper, plus earned commissions. "We give him access to North and South America," Father had said. "The Jardine Matheson British firm gives him Europe. Howqua gives us China. He is a very valuable Chinese resource."

Richard could not hold back his excitement at a chance to meet Howqua, experience China—the land of exotic architecture, men in robes, and cities of pagodas. Perhaps Howqua could be the Chinaman needed, according to Blake, for a personal venture. "When do we leave?"

With two days to go until this scheduled departure, Richard found Dora at the stable readying her white pony to ride.

"I'm leaving Hong Kong in a few days," he said. "Your father has asked me to go with him to Canton."

"You are? Why did I feel something might send you away?" Her teasing demeanor struck him as more emphatic than usual. He gave her his hand as, clutching her skirt with the other, she placed her high boot onto the step to mount the pony.

"Good luck in Canton," she said, still holding his hand. "I need to tell you, I'm leaving, too. Mother, Sara, Louise, and I are going to visit Japan soon. It is next on our travels."

He said, "Have a wonderful trip. I'll see you when you get back."

"After Japan we go to San Francisco. We won't come back to China."

He let go of her hand. "When do you go?"

"We may not be here when you get back from Canton. So I must say good-bye now, too."

She sat on the sidesaddle, pulled her legs up and smoothed her skirt.

"I'll miss you," Richard said. Pangs of disappointment swirled through him, although he always knew that one day their fun would end. "There will not be another like you in China."

She blew him a kiss. "Bye," she said softly as her horse walked away with her.

WARREN DELANO, RICHARD, William Hemsley, and consular translator Robert Hitch left on the company steamer *Empress* early in the morning. The steamer smoothly circled Hong Kong Island, entered the bay, and headed for the Pearl River. Delano had very strong convictions on every subject, and during this trip Richard wanted to study the character of a successful China trader.

A sleek British merchantman sailed before them on a course to three-mile-long Lin-Tin Island, where several Western sailing ships lay at anchor. None flew identifiable ensigns.

"Opium ships dock there. Away from Canton's customs officials," Delano told the clerks. A many-oared junk, sails folded, sped its way toward the island anchorage. "That's a smugglers' warehouse ship. Going after a load of opium. It'll take it ashore up a creek. Try to beat government gunships."

Richard suddenly wondered whether Blake's reluctance to tell about his venture with Forbes meant that they had traded opium with smugglers. People at the firm had never talked about opium trading, at least to new clerks. He looked directly at Delano. "Has Russell & Co. sold to opium smugglers?"

Delano looked away. "One doesn't ask." Delano plainly did not want to say more. "It doesn't matter to us what buyers do after we've sold."

To Richard, it did matter what was done with opium after it is sold, particularly if it was smuggled in or abused. Smugglers avoided duties and controls, and the drug destroyed lives. There were some sensible uses for the drug, such as the legal medicinal laudanum that he kept in his room, but he would not touch raw opium even if it became legal and made him money. Delano's remark troubled him. It was wrong-headed. He would not mention opium again.

The river soon pinched between cliffs, the water turned turbulent, and the *Empress* passed through the Tiger's Mouth, the Bogue, legendary entrance to China for years. On the cliffs, forts lined up like teeth—an open jaw that foreigners had to pass. Richard had entered China at last.

In a few days he would meet the fabulous merchant Howqua and set foot on the exotic land he had only previously imagined. He surveyed the passing scenes like the tourist he had been one summer on the Mississippi. For the next thirty miles barren hills, cliffs, and rocks overlooked the river. Red-sailed junks with blunt upswept bows and rotting hulls plodded upstream and others drifted down. An occasional lonely pagoda, overgrown with weeds and vines, jutted from a hillside rock.

They reached Whampoa, the last point of navigation for European ocean-sailing vessels, where an English clipper and several schooners lay anchored. Small steam lighters and sailing cargo sampans passed among them carrying goods to and from Canton. A white eye painted on the bow of an anchored red-and-black cargo junk spied on the foreign barbarians.

"Our ships used to pack this harbor," Delano told the two clerks. The anchored British blockade ships upstream of Whampoa let the well-known *Empress* pass without question.

Beyond Whampoa the shore spread out to flat land, and the river narrowed and wound around islands and past tributary deltas. On shore, water buffaloes were kept moving by switches and the cries of young boys under wide conical hats, walking in circles to turn water wheels that irrigated rice fields. Houseboats and cargo-burdened sampans, some sailing, some rowing, some sculling, some drifting with the current, floated downstream or tacked and rowed upstream. The simple drawings in his childhood books about mischievous Tin-Tin with a pet duck on his sampan came alive.

As the *Empress* neared Canton, the river water clouded. Effluent gradually became muddy and streaked with green slime. When the steamer passed through a sickly yellow-brown streak, a stench of mixed urine and rot wafted up. Insects swarmed on the putrid patch of water.

Richard glanced down on the muck. Suddenly every system in his body turned to ice. In green gunk amid the flotsam floated a naked baby, belly up, white like a sick fish. The tiny apparition transfixed him. The ship knocked into the little body. It passed into the bow wave, was swamped under, and sank out of sight. Unable to move, Richard fought the bile rising in his throat.

"Are you all right?" Hitch asked.

Richard managed to nod and swallowed the bile. He looked at Delano. Then at Hemsley.

Delano, apparently undisturbed, said, "Families throw away babies they don't want. Toss them in the river. Girls especially."

Richard swallowed again. He could not look down at the water any more. He stared at Delano, unable to believe what he just heard.

"It happens frequently," Delano added. "Girls are second-class citizens. When a girl matures, her family might sell her for cash to a husband or brothel."

"Barbaric ..." Richard managed, and turned away.

"Yes. Once saw a man fall into water. He couldn't swim. No one tried to help him," Delano said in an unemotional monotone.

The little ghostly body of a wasted life haunted Richard. A sailor had drowned in the dark. Now a body in the river. He had never before seen a dead body. People of the oldest civilized land in the world throw away human life? Delano's callous reaction surprised him too. What did this place do to a Christian man?

They overtook a small sampan packed with families. A woman and two naked boys huddled in straw cabins and stared up at the steamer. He saw no little girls. A man of the family stood on a raised stern with his skinny arm draped over a single steering oar levered in the stern. Everyone seemed coated with dirt and smudged in sweat. *Empress* steamed on, passing boatmen who jabbered and screeched in their incomprehensible language. Books and etchings portrayed a romantic Chinese life on the river but never hinted at the reality he now saw—poverty, dead babies, stench, dirt, and insensitivity to life.

Through progressively heavier river traffic and shores lined with rounded sampan matt roofs and bare masts, the *Empress* arrived at Canton and docked near the remains of the burned-out European trading houses and factories.

"This is where British wars with China started years ago," Richard said to no one in particular, trying to picture the warships bombarding the city, the hillside cannons firing in ineffective defense, the mobs rioting. Father had told him of the war and the treaty to cede Hong Kong to Britain and open other ports. Since then, Chinese political squabbles had rarely made news in New York, and his father, away from home for over two years before Richard sailed, had not written about any more conflicts in China. Nor had anyone in Hong Kong mentioned recent fires in the factories. Richard asked Delano, "Our factories burned just two years ago. What happened?"

中国

The *fanqui*, the barbarian devils, the Europeans, lived at the foreign factories across a creek from Canton. Every day Kou Chi-chi had laid out the hated British merchants' dark heavy trousers, pressed their shirts in the morning, stacked their cumbersome crates in the godown all day, served them five courses of unpleasant food, stooped to pick their clothing off the floor in the evening, and no *fanqui* ever acknowledged his presence or thanked him. Only more orders for more tasks. His hatred for the hairy long-nosed barbarians who controlled his life grew until one day he refused to return to the factory. Kuo walked away from his servant's work, no longer to cater to the barbarians.

After a few days enjoying time without *fanqui* demands, Kuo stepped down the stones covering a drainage ditch in the muddy street between a row of shops and into a teahouse for a drink and companionship. The men in the undecorated room murmured loudly, their voices distressed and talkative. An air of tension hung around the conversations. Kuo heard an angry tone next to him, "One day ago flower flag barbarians capture Canton Barrier Fort."

Flower flag barbarians were the Americans. Kuo knew that British gunships also had fired into the Canton walls.

"The *fanqui* do not dare fight Commissioner Yeh's army," someone shouted. "*Fanqui* coward fight from ship far away."

Kuo soon caught the fever around him. He had heard that a British captain demanded that Commissioner Yeh let all *fanqui* enter the city. That could not happen. Kou turned to the man next to him, a tired looking coolie, and said, "What can we do?"

The door flew open. A frantic man with fire in his eyes ran in waving a gun. Outside a mob had gathered on its way to the creek that separated the foreign factories from the city. "Come. To the factories. Join us. Show the *fanqui* we don't want them."

Patrons rose and rushed out, crying slogans. Kuo went with them, and before long the cry, "To the factories!" became "Destroy the *fanqui*!"

Kuo yelled with them. "Destroy the *fanqui*!"

He headed to the creek with others who picked up rocks, weapons, and staves as they passed down the dirt streets. Kou picked up a stout board. Two soldiers watched the mob surge to the factories and did nothing to calm them. More men joined them, and at the creek they met others who had come down other alleys. They all stampeded over the bridge, an undisciplined group with a common mission.

Before them stood the first of thirteen *fanqui* buildings lined along the waterfront. Groups began breaking windows with rocks and staves. Ruffians spread out by the dozens and headed down the back side of the factories. Dozens more angry Chinese spread along the waterfront. The disorganized demonstration became a riot.

Up ahead, Kou saw four *fanqui* run from a factory, leap onto a boat tied nearby, and shove off. "The cowards flee!" He was tempted to laugh, but he was headed for the British factory where he had taken so much abuse. It was the third building. Knowing what was inside, Kou became the leader of the rioters following him. On his motion a rioter carrying an axe chopped down the door.

Inside the factory, Kuo immediately rushed to the warehouse where household supplies were stored. "Follow me. This way."

He found the barrels he knew were filled with whale oil that lit the *fanqui's* lamps and lanterns. He rolled a barrel away from the others and tipped it over, careful that the whale oil would spill out away from him. He called to the axe man, "Smash barrel."

Thirty gallons of the fishy flammable liquid splashed out and flowed under the goods and stores. Kou took a flint from his pocket and struck it on an iron barrel hoop. Sparks jumped off and ignited the whale oil. He watched the flame spread until stored crates began to burn.

"Take barrels outside for others," he called, then turned and ran outside.

Rioters found rags, wornout clothing, anything to make torches. A quick dip in the flaming oil, one torch lit another, and soon torches were running through the factories. Smoke billowed into the air. An explosion blew down a wall. Kou ran with the others, setting fires at will. *Fanqui* fled to their boats. When another warehouse exploded, the rioters cheered. Flames engulfed the entire foreign factory row.

中国

"The British military eventually decided to retaliate," Delano said. "They attacked Canton. Installed a peaceable Chinese commissioner in place of Yeh. Now the British navy blockades the river and controls Canton." Richard had seen military restlessness in the harbor and drilling grounds, but the blockade and burning had escaped his notice in Hong Kong, where he had been spending time with Dora or with his head down focused on papers in front of him.

Delano showed his charges what was left of the American house, a broken, burned hull, a row of ruined factories to either side, none showing any effort at rebuilding. He silently looked over the ruined building, which had weathered enough to lose any odor of ash. Delano explained, "Partners can't agree to rebuild it until a new treaty is signed. Someday, perhaps. Nothing salvageable here. We need to build an entirely new building."

The Americans spent the night aboard the steamer. Over a shipboard dinner the four discussed the previous fighting, the newly opened ports, and the Chinese and British intransigence until Delano ended the conversation for the night.

"Out of stubborn pride the two governments refuse to treat each other as equals," he had said. "President Buchanan's policy is that we be neutral in their fight. Under the most favored nation treaty, we receive any concessions they give the British. Remember, this leaves American businesses here under no control, subject to no law, except that of self-interest."

As Richard lay in his bunk that night, he contemplated the day, the continual fighting, the contrasts between his expectations and reality, the picturesque but stinking river, the arrogant British, the stubborn Chinese, and the heathen, poverty-stricken, lawless land.

"The Chinese hate foreigners," Father had said. Richard could understand why.

7

DELANO HAD SENT a boy to inform Howqua that they had arrived and he had returned promptly with the time and place arranged.

"To get there," Delano explained, "we will ride. To maintain appearances." Will had mentioned the partners' same excuse for riding in Hong Kong when they could walk. Who were they trying to impress this time? Delano climbed into a curtained sedan chair where no one could see in; nor could Delano see out. Coolies carried Hitch, Hemsley, and Richard, each in an open-air bamboo frame chair that twisted and swayed, seeming ready to collapse at any moment. Six knees, six elbows, and six feet protruding awkwardly, arms and legs bracing for a collapse, Hemsley and Richard laughed at each other in their flimsy frames. Silliness was the only appearance they could maintain.

Off they swayed over a footbridge that connected the charred foreign concession to the city. Richard's forward carrier stumbled when he stepped off the bridge, nearly tumbling Richard into the street. The Americans clutched their chair frames while the coolies, who could not understand a word of instruction, trotted and swung them as they followed Delano through the city.

Richard's first look at a Chinese city street belied the bright colors he had imagined after viewing Thomas Alom's neat etchings of unique architecture and strange costumes. Streets were dirty, colors were faded, buildings were drab and damaged, the natives wore rags, and the entire street smelled of urine and spices. An unkempt nine-story pagoda, plaster peeling off its drab brick, towered in the distant sky over brown tile roofs darkened by soot. Unwashed brown men bent under bales or piles of sticks stared at their own shuffling feet with hollow eyes. Barebacked men jabbered around a coolie fuming over a spilled wheelbarrow of bricks. A vendor touted rat corpses, skinned rabbits, and eels amid sharp spicy odors surrounding an eating-house. Richard tried not to stare at slovenly, blank-faced men lounging in corners with long-stemmed pipes. Only a few bothered to look at the American caravan. The war, blockade, and opium, Richard thought, must have caused this ruin and poverty.

The bouncing Americans crossed a canal over an arched stone bridge, soon arrived in a prosperous residential street, and the sedan chairs stopped at a small wooden gate in a plastered brick wall. They dismounted the chairs, a houseboy opened the gate, and they entered a garden beyond which stood a clean, red-trimmed yellow dwelling, a row of tiny gargoyles perched on the ridge of its roof. The boy led them over another stone bridge, along a meandering rivulet, past weirdly gnarled trees and shrubs, until they stepped up a landing into a spacious hall.

An intricate frieze of polished dark wood carvings ringed the ceiling. On the walls hung silk panels painted with delicately entwined trees and bright red, white, and blue birds. Chinese calligraphy decorated red lacquered columns like advertisements. Pointing to the characters on one of the columns, the boy said, "*Kung Fu-tzu.*" He then read the characters slowly so Hitch could translate.

"Words of the Great Master, Confucius," Hitch said. "He says that one reads: 'By nature all men are alike.'"

Richard snapped away from admiring the richness around him. An emaciated little man in a red silk robe with a brilliant peacock embroidered on its breast had stepped out to greet them. Unlike anything he had imagined, Howqua looked meek, yet serene. Pearl and jade beads hung around his neck. His large head was bald, except for a few wisps of gray hair lying over the scalp. Traces of a thin white mustache dropped from the corners of his upper lip. His large eyes looked more vacant than shrewd, and they were inscrutably calm.

"Welcome to humble home," Howqua said in heavily accented English.

Warren Delano returned Howqua's welcome with a broad smile and gentle handshake such as Richard had not seen from him. As if introducing an old friend, Delano presented his companions. Howqua spoke polite greetings, and, one at a time, extended his small hand as if he was meeting a merchant as equally prominent as he. Helmsley and Hitch, taking the cue from Delano's handshake, softly responded, took Howqua's hand, smiled, and mumbled, "Honored to meet you."

"You have pleasure with first visit to China?" Howqua said when it was Richard's turn. "I know father."

Richard felt awed in the presence. There seemed to be some magical confidence about him. "Father speaks well of you."

Howqua escorted the four men into an adjoining room elegantly decorated with intricate carved designs that bordered the ceiling like a collar of chocolate lace glistening with lacquer. The room opened on one side to a garden and a placid pond filled with lily pads. They all gazed at the garden. A school of golden fish circled leisurely among the lilies. Twisted gray pines grew among head-high rocks pockmarked as if hellfire had pierced them.

A white body drifted among the fish. Richard jumped with horror. Then he realized that the body was swimming. He shook his head to dispel the dead baby image before daring to peer again at the pond in the twisted but peaceful garden. He took a deep breath; a single ghostly white fish swam peacefully among the golden koi.

The only furnishings in the elegant room were polished wooden chairs with flat, hard seats and a small table with writing brushes, ink, and paper neatly placed upon it. The perfect host, Howqua bent over each guest's hard chair in turn, sweeping the seat with his oversized silk sleeves. The Americans seated themselves where their host indicated.

The meeting would be long. Richard expected to leave this luxurious house with a clean but sore bottom. He wanted to learn all he could by listening, but as time dragged on he could not keep his mind from wandering to his first impressions of the city. Squalor was in the streets around this elegant house in this ancient civilization, a civilization evident only in this house. Certainly the Chinese were not all alike, yet Howqua's wall proclaimed: "By nature all men are alike." Americans had different skin, different speech, different eyes, different food, and different gods than Chinese do, yet Americans also declare, "All men are created equal." Richard could see that all men were certainly not alike or equal. Why such similar …? Richard snapped out of his musings.

The tall white man and the diminutive yellow man, one in a black suit, the other in a brilliant red robe, began talking. When the business required clarity they turned to Hitch or Howqua's interpreter, who sometimes talked among themselves and then reported to their respective bosses. Hitch translated Howqua's response to a question: "He says that British and French warlike behavior have hurt trade here. Trade business is now growing in Shanghai. That old fishing village will become important."

"I believe that too," said Delano.

The conversation continued. "The *Dagmar* with your shipment of Enfield rifles has left Manila," Delano said. "It will arrive shortly."

"He said," Hitch translated Howqua's response, "that a young American has asked his broker to buy British rifles."

Richard straightened up. He recalled recent conversations with Simon Brown about Carolina's threats to secede from the Union. Brown was developing relationships with the British trading firms and had said that England might support South Carolina to ensure receiving its cotton. He assumed that Simon Brown certainly would be able to buy a shipment of quality rifles to support his state.

On a whim, Richard spoke up, "I may know this American."

With surprise on his face, Delano looked at Richard. To Howqua, Delano said, "Some Americans are anticipating an unlikely possibility of war among some states."

Richard fancied to help his country. The latest papers from home had articles reporting that some South Carolina politicians had threatened to secede if necessary to continue slavery. Uncle Samuel could surely sell high-quality rifles to Massachusetts or New York militias. Richard would buy Howqua's rifles but had no way to pay for them. He mentally crossed his fingers and said to Delano, "Would Russell & Co. buy them?"

Delano thought for a moment, smiled, then said, "I think a speculation for a good reason will show you young fellows just what it entails." He turned to Richard and Helmsley. "Would you both share in the costs and risks with Russell?"

Howqua spoke without expression. "You want buy rifles?"

Richard quickly said, "Yes, but I will need credit to buy my share. I can pay it back when the resale is made." Helmsley did not want to share. Hitch, a consular employee, could not.

Howqua, having already paid for the rifles, said through Hitch, "I sell to you. Yes. Yes, you have credit. Howqua profit same when sell to American or Emperor or rebel. Mr. Delano agree to handle resale in America?"

Russell & Co. had already earned its finder's commission and shipping fees on these rifles. Delano said, "Russell and Mr. Starr will share the purchase price and the profit equally. There also will be expenses for shipping, insurance, broker's fees, and, for Mr. Starr, interest on his loan."

As the experienced trader ticked off this list of additional costs, Richard despaired that, with no way he could control it, any profit for him in this deal could easily dwindle to very little. The time to ship, sell, and receive the proceeds meant that as many as six months could pass before he knew his profit—if any. He realized that Delano had purposely wanted him to know that making money quickly with a speculation was much harder than he had imagined. He had spoken too quickly, had not fully thought through this first personal speculation.

The three men decided that Richard would meet the *Dagmar* in Hong Kong, off-load the rifles, and deliver them to Captain Devens for the *Fearless,* soon to sail to San Francisco, where they could be sold or sent on to the East. Howqua agreed, and the agreement was concluded.

Shortly after Richard made this rash rifle speculation, the meeting ended. The merchants relaxed while a demure woman shuffled in to serve tea and dried fruit. Boosted by his first venture, Richard joined in conversation and asked questions of Howqua and Delano. Hemsley remained silent, speaking only when spoken to.

Richard looked again with awe at the fish swimming among water lilies, the fantastic shapes in the rock garden, and the philosophical characters on the columns, and, as they left, his bottom sore from the hard seat he pondered the contradictions between the miserable city and the lavish wisdom in the strangely peaceful heathen home and its remarkable owner.

8

H E COPIED PAPERS and learned as before, encouraged by the thoughts of the ancient Chinese merchant who had given him credit for his first speculation, but as he became more efficient at the clerking routine, the work bored him at times. The slowdown in the firm's business and in opportunities for promotion worried him. He needed a break from routine.

The first chance after returning from Canton that Richard had to talk with Blake, he boasted about the investment he'd made with Howqua. "Just like your trade with Forbes, I had a partner's connection, and a Chinaman was part of it."

"Good luck with finding another investment," Blake said. "I've been clerking for three years. Enough of that for me. I'm going home soon. That will be a welcome change."

On an impulse, Richard said to Blake, "The trip to Canton whetted my appetite for adventure. I need to find some change in my routine. Do you want to go visit the Chinese section?"

The next day after work, they walked out of the city and into the maze of single-story brick and mud houses and shops, not unlike the poorer streets he'd seen in Canton—mostly dirt streets, some paved with stone slabs covering drainage runs, some brown buildings draped with unreadable dirty signs. Nothing to lift a man's mood. Women sat about on the residential street while naked children played in the mud. Men, some probably servants to the British, strolled the shops and drinking houses. The streets were dim, and, as darkness came, Richard and Blake turned a corner and wandered into an alley where red paper lanterns lit several doorways. The tuneless twanging of music drew them on down the alley. *We could listen to squeaks and thumps that passed for music for a short while,* he thought, *and there's no sin in that.*

The sickly-sweet, flowery, yet pungent smell of opium curled Richard's nose as they entered a door. Carousing Chinese men sat at tables drinking and laughing. Except for the opium, this seemed no different from the seedier bars in New York. For a few moments, the two Americans stood still as oriental faces turned, frowned, and stared at them. Girls danced topless in skirts slit to the thigh and the men soon turned back to the girls. Blake chanced to peer into a side room where bright colors showed and beckoned Richard to follow him toward more music and laughter.

Two eager Chinese accosted them. "Wanchee girlee?' said one with crooked teeth.

Richard gawked at bare breasts—sights he had only seen from a ship in a Malay proa—and shook his head.

The man laughed. "Pretty girlee? Come, I show." He took Richard's arm. "Yes?"

Richard shook his head again but saw that a Chinese hustler had Blake by the hand leading him toward a doorway curtained off by stringed beads. The opium made him dizzy, the music jarred his head, the topless dancers swayed, and Richard let himself be led through the curtain.

Naked and half-naked bodies writhed on the floor, on pillows, on beds and on chairs. In a smoky haze, men with women, men with men, women with women caressed, wrestled, and heaved in a pit of debauchery. Body odors mixed with tobacco assaulted his senses. His head spun to cries, moans, and groans of ecstasy. Thirsty from the smoke, woozy from the smells, and revolted by the scene, Richard felt a glass of liquid in his hand. He took a swallow of a smooth but bitter wine. His inner sense screamed, "Don't drink it!" He swallowed again and dropped the empty glass on the floor. He staggered from the room, the hustler's laugh echoing behind him. He stumbled through the crowd and out to the street.

Breathing again, he gasped, "A vision of hell from Grandfather's sermons."

Presently, Blake appeared beside him. Both too stunned to speak, they helped each other find their way back to civilization.

The next morning, the most splitting headache Richard had ever experienced kept him in his room. The few coins he had had were gone. He remembered a blur of writhing people after he'd heard a jingling of beads and a twanging music, in the midst of inexplicable and intoxicating odors. Had he committed a terrible sin? He couldn't remember. He had inhaled opium. He drank something. He had witnessed appalling scenes. He prayed for forgiveness and asked God to block it from his mind—except to prevent him from ever doing such things.

He spent the day trying to shake off the hangover brought on by the terribly mistaken decision to enter a Chinese bordello and, fighting sleep the while, accomplished little work at his desk.

The next morning he was summoned to P. S. Forbes's office. Disappointments with his months in the new job, disillusions about living in China, and the absence of proper girls tumbled and mixed in his sore head. He thought of home. He missed Meto. He wanted to see old Toodla, feel his soft nose, rub his ears, feed him an apple, climb on his back. He was the newest and least experienced clerk with much to learn; the employee that would be first to fire when business was poor. As far as he could see, he faced more clerical duties for the future, repeatedly writing out invoices and bills of lading for stiff and demanding men who valued nepotism more than good work. Nevertheless, he believed that this job was similar to what he'd be doing if he had stayed in New York or Boston. He had come to China to do a job and had not been at it long enough to feel so discouraged. Stick it out longer, he told himself. If ... the firm wanted him.

He stepped into the partner's office. Warren Delano and P. S. Forbes sat at the conference table, a few papers spread on the table before them. They seemed to look him over for an extended time. Their serious expressions made no greeting. Instead they seemed thoughtful.

"Sit down, Mr. Starr."

Richard sat down at the table to take the news.

Forbes began, "Business here has dropped to the extent that we are not comfortable. It will be necessary to reduce our clerical staff."

That was it. He had looked forward to working in China. He had tried, and it had not worked for him. Father would be disappointed. Meto would be disappointed, too, but glad to see him safely home. He would be resigned.

Forbes said, "You remember your visit to Canton last week."

He vividly recalled the visit to Howqua. "I do."

Forbes said, "Mr. Delano has reported to me about your visit to Canton."

Then Delano spoke up. "You showed me excellent initiative when you agreed to an arrangement that will profit all of us in spite of your additional personal financial risk. Throughout the trip, your questions about business and China impressed me with your eagerness to learn."

Forbes added, "Your work in the office has been excellent. You made no complaint when my son Will did not apply himself."

These words surprised Richard. Would he be staying or not? If clerks needed to be cut, Blake's departure would do that.

Richard shifted position in his seat. "Thank you. I appreciate your help with the rifle trade and the opportunity for the Canton visit. I have tried to do well."

Delano turned to him. "Howqua believes that business is moving north to Shanghai. Particularly for tea. We concur with that assessment."

Forbes said, "If you agree, we have a position for you in Shanghai."

Richard sat up. He was staying. Business would improve with the complete change of scene. He would experience more of China. Although Delano had discouraged private speculation, a move to a place where business thrived should offer more and better ventures. "I look forward to it."

"Good. We have notified Edward Cunningham, head of the house there, and he will be expecting you."

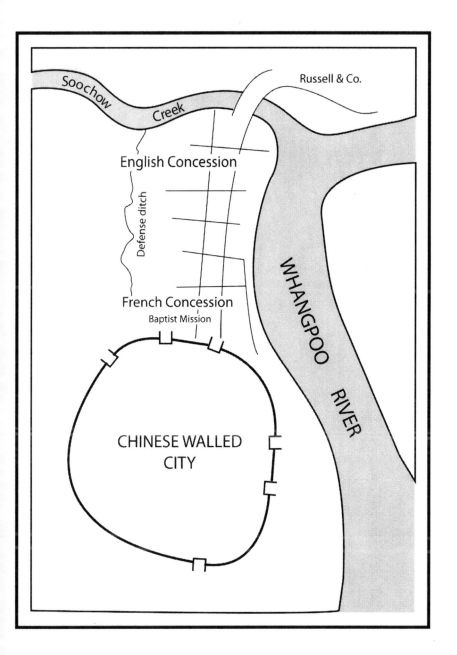

SHANGHAI 1860

PART 2

Shanghai

JULY 1859 TO JULY 1861

Bright painted hulls and a thousand masts adorn the harbor.
With northern goods and southern treasures
hidden away in their vaults ...
P'an Lei, Chinese poet

9

Ominous weather forced the Shanghai-bound coastal steamer *Yangtze* close to the mainland shore where uncharted shoals and rocks lurked. For five days in drenching rain, the *Yangtze* pounded directly into the wind and waves and each evening she anchored in some lee cove to weather the worst of it. The storm abated on the sixth day, and in four smooth days Richard and the battered steamer entered the Whangpoo River in the estuary of the great Yangtze-Kiang.

Anchored at Woosong, clippers, sloops, steamers, and junks bobbed among merchant and war ships. The huge steam-and-sail American *Mississippi* lurked near a cluster of more sail and side-wheeled steam warships, each bristling with guns and flying Union Jacks or French tricolors. Soldiers and sailors aboard them worked, trained, and drilled. War was in the air.

Richard transferred from the coastal steamer to a small steam shuttle and chugged on. Soon, the heavy mud-brick wall surrounding the Chinese city loomed on the south shore. Tents and wooden shacks clustered around the wall, wisps of cooking fire smoke rising from them. Sampans and houseboats two and three deep lined the riverfront below the wall. The low city of slum-like brown houses enveloped the city, and monsoon weather threatened again from gloomy skies.

Farmers, peasants, and the ruined rich, landless landlords and merchants, with their hidden silver, jade, ivory, ceramics, furniture, and icons, had fled the Taiping rebel armies and swarmed into Shanghai city and its foreign settlements. A movement called The Taiping, or Kingdom of Heavenly Peace, led by Hong Xiquan, a mystic who believed he was Jesus Christ's brother, had become a bloody revolution aiming to topple the Ching Dynasty, and its armies had scourged the land from southern China north to the Yangtze River and down the river toward Shanghai, collecting followers who joined the rebellion rather than face bloodshed, fire, and rape. When Richard arrived in Shanghai, Taiping armies had captured Nanking and made that Yangtze River city their capital, from which they raided river shipping and nearby towns.

Richard stared with opened mouth at the passing houseboats, shacks, and tents that sheltered the masses of people, many hundreds of impoverished refugees, around the city in which he was to begin work. "What goes on inside those places?" Richard said to no one in particular.

The shuttle passed a row of granite and brick European godowns, with sloops, small steamers, and junks tied up before them. Behind the godowns spread tile-roofed homes, shops, slums, and scattered temple and church spires. Chinese shopkeepers, launderers, tailors, laborers, servant boys, and coolies of all sorts mingled in large numbers.

The stars and stripes, the red, white and blue of which prompted the Chinese to name it the "flower flag," flew over a godown next to a tributary stream called Soochow Creek. The Whangpoo veered north, turned into fast, rough, white-capped waters where the creek entered, and in a few hundred feet the shuttle deposited Richard with several other passengers onto a waterfront dock.

"Richard Starr?" said a young fellow dressed in top hat and black suit typical of foreign merchants. "Harold Doyle. Pleased to see you. I'm one of the Russells here. A clerk. We'll be working together, or at least alongside each other." They shook hands, exchanged a few pleasantries and chatted about the storm. "The boys will bring up your luggage."

Behind protective walls, a broad lawn sloped up to a mansion with columns and portico resembling a southern plantation home larger than any American building in Hong Kong. The clerks lived on the second floor above a well-appointed billiard room, lounge, and dining hall. The two Russell Shanghai partners, Henry Grew and Edward Cunningham, resided in princely homes near the clerks' residence. The luxury far surpassed that in Hong Kong.

The managing partner, Edward Cunningham, received Richard in an upstairs office in the mansion. The tall trader who would be his boss stepped around a polished Chinese teak desk supported by carved lions. Neatly piled papers sat on its surface, a pen holder, ink stand, and blotting pad took the center. Prints of old Russell & Co. partners shared wall space with British and American square-riggers broadsiding each other. "Welcome to Kee Chong, Mr. Starr." Cunningham's friendly and sun-crinkled face smiled broadly as he extended his hand to Richard. "We are glad to have you. Things are getting busy, and we need you."

"Delighted to be here, sir … Kee Chong?"

Cunningham laughed. "Kee Chong has always been the Chinese name for this area. It's not part of the British or French concessions." His mutton-chop sideburns bobbed comically. "Few Orientals in Shanghai know Russell & Co. by any other name. 'Kee Chong' is used in many transactions."

"I'll have to get accustomed to that."

They chatted briefly, and then Cunningham showed him around the firm's facilities.

A godown of warehouses and offices shared by all the American trading houses had been built across Soochow Creek and faced the broad Whangpoo River embankment alongside similar French and British godowns. The partners, a tea taster, a silk inspector, and counting house clerks occupied offices there. Compradors, essential Chinese who served as liaison and facilitators with the Chinese, also had offices, quarters, and a common room far down the hall in the rear. Richard will walk or ride a shuttle there for much of his work.

Cunningham told the house comprador, Sunchong, to cash Richard's checks and to administer to his needs. Richard met Hop Tzu, his houseboy, with a two-foot-long queue, a passive face, and a friendly slant to the eyes. Hop Tzu very quickly learned to lay out Richard's wardrobe, wait upon him at meals, remove his chair when he rose, and hand him his stick and hat when he went out. Richard could go to bed without finding a mosquito under his mosquito bar, and when he awoke Hop Tzu brought tea and toast and laid out his clothes.

Amanda Williams, wife of a merchant captain, commented to Richard a few days later, "Don't you think China is just the best place in the world to live? One is so nicely waited upon." Hop Tzu was a perfect servant.

Richard hung a daguerreotype of Meto over the bed. He would buy more furniture later. He quickly adopted Ben Franklin's maxim, "Early to bed and early to rise." He worked beside Doyle processing papers similar those he had worked on in Hong Kong, noticing subtle differences in procedures, products, and prices. Before meals he played on the grand piano, missing Dora's accompaniment, and billiard games often followed after.

On his first break from his clerical duties, he borrowed a small dinghy and set out up Soochow Creek. He had enjoyed rowing a shell while at Columbia, and decided that Soochow Creek made fine calm water on which to exercise during free times. The resistance of its current gave regular heft to his sinewy arms that pulled him along.

He passed by the European architecture of the foreign godowns, and then by the houseboats and sampans crawling with families along the creek shore. They looked destitute. *Must all be refugees from the Taiping raids*, he thought. On one boat, he noticed a man fishing, obviously the father of two toddling children who scrambled at his feet. One of the urchins, a black-haired girl, reached down to the water to investigate a piece of flotsam. Suddenly, she lost balance and fell into the water. Her father heard the splash and looked down at the water. He did nothing. He stared a moment until the splash dissipated, then returned to his fishing.

The image of the dead baby in the Pearl River flashed through Richard like a lightning bolt—*this man will let his own child drown.* A few quick strokes, and Richard was beside the boat. A small, still arm was visible just under the water. He reached down, seized the little child, raised her out of the water, and laid her on the floor of his boat. She spluttered, coughed, and then started to cry.

Richard paddled over to the father, lifted the child, and set her at his feet. The fisherman stared wide-eyed at Richard. The mother quickly appeared from within the bamboo roof and hugged the little girl to her bosom. Satisfied that the child was safe, Richard drifted back into the stream and continued rowing. Without a word, the father followed him with his eyes.

As he rowed, Delano's horrid words came back to him, 'Families throw away babies they don't want.' He would never get accustomed to such heathen callousness. His oars dug at the water hard, again and again, arms aching, breathing hard, trying to splash away the awful memories.

Pulling past the miserable families in the houseboats, he looked across into the close-packed Chinese buildings behind the godowns, trying to picture the people living in tenements and hovels much like the Chinese section near Hong Kong. The squalor was endless as far as he could see from the water. The people he could see looked dirty, sad, and poverty stricken. He heard cries, yells, and the general hubbub of crowded streets as he rowed. When in the godown, the Russells sometimes heard such racket and attributed it to minor riots over some local grievance and thought little of it.

中国

A SPEAKER DRESSED in a soiled deep blue Chinese robe stood on a box exhorting a small crowd of impoverished natives and refugees. "Gold in California. Gold lie on ground all place," he shouted. "Get rich easy. Come to ship." Mingling in the crowd, two American sailors passed out brochures printed in Chinese. Those that could read studied the brochure as the speaker shouted on. "Come back soon. Bring gold for family. No more starve. Gold in California."

Gold lying on the ground waiting to be picked up was something his audience could not imagine. Gold meant untold wealth. Many had fled poor farms and starved in the city. Others worked for scraps from the *fanqui,* and all wanted a better life. This man promised they could have that life. Word spread, and more thin, struggling men joined the crowd.

Wen Chi-chong pushed his way to the front. Pushing behind him, four other men joined him and edged closer. Wen shook his fist at the speaker. "You lie,'" he shouted in Chinese so all could hear. "You steal my father. Ship no go to gold mountain. Father no come home. Where is gold?"

The speaker ignored him. The four with Wen began telling the crowd, "No go with *fanqui.* You no come back. No real gold."

Two destitute men stepped forward to take pamphlets from the speaker. "You smart fellows. Get rich. Bring back gold for family," said the speaker.

Wen pushed a ragged man away so the man could not reach the pamphlet. From a secluded place, two rough sailors swept up two gold-seekers and, before anyone else noticed, hustled them out of sight. Wen knew that these two poor men would sail for a month in a dark hold with the stink and illness of hundreds of others. There would be little food, much filth, no air, no water, and many would die.

Wen shouted again to his neighbors. "No go. No gold. You never come back. You die."

Others joined in the shouting. To many refugees the risk was worth taking. Fathers fought with sons, brothers argued with brothers. Someone threw rocks at the speaker. A demonstrator was hit and retaliated. Soon a desperate man threw a fist at one who had lost a relative. The clamor turned into a riot.

Suddenly, the thunder of hoofbeats burst upon the melee. Mounted uniformed troops galloped into the crowd, swinging swords, banging shields, and yelling threats. A horse knocked an emaciated man beneath his hooves. The soldiers turned and roared back into the agitators. The demonstrators scattered.

The speaker jumped off the box and ran into an alley. The sailors fled. Wen clutched a cut on his shoulder from a sword blow that narrowly missed taking off his head. He fumed against the *fanqui* who had kidnapped his father, raged against the Chinese who helped them, and raged at the official brutality.

RICHARD ROWED BEYOND the city's noises and could have heard none of this.

10

"Mr. Starr, I am assigning you the primary responsibility for the house's tea business. Your duties will include negotiating prices and weights, seeing that tea is properly packed, sorted, and transported to the correct ships on time. Your salary will be $80 a month." Cunningham folded his hands on the desk.

Richard let his shoulders drop, but the tension in his neck remained. "Thank you, Mr. Cunningham." This substantial raise in both salary and responsibility made him apprehensive as well as eager to get started. He knew no Chinese words, knew teas only by names on shipping papers, knew shipping only on paper, and knew he could do the job. "I'm sure I will repay your confidence." He failed to suppress a nervous grin.

"Ahyue and Mr. Boyd, our tea-taster, will help you get started." Ahyue, the firm's oldest comprador, a Chinese who once helped facilitate trades, would serve as a translator. Cunningham said, "Be prepared for each negotiation. Be firm and honest in your negotiations, and you will have no trouble with the Chinese."

"One more thing," Cunningham said. He got up from his desk, crossed to a black lacquer Chinese cabinet in the corner, opened it, and pulled out a revolver. Cunningham turned the revolver, held it by the barrel and presented the handle to Richard. "I want you to have this."

He took the handle, quickly turned the weapon to the ground away from his boss and immediately examined the cylinder for loaded bullets. Richard knew guns well, had shot pistols at targets and small animals, and automatically checked whether one was loaded. Then he stared at Cunningham. Was a weapon necessary to buy tea? To threaten for a good price? Was this for defense? Did the Chinese hate the foreigners that much? Cunningham waited while the astonished Richard looked over the Colt six-shot weapon.

"We have occasionally found a revolver useful when in Chinese parts of the foreign settlements," Cunningham said. "You may never need it. I hope you don't, but keep it safe and carry it with you whenever you leave our compound. Here is a box of ammunition. Load it, and use it as you need," said Cunningham. "But don't kill anybody. That brings big trouble for us."

Richard left the office pleased with the promotion and new responsibility but nervous about what he might need to do. How could he shoot if challenged and not risk killing someone? He would have to avoid any debauchery, angry crowds, or rowdy sailors, and any situation that might turn violent. He walked to his room in a soft drizzling rain.

That afternoon Richard met Herbert Boyd in his tea taster's office. Jars of tea lined the walls. Papers, boxes, and record books jammed the tight space suffused with blended musky, floral, and toasty aromas. "Tea comes here from the country over the mountains, down the Yangtze, or by steamer up from Canton," the precise little man explained.

"I'd like a sample of the teas I will be buying," Richard said. "So I can compare."

"Here's a muster of lapsang souchong. Take a little."

"Muster?"

"Same as sample."

Richard opened the canister marked with a chop, the Chinese character identifying the grower's crop, and fondled and sniffed the leaves as he had seen others do. "Now try a Chinese oolong." Another sample hardly smelled any different. Boyd said, "In time, you'll be able to distinguish differences in texture, aroma, and color, and develop a sense of value. I value the tea according to a standard agreed upon between our house and the tea guild. You will be concerned with the quantity, the packing, and the weighing, and you will negotiate the total price of the entire shipment based on the values I give you." He handed Richard a book with values listed alongside the chop markers and dates. "Take this book. Learn it well. When a purchase is completed, you report to me, and I complete the record."

A few days later, Richard, dressed neatly in a black suit and top hat, walked with Ahyue over the wooden Soochow Creek bridge to the godown. The old Chinese comprador wore his typical merchant's deep blue robe and made no conversation during the walk. Meanwhile, Richard's thoughts raced in anticipation. His father had called the Chinese the most scandalous rascals and scoundrels in the world for they lacked Christian morals. In negotiating, father had advised to remember to be truthful and impersonal, to always keep your promises, and if something is confidential, say so without revealing it. Cunningham had once said, "Asiatics might consider honesty a strange habit. They nevertheless appreciate the truth, and it greatly facilitates business." Richard vowed to himself to be honest even with a scoundrel.

Inside the packing room, filled but open crates lay on the floor. In a building behind the godown, sweaty laborers wearing only loincloths stomped knee deep in crates to pack the dried tea leaves. Under the eyes of merchants, laborers heaved the filled crates onto a nine-foot-tall balance hung from a tripod of stout poles while a Chinese supervisor adjusted counterweights.

Richard walked around inspecting open crates, putting on his most knowing frown as he looked over his first shipment. He could not tell whether crates were unusually heavy or light, whether they held bricks, were packed ruinously or dried poorly. He knew that everyone could see he was a novice.

Ahyue introduced a beardless young man as Kuan Yingho, with whom Richard would negotiate. The pleasant-looking Chinese purser nodded, and Richard returned the nod. A tight-fitting skullcap with a tassel remained on the oriental head, so Richard kept on his stovepipe hat. Each negotiator remained silent while scrutinizing the weighing. Richard selected four heavy but empty crates to determine the tare—the average empty crate weight—to subtract from a loaded crate's weight to determine the tea's weight. Kuan, the seller, selected four light crates. They compromised on the tare, then sealed in the tea crates and began weighing. Richard and Kuan sat on opposing sides of a small table, and Ahyue remained silent as the two traders alternately called the weights. Kuan's fingers flew over a counting board flipping beads with extraordinary speed. Richard's fingers scratched and blotted on a paper at a plodding rate.

"Stop," Richard called out after eight full crates had been weighed. The ninth crate weighed over a kilo more than the average of the others. Able to communicate only through Ahyue, he faced Kuan's blank face as Ahyue translated: "Crate weigh too much. He want to examine it." Kuan waved his hand quickly.

A deep Chinese shout from behind Kuan stopped all activity. A husky Chinese merchant rushed at the table. Richard blinked, Ahyue started, Kuan jumped. The merchant slammed his fists on the table, and barked an unintelligible diatribe at Richard. The baggy sleeves of the man's robe swung as he pounded the table repeatedly. His shouting continued for several minutes, giving Richard time to adjust to the surprise.

Ahyue sat calmly to tame the words he had to translate. The merchant's cheeks shook in vehemence as he stifled his anger while waiting for the translation. ""He say exam no necessary. He say no Kee Chong ever doubt him."

Richard, utterly taken aback, straightened his shoulders, fought to look firm, and faced the man. For Ayhue's relay he said, "I don't doubt you. I just want to examine the crate."

The angry man suddenly spoke pidgin, "You new. You young boy. You no here before." Then he leaned on his fists again to deliver another blast of Chinese screeches. Richard thought he could adjust to the tirade, but he did not. Even without understanding a word, he knew that the man was insulting him and prayed that his hurt did not show. Should he shout back? Was this the time to show the revolver? He forced himself to sit tall and lean forward, thinking that this offensive heathen would only understand stiffness and hard argument in response. Be firm. Be honest. He braced. "Please do as I say," he demanded. "Open the chest." Ahyue translated, and they waited through the man's retort.

Ahyue reported, "He say you wrong. Other crate very light. He say he no complain about that."

The harsh dark eyes narrowed into an accusation that penetrated Richard's core. "You lie. You cheat," the heathen said, startling Richard with English. Richard silently fought the insult and the startle—the accusation was outrageous. Don't be affected, he told himself, but it did affect him.

"We waste time. Open the crate." Richard's words were clear without translation.

After another incomprehensible outburst, the man said in pidgin, "Go look. I report you to Kee Chong boss." The man folded his arms, turned, and scowled away. Richard knew he must report to Cunningham before this scoundrel did.

A laborer dug in the tea and, reaching the bottom, lifted out a brick. The big merchant watched from the side, slowly stroking the hair growing out of a black mole on his cheek.

Immediately upon his return Richard reported to the head of the house. "When I questioned the weight of a crate, a Chinese merchant accosted me. He interrupted and used abusive language. He tried to intimidate me. A coolie did find a brick in the crate."

"Was the man big for a Chinaman, with bad teeth?" Cunningham asked.

"I think so. Yes."

"Mouth like one of those infernal temple guard lions that we call Foo Dogs?"

"I'd say so, wide nose, scowl."

"A gross mole on his cheek?"

"That's him."

"That was Kung Loong," Cunningham said. "Kung owns the hong tea house you were buying from. Your purser and the laborer who found the brick were Kung's men. They were testing you."

"They knew this was my first negotiation. Father said the Chinese were scoundrels."

"A new man can expect rough treatment," Cunningham said. "The brick in the chest was a test."

"You said to be firm and honest and I'd have no trouble. I guess in the end I didn't have trouble."

At times, Cunningham managed by teaching lessons, unlike the aloof management of Forbes and Delano in Hong Kong. "Kung probably faked the anger. You did well to face it. And you passed the test. Kung and others will respect you for that."

It struck Richard that Cunningham had tested him, too, by throwing him to the wolves without warning. Richard said, "It seemed that his vehemence was unnecessary."

"All Chinese know well the arts of intimidation, half-truth and stonewall. They have peculiar standards and priorities developed to dodge official pressures and bureaucrats." He said to Richard, "If you sense misrepresentation or lying, be firm about it. Correct the culprit and confront him directly as you did. There is no need to be diplomatic. He knows where his profit will ultimately come from."

Cunningham paused as if he were about to say more. Richard waited. "You can be sure that most Chinese are honest and intelligent," Cunningham said. "I'm not sure about Kung."

Richard relaxed with relief that Cunningham thought he had passed his first test, but if he were to see Kung again, his boss's doubts about Kung concerned him.

"You will likely see more of Kung."

11

RICHARD LEARNED MANY negotiating tactics by observing Kung Loong, a veritable Edwin Booth, and, in a way, Richard became an actor too. In a few months time, he had observed enough of Kung's tactics, expressions, and mannerisms that he felt he could trust his instincts and react so as to earn Kung's trust in return.

When they had finished trading one day, Kung Loong, acting as friendly as he could, twirled the hair of his mole and said to Richard, "Come to singsong performance in city. We have meal. Come east gate tomorrow. At midday."

Kung smiled as he extended the invitation, but the twirl of the mole hair meant more than the smile did. Richard had noticed the involuntary twirl when Kung held a hidden motive behind something he was saying, a sign of nervousness or treachery, an unintended signal to Richard to beware. The opportunity to see a singsong performance and more of a Chinese city than the slums of Hong Kong or a street in Canton nevertheless tempted him. The chance to look behind those big city walls enticed him.

Although wary about the real reason for the invitation, Richard said, "I will, Loong. I've wanted to see a singsong theater. Thank you."

Richard and Walter Tanner, an American clerk from Augustine Heard & Co., arrived first at the east gate, its heavy, wooden doors braced open. They had dressed for the occasion in coats and light trousers, casual and cool, pleased to be out of hot black business suits now that the air was warming. The city's worn and sooty brick walls towered twenty feet above them. A rancid stench assaulted them as they neared the gate. It reminded Richard of the discarded raw meat in Wheeler's butcher shop in Massachusetts.

Three weathered Chinese heads jammed onto ten-foot pikes flanked the city gate. Two matted queues hung down, host to black flies swarming and picking at dried blood. A third head seemed almost alive, recently severed, still dripping blood into a coagulating puddle on the ground. Several disembodied arms and a leg lay in the dirt; flies feasted. Mesmerized, Richard stared for a moment, then hurried past the mess into the city. Tanner did not speak and followed into a crowded square.

"I can't eat after this," Richard said. He gagged and swallowed bile. In silence they moved away from the gate and looked around. Not much different than Canton, Richard thought. Except the horror at the gate.

"There's Kung. Someone is with him," Richard said. Kung and another Chinese merchant, both elegantly robed, emerged from the busy swarm of Shanghai residents. Many street people seemed to move to open a path for these two, as if they feared the wealth displayed in their garments. The two Chinese bowed; Richard and Tanner returned the formality and said, "*Ni Hao* … hello."

Kung introduced his companion, "Yang Fang." Then he said, "Follow us," and turned to lead them across the square. *Who is that man?* Richard thought. *Why is he here?*

The Americans followed the two merchants through narrow streets, streets that angled in no discernible pattern—streets that bore the city's commerce on foot, wheelbarrow, and wagon, streets on which people lived, ate and drank. The four merchants passed open-air food shops; from one, a wretch waving a bony arm hawked small animal carcasses, and nearby, three haggard women stooped over a kettle popping with pungent bubbles. Richard shuddered at the sharp, spicy odors, unable to imagine what might be in those pots. On his left, as he stepped over an arched stone bridge, a naked child defecated into a gutter that let into a canal. Farther on, against the wall of a teahouse, slouched a smeared face in a pile of bunched rags, Richard saw an arm scratch at a crotch and bring its pinched fingers up to the smeared mouth, where rotted teeth nibbled on a louse.

"Taste good?" Tanner said.

Richard winced at the sarcasm, as he had winced at acidic spices, the louse a sign of misery that contrasted with the lavish living at Kee Chong and Howqua's residence. He wondered where Kung lived.

Inside the theater, a large round space of red and yellow trimmed windowless walls, a short runway led to a center stage, next to which Kung escorted them to a private table and seats on a level floor fenced off from the rabble. Kung boasted that he owned the club where the performance was to take place as well as other property speculations in the city and in the French concession. Richard expected that, like Howqua, Kung squeezed commissions from every step of the business—construction, sale, resale, lease, and sublease.

Surrounding the stage a noisy audience sat jabbering and drinking at the tables. The Americans sat with their hosts, and a waitress placed drinks of wine and juice before them. Suddenly, gongs crashed, drums pounded, and a dozen dancers in harlequin-like costumes bounced and tumbled onto the stage as if they had springs for legs. Next, shirtless acrobats twisted and gyrated while balancing on tall poles. A scantily clad dancer bent herself backward while juggling four balls. Another twisted herself into grotesque contortions putting her feet behind her head backward. The athletic mayhem on stage set the audience whooping and hollering while they laughed, drank, ate, and jostled each other.

After a finale that included impossible flips back and forth from seesaws and finally onto a three-person-high human pyramid, Kung's party moved to a banquet room. Boys brought pepper-salt spare ribs, braised prawns, and fried dumplings for the Chinese, beef, chicken and vegetables, dry and overcooked in the English fashion, for the two foreign guests.

Kung, much more adept at English than Richard was at Chinese, said, "Help yourself." They often talked to each other in pidgin now, Richard trying to pick up some Chinese words.

The Chinese diners snatched the delicacies with their chopsticks. Seeing Richard and Tanner slowly manipulate the bamboo sticks, Kung reached over and placed ribs lathered in shiny brown sauce before them. The Americans lifted slices of dry beef with their chopsticks, and, having seen Kung and Fang do so, tried the surprisingly good ribs, dumplings, and prawns with their fingers. Sparse polite comments about the acrobats and the food, and mutual amusement over the Americans' efforts with the chopsticks punctuated the meal.

When a clear soup with noodles had been consumed, Kung turned serious. Speaking in pidgin, he said, "Young Americans want make money. I want help you." The Americans looked at each other. This was a pleasure meal, Richard thought, and had not brought a translator as he surely would have done had he expected any business to take place. Knowing Kung, Richard suspected some chicanery with the two novice traders.

"Your business slow. You buy Chinese good for sell in America, yes?" His listeners nodded. "You need money for buy."

A silent glance passed between the Americans. Kung turned to his thin companion, who had so far said nothing but a few words of Chinese in apparent praise for the acrobats. "Yang Fang partner in bank with me." The expressionless Yang paid no attention, as if he didn't understand the pidgin or knew well what Kung was about to say. "We lend money so you buy Chinese good." Kung pulled at the black hair from his mole.

Do not agree to anything now, Richard told himself. "I like your thought." Richard said. "But why us? Others at Kee Chong trade more."

Kung was ready. "You young. Work hard. Deserve help and money."

"Right now I have no purchase in mind. Desirable items are not available," Richard said. He had noticed the mole hair pull.

Tanner began to speak, "I have an idea ..." Richard kicked him under the table. Tanner said no more.

Kung looked to Tanner. "Goods I get you."

"How?" Richard said. "You know rebels stop trade."

"I find." Kung's folded face battled a smile. "No ask how."

Richard had no intention of borrowing money from Kung to buy anything from him, and wanted to stop any more talk about it. "I respect our business relationship." Emulating a Chinese stalling tactic that usually meant no, he said, "I will consider what you offer."

"We talk more," Kung concluded.

Richard remembered what Blake had said about personal ventures. Kung could be a Chinese to work with, a source of money and contacts ... If he dared.

A FEW WEEKS later Richard chanced to speak at dinner with visiting American Captain Josiah Kilton, an affable but coarse man who told good sea stories. After a tale about his ship almost capsizing in a storm because it had been top-heavy, Captain Kilton mentioned that he was looking for ballast to load before he left for home later in the week.

Often, low quality Chinese porcelain made weight for ballast in tea ships and could be sold for profit at the destination. As Russell & Co. did not deign to sell ballast, Richard spotted a chance for a personal profit. This might be an opportunity to test Kung's offer to lend and procure goods with relatively little risk.

He dared to try. "I think I may be able to get you some porcelain," Richard said. Richard estimated the approximate weight and price from his memory of shipping papers. Soon they reached an agreement to reimburse the porcelain's cost plus a markup in cash upon delivery to the ship. If he couldn't get the porcelain, he'd tell Kilton by the next morning.

Richard went to Kung Loong to take him up on the offer to lend money and to buy goods with it. Kilton's commitment to pay right away meant that the loan would cost Richard virtually no interest, and the marked-up price would allow a profit. If Kung gave reasonable terms and did what he said, there was no risk.

The Chinese banker seemed eager to make a loan. "*She de—* yes. I get you porcelain." Over the next several days, with Ahyue to translate, they had negotiated the price, a broker fee for Kung, a low loan interest, six months to pay back, and planned delivery of the porcelain. Three days later, Richard stood on the dock to collect his payment and to see the ballast loaded onto Captain Kilton's small three-master.

Next to Kilton's ship a group of twenty or thirty Chinese men grouped silently and close together, bare-chested, thin, dirty, and destitute. Sailors held staves and weapons and stood watching the Chinese. Two of the sailors had whips.

Richard approached Kilton when the last crate had disappeared into the hold. "The porcelain is aboard," he said. Kilton handed Richard a sack of silver coins, which Richard counted and pocketed. "Thank you, Captain."

The sailors began to herd the Chinese onto the ship, shoved and poked them with the staves to keep them in order. "Who are those men?" Richard asked.

"My passengers. They want to go to California for the gold."

"Your men are treating them like slaves."

"No. They have paid for their passage. They are not slaves."

As the group of slaves neared the gangplank, one of them burst away and ran. In a few steps, a sailor tripped him with a stave and dragged him back toward the ship, where another sailor flogged him twice with a whip. Richard struggled to control his passion. "That doesn't look like a volunteer."

"You've got your pay. I've got my ballast. The rest is none of your business."

It was none of his business, Richard thought, but he had helped a slave trader. Slavery is wrong. Delano's indifference about opium used after sale and Simon Brown's attitude about slavery had repelled him before, and now his conscience again spoke. He should return the money he'd just received. But he needed it to repay Kung. He continued to argue with his conscience as he trudged along the waterfront, until suddenly a troubling thought burst from nowhere—did Kung and Kilton together arrange to take slaves to California and use Richard to help them?

Richard repaid Kung.

12

WHEN THE FEBRUARY mail boat delivered the Russells' package of dispatches, letters, and papers, Richard saw among his letters a message from the ship *Dagmar*, which had sailed for Boston via San Francisco carrying his shipment of rifles. He had not expected to hear about the rifle venture this quickly and had not been thinking about it.

> *Your shipment was sold to Kratze Brothers gun dealers in San Francisco. Few fine guns are available there. All prices are high. We were able to negotiate a particularly good price. Enclosed please find a note drawn on Wells Fargo for your one-half share of the net profit. The other share was delivered to Wells Fargo for the account of Russell & Co., New York. Signed, George Fowler, supercargo.*

The note amounted to more than he expected. He promptly took it to the firm's accountant, paid his debt to Howqua, his debt to Russell & Co., and credited the remainder to his account. Now, freed from debt and nepotism incurred in Hong Kong, his financial situation looked better. With the small profit from the porcelain sale to captain Kilton, his saving had begun.

RUSSELL & CO. welcomed military and civilian ship officers for board and to eat with them when their ships passed through

Shanghai. Contacts led to business. One evening Richard chanced to dine next to Captain Hugh Nicholson of the *Mississippi*. He knew that the American naval frigate was on its way home from Japan carrying Consul Townsend Harris, who had negotiated to open Nagasaki and Yokohama to American trade. The great warship's enormous guns, giant paddle wheels, and sails worked together to make a powerful fighting machine.

"Would you like to tour the ship and meet Mr. Harris before we go?" asked Nicholson. "Come out for a late breakfast tomorrow."

Good as the Russell's cook was, he could not make corned beef hash, codfish balls, cornbread, or pancakes that matched a ship cook's breakfast. Richard's patriotism also meant that he must visit this military marvel. "I most certainly would. Thank you."

The next day dawned clear and sunny. No tea meetings had been arranged, and his time was free. A brisk breeze persuaded Richard to spend his day sailing out to the *Mississippi* and back by himself. He had always had relaxed and enjoyable solitary short sails around Lake Mackinac in the Massachusetts hills. Confident that he knew the nuances of wind-powered travel, he sent a message to the godown to ask that the Russell's thirty-foot sailboat *Adrian* be readied for him and brought to the dock.

An hour later, Richard spied two coolies rowing the *Adrian* toward the dock and headed down to meet it. When he reached the waterfront, he was surprised when Simon Brown, last seen in Hong Kong, hurried along the bank toward him.

"Good to see y'all, Richard," the tall redheaded Carolinian said as they met.

"A surprise to see you here. What are you doing in Shanghai?

They shook hands vigorously. "I came for better luck," Brown said.

"I'm on my way to the *Mississippi*. The captain promised me a tour."

Brown had tied his uncut red hair into a ponytail. He looked beyond the ships over the choppy water. After a brief explanation for his presence in Shanghai, Brown said, "I'm glad we met up. I need someone sensible to talk to. The missionaries I live with are too possessed with religion to understand. It's the news from home. In Charleston there's talk of war."

Richard motioned that they sit on a bench at the foot of the dock. "Yes, I've read about it," Richard said.

"This new politician, Lincoln, is an abolitionist agitator," Brown said. "I hear he's a backwoodsman and something of a monkey." Brown spread his helpless hands. "Carolina may leave the Union if he's the next president. Or sooner."

"Breaking the Union would be a great tragedy for our country."

"I'm thinking I should go home to support my people." They gazed over the water in silence, watching a Russell shore shuttle puff past. "I can't support my home from here."

Richard did not want to get into a lengthy discussion. The coolies with the *Adrian* were landing. "Because Carolina may secede? I don't think it will come to that." Richard looked for his boat.

"My uncle thought I could help our cause because he believed that the British here would support the Southern states with cotton and tobacco orders. Not much luck with that. I did almost get some good British rifles in Hong Kong."

Richard tensed. It was Brown who had asked to buy Howqua's rifles, as he had guessed.

After a moment, Brown said, "A snake of a Chink broker refused to sell it to me. Somebody bought it out from under me. I could do nothing." He shrugged.

Richard's first instinct was to confess his purchase. He wanted to be honest. He began, "Simon, I ..." and stopped. Brown had blamed his Chinese snake broker. He realized that Simon didn't know who had bought them. If he confessed, should he deny that he knew Brown wanted Howqua's rifles, or throw the blame on Delano? Brown thought he had been undercut unfairly, and confession could ruin Richard's business reputation. No, he shouldn't lie. The *Adrian* landed, and its rowers were preparing the sail to the *Mississippi*.

"I ... am really sorry," Richard said, hoping his face wasn't red. "I mean, who would ... It's not right when that happens." He hoped he sounded sincere. "Business is business. Tough at times."

The Russell coolies had raised the *Adrian*'s sail and waved to him. "Here's my ride. I hope you will stay in Shanghai. Good luck. See you again."

They stood, shook hands, and Richard cast off into the river. Brown quietly said, "See y'all," and returned to his walk.

He hadn't directly lied to Brown, but his conscience knew that silence about the rifles had been a lie. *Was it necessary to lie to protect my reputation for honesty?*

13

INVIGORATED BY A stomach filled with the *Mississippi's* buckwheat pancakes, Richard sat again before Cunningham's desk. He reported on the month's tea transactions with Kung and others, concluding that a lesser amount of tea had been available than in the previous month.

Cunningham said, "The partners want you to travel to our house at Foochow. Lately, Chinese merchants do not bring tea on the Yangtze because they fear the Taiping will rob them on their return upstream. Though for different reasons, exports suffer here as well as in Canton. Foochow is closer than we are to tea-growing mountains and may afford a base to maintain Russell & Co.'s tea exports. We want you to assess the business opportunities there."

Foochow lay halfway south from there to Hong Kong and up the Min River. Richard jumped at a chance for a change from office routine. "I can be ready for Foochow in a couple of days."

Two days later, Henry Grew, the second of the two Russell partners in Shanghai, carried to Richard's room a shotgun, broken over his arm. "Take this," he said as he held out the gun. "You might need it to get to Foochow. You can leave it there."

Richard took the weapon, felt the heft and balance of the battered heavy ten gauge single shot. He sighted inside the barrel, and rust spots showed inside. He could not believe Grew seriously expected him to use it. "This is a well-used gun, Mr. Grew. Did all this abuse happen in Foochow?"

Grew laughed. "No. Showing the gun is a good threat." He stopped laughing and turned serious. "Chinese boatmen around Foochow are not just cheats. They have a reputation as pirates. You will have to hire a boat to take you up the Min. You need to make sure they take you where you want to go." Grew produced a box of ten-gauge shells. "Your course will take you directly through Fookie Tom's favorite playgrounds, too."

Stories in every foreign settlement in China described a desperate Englishman called Fookie Tom, whose gangs of marauders hid in the coastal islands and raided vessels they thought might have silver or opium. The pirate spoke English and Chinese, killed at will, and stole anything from opium and silver to clothing, weapons, and men for his gang. He had been seen, evidently, in virtually every river delta on the coast. Some claimed the legendary pirate was actually many different men.

"Thank you." Richard held the broken shotgun to the window and sighted again through the badly pocked barrel. Another weapon? Wasn't his revolver enough? "I hope I never have to fire this relic."

He took the ammunition Grew offered. "Perhaps there are ducks in the Min," he said with smile.

With a sizable bribe and a mild threat about Russell's future shipping business, Grew persuaded the coastal steamer captain to let Richard take a ship's longboat fitted with a gaff-rigged sail. Grew's warning made Richard think that sailing a boat to take him up the Min risked attracting a Fookie Tom. A new Russell comprador named Apun suggested a deception. He bought a dirty red sail from a houseboat owner and fitted it to the gaff. A large, flat Chinese peasant's hat from a Hog Alley shop completed the plan, and Richard went along with it. From a distance the long-boat and its skipper would look like a lone Chinese fisherman.

Richard packed the shotgun, unloaded and broken for safety, in his duffel bag along with the shells, his pistol and its bullets, and clothing. Four days steady steaming down the coast brought the steamer near the White Dogs, small uninhabited islands at the entrance to the Min River.

The steamer captain searched the midmorning horizon. "I see no other sails. Off you go. Good luck."

A deckhand tossed his duffel and case into the boat. Richard clamored down a swinging rope ladder and lurched into the rock-ing longboat. He tucked the duffel containing his revolver and shotgun under the stern seat and, taking a deep breath, signaled to cast off from the steamer.

The boat was light to pull as he rowed away before setting the red sail. Northeast winds riled the China Sea's swells. The strong following wind and incoming tide then sped him into the mouth of the Min, twelve miles from Foochow city. When the steamer dwindled to a distant plume of black smoke, the only sign of civilization was a lonely longboat with a red sail, one pretend Chinese fisherman at the tiller.

He sailed for an hour before he could see a shore. The big hat that marked him as Chinese repeatedly blew off, so he tucked it under the seat. He ate a buttermilk biscuit and a container of beef stew and sailed on, keeping within sight of shore but far off. He decided to parallel this shore until he saw the other shore, and then to sail as equally distant from each as he could.

The longboat sliced the water easily and rode smoothly, and hours passed. The sky remained clear but for occasional white clouds. Their shadows on the water relieved the bright sun's re-flections. To pass the time, Richard tried to remember seamans' ditties he'd heard on the *Alfred Hill* but could only sing a few lines. "What do you do with the drunken sailor?" He laughed at his efforts to make up words to the answer and fit them to the tune. In his versions of the verses, the drunken sailor was thrown into the longboat, hoisted to the topmast, thrown in bed with the captain's daughter, had his belly shaved with a rusty razor, and more. When he had exhausted his imagination, Richard put his feet up on the bulwark, sat back, closed his eyes, and imagined that he sailed the Berkshire lakes on a balmy summer day. Time passed. Gradually the river shore curved so that, unnoticed, the wind no longer blew directly upstream.

中国

FOOKIE TOM TORE at the red fish he had pulled off the campfire, spat out a bone, and chewed the harsh flesh, his long, thick black beard sticky with fish oil and saliva. A cave lay behind him to his left, before which five rifle barrels formed a pyramid. Inside, four dirty Oriental thugs, barefooted and in shirtsleeves, sorted through a trunk, laughing drunkenly as they argued how the four could share three gold pocket watches.

Fookie Tom gazed over the white-capped waters of the river. There had been slim chance of a good raid during this trip to the Min. Their last day in the cove, he decided. Seize the next small boat that came along, whatever it was. Nothing on the water. The sun shone directly overhead. Then he saw it. First a spark, no … a reflection. Then the top of a single red sail.

"Boys. We sail," he said in English.

In a few moments, Tom gathered his battered English captain's coat with brass buttons and epaulets, and his men brought rifles, swords, and pistols and rowed out into the river, where they set out after the lone sailboat. With larger sail than the gaff-rigged boat and a good shore-hugging breeze, they gained on it. The boat was smaller than Tom had thought at first. Only one man sat in the stern. The sail was not a Chinese design; it looked more like those the Europeans sometimes used for small sailers. He could see no fish nets and no cargo. Small and solitary in the river, it might be smuggling something, or trying to slip treasure—gold or silver—into the foreign concession at Foochow.

Tom trimmed his sails a bit so they could close the distance. The red sail had slowed. The wind had nearly died around it. His quarry now wore a Chinese peasant's hat. Tom laughed out loud. *He's seen us and wants to look Chinese,* Tom thought. Tom would toy with him, play Chinese too, and go along with the pretense. If needed, he knew English well, and a little French. In Chinese, he ordered his crew, "Lower sails and row."

Soon they were close enough to hail the sailor at the tiller. Tom stood up, donned his old English captain's jacket, stuck a loaded pistol in his belt, and was ready to play his game with this foolish fake fisherman. The four crewmen watched.

To frighten the man who thought he was disguised as a Chinese fisherman, Fookie Tom fired his pistol into the air and shouted in Chinese, "*Ting.* We come board."

中国

RICHARD HEARD THE gunshot. The standing man looked to him like Blackbeard resurrected. The pirate shouted at Richard in Chinese. He had no answer for Chinese words he did not understand. The heavily bearded pirate shouted again. Richard had not seen so much beard on a Chinese. Was it Fookie Tom? Again he made no answer. The pirate oars went back in the water.

Richard dug in the duffel. The shotgun came out. He had not dared load it, so he set it aside. He took the empty revolver, laid it next to him on the seat, and felt in the duffel for its bullets. Not in that end, he tried the other end. The pirates came close. Richard found bullets, grabbed the pistol, and snapped the cylinder open. Rushed too much. Dropped a bullet. No time for another. Two guns, neither loaded. Don't kill anyone, Cunningham had said. He wasn't going to.

The pirates had pulled alongside. Richard saw Blackbeard, standing taller than the others in a soiled English captain's jacket, brass buttons and epaulets, long two-pointed beard, and pistol in hand, poised to step aboard his longboat. Four dark-skinned, unwashed men stood behind him, waiting for orders.

The black beard barked gibberish at the rowers. He pointed his pistol ahead as he stepped onto the bow seat, two ruffians right behind him. He delivered orders in Chinese.

Richard raised the shotgun, threatened with it, and said, "What do you want? I have nothing."

He aimed the shotgun at them, finger on the trigger, and held it at his hip, swinging it from one pirate to the other. His words in English, his face exposed, his leather boots obvious, his disguise was useless. The three stepped toward him.

Blackbeard put a sinister smile on his face and his fists on his hips. "Well, well. What have we here?" he said in perfect English.

Richard started. This surely was the Fookie Tom he'd heard about. "There is nothing here. Get out. Go back."

"American, looks like." The pirate's pistol aimed directly at Richard's chest. An order to the two brutes. They rushed at him. Instinctively, his trigger finger tightened. Click.

Fookie Tom lowered his pistol and laughed—long, harsh, and malevolent.

Richard shouted, "I have nothing. What do you want?"

Fookie Tom eyed the duffel behind Richard. "Give me the duffel."

A pirate crewman grabbed for the shotgun, Richard jerked the weapon away from him. Fookie Tom barked at his men again. Richard bent down to reach for the duffel under the seat. His hand dropped near the unloaded revolver. A crewman seized Richard by the arm, making him knock the pistol to the deck, and pulled off the big hat. The other grabbed the duffel. Richard grabbed it too. The two tussled with it for a moment, then the pirate struck him on the face. Richard felt blood run from his nose, staggered, and nearly fell. He regained his balance, summoned a lesson from the gentlemanly art of self-defense, and punched back. Someone swung the duffel at his head, an oar caught him in midsection, and his breath was gone. *Father said to let them take what they want. He was right.* Before he could shout, "Take it," Fookie Tom struck him with the butt of his pistol, and all went black.

14

Two hours later, Richard gained consciousness, splayed across the seats in the longboat, groggy, and having no idea how long he'd been unconscious. As his aching head cleared, he realized that his boat had been beached behind rocks on a small cove. He climbed out, stretched in an effort to see what worked, and splashed water on his face and head, hitting a touchy knob on his head as he did so. Caked blood on his lip broke off with the water. He winced when his thumb bumped his nose.

The smell of a driftwood fire drew him. He stumbled in bare feet toward the smell, fell once onto the sand, and ached at every joint. Slowly his memory of the Min River and of men boarding his boat crept back to him.

About twenty yards away, the five pirates camped in a cave partially disguised by gray shrubs under an overhanging rock. The bearded leader squatted next to a fire staring past Richard. Sticky, tangled hair hung around his face, filthy shirtsleeves rolled up, tight muscles rippled as he stirred the fire, and he wore Richard's leather boots.

"Where am I?" Richard said.

The pirate chief turned and stood up. "On an island."

Richard said, "Where are my things?" He kept three steps away from the man.

"What things? A worthless old shotgun and a six-shooter. Money not worth the effort to chase you."

"My duffel and boots. Give them back. They are no use to you. I told you I had nothing. Are you Fookie Tom?"

"Some may call me that." Fookie Tom looked Richard up and down quizzically. "Who are you? Why are you sailing alone in these waters?"

"I'm traveling to Foochow."

"You are alone. That is strange for a *fanqui*."

"You were supposed to think I was a fisherman."

Tom laughed "Your sail was not Chinese. Chinese fishermen do not carry duffels, take off hats, or wear leather boots when fishing. Foreigners have things worth stealing."

"What do you want with me? I need to get to Foochow."

"You should not have tried to shoot me. No one has ever fought me alone. You are either very clever or very stupid. Why did you fight for your duffel? You have nothing that I can sell or blackmail anyone with. You're not important enough to hold for ransom.

Richard bristled at the insults, clenched his fists, but relaxed them quickly. No sense in more talk. Hunger gnawed at him, still sore and tired. He had nothing but the clothes on his back. He turned away from the pirate's den and walked down the beach past his boat. The tide was lifting the water close to his boat. Oars, sail, and mast lay on the seats.

He reached rocks and shrubs that blocked walking farther, turned and came back to his boat. The pirates ignored him while they talked among themselves and dug through chests of previous loot, apparently still squabbling. Fookie Tom pulled on a brandy bottle, keeping an eye on the crew. Richard, moving slowly to avoid catching their attention, snuck back to his boat.

He set the mast and in several heaves, slid the longboat into the water, shoved into the river, and leapt in, banging his shin.

"Aieee!" a Chinese yelled.

Richard slammed the oars in place and pulled as fast as he could away from the shore. The pirates ran to the shore but stopped ankle deep, let out sounds that could only be curses, and one fired a wild pistol shot. Fookie Tom said something in Chinese, and they let him row away.

Three hours later, Richard drifted past an anchored two-masted British merchant ship and up to little Nantoi Island, the foreign concession at Foochow. A stone arch bridge that Richard later learned was the Bridge of Ten Thousand Ages crossed to the Foochow mainland. He managed to step across his boat and lash it to a low floating dock, every movement of his bruised body painful. Two Americans looked down on him from the shore.

The two Americans lifted him out of the boat and escorted him to the Russell & Co. compound. "What happened to you? Where have you come from?"

"Shanghai," he said, and they stared, as if unable to believe he had sailed so far in the little boat. "You fellows are a sight for sore eyes."

A night and food rested his exhausted body. The firm furnished new clothes, a wash basin, and a comfortable room. Still stiff and sore, he walked slowly into the head partner's office and presented a letter from Cunningham. Thomas Sloane greeted him and immediately asked. "What happened?"

"I ran into pirates when I sailed up the Min. Didn't go well."

"You incurred a foolish risk," Sloane said. "Sailing alone." His frown conveyed the seriousness with which he spoke.

"Thank you for the clothes and shoes, and the rest and good food."

"Troublemakers on the Min have caused most unpleasant incidents for foreigners. Fortunately, you made the voyage safely. You can congratulate yourself."

He did not deserve congratulations. "I'd been advised to give the pirates what they wanted. So I did." It was a white lie, but the memory of his foolishness was too raw to admit. He had been lucky.

His mission to review the operations of the Foochow office occupied their conversation thereafter until Sloane, disliking the Shanghai office inquiring into his affairs, stopped answering Richard's questions. "You can see our records. Talk to the clerks, and do what you've been sent to do."

The following day, Richard met the clerks, inquired into their business methods, and looked into the books. The Foochow traders lived in regal style, bowling or playing billiards for amusement. After two weeks talking with Sloane and the Russells and British merchants, and observing export-import activity on the island, he learned that a thriving business did indeed come through Foochow. If the Taiping and the British military continued disrupting everyone's tea trade on the Pearl and on the Yangtze rivers, and pirate activity on the Min could be controlled, Foochow could be a successful alternative port to get more of Russell & Co.'s tea to market. The British firm Jardine Matheson dominated most of Foochow's tea business and was strong competition. A serious effort would be necessary to build up the Russell office's business.

Richard's candid report completed, he found passage on a British steam shuttle to take him out the river to meet the next northbound coastal steamer. By the time he left for Shanghai, he felt completely recovered from his encounter with the pirates.

Meanwhile, French and British men of war were steaming north too. Their military officers had persuaded their respective diplomats that a collective show of foreign might would intimidate the stubborn Imperial givernment to accept the diplomats' demands for resident agents, more open ports, and legal opium sale. As the shuttle carrying Richard entered the Whangpoo River to Shanghai, steam and sail warships from Canton rendezvoused in the distance around Chung-ming Island.

15

CLERKS AND OTHER Russells chattered about Richard's exploits in the Min River for days after his return to Shanghai.

"He fought with Fookie Tom and lived?"

Doyle shrugged. "That's what I heard."

"Fookie Tom doesn't let people go. He must have beaten Richard. Did he have his revolver?"

"I don't know, but he had bruises and a cut lip when he got to Foochow."

Thinking that Meto might hear the stories about his adventure with the pirates from some acquaintance, Richard wrote her, "Foochow is a very pretty and picturesque place, but one cannot ride there on land, and, in spite of what you may hear about my journey, I am safely back with no untoward consequences. The current in the river is much too swift to make boating pleasant or safe," and thus had described for her the adventure on the river.

The partners heard the stories, too. Richard was embarrassed to have been foolish enough to sail alone in waters known to be dangerous. When he protested that all he did was follow his father's advice to give pirates what they asked for, his reputation for courage grew.

Richard reported his Foochow findings to Cunningham, who, after passing them to his partner, pronounced it satisfactory.

Richard braced for negotiating sessions with Kung Loong and settled again back into his work and relaxing pastimes.

IN THE LOUNGE before dinner, a session at the piano became particularly enjoyable, for it reminded him of the duets with Dora. He played ditties, songs, and a few classical pieces with occasional slips and fumbles. No one seemed to mind the mistakes, if they noticed them at all, and everyone seemed to enjoy the background music while they read the *North China News* or the latest papers from home.

One day, a Russian merchant, Boris Sauermann, temporarily joined the Russells for room and board while, he said, he followed up on orders from the Russian western provinces that his countrymen wanted placed. No Russells really knew exactly what the likable Russian did in Shanghai. He had mingled freely with the partners, clerks, and visiting military officers alike, but they all thought him a singularly private fellow. He visited the British and other foreign offices as well for meals and drinks. When Sauermann dined with the Russells, he often shared the piano with Richard before meals, playing duets, and they became friendly piano partners.

One day not long after the Foochow trip, Charles Parke's voice pierced the tuneful quiet in the lounge: "What can I do for you?"

A stranger had entered the room. Richard looked up and stopped playing. He leapt up and ran to the door.

"Augustus!"

His friend and cousin, Augustus Hayes from Boston, posed in the doorway, grinning that silly grin of his. They clasped hands and looked each other up and down.

"What brought you here? How good to see you. Where are you living? How is your father? Tell me everything," Richard said. The cousins had the same tousled dark hair, deep brown eyes, and tanned outdoor complexion, but Augustus's ears protruded.

Immediately they commanded the best available seats in the lounge and throughout dinner caught up on friends, home, family, and girls. Augustus said that an agent for Olyphant & Co. had offered him work in Shanghai. He had arrived the previous day and was staying at Olyphant's house until a room became available. He told Richard that their friends had not forgotten him.

When dinner was over, the cousins repaired to the salon to continue their revelry, enhanced by fine French Bordeaux. Richard joked about the Russells' life, his work with tea brokers, his negotiating adversary Kung Loong, and the trip to Foochow. They downed brandy together until late in the night and then parted, spinning from the wine and showering each other with avid promises to meet often.

Business went on as usual when Richard realized that Sauermann had not joined him at the piano for three days. Curious, he asked about the man. No one else had seen him either, or heard where he might be. Richard played on, and the Russells worked on and forgot about the tall Russian that nobody had really known.

THE EUROPEAN MILITARY patience finally broke. After two frustrating years of negotiating, threatening, blockading, and pestering coastal cities to enforce the still unratified Nanking treaty, French and British fleets loaded with battle-tested soldiers, field cannons, and howitzers pulled out into the North China Sea intending to attack the Tagu forts, take Tientsin on the Peh-ho River, and go on to occupy Peking, the Emperor's capital.

According to US President Buchanan's policy of neutrality, Americans were not to fight the Chinese. However, the American East Indian squadron flagship, *Hartford,* with its massive side wheels and eighteen guns, and the similar warship, *Powhatan,* accompanied the fleets to support the troops.

"Why are our ships joining the fight against the Chinese?" Richard said to his cousin. "I wish we could stop fighting and just go about our business. What right do the English have to force their way to Peking anyway."

Augustus laughed. "The Chinese need a good beating so they'll take us seriously."

"Why do they resist? European trade helps China as well. The celestials should know that."

"Goodness, you are full of why's. The Emperor doesn't understand that trade helps his country. He thinks scoundrels like you and me take the squeeze he would get instead."

Richard raised his glass. "I wish I did."

"Ha-ha. Here's to the Brits' victory—and our future luck!"

16

A TIRED HORSEMAN RODE his mount into the camp on the river near the Tagu forts guarding the route to the imperial capital. He dismounted, a stable boy took the foaming horse, and the rider walked stiffly to the Russian commander's tent.

Colonel Alexey Ivanoff stood as the rider stepped in. "Lieutenant Sauermann, good to see you."

Sauermann had sent couriers to Ivanoff with sealed reports on the British preparations for the expected attack. His clandestine reports had been passed on to the Chinese commander, Prince Seng Kolin-Chin, and had spurred the Russians to deliver to the Chinese ten thousand guns and fifty cannons they had promised two years earlier. Sauermann saluted. "The fleets are on the way here. They plan a direct assault on the Tagu forts as soon as all ships arrive. Less than a week."

Tsar Alexander wanted to keep the British military engaged in China. Coastal fighting and the native rebellions kept Chinese forces away from western frontier provinces that Russia coveted. Ivanoff said, "The Peking government has seemed ready to let the Brits come in to negotiate. Our task is to keep the fighting going."

"We must find Prince Seng immediately," Sauermann said.

The Chinese had built barriers of heavy chain and logs to block the river and added guns and cannons to the Tagu defenses. "Seng has so far kept secret the added cannon and the river barriers," Ivanoff said. "He thinks the Chinese defense can stop the British."

The two Russians mounted horses and galloped to the Tagu forts.

A week later, thirteen British gunboats and four supply and troop ships, and two French gunboats lay arrayed at the mouth of the Peh-ho River and just off the Tagu forts. On board the British flagship, *Plover,* Rear Admiral James Hope's reconnaissance had spotted spars and logs stretched across the Peh-ho, and he had sent a ship ahead to blast the barrier apart. During the night Chinese soldiers repaired the damage.

Hope dressed in his splendid blue uniform with brass buttons, gold braiding, and epaulettes as was proper to identify the commander. He reviewed the scene from the quarterdeck as he envisioned the attack. The gunships had been pounding the forts for two days, and now the gunboats and troops would enter the river and land troops to storm the weakened forts. To his captain, Oliver Shadwell, he ordered, "Go at the barriers. No Chinese have ever stopped a solid British attack. The *Opossum* will go first, then the French in the *Duchala.* We'll go next, and the others will follow as planned."

The *Opossum* rammed the first barrier but snagged on unseen chains in the second. Four other gunboats close behind were trapped. Immediately, forty Tagu cannon and hundreds of rifles, all preaimed at the trap, began their barrage. Conspicuous Admiral Hope was one of the first officers hit. Shadwell took command, other ships became disabled, and as night fell, the tide fell with it, stranding four ships in mud. Determined to press the attack, Shadwell ordered marines to land and storm a broken length of the fort's wall. Two hundred marines jumped overboard into waist-deep water, taking scaling ladders with them.

Canadian John Powers, marine, fought forward with his comrades, struggled, mud sucking at every step, refusing to let go of his feet. For one hundred yards, they battled ahead. Men fell and got up dripping mud. Chinese guns wounded or killed the exposed men. Hit by cannonballs, their scaling ladders now floated in worthless pieces. Almost out of the swamp, Powers and surviving marines slogged into a fifteen-foot-wide ditch filled with mud at the base of the walls. He looked up at the looming fort. He saw a soldier in a Russian fur hat talking with a blond-headed officer on the parapet. The Chinese have help, Powers realized. *We'll never take it.*

A buddy urged him ahead, and he pressed on. Exhausted, he crawled out of the ditch and collapsed. Rock piles and broken wall towered over him, protecting him from gunfire. Everyone huddled under the rocks around him was caked in mud and blood; weapons were soaked, ruined, useless. Mayhem left behind them; marines that had begun the assault lay trapped without working weapons, protected only until they moved. The rest were dead.

The cocksure redcoats had failed.

THE CHINESE STOPPED their cannons when the fleets began to leave. This allowed the trapped marines to return to their ships. One by one, the defeated fleet and remaining soldiers returned to Shanghai, minus six wrecked and abandoned gunships and eleven hundred men now dead. Soldiers and restless sailors shook off their frustration and anger by flooding into the singsong houses, bars, and brothels in the European settlements of Shanghai. "The Chinese had foreign weapons of all kinds," said a returning sailor.

"Russian officers helped them," said another.

"The plan of attack was secret, but they knew it was coming," a redcoat officer reported, "Spies are among us."

"The whole coast of China will erupt now!"

The Russells discussed the defeat for days. The Russian, Sauermann, had disappeared shortly before the assault. One evening at dinner, Richard told Doyle, "He may have been a spy."

"He often mingled among military officers who talk too much," Doyle said.

Richard enjoyed a British put-down. "I think they quite deserve their defeat."

"What do you mean?"

"They're too arrogant by half." Richard stopped eating. "The Chinese took them down a peg."

"The Brits will try to reach Peking again. Revenge will motivate them now," Doyle said. "A war with the Chinese might be to our advantage."

"Yes, the Brits will stir them up with a long pole for the reception at the Tagu forts," Richard said. "Tumult and repercussions will come to Shanghai in one form or another."

Henry Grew reminded everyone that American Minister Frederick Ward had negotiated a most-favored-nation treaty with the imperial mandarins. "Any concessions the British force from China will also be ours."

That night, Richard wrote to his mother the first letter to mention any troubles. She doubtless would hear of the British defeat. "I fear that the consequences will be dreadful, and that the whole coast of China will be in an uproar," he wrote. "I cannot say how trade may be affected, but could the Americans manage to keep out of it, it might be of advantage to their commerce. The tea market will doubtless go up at home, and I should much like to have a cargo on the way. If Americans continue to mind their own business in these stormy times, their ships should do the carrying for the world."

At about nine o'clock that night, unusually loud gongs, gunfire, and explosions from the slums near Suchow Creek unsettled the Americans enjoying their brandy and cigars. Russell & Co.'s compradors with sources in the Chinese communities reported that sailors and soldiers of all nationalities infested the bars, dance halls, and pleasure houses along Foochow Street in the French settlement. They said that roughnecks among the troops humiliated at Tagu made sporadic night raids to assault Chinamen, and Chinese troublemakers retaliated. Three foreign sailors had been murdered. Fighting between European troops and Chinese had provoked anger in the populace. The compradors said that many Chinese worried that the hated *fanqui* would never go away or leave them alone.

This night, drunken European soldiers eager to beat up Chinese left the bars and bawdy houses to scour the streets for targets for their sticks and fists. When they found a scuffling crowd arguing about leaving to find gold in America, the Chinese mob turned from each other to the foreigners. The melee grew into a riot, and the riot became a battle. A French legionnaire clubbed a skinny Chinese and ran over him to smash another in the gut. A stave whacked a Brit fresh from the Crimea, and blood ran from his ear as he crumpled to the ground. Four Chinese men wrestled each other shouting and screeching. Adding to the violence, mounted government enforcers thundered in with their swords to sweep and swipe and stomp in indiscriminate assaults on all rioters. Foreigners and Chinese alike turned on the troops. Two horses were pulled down, their ridersbeaten, their weapons taken. Blood splattered and the fight went on.

Foreigners in the settlements and the American house heard the cries and noise, louder and more violent than ever before. "The Chinese are about to attack the foreign settlements," someone shouted. The story spread. Chinese servants confirmed, "Rioters want attack *fanqui* settlement." The Russells gathered their arms.

"The walls will protect us," said tea taster Boyd. He looked at others. "Won't they?"

"It's probably just a ruckus like any other," said Doyle.

A determined army might reach the American houses, Richard thought, but not a mob. "Riots happen all the time," said Richard. "Nothing ever comes of them."

The racket continued all night. French legionnaires and English redcoats appeared at dawn to guard their respective settlements. The *Hartford* sent American sailors ashore. Daylight exposed the agitators that had been hidden by the night. Intimidated by neither the foreign military nor the Taotai's enforcers, riot instigators scattered to protest another night. The riot gradually spent itself. The foreign soldiers and sailors returned to their ships. The government troops jammed severed Chinese heads onto pikes for public display and rode through the streets parading the bloody heads.

That afternoon Richard rode to the godown with Augustus, the shuttle boat slapping over rough water. They avoided any possible trouble on the streets and did not see the pikes with heads. "That scare's over," said Augustus. "There may be more. It seems that everyone wants to buy guns."

Richard had missed his chance to get a rifle from Howqua. "Dealers here sell used guns of all sorts, but good ones are hard to find."

"Impossibly expensive."

"I'd be afraid that any used firearm bought here would blow up in my face."

That night, Richard asked Meto in his letter to send his rifle. To allay her fears, he told her he hoped to have the opportunity to do some hunting.

17

THE TAIPING REBEL armies were on the move, moving toward Shanghai's arms and supplies, its access to the sea, and its foreign riches. They raided from town to city, slaughtering anyone in their way and burning farms, villages, and forests as they neared Shanghai. They had taken Soochow, fifty miles away. Shanghai's government armies, its guards, its citizens, and its foreign settlements and compounds all began preparing for the attack which seemed certain to come.

Russell & Co. bustled with preparations, too, and had accepted a request to meet with the imperial administrative and military official responsible for law, order, and defense, the newly appointed Shanghai Taotai, Wu Hsu. The house comprador, Sunchong, had guided his staff to prepare a dinner party for Wu including flowers and fruit on the long table set with carved roast beef, boiled potatoes, and vegetables, and, for the Chinese, boiled duck cut in bits, pieces of ham, pork, onions, carrots, and pea shells. The Chinese liked a ceremony of continual toasts, in which each glass must be emptied and displayed to the host, and French and Chinese wines arrayed on the sideboard to be constantly poured.

Cunningham hoped to introduce the Wu Taotai to Russell & Co. and its business and establish a working relationship for defense. The partners of Augustine Heard and Olyphant & Co., the two other significant American firms, would also attend. Cunningham had explained to the Russell diners, "This man, before his appointment, had a reputation of working with foreigners as long as he got his squeeze, in whatever form it might be. He is reputed to be one of the richest mandarins in China."

Wu Hsu, a short, skinny man with hollow cheeks, a shrewd expression, and sparse mustache, entered the Russell dining room in a resplendent robe of brilliant green silk, fringed in yellow. The robe displayed an embroidered horned owl, a fearful bird whose call some Chinese believed to be a portent of death. A white jade button in his hat denoted sixth mandarin rank, a regional official responsible for local administrative and military matters.

Edward Cunningham led Wu to the honored seat to his east and left. Wu's assistant and a translator accompanied him. The diners completed elaborate mutual compliments and introductions, and conducted, through interpreters, the customary toasts to each other, to peace, to health, and to friends. The business talk began as the eating continued. Richard's houseboy, Hop Tzu, and other houseboys hovered unobtrusively, serving a never-ending collection of delicacies, refilling wine glasses, and silently responding to abrupt orders from American and Chinese diners alike. Translators repeated all conversation for best understanding.

"Americans appreciate good relations with you." Cunningham said to the Taotai, and the other Americans nodded.

"Best for Shanghai and China that we remain friends," said Wu, through the American translator.

The Wu Taotai burped boldly and wiped his chin. "Foreigner from Europe fight Emperor ... Taiping rebel fight Emperor." He looked over a fresh serving of wontons and vegetable rolls. "Emperor worry about rebels. He worry less about British threat. Taiping rebel are near Shanghai now. We fight soon.

"American," Wu went on, "send no army. They no fight Emperor. American neutral in Chinese war ..." Wu gestured toward the pictures of battling European and American warships on the walls around them. "No matter. American fight to defend house and godown."

David Olyphant, who preferred peace, muttered in protest, "We are not soldiers."

"No matter," said the Taotai. "Your interest and Taotai interest depend on defense."

Cunningham took a sip of wine. Taiping officials had told Europeans that they intended to defeat the emperor, not the foreigners, but the foreigners knew that great wealth sat for the taking in the settlements and godowns. If Taiping troops smelled loot or valuables, they would not resist temptation. Cunningham said, "The rebels do not concern the foreign settlement much. They have not shown any serious hostility to us ... up to now."

"Do you really think that the rebels will attack as large a city as Shanghai?" asked Henry Grew.

Wu leaned forward as much as the table allowed. The embroidered owl on his chest peered at the Americans from hooded eyes. "General Li Xuicheng now raid city near Shanghai," said Wu. His narrow eyes shifted directly to Grew, then to Cunningham before they fixed each American in turn around the table to impress them with his seriousness. "We must prepare." Richard's boy, Hop Tzu, quietly filled Wu's wine glass.

Wu had the attention of the barbarians listening. "Shanghai people nowhere to flee. Many no fight rebels. Many help rebels." Wu plucked another drumstick from the pile in front of him. "I need stop people desert to rebels."

"The Imperial Army defends between the rebels and Shanghai," Grew pointed out.

Cunningham rubbed his bushy sideburns and spoke. "The Imps have not been able to stop the Taiping. The British and French are likely to attack Peking again. The rebels may well attack Shanghai when they do. The Imperial Army cannot fight two wars at once."

Wu smiled at Cunningham's words as his translator spoke. He looked around the room again to sense the reaction of the listeners. Wu again glanced up at the pictures of square-rigged European warships sending broadsides at each other. "You fight," he said. "Imports bring customs duty and tax to Shanghai. Profit me. Profit American. We both want keep trade. Yes?"

The Russells listened to Wu's speech, eating in silence. Wu's cheeks no longer hollow but chock-full of chicken parts, he continued. "I need ammunition—bullets, balls, and powder," the Taotai resumed, "and weapon to defend city. Taiping army capture normal city supply place. More gun and ammunition in Singapore."

The Taotai would normally commandeer Chinese sailing junks from Shanghai—a good wind would take three months to blow the fastest junk the thousand miles to Singapore and back. He needed a steamship not dependent on the weather for speed. "Kee Chong ship cargo Singapore to Shanghai for me?"

With a nod to the others, Cunningham agreed to Wu's request. The Russells easily understood that good city defense helped protect the foreign settlements. The serving boys refilled everyone's wine glasses.

Wu picked up his glass and raised it to the diners. Automatically, the Americans reached for their glasses. "*Gan bei*," Wu said. "Bottoms up."

THAT EVENING, CUNNINGHAM called Richard into his office and told him of the Taotai's request. "The Taotai wants a Russell ship to get arms for him. Meet with Wu's men and learn the details.

Then send an order for whatever Wu wants to Hong Kong on the first steamer. There Delano can order Singapore to make the shipping arrangements for prompt return. Use Ahyue to translate and help."

Cunningham must be reaching for business, Richard thought. *He needs good relations with the Taotai; some time he may want a favor from Wu.*

Richard met with the Taotai's mandarin in charge of supply, a dour man who consulted an armful of scrolls. Ahyue translated, "He say they need rifles, swords, powder, bullets, shot, and cannon balls. He write how much in order."

"Ask him for instructions the steamer captain will need to locate the supply," Richard said.

The bureaucrat handed a paper written in English, with a name and address, and a Chinese language order form that was unintelligible to Richard. He showed it to Ayhue, who shrugged. "The sale man understand."

The Taotai's mandarin then spoke, and Ahyue translated. "He say order one hundred rifles for you, Mr. Starr. That your squeeze."

"No. A kickback like that is unethical. I want no part of it," Richard said. He muttered to Ayhue, "I suppose the mandarin gets one hundred rifles too? Don't translate that."

A good idea to have protection from violence, Richard ruminated. He had lost Grew's shotgun and his revolver. It would be months before his own rifle would arrive. He realized that he could use a new rifle now.

"I will not take kickback rifles," he said again, as much to himself as to the mandarin.

Ayhue spoke to the mandarin and translated his reply. "He say, if you no take squeeze, Taotai think you no finish job."

"I will do the job. My word is good."

"When guns arrive, you take. Gift from Taotai."

He had a job to do, so he stopped arguing. He was resolved not to get involved in such immoral deals. When the guns arrive, they could do what they want with them.

Under Richard's direction, Russell & Co. resources went to work, and in a month the steamer *Cumfae* dropped anchor at Woosong with fifty-pound bags of powder and crates of rifles, swords, bullets, and cannon balls stowed deep in its lower deck. The Taotai's men unloaded it all and carried the cargo into the city, to be distributed as needed or stored in an armory.

The next day a courier found Richard working in the godown. Unable to speak English, the courier handed him a package wrapped in parchment that looked suspiciously like a new rifle. Richard refused to take it. He set the package at Richard's feet, bowed, and left without a word.

I shouldn't take this. He left it a moment. Then picked it up, and liked its feel. Thought awhile. "Well, if they insist. This one time. It's only one gun."

AFTER HE HAD made the orders for Wu Taotai's armaments, Richard had returned to work. In his spare time, he wrote his mother to assure her that things were going well for him with Russell & Co. He spared her any further suggestion of danger, poverty, or violence. They had parted so long ago that he was finding it difficult to think of new ways to express his feelings to her. When he finished writing, he thought it was time to send her some gift that would suggest he still missed her.

Looking for some curio he hoped Meto would enjoy, he entered a shop where Chinese sold jade and porcelain statuettes to foreigners and picked out a delicate and skillfully made carved jade scene with gnarled rocks and a peasant holding a basket. He bought it in spite of an exorbitant price and carried it back to his room to await the next ship to New York.

That night, he talked with visiting Captain Frederick Macondray of San Francisco, a friend of his father from San Francisco, and a responsible client of Russell & Co., and learned that the captain was loading his ship with a cargo for which he needed extra ballast. Richard remembered that Kung had before loaned him money to buy porcelains and offered to find some for the voyage to San Francisco. This time he knew that Macondray did not sail a coolie slave ship. Macondray quickly accepted the offer.

The next morning, Richard met Kung Loong at a small seafood restaurant near the waterfront. The oriental merchant smiled his yellowed teeth at Richard. The fishy smells in the shop filled the air around them. Richard acted firmly; Kung fingered his mole hair, and they agreed that Kung would lend him the cost of a shipment of jade green porcelain dishes, bowls, and cups. Richard, after noticing the fingered mole hair, suspected that the cost of Kung's money would rise this time and argued that he had to sell the cargo in America before he could repay. Kung wanted a half percent increase in interest in return and agreed to one year to repay. Richard knew that he could avoid interest because Macondray would pay right away, and he accepted the increased interest.

Kung procured poor-quality goods, but they were only ballast, and Macondray judged that quality would be little problem for the extravagant wealth in the California frontier port. Macondray bought the shipment for the amount Richard asked. The exchange rate and the sale price gave Richard a profit to save. Kung expected at least six months of interest and was furious at the prompt repayment.

Two days later, as Richard dropped onto his bed to rest before Augustus arrived from Olyphant & Co. for dinner, his eye fell upon the table where he had set the statue. The jade was not there.

A thorough search did not locate it. Houseboys might take things when they knew that the foreigners no longer needed or wanted them, but Hop Tzu denied anything, saying he never touched it. The Russells believed that every Chinese employed in the house was honest, so Richard did not want to accuse anyone of a crime without proof. To mention the theft to Cunningham or the house comprador could cause an investigation and unnecessary recriminations. Meto's gift was lost.

"It will turn up," Augustus said. They sipped after-dinner brandy. Augustus's company usually cheered Richard.

Feeling depressed, Richard talked about Kung's loan and the coolie slave ship, the likelihood of war coming to Shanghai, and the lack of business. Everything discouraging about Shanghai bubbled up from him. "Have you seen up close severed heads on pikes? Make me sick. Why do they show off such killing?"

"A beheading is made to show off," said Augustus. "Supposed to deter criminals."

Augustus's company had not lifted his mood. "Death is everywhere in this godforsaken country."

"Enough depressing philosophizing," Augustus said. "What you need is a good time with some girls."

"Married society ladies don't hold any attraction for me." He pictured sparkling Dora trotting beside him on her white pony, and carefree Annie dancing and laughing with him. "Girls are a grand idea, but where?"

"I've heard about the ladies that populate the French quarter clubs. It would be amusing to visit them," Augustus said.

"I went to a club in Hong Kong. Not eager to do it again. Maybe if we go where foreigners go. Not with Chinese."

Bright red and yellow signs hung in a confusing mixture of languages advertised amusements behind closed doors on the seedy streets off Foochow Road. Enough dim light glowed from oil-lit paper lanterns to see shadowy outlines along the dirt street. Tinny music and drunken laughter resounded from the theaters, teahouses, and Western bars. Men, battle-hardened in the Crimea and Africa, packed the dens along with tough legionnaires, mercenary adventurers, deserting mariners, and soldiers bent on revenge for the Tagu fort fiasco. Four French sailors stumbled out of a door arm in arm, holding each other up and shouting a drinking song until they rocked into another door. Augustus peeked into an unmarked door from which the unmistakable odor of opium leaked. He reported to Richard. "Nothing to see there. Lots to nauseate."

Farther on, a doorway decorated with bright red paper strips, Chinese characters, a paper lantern, tuneful music, and laughter enticed them to enter. Foreign soldiers and sailors stood about; others at tables laughed, argued, and sang. Long-stemmed pipes and cigars enveloped everything in smoke. Richard felt more secure among Europeans than he did in the similar all-Chinese place he had seen with John Blake. European women with overdone lipstick, tight low-cut dresses, and bare shoulders mingled among the drinkers.

Richard and Augustus had seated themselves at a table with French soldiers and ordered beer-like *pijiu* when twanging and banging Chinese musical instruments started to play, and eight or ten gaudily dressed Chinese girls began to wind among the tables. Their smooth faces were unnaturally painted and powdered, their lips glossy, and their tight silk dresses slit to the thigh. Undulating muscles in their exposed legs aroused Richard; sensuous arm motions and hand gestures tempted the men to hoot and holler, reach out, and slap and pinch the girls. Some of the girls smiled, laughed, and joked in return. Others looked vacant and tried to avoid the groping.

Richard stared at sensual legs, cleavage, and hips. The Americans' weak attempts to flirt failed, and each of the two legionnaires at their table soon trapped a passing girl. The Frenchmen kissed and fondled them; the girls giggled. The colorful sexy girls, the drunken men, and the raspy music were indeed entertaining, if noisy, smoky, and fascinatingly depraved.

Richard and Augustus sipped the *pijiu* and sampled doughy Chinese finger food someone dropped on the table.

"So this is what we've heard about," Augustus exclaimed. Richard was staring at a long bare leg hooked over one Legionnaire's knee. He was too absorbed in the leg and scene around them to respond to his friend. A table of American sailors tickled a girl, who bounced among them, her laughs, her squeals, and her elbows playing in mock protest. Several British officers to his left drank *pijiu* while an earnest young Chinese talked to them. Richard's eyes, unable to see clearly through the smoke, surveyed the room.

After studying the serious expressions on the young Chinese for a few moments, he thought, *Hop Tzu?* Was that really his houseboy? What was he doing here? Richard had never thought about what the houseboys did when they weren't waiting on the Russells. He could not help repeatedly glancing over to the table at Hop Tzu. The boy bent forward over the table, talking intently to the Brits, one in particular. The Brit seemed to listen to him passively, acting bored and aloof, then turned and watched the girls.

As Hop Tzu stood to leave the table, he placed a jade green statue of a peasant holding a basket on the table for an instant.

"My statue!" Richard jumped up, ready charge over. Cunningham had advised to confront a cheater. Surprise the boy and take the statue back.

Augustus grabbed Richard's arm. "Wait! Don't accuse him here. There are Chinamen here. We don't know who his friends are. You could start a fight. We don't want trouble. We shouldn't even be here."

Augustus was right. Ill feelings among drunken fighting men often begat brawls. An angry confrontation in the midst of nationalities at war could start a donnybrook. Richard sat down, helpless.

"Let's get out of here," he proposed a moment later.

THE NEXT DAY, Hop Tzu greeted Richard in the morning as usual and again denied knowing about the statue. After breakfast, Richard located Sunchong, the mild-mannered Russell comprador and sometime translator, who was manager of all the houseboys and coolies. Proof of Hop Tzu's guilt now certain, Richard told Sunchong of his statue, its disappearance, and what he had seen at the club.

"Except for this theft, Hop Tzu has done a good job for me," he said. "I have no complaint with his work. He has been a perfect servant. I don't know how to discipline him. I must get my statue. What do you think I should I do?"

"I punish Hop Tzu," the manager of all the boys in the house advised. "Punish to avoid punishment. He no more take."

Not sure what he had just accomplished, Richard ended the short meeting. Perhaps he should have confronted Hop Tzu himself. What will Sunchong do about this personal matter?

That night a new houseboy emptied his chamber pot, laid out his nightshirt, and set up his mosquito net at bedtime.

18

ONLY FARMS AND villages remained between the Taiping army's marauding troops and Shanghai. A small family huddled around the table in their wooden home at the edge of a small village in the army's path to Shanghai. The elderly head of the family spoke carefully to his descendants. His white beard trembled. "Grandfather and father and family work land, and prosper by hard work. Now trouble come in our land."

Fan Li-gong, the old man's son, turned to his wife, Wuxi, and their two teenaged sons. "We must defend our land always. Locusts no take land from us. Flood and drought no take land. Land our home. We stay and fight. We have gun and sword."

"No" Wuxi cried. "Respected husband, we must leave. Land always stay. Rebels kill people. No kill land. We go Shanghai. Emperor army protect us there. Maybe barbarian protect us too. We live. Come back."

The family discussed these troubling arguments, and consulted long-gone ancestors at their shrine, a carved shelf holding an ancestral icon and a valuable jade incense burner, in which grandfather lit fresh incense with a shaking hand. Outside, the clamor of drums, gunshots, and screams drew close. Sooty smells began to seep through cracks in the walls. Fan peered out to the woods at the far edge of their field. Flames engulfed the trees.

Grandfather sat during the decision making, his head and hands quivering with age. "Too old travel. Too old fight. I stay here with ancestors."

"Good wife, go now, flee to Shanghai," said Fan. "Number two son go. Help mother. Number one son stay. Help father and grandfather. We fight to save home."

The family gathered rice, bread, and fruits for the two who would flee the Taiping. Other families ran past their home. A frightened neighbor burst into their door. "Come. Village burning. They are here."

"Go quick," Fan said, and his good wife, Wuxi, and son joined the flight of friends and villagers. Torn by his decision to divide the family, Fan got to work. "Shan, barricade door with table," he ordered number one son. The boy worked while Fan shuttered the window. They piled rocks. They each had old swords.

Shan picked up a rock, "I throw at intruder. Kill."

Fan retrieved the great old blunderbuss he sometimes used to shoot rodents. He packed into its barrel all the gunpowder he had while Shan broke dishes and gathered pebbles. Then they poured dish shards, pebbles, rusty nails, and anything small and sharp into the gun's yawning barrel. Fan rigged up a chair and tied the loaded blunderbuss to it, fixed a short fuse, then shifted the gun to aim directly at the door. Defenses ready now, they waited.

Then the door shattered. The table went flying. In he came, the red bandana of the Taiping fighters sweaty on his head, long greasy black hair swinging. Fan lit the fuse and an explosion of smoke filled the room. The blunderbuss load struck the rebel in the chest. Blood splattered the walls and floor. The man fell out the door, his entrails spilling out and pumping red from a crater in his middle.

Another rebel leapt over the fallen mess, landing inside. Shan threw a rock. It bounced off the rebel's head. A second rock struck his leather vest. The rebel ran to the shrine and seized their revered icon and jade incense burner. At the appalling sight of his ancestors being stolen, grandfather stood, and with a prodigious effort, plunged his ancestral sword into the rebel's stomach. The rebel fell to the floor, dropping the stolen valuables. Grandfather's chest tightened. A great pain engulfed him. He clutched his heart and collapsed. He landed beside the icon, looked at the treasured figure, then at the shrine for a moment, and joined his ancestors.

Another rebel crashed through the door. This one had a sword. Number one son Shan swung his sword at the leather armor, causing only a thump. Angered by the blow, the Taiping soldier with one swipe of his sword took off Shan's head.

"Aieeeeeee." Fan ran at the man with his old sword. It struck the raider's parry and snapped. Before Fan could react, another rebel barged in with a torch and set fire to the smashed table and the bedclothes.

"What do with this one?" the first rebel said, motioning at Fan.

"Knock him out. Let him burn."

Fan heard this. The rebel kicked Shan's bloody head toward his dead grandfather. Fan knew he could not defend their home. He knelt beside his father, turned his broken sword on himself, and fell on it to push it into his chest as far as he could. His last thought was of his good wife and son safe in Shanghai.

The Taiping rebels moved on to bring their Heavenly Peace ever closer to Shanghai.

WUXI AND NUMBER two son had followed their neighbors out of the village and soon mingled with other refugees. She clutched her bundle of food in one hand and reached for her young son's hand with the other. "Stay close to me, Li-tu."

They hurried on with the neighbors, keeping in woods or shrubs until their burning village disappeared in the distance. The refugees soon found the road leading to the coast. "Horses catch up soon on road," someone called. "Get off road."

"We go fast on road," a friend said, "I drop back to watch."

On they trudged, sharing the weight of their belongings, listening for hoofbeats, gunfire, or shouts. "They come! Quick."

The group scattered to either side, stumbling, slipping into woods. Wuxi and Li-tu dove into underbrush and lay still, while the branches settled down and all became still. Three horsemen, fierce red bandanas blowing behind them, trotted past. Breath returned to Wuxi when the men turned a corner in the road. Slow, careful, silent movements stirred in the woods. One by one, family by family, the fleeing villagers gathered.

All immediately agreed, "We stay in woods. No road. They come back soon." Night was falling.

Hours later, seven men, eight women, and twelve children approached the city walls visible on the early-morning horizon. Renewed spirit lifted them many yards across a broad field. They clamored down, across a stream, up the other side, and emerged they knew not where, but breathed the protective air of many other local citizens.

Refugees, residents, and foreigners pressed against the wide Whangpoo waters. Soochow Creek choked on boats containing families who thought themselves safer near the foreigners. Mounted soldiers under Wu's control regularly charged through the hovels burning to clear open spaces to expose residents likely to loot and steal or defect to the Taiping, and indiscriminately trampling or slaughtering anyone who stood in their way. Bloody heads with red headbands appeared on pikes throughout the city, advertising what happens to Taiping supporters.

Wuxi and Li-tu settled as best they could under a rough tent they shared with families already camped. Their companions found spaces nearby. Wuxi broke off a piece of bread to share with Li-tu. "Where find more food?" she asked a man lying nearby.

"We no know. Wife look now."

When the Taiping come, she thought, they would bring food. "How get money?" she asked the man.

"Some steal. Some sell—icon, jewel. Some work for Taiping or barbarian."

She held her son close. There were no answers now, but maybe tomorrow. She thought of her proud and faithful husband and son Shan at home.

Li-tu asked, "When will we see father and Shan again?

Wixi wept.

中国

THE DIMINUTIVE MAN flipped his queue over his shoulder to avoid the flame. He blew out the candle that had lit the tiny room where his wife lay shivering with fever. Their small daughter slept in the corner on the earthen floor. Her mother had their only two blankets. The man picked up the baby girl and nestled her gently on the blanket against his wife's huddled form. The husband tiptoed out of the room, made his way to Soochow Creek, climbed aboard a small flatboat and set out up the stream sculling a long oar, careful not to splash. A brooding overcast had covered the stars.

After nearly two hours of arduous and silent sculling, he had slipped past houseboats, slum buildings, an old joss house, and farm fields, until he arrived at a small inlet where shrubbery hung over the water. He seized a branch, eased the boat into a hidden cove, and pushed the prow onto the shore. There he waited.

A twig snapped. He looked up. Two men on the bank above him stepped out of the underbrush toward him. One held a leather packet, the other a rifle, his shaggy hair held back with the deep red bandana of the Taiping. The man with the packet approached. His stiff bearing marked him as a military officer. He beckoned and said nothing. The diminutive man in the flatboat climbed onto the shore, and they stood close to each other.

"I have report," the boatman whispered, speaking Chinese. "Wu Taotai want guns and bullets. And swords." He did not look at the officer's face. "Kee Chong get weapon for Taotai soon."

"When?"

"From Singapore. Order go on steamboat last week."

"How many gun?"

"Many. I no know number."

The officer grunted. The fact that foreigners had helped the Taotai prepare for defending Shanghai was important news. The *fanqui* will fight too, came the clear message. "Come back with something useful about barbarian defense of city." He dismissed the man. "Go."

The officer drew a small cloth sack from his leather packet and tossed it into the boat with a clink, and the man climbed back in to retrieve it. Raising his foot, the officer pushed the flatboat back into the creek to let the current carry the man and his sack of copper coins back downstream.

When the man snuck back into his room an hour later, his wife stirred, and he heard her feeble wheeze.

"Where … have you … been … Hop Tzu?"

19

THE UPCOMING TAIPING attack caused turmoil and riots among the local Chinese. The clamor of riots in the city had dissipated as the Taiping neared and was being replaced with a somber murmur of a frightened populace, divided over whether to defend or to join the rebels.

That decision did not trouble the Americans. When the time came, Americans would be neutral but knew they would defend themselves from looting if necessary. Otherwise, they expected to continue trading with whoever would eventually control the city.

With little else to do on a hot July day while time passed before an attack, Richard and Augustus decided to go rowing on Soochow Creek. They acquired a rowing shell from the British godown, rigged it for exercise, and tossed in a water bag, some food, and dry clothing in case they needed it. Richard balanced his oars on his shoulders as if they were slung with water buckets.

"We'll have no trade, no peace, and no quiet until we allow the Taiping to take the city … or they take it in spite of us," Richard remarked as he and Augustus set up the narrow shell. "They might attack in a few weeks."

"Or days," Augustus said. His first oar dropped into its place, slapping the water with a sound like a gunshot.

All four oars in place, they climbed in, Richard in the bow. When they maneuvered the shell through the crowd of houseboats, rafts, and sampans it bumped hard into some underwater object. Richard reached into the water and pushed down to loosen it. A foot bobbed up.

"A body." He swallowed disgust, rinsed his hand, pushed the body away with the oar, and pulled on.

"This is a country of ten thousand deaths," Augustus said.

"So much unnecessary death depresses me," Richard said, "but that poor fellow probably was lucky to avoid Taiping slaughter."

They squared the shell into the stream and pulled hard and strong.

In half an hour they had rowed into the current two miles up the creek and into an area of deserted small farms. Dripping sweat, they pulled up to a landing. Any farther upstream they might enter rebel-controlled territory. Nearby rose a low hill topped by a small joss house at which fishermen once left prayers for good fortune. Pale and chipped paint now decorated the once brilliantly colored little temple, and devilish carved beasts, many broken, lined the ridges of its upturned roof. A Union Jack hung listlessly on a pole jammed into a crevice in its wall. British soldiers strolled about a field of tents spread out farther around the hill.

They secured the shell, and Richard and Augustus began climbing up the hill. A tall unshaven fellow wearing only an undershirt and uniform trousers unfolded from a group of soldiers sprawled on the ground. "Say, who comes?" Another, shirtless, wearing an unbuttoned red army jacket, and a third, bare-armed in a sleeveless undershirt stood. "Looks like Yanks," the third said with a smirk. "In civvies," the other pointed out.

Augustus called back. "Hello! We rowed out from Shanghai. Need to refresh."

"Be me guest," said the unshaven fellow, bowing and sweeping his arm to the ground. "At yer service." He stumbled and caught himself. His friends laughed.

Richard and Augustus continued on up the hill. The three soldiers followed them up. "Look wha' we dragged in," the red coat called out. A soldier leaning on the joss house door frame hitched up his braces and stepped aside to wave them through with a half-full bottle of gin.

Scattered clothing and knapsacks filled the one-room house, bayoneted rifles leaned against a wall. A red uniform jacket was carelessly draped over the head of an unhappy and dirty Buddha who serenely accepted the rifles piled against him. A few soldiers lounged about half-clothed.

The Americans visited for a time, tolerating British boasting and taunts at the United States. After they swallowed some gin and endured few awkward moments, they found a common object of derision and became friendly, trading disparaging remarks about the Chinese. The meeting turned boisterous. More laughter when Richard asked whether they thought any Imperial Army guns could hit a Taiping.

"Bloody 'ell, no. Heathen clots ain't worth the powder behin' a bullet," said one tipsy redhead, rolling on the floor.

"'Ere ... 'ere, me man, take a snort." The giggling soldier held out his bottle. Richard took it, tipped it to his lips, and pretended to swallow.

The rollicking went on for a good twenty minutes. By then, Richard had had enough. He looked at Augustus, who winced as a hairy arm flopped around his shoulder and the unshaven slob tried to sing something in his ear.

"This has been fun, fellows," Richard said. "We have to get back to the settlement."

Cries of "No! No! 'Ave anotha'," and "You Yanks be good for laughs," greeted this announcement. Augustus extricated himself from the hairy embrace, and soon he and Richard were in the open air. When they reached the creek bank, their shell had gone.

"Where the bloody 'ell is our shell?" Augustus said, mimicking the British pronunciation.

Then they heard a shout, a splash, and a bang. Out in the creek a soldier in his undershirt stood in their shell, drifting downstream, and waving his arms for balance. An oar floated just out of reach. The boatman leaned over to reach it, lost his balance, and the boat rocked. He swung a uniformed leg trying to steady himself. As he did so, the boat instantly capsized. Grates, packs, water bottle, food, clothes, and Brit dumped into the creek. Richard ran into the water to try to keep their belongings from being swept downstream. Augustus tried, too, but having had more to drink, slipped and fell in.

The men on the bank laughed at their spluttering comrade. The flooded shell kept drifting downstream.

"Jack, ye oughta join the navy," shouted the redhead.

"Look out for the shark!" another wag yelled. They doubled over in laughter when the hapless swimmer's eyes popped, and he whipped his head around looking for the shark.

Less amused, Richard and Augustus plunged into the water to retrieve their belongings. Two soldiers dove in and helped, and soon the water-filled boat, its gratings, and all oars were dragged ashore with the dripping Jack. "That were bloody refreshing," Jack said, wringing out his shirt. The soldiers sniggered some more at their embarrassed mate.

When they had cleaned as much as possible and loaded their soaked belongings, Richard and Augustus stepped into the shell, thankful that Jack had not put his foot through its bottom. They took the oars and set out into the stream to a drunken chorus of good wishes from the British army.

When they were well on the way back to Shanghai, Richard remarked, "Please tell me that that schnockered bunch is not our only defense."

"Posted out here, those drunken sots will be the first to greet the rebels."

"God help us." Richard pulled his oar harder.

20

"WHEN TROUBLE COMES we will have to protect ourselves." Cunningham spoke before a group of concerned American merchants, all of whom knew that the rebels
had paused to prepare for an assault on Shanghai. "We can expect
the Taiping to attack here when the military leaves to advance
on Peking again."

American minister Frederick Ward reported, "The British
are certain to return to Peking. In spite of the recent defeat at
the Tagu fort, their envoy, Lord Elgin, and France's Baron Gros
have confirmed orders from their capitals to force the Emperor's
government to accept demands for trade privileges."

Henry Grew pointed out, "The Brits and Frogs will take
their armies and warships north to attack Peking. There will be
few soldiers left here to protect our settlements from the rebels."

"The British will defend themselves first, for sure," said
Cunningham. "They won't defend us."

"We are supposed to be officially neutral in any fights among
the Chinese," said David Olyphant, a Quaker. "We should not
be fighting anybody."

"Protecting ourselves is neutral, isn't it?" Cunningham said.

The group determined to organize a volunteer defense corps.
Henry Grew agreed to coordinate the Russells as well as other
American volunteers and independent adventurers. The young

Russells would comprise the largest contingent. "We should not depend whatsoever on our Chinese servants or employees."

Grew asked all the young men attending to sign on for defense. Richard volunteered, ready to do his duty. He had lost Grew's shotgun to Fookie Tom and had not yet received his own rifle from home, but he did have a gift rifle from the Wu Taotai, and he soon procured another revolver from Russell & Co.

Two days later, the French and British fleets, augmented by fresh troops and ships from Hong Kong, steamed out of the anchorages around Woosong and Chung-ming Island. The American warships *Hartford* and *Powhatan,* with their full complements, went north, too. The only ground forces left behind were the small drunken unit at the joss house and a unit of Hindus, called the Loodiniah Regiment, recruited in India and deemed too unreliable to take north. The entire British, French, and American military forces in Shanghai had left.

"They were supposed to protect us, weren't they?" said a nervous clerk from Olyphant.

中国

"*Bu yao tzo*—DON'T go, Hop Tzu." the girl gasped. Her pale skin reddened with the effort to speak. She looked up, pleading with her eyes.

"I must," he said. She collapsed back onto the pile of rags that cushioned her head. "Money bring healer. You get better."

The venerated old healer, long facial wisps suggesting great wisdom and experience, had arrived that afternoon with his drawers of roots, animal parts, and herbs. Sweet but goatish smells and the thick cheese-like coat on her tongue had told him that the girl's *chi* was weak—her elements out of balance. He prescribed an herbal formula of *ma huang*—ephedra—assisted with *xing ren*—apricot seed—to relieve her shortness of breath.

The healer had left, counting his proceeds from a stolen jade statue. Hop Tzu needed more money to pay for the medicine.

"I come back," he said. He patted her arm and stole out into the night.

The trip up Soochow Creek seemed particularly arduous that night. Anxiety to cure his wife's illness powered his tired body. He sculled against the current as he had many times before, through the houseboats, out of the city, past the farms. When he reached the British soldiers' encampment near the old joss house, he crept close to the far shore where the shrubbery would hide him. A distant grating sound reached his ears. The sentry's snoring. Hop Tzu's luck held. The silent spy slipped by and sculled on until he found the usual landing, grounded the boat, and stepped ashore.

"Barbarian armies gone," Hop Tzu reported to the Taiping officer. "All warship go north to Peking." The rebel smiled. The barbarians were attacking the Emperor. The *fanqui* might topple the Manchu dynasty for them.

"What foreign soldier stay in Shanghai?"

"One barbarian regiment of Hindus south from city."

"Any more?"

"Small army near joss house. Few soldiers in city. No land army. *Fanqui* have volunteers to fight."

The officer knew that Hop Tzu no longer worked for the barbarians. "How you know all this?"

"Servants report. I see ships go."

The clandestine meeting over, Hop Tzu secured his payment under his shirt, returned to his boat and drifted away, relieved and exhausted. The farms, the joss house encampment, refugee camps, and boats were all dark as he floated down with the current. He would not make this dangerous trip any longer. He had enough money for the medicine. Now Mai will recover. Little Joi will grow. When the rebels entered Shanghai, the officer had promised, the Taiping would treat his family kindly.

Reaching the settlements, he landed at the usual spot. He quietly stowed the steering oar and crept over the old flatboat, stretching past the seats and mats in his path. Rocked by his haste to jump ashore, the boat tipped. Not much, a common movement, but it tipped just enough to throw him off balance. His foot flew out and knocked over an empty bailing tin. The clang echoed into the night like a terrible gong announcing the Emperor's arrival.

Hop Tzu froze.

21

TAIPING NOTICES APPEARED on doors and walls in the foreign settlements: "Do not oppose us or you will be killed." Richard and other Russell volunteers helped pile up sandbags, rubble, stones, wood, spars, and anything that could barricade a force wanting to enter the settlements. Four men dragged in the hull of a wrecked sampan. Natives drove sharp pointed pilings into the ground to make palisades across major streets outside the city walls.

After five hours of this work, Richard trudged back to the Russells' compound with Harold Doyle, their route taking them through Chinese tenements where hopeless souls lay, sat, or leaned among tents, old ship's parts, bamboo mats, broken doors, and rubble. A dirty child with a finger in his nose looked up at his hollow-eyed mother, pleading with his big eyes. It seemed that in this desperate place everybody was exhausted.

A buzzing murmur drew the two Americans into a crowd gathered in an open courtyard. "What's happening?"

Richard and Doyle gently elbowed men and women aside until they could see that soldiers had spread the people out into an open circle. In the center stood a shirtless young man, his hands roped behind him. "They have a prisoner," said Richard as Doyle came up behind him. Blood striped the man's back like that on a flogged sailor. A rough-looking brute in patched clothing stretched the man's queue, leading the unfortunate about with the hair as leash.

A large soldier stood beside the poor man, speaking harshly to him. Richard could not see the guard's hands. Suddenly, the first guard yanked hard on the queue, jerking the head forward. The prisoner fell to his knees. The soldier raised his arms overhead holding a broad sword. The crowd hushed.

One blow severed Hop Tzu's head. It rolled a few feet and stopped, eyes open and staring. Blood squirted out of the neck. The body fell over, twitching. The ground turned red. Richard retched violently.

Doyle had turned away, unable to watch. Neither man could talk until they had reached the house.

Richard didn't eat dinner; a little white wine was all he could stomach. Guilt kept him tossing that night. He had exposed Hop Tzu for stealing, and the poor boy had been decapitated. He couldn't sleep. If he had talked to the boy himself, if he had found some sort of discipline himself, the boy would still have a job and his head. He had not imagined that Sunchong would turn the boy over to government authorities. How could Richard have known that anyone would cut off a head for petty theft? *I caused my boy's death over a triviality.*

"Richard, it makes no sense," said Augustus in the morning, worried about his friend. "The boy must have done something else." Richard could not be mollified. "Why don't you go talk to the comprador?" Augustus suggested. "He may know more what happened."

The next day, Richard decided to see Sunchong. He found the comprador in his room, sitting in a chair, bending over a small lacquer box on the floor. Sunchong slammed the cover on the box, pushed it under the chair with his foot, and straightened up. He remained sitting, his oriental face betraying nothing.

Richard decided to stand so he could look down on Sunchong. Did he put money in the box? "Some time ago I told you that my houseboy Hop Tzu had stolen an item from my room. You had him replaced."

"I remember."

"You said you would punish him."

"I get you new boy. You no happy?"

"I saw Hop Tzu beheaded yesterday." Richard had to blurt it out.

"Poor man," Sunchong said.

That was a surprise. Sunchong did not sound regretful. Cursed heathen indifference to death. "Answer my question."

The Chinaman sat straight. His narrow eyes stared back at Richard. "Taotai behead only spies. Punish to avoid punishment. Make example for those who desert to rebels."

There was too much avoiding going on here. He was not telling all he knew. "Was Hop Tzu a spy? For who? You told me punish to avoid punishment before," he said. "You make no sense. Murder is not punishment. It's inhuman and cruel."

Sunchong remained stoic, unperturbed. "Cutting off head is merciful. You think man in *canque* merciful?"

Beheading merciful? Unthinkable. *What was a canque? Some Oriental torture? Don't let Sunchong change the subject.* He shot back, "Do you think that Hop Tzu was a spy?"

"I hear about Hop Tzu. Always rumors." His hands folded in his lap. "They say he need money. They say wife and child sick."

"Is that true?" He clenched his right fist. *Wife and child?* He had never imagined that a young servant would have a family.

"Servants talk. There are rumors."

"What is her name?" Richard had to know now. "Where did they live?"

"I manage servants here. Nowhere else."

"Where did Hop Tzu live? Was he a spy?"

"That his business." Sunchong turned away as if he had better things to do than answer to this young pup of a clerk.

Richard turned his back and left, slamming the door. He heard Sunchong get up and lock the door.

Richard returned to his room. His mind tumbled and raced. The exasperating Sunchong was no help. The comprador had led him in circles. He had only learned that the boy had a family. Was Sunchong responsible for Hop Tzu's death? No. Richard had reported to Sunchong. Maybe the boy had spied. As a waiter, Hop Tzu could have heard conversations valuable to others. Was Sunchong also a spy? Did he put illicit money in his box? Richard had not intended to make a criminal charge and knew nothing about spying, but he could not shake the thought—*Hop Tzu is dead. It's my fault.*

He sat on the edge of his bed, his head empty of answers. His mother's unsmiling daguerreotype looked down on him. She seemed to scold him. He reached out for her latest letter. The touch of home in her letters had always comforted him, even though she was far away and had no idea what was going on with him. He had told her about the firm, its food, and the unpleasant wives of the settlement, but only in most general terms did he report his life to her. As a result, the longer he was away the more unsatisfying her replies had become. He hoped even old news from home would help take his mind off the headless houseboy.

He read again that sister Etta had become engaged to a young man from Cuba. Meto liked the Spaniard, but the thought of a foreigner in the family did not comfort Richard. His brother Willie was determined to enter the Naval Academy, but the navy types Richard had seen did not give Richard comfort about his undisciplined young brother joining those ranks.

Then he remembered Meto's parting gift, the Bible in which she had inscribed: "When you read ... feel as if your mother's hand was on your head, praying for a blessing on her son." He opened her gift. It fell open to Matthew, chapter 6.

"After this manner therefore pray you," he read. "If ye forgive men their trespasses, your heavenly father will also forgive you."

He collapsed into bed, so very tired. He did not often pray, but this was a good time. He closed his eyes. "I forgive Hop Tzu. Forgive me, Lord," he prayed over and over until he fell asleep.

Suddenly Hop Tzu's face looked down at him from a city gate. A bloody, dripping, leering face. Richard snapped awake. He shivered, got up, walked around the room, splashed his face with water, and tried to go back to sleep. He had to think of something pleasant. He thought of his "dears": Annie Wiley, Mary Collins, Nellie Rockwell, and Dora Delano. Richard saw the girls' joyous smiles, their flirtatious manners, and their melodic laughter. Dora trotted on her white horse and smiled at him. He was holding her hand under the stars. Suddenly Hop Tzu's yellow grinning face, oozing red tears and shrieking, swooped toward him and fell on Richard. He jerked awake with a shout, flailing to get the horrid apparition away. He got up again and paced in bare feet on the wooden floor. A cold sweat soaked his nightshirt.

Death and violence out of control surrounded him. More was sure to come. His heart was at home. Why not return home? He would ... if they were not about to be attacked.

22

S MOKE WAS RISING over the western horizon. The rebels devoured their way ever closer to Shanghai. The anxious Russells yearned for trade goods to fill the holds of ocean ships lying dormant at Woosong. For months Russell partners had encouraged their Chinese compradors to try to contact the Taiping to persuade them to allow tea from areas they controlled to sail down the river on junks and sampans. If and when the Taiping captured Shanghai, the Russell partners wanted to be on good terms with them, so trade could continue rather than start anew.

Two days after his confrontation with Sunchong, a discouraged Richard Starr, depressed over Hop Tzu's fate, perched on the spare wicker chair waiting for the head partner to tell him why he had been summoned. Edward Cunningham now sat behind his desk. Old Mr. Russell on the wall frowned.

"Mr. Starr, I have a job for you."

"Good." *Perhaps this will get my mind where it belongs*, Richard thought. He had had too little constructive work.

Cunningham rubbed his eyes, stopped, looked out from under heavy lids, and spoke slowly. "Richard, we need tea." He leaned back. "Sunchong has made contacts within the rebel hierarchy. He has recently negotiated an agreement to trade with Russell for tea. I want you to go up the Yangtze with Sunchong and bring the tea to our godown."

Sunchong had recently avoided answering his questions, had been cold and virtually pushed him out the door. He thought that the man might be a Taiping spy and might have swapped information for tea. Could Richard cooperate on such a job with this two-faced man? Their mutual boss was sending both together to the rebels. He wanted something to do, so he would go with Sunchong, and be careful.

"Where is the tea?" Richard asked.

"Sunchong says it is with the rebel army now. They want to sell it soon. It burdens their soldiers, who have to carry loads useless to them." Richard listened without comment. Would Sunchong translate accurately for him? Cunningham continued, "Wu Taotai picked up his guns and ammunition from the *Cumfae,* but Captain Graves also has rifles, pistols, powder, and ammunition from Singapore consigned to us. We will trade those weapons for the tea."

"Wait a minute." Richard's eyes widened. He stiffened in his seat. As far as he knew, Russell & Co. was asking him to work with a suspected traitor. Instinct told him he shouldn't do it. Cunningham was as double-dealing as a Chinese pirate. The firm's head partner had acquired munitions for the Wu Taotai to defend Shanghai, and now he was helping the rebels attack Shanghai. Richard shook his head at the irony. In no place else in the world do principle and patriotism mean so many conflicting things.

Richard thought about it. Cunningham didn't need to sell weapons; guns and swords were available anywhere. Shanghai's alleys sheltered stores of weapons, powder, percussion caps, and other implements of war readily for sale to the Taiping as well as to imperial officials, foreign mercenaries, and merchants. His New England conscience rebelled at such conflicting business deals.

"We are arming both sides of this Chinese fight?"

"We are bound to be neutral, are we not?" Cunningham said with a straight face.

Russell partners never ignored a business opportunity. The Taiping might control Shanghai any day. The firm paid Sunchong and other compradors to develop business relationships with Chinese traders, to negotiate purchases and sales, and he had done what he was supposed to do. Good relationships with both the Taiping and the local Taotai were essential. Working both sides of war was a common Chinese game.

"When does the trade take place?" asked Richard.

As THE SUN reached higher over the Yangtze, Sunchong paced the deck. The junk, midsized, with rusty square sail, green wales, and a suspicious oriental eye on its bow, having left the steam tug that had towed it against the current, crept close to the shore. Sunchong took intense interest in the surroundings, studying the shoreline, occasionally speaking to the captain, and gesturing toward the western shore.

Sunchong seemed to have this job in hand. Richard fidgeted near him, also searching the shore. He wore a light shirt, boots, and the small revolver he had been given as a defensive volunteer. Sixty crates of rifles, thirty bags of powder, pistols, machetes, and ammunition lay piled about them in the hold and on the deck. He was about to deliver weapons to religious fanatics who in the name of Heavenly Peace slaughtered more of their countrymen than Ghengis Khan had slaughtered in a lifetime. Richard began to perspire. Adrenaline coursed through him. He stepped to the bow, held onto an overhead line, and urinated overboard.

The oarsman pushed hard on his steering oar, and the junk veered toward a clearing on the shore. The current pushed them close, and two crewmen threw overboard a large rock tied to the bow to anchor the junk. On a wide path, four men in Taiping bandanas appeared dragging a small flatboat to the water, and the

155

boat soon appeared beside the loaded junk. Sunchong motioned to Richard to get in. He knew what to do. *I'm his boss*, Richard thought, *but he's treating me like his underling.* He told himself, *don't resent his help—think clearly.* He patted his revolver to make sure it was still there.

Sunchong said nothing as a soldier skulled the two Russells ashore. A hatless rebel in black trousers and soiled white shirt appeared on shore and waved his hand, palm down, at them. The fellow led them inland past brittle shrubbery that clawed at them, until they came upon a clearing where cloth bags, tea crates, and baskets were set out. Wagons and draft horses waited deeper in the forest. Bearers and armed soldiers lined the clearing.

Behind Richard, a guttural, violent voice exploded. *"Ni shi shei! Ni wai mashi wasi shi!"* He whipped around to face a tall soldier with unkempt beard, long hair, Taiping red scarf, and blue jacket. An angry bear could not have startled Richard more.

Sunchong stepped up and said something in Chinese. Richard smiled in nervous greeting. The soldier, evidently the officer in charge, could strut standing still. His dark face scowled from hairline to chin bush, as he looked the barbarian up and down. These soldiers had been camping, marching, and fighting for weeks. They looked ready to kill and burn at any excuse.

The Taiping officer roared orders. As his carriers brought the weapons from the junk, box by box, slung on poles across their shoulders, the officer had each crate opened so he could inspect the contents. Without comment, the officer strutted from one to the next while Richard walked around absorbing the long swords and arrows, rifles and hand weapons, bayonet blades, pointed knives, and bags of gunpowder that he had delivered. His puny pistol poked his ribs in jest. The sun flashed on the exposed blades. Richard counted the crates as the rebels brought them ashore. Hours ticked by; the sun climbed. He stepped behind a tree to urinate again. He had reached a count of forty-seven crates when he paused, and soon he realized that the delivery was going to be short of rifles. He was not going to deliver the sixty crates that Cunningham sold. *They have more than enough weapons to slaughter us in a flash.*

"Sunchong," he whispered, "We are short about ten rifle crates on this delivery. Some are missing here. Are more on the junk?" His voice shook and his eyes flashed. "Be ready for the Taiping to find out."

Sunchong remained stoic. "All here. Delivery okay."

"It's not okay. We agreed to sell sixty crates. Not all are here. Did you count when we loaded?"

"No worry," said the comprador and turned away. "Nothing happen."

Damn that Chinaman's evasion. Richard had to rely on the inscrutable comprador and his cryptic talk. The oily smell of gun oil drifted over the clearing. Hot waves pulsed up into the overhead brilliance. Maybe the soldiers will not deliver enough tea either. Cunningham would not have him flogged for bringing back a contaminated load, or bags diluted with shrubbery, but his reputation would certainly wither if he brought back less than the agreed amount of tea. Sweat poured down his back, soaking his shirt.

"Sunchong," Richard said. "Have the tea crates and baskets opened so I can inspect them."

Sunchong spoke to the rebel commander, and then sent a runner to fetch crewmen from the junk, who soon were at work opening tea crates and baskets following Richard's gestures. They could not open the bags, for there was no way to reseal them. The bags could easily have been filled with straw or weeds. Richard and Sunchong looked, sniffed, felt, poked, and counted, recording all until Richard judged that a sufficient amount and quality had been delivered to cover the weapons' cost. Meanwhile, the sun beat on the clearing; the shrubs seemed to toast.

Richard found the comprador talking with the Taiping officer partially hidden in a tree's shadow. Sunchong slipped a small brown sack under his robe. He got his commission.

"Get loaded as fast as you can," Richard called.

Loaded and piled high with tea, the junk soon swept into the current, picked up a crosswind and sped downstream toward Shanghai.

Richard and Sunchong sat on a bench together, Sunchong seemed pleased that they had accomplished the task, and Richard relaxed that it was safely over.

After a time, after the sun had lowered to the horizon, Richard ventured to bring up the troubling subject that Sunchong had avoided earlier when Richard had asked about Hop Tzu.

"Sunchong, you said Hop Tzu had a family ... a wife and child?"

The Chinaman looked at him, his face serene. The evasive manner of the day before seemed to be gone. "Yes, sick wife," he said, "and baby girl."

"What will happen to them?"

Sunchong paused thoughtfully before answering. "I not know. The wife not get well, perhaps. Abandon baby or sell. Maybe throw in river."

During the trade, except for his odd response to news of missing rifles, Sunchong had been cooperative. Richard hoped that he might regret his abrupt dismissal of Richard's previous concern about Hop Tzu, that compassion for a grieving widow might overcome his previous reluctance to talk about Hop Tzu.

"Sunchong, I want to help the family, if I can. Do you know where he lived?"

Sunchong looked deeply into Richard's brown eyes. "I find ... maybe."

"Will you come with me to see his wife? To translate?"

After several moments' thought, Sunchong agreed. Richard had correctly understood an enigmatic Chinese face this time.

THE JUNK LANDED near the Russell godown, and Sunchong negotiated with the captain while the crew unloaded the tea. Richard made sure that all the tea had been placed on the dock and that Russell coolies had begun transferring it to the godown. He made one last look into the junk's hold. A stash of ten narrow rifle crates from the *Cumfae* lay stowed far under the ship's bow. Richard's count confirmed that they had not delivered all the rifle crates, yet the trade had gone smoothly. Sunchong must have promised the Taiping to deliver only fifty crates for the same price Cunningham had asked for sixty.

Should he question Sunchong about the extra rifles, and his commission from the Taiping officer? Should he admit to Cunningham that they had failed to deliver everything? The Taiping had accepted all the rifles without complaint, and they had returned with all the tea. As he thought about it, he realized that a Chinese squeeze had been worked. Sunchong and the junk's captain could sell those additional ten guncrates easily and divide the proceeds. The oriental device compensated Sunchong and the junk's captain for accomplishing a profitable trade. He shrugged and decided not to tell Cunningham about Sunchong's squeeze with the rifles.

23

THE NEXT MORNING, Richard followed Sunchong into the tenement slum in the French settlement near the walled city. Spice, smoke, urine, and death surrounded them. A pale man flopped against the wall, drunk, dead, or asleep. A rat scurried out of their way. A skinny man spat in the dirt. Sunchong paused, addressed a man whose threadbare clothes hung on his bones, and, heeding the point of his shaking finger, they walked on to a mud-brick hovel with no windows.

Sunchong called inside, and an old woman came out, cradling a sleeping baby in her arms. The wrinkled face, lined with fatigue and age, looked kindly and sad. The woman was clearly frightened. Sunchong spoke to the woman.

She said nothing and shook her head. Sunchong spoke again. She nodded. They talked quietly and briefly.

She dropped her head. Her shoulders fell. She spoke softly.

Sunchong turned to Richard. "She say Hop Tzu wife dead."

Richard's arms suddenly became heavy. He could not talk for a moment. In the dusk, little light penetrated the ally. He looked at the woman. Gray streaks marred the black hair pulled back from her face. The baby stirred in her arms, then began to cry softly. Sunchong did not speak.

"Ask her if that is Hop Tzu's baby." His words came out weakly.

Sunchong did so, and told Richard, "Yes, she says."

"What will happen to it?" Richard asked. Sunchong spoke quietly with the woman. His easy manner seemed to calm her.

"She say she live next house. When Hop Tzu die, she help wife, but she too sick. Woman can do nothing," Sunchong reported with equal calm and kindness. "Now she afraid. No food for baby. Husband take girl baby away tomorrow."

The specter of the floating dead baby returned. "Ask her if she can keep it for one more day. Tell her that I will try to get some help for Hop Tzu's baby."

Sunchong asked Richard, "What will you do?"

"Tell her I will try to find a home for it." Sunchong translated, but the worried old matron did not show any relief. The two men left, promising to come back the next day. The tiny wrinkled girl in the kindly old woman's arms kept crying.

Immediately upon reaching his house, Richard summoned a runner, a young boy the firm had recently used named Li-tu, gave him a coin, and asked him to take a message to Simon Brown, who had contacts at the American Baptist Mission not far from Hop Tzu's house. The message explained the situation and asked whether the missionaries would be able to care for an orphaned baby. He wanted to meet a missionary in the morning.

The next morning, Richard and Sunchong met Rev. Abner Whipple at the mission, and the three returned to the dusty alley. The Reverend wore a clerical collar, but otherwise dressed in a typical missionary's black suit, and wore a wide-brimmed hat to shield the sun. When they reached Hop Tzu's hovel, Sunchong called for the old woman. The two Chinese exchanged a few soft words. Then Whipple stepped forward, doffed his big hat, introduced himself, and, Sunchong translating, said he would be happy to raise the child as a Christian in the mission in the city.

"We will, with God's help, make a good Christian child." He wet his dry lips with his tongue. "Raised in the ways of Jesus."

This was meant to reassure the old woman. She objected to the proposal with a torrent of Chinese that only Sunchong could understand.

"She afraid," Sunchong told the Americans. "She want baby. Husband take baby away soon. She not know what to do."

Richard proposed, "Let her see that we can care for it. Maybe I could hold her. See if it will remain quiet with us. That may pacify her." The woman did not like that proposal either, wailing and fussing so much that she set the baby to wailing too. In the confusion her protests caused, Sunchong pulled Richard aside and said, "I no like to say before ... she think barbarian missionary take new baby to eat."

"What?" Richard said. "That's absurd."

"Yes. Many peasant believe."

"Tell her it isn't true," Richard pleaded. "Tell her this missionary does not eat babies."

The old woman calmed down a little at Sunchong's soothing voice. He seemed to understand the woman's fear and to be concerned about the baby's care himself. Richard wondered whether Sunchong had children of his own.

"Tell her that Hop Tzu worked for me." Richard lowered his voice. "Say Hop Tzu wanted me to care for the baby!" It was a lie, but it might help.

Some more calm assurances by Sunchong, and a few words in Chinese and translated English from the Reverend promising repeatedly that no one would eat the girl, stopped the old woman's wailing. The baby quieted too. Slowly, hesitatingly, the poor caretaker held the baby out to Richard. He took the tiny bundle in his arms. He had not held a newborn since his mother let him hold his little brother Willie seventeen years ago. Afraid that she would start crying again, he nervously held the living doll as long as he dared, then passed her to Rev. Whipple. Sunchong put his arm on the woman's shoulder. The missionary caressed Hop Tzu's baby with care and a tender look. If only he had not chosen this moment to wet his lips again. The woman saw the gesture and shrieked. She reached toward the baby.

"Time to go," Sunchong said. "No give back. Baby will be killed. Take baby away. We can do nothing more."

With the baby safely and comfortably cradled in his arms, Whipple turned without a word and stepped away.

"Please. The baby will be cared for," said Richard. The woman wailed again. Sunchong spoke to her at length, soothing, taking the time to quiet her wailing. Whipple and the baby, followed by the two merchants, walked out of the alley. As they turned the corner they heard the old woman's heaving sobs.

24

WITH THE EUROPEAN warship flotillas and armies gone far to the north, Wu Taotai had promised to defend the foreign settlements, but no one had seen his troops except when they sought to discipline his own citizens. In hopes that the sight of foreign red and blue uniforms might intimidate the rebel troops, a few British and French soldiers mingled with Chinese troops on the fortified city walls to help aim and fire cannons.

Coolies and servants from the foreign houses and volunteer corps had helped the natives enlarge a small stream, excavating dirt into a low rampart behind the ditch that formed a meandering border obstacle in front of the foreign settlements and reaching from the native city wall to Soochow Creek. The Taiping army would need to cross a broad field before facing the walls and the defensive ditch and rampart.

The Taiping army stopped out of sight behind low hills and woods. Several test rebel cannon shots fell short but told the Taiping commanders the range. General Li sent a warning message to the barbarian houses. "Foreigners should fly a yellow flag at their houses to signify that my soldiers should not attack them." Yellow flags appeared within the settlements. Dark smoke from burning villages behind the camping troops still drifted up through the dust.

The day after Richard and Sunchong had delivered weapons to the Taiping, many of the Russells and other Americans and their Chinese employees climbed to the Kee Chong roof to spy on the battle staging. The Chinese servants jabbered quietly among themselves. The Americans, including Richard, watched the action—some anxious and some curious.

"The drunks at the joss house will be of little use," Augustus said to a small group of clerks looking over at the city. "Except for the imperial troops, we have no other military help."

"Where is the Loodiniah Regiment?" Doyle asked. "They are British trained."

"They're not the great Sepoys that fought for the British in India. They're just Hindu recruits," said Tanner.

Augustus answered, "The Hindus are south of the city walls ... far from here."

"Keeping a guard at a great distance from what is to be guarded seems useless," Richard said.

"Imperial troops are setting up camp," said another. "Before the city, not in front of our settlements."

"Those damnable Imps have fled any fight so far. Their backs are to the river. Suppose they desert now?"

The small coastal steamer *Cumfae* had been at anchor off the Russell dock for days. Nearby floated two little British gunboats, *Nimrod* and *Pioneer*. Shanghai's people massed along the shore like scrambling ants to find something floating to get them away from inevitable slaughter. The waterfront from Soochow Creek to beyond the city walls teemed with houseboats, sampans, barges, steam shuttles, and rowboats.

Edward Cunningham turned to his partner and said, "Henry, see to it that any of our ladies who want to leave get out to the Woosong anchorage. Use the shuttles. The *Sea Serpent* should take them aboard until this passes." Then he left the roof. "Starr,"

Cunningham called, "come." His anxiety showed in his unusually forceful tone.

Immediately upon closing his office door, Cunningham paced back and forth; arms swung as if swatting flies. Richard stepped aside. He had never seen a partner so agitated. "Our treasure is in the vault in the godown," Cunningham blurted. Treasure—gold and silver bullion and coins that underlay all financial transactions. "Go to the godown. Get it to safety."

"All of it?" he asked. His voice sounded strangely high-pitched.

The head of the house was indeed agitated. "All of it. The silver and the gold. Get it to the *Cumfae* as quickly as possible. You'll need a comprador's men to help. Find Apun or Sunchong, and tell him I said to work with you."

Richard would have to pack the gold and silver coins and ingots, cross the broad waterfront, navigate through the crowd, find a boat, and row or steam several hundred yards out to the *Cumfae*. Every looter would know what was in the heavy loads.

Richard changed into a black navy-style jacket, dungarees, and boots. He picked up his revolver, loaded it, stuck it in his belt, buttoned his jacket over it, relieved himself in the chamber pot, and headed across Soochow Creek.

Seeking to escape to the shore, men clutched bundled belongings and women carried crying children. Gangs scoured deserted tenements looting and wrecking, and scoundrels tried to rob fleeing families. European women abandoned their compounds, terrified that the native servants and coolies would rob them. All fled, pushed, and fought to the water's edge, seeking a boat to take them across the river. Mounted soldiers rode through the mayhem ready to quell any violence. Richard quickly bulled his way to the godown and found the comprador's room.

There sat the burly comprador that should look intimidating going through the crowds. Richard had worked only briefly with this comprador before.

"Apun, Mr. Cunningham has asked me to do an immediate job for the house. Will you help?"

"*She de.*" Apun nodded and stood.

"Come with me." Richard led Apun through the warehouse to the vault. He explained the task and learned that Apun understood English well.

Richard knew where the firm's vault was, but he had never been in it. The volume of stacked ingots and bagged pieces of eight surprised him. "We need loyal Russell coolies. Six or seven volunteers. Right away. Bring them here." Apun nodded, disappeared, and then reappeared a few minutes later with six muscular men. Richard suspected that Apun had made liberal use of expense money the firm allowed compradors.

Apun directed the coolies. They packed the ingots in used tea crates of varying sizes and chops in an attempt to disguise the contents. Apun beckoned one of the coolies to come to him. "*Leo liang liu koong je,*" he said. The coolie removed four ingots to empty a crate and set them in another. Apun delivered more incomprehensible orders to the coolies. One man left the godown. Richard watched carefully but had no idea what was going on. He fingered the revolver in his belt. Although he had no reason to distrust Apun, if these coolies stole anything, he had to be ready to get it back. Apun's men worked silently.

In a moment the man returned carrying four buckets of coal, which Apun pointed and gestured that the coal be dumped into two of the empty crates. Richard quickly realized Apun's idea. If someone stole a crate filled with coal, he'd think they were carrying fuel and leave them alone. Impressed and amused at Apun's trick, Richard took a chance on leaving the comprador unsupervised with his coolies packing crates. He ran to the waterfront to find a boat to the *Cumfae*.

He spotted an American flag on the bow of a longboat creeping close to shore. Four rumpled sailors slowly drifted near the shore looking for extra cash from fleeing foreigners. The sailors rejected any Chinese, and the Americans rejected the crew's unsavory appearance, but Richard pushed his way toward them.

"I need a boat for a cargo to the *Cumfae*," he called out.

One soiled fellow in a striped shirt doffed his cap and with a smirk, said, "What ya got, mate?

"What's your name?"

"They call me Lokker."

"What ship you from?"

"The *Sea Serpent*'s me home, mate." The extreme clipper out of Boston had arrived the day before after three months at sea. It was a good enough reference.

"Will you ferry my goods to the *Cumfae*?" They rowed closer; the smell of rum polluted their boat.

"What you offer, mate?"

"A handful of silver when you're done." Richard pictured letting him dip into a sack of coins once they had delivered all the treasure to the *Cumfai*.

"A han'ful for each o' me mates."

"Done." Richard had just told Lokker that he had something valuable. "I'll be back with the load."

Lokker saluted with a grin and held his boat away from the landing. "Aye, aye … sir."

Apun's coolies had packed eight crates, about half the total. No one could tell which ones contained coal. More treasure remained. Richard put several handfuls of silver coins in a small canvas sack and pocketed it in his jacket.

"Take the first load, Apun. I hired a boat. Hope it's still there."

Four coolies each slung two chests on a bamboo pole, heaved the poles to their shoulders with grunts and headed out into the churning mob, alert to thieves and ruffians. The bending poles advertised to all that they bore heavy weight. Carrying a stout stave for a weapon, Richard supervised from behind. To open a path, Apun shoved aside a man with bad teeth. Suddenly, a bandit grabbed a pole and jerked the rear coolie off balance. The chest crashed to the ground. Its wood split but held. The coolie shouted. A second thief knocked Apun's coolie aside, clutched the chest and lifted. Richard whacked his weapon hard on the thief's shoulder. The would-be thief swore and let go. The chest dropped again. It split open. Half a crate of coal spilled out.

The thieves disappeared into the crowd, and Richard smiled inwardly. The coolies quickly carried the rest to the landing.

"Get this to the ship now," Richard ordered the sailors. "We'll have another for you." As the four sailors climbed into the boat, he suddenly decided that he had better go with them, better stay with the treasure now in the control of strangers who smelled of rum. "I'm going with them, Apun. Get the next load ready."

A Chinese comprador and coolies he barely knew now controlled the remaining treasure. Since he couldn't be in two places at once, he had flipped a mental coin to decide. Either way, he'd worry about the other. With qualms about leaving the open vault, Richard climbed into the stern, where he could watch the crew and the treasure chests. The four men pulled and splashed with rum-aided gusto.

As they neared the *Cumfae*, Lokker said, "Hold up, boys. Way enough." The longboat bobbed to a stop. "Y'say you have another load for us? How many loads you got?"

"Maybe one, maybe two more trips," Richard guessed.

"That'll be ... a silver handful each man each trip," said Lokker. The boat drifted with the current.

"No. That's robbery. You haven't delivered anything yet."

"No man calls me a robber." Lokker put on an angry face. Richard rolled his eyes at the blatant blackmail, but the treasure had to get moved.

"I'm not going to argue with you," he said. If he showed too much concern here in the middle of the river, this crew would be convinced that they had valuables. Did they suspect what they carried, anyway? He did not want to pull his revolver on an American. Richard decided that he, not Lokker, would measure the silver handfuls. "All right, you blooming blackmailer. You pushed too far." The sailor smiled at his friends. They smiled back.

"Heave-ho, me boys. We got another job."

They soon reached the *Cumfae,* and Captain Graves soon appeared. "Starr. Back on our ship again, I see. What do you need?" His weather-worn face and soiled overcoat spoke of years cruising the pirate-infested coast.

"Take a small cargo," Richard said. "We'd like you to store it for us."

"What you got?"

"Eight crates, now. Maybe about sixteen crates in all." While they talked, the tipsy sailors with help from *Cumfae's* crew began unloading the boat. "Please store it in the hold below deck."

"How long you want it stored?"

"Probably as long as this disturbance lasts." Richard was impatient to get back to the Chinese left alone in the vault. "Several more boatloads will come out in the next few hours." *God willing.*

The experienced captain nodded. "Tea for an important client, eh?" he said with a wink.

"Okay, sailor," Richard called to Lokker, who was in a parlay with two of *Cumfae's* crew, "Time to go back to shore."

"Where's me silver, mate?" Lokker looked serious.

"You'll have it when we get back to shore," Richard said.

"Oh, me mate, you said, 'when we're done,'" Lokker smiled. "We got her here, didn't we?"

Richard fumed and raised his voice, his confidence sharpened against pirates. "Get your fat arse in the boat and take me back."

"Oh, now he's mad, is he?"

"Now." Richard stepped close to him, glaring with a glare developed negotiating with Chinese traders. The rummy stench of ship's grog on Lokker worried him. "Or you'll not get a red cent. Now."

"Okay, okay. Hey, mates, time to go."

They rowed back in silence. From his stern perch, Richard saw black plumes rising near the city wall. The smoke drifted over the troubled walls.

Apun was waiting with more crates guarded by the coolies. Richard climbed ashore, leaving Lokker and crew rocking in their boat. "Wait here," he told the sailors, "I'll see what we got next."

Right away he told Apun about the costly blackmailing tactics of the tipsy crew leaning on their oars nearby. "Blackmail useful," Apun said. "You pay too much. Chinese boatman not much money." Richard had promised, or at least had told Lokker, that there was another trip. He didn't want to go back on his word, but the man's insolent attitude gave him good reason, and he would go back on it if necessary. The four sailors slouched in the boat. One held a small rag, which he raised to his lips, then passed the rag to his mate. Passing around the rum.

"Apun," Richard said, his anger with the sailor returning. "I will hold this boat of galoots while you see what other boatman you can find." Soon a small sampan came sculling toward them. Apun stood on its bow pointing at the crates waiting on the landing. Richard needed to get rid of the sailors. He fished for his hidden bag of coins readying to use them.

"Ahoy, mate. You got our cargo?" Lokker stood up in his boat and stepped toward shore. The boat rocked, and he tottered onto his companion. He bent over to balance and swung his arms in a circle. "Ha-ha … Losht me bearings there."

"I've got your silver," Richard called. "Here. Take it and cast off." Richard tossed the small bag of coins into the boat, bent over the bow, and shoved hard. Lokker lurched after the coins, lost his balance, and fell hard. His face smashed on the seat when his hand missed the gunwale. The boat shot from the landing and carried the drunken sailors into the current. Lokker spat blood overboard.

Some Chinese had jumped into the water, hoping to commandeer any drifting boats. The sampan swung past them into the landing. Shouts rose from shore. Richard whipped around. Pushing through the crowd, nasty-looking men threatened to overrun the chests piled ready to load on the sampan. Apun's coolies heaved the chests onto the boat and then turned with their poles to face the mob, keeping them away while Apun's boatman backed away from the shore.

With his heart in his throat, Richard watched the sampan, hoping its crew did not hoist sail and head for the open sea. After assuring himself that they headed in the right direction, Richard led the coolies back to the godown, where they filled the remaining crates with coal and silver, loaded up, and headed back to the shore in time to meet the returning sampan. They quickly loaded the final crates. Richard decided he would go on this last trip. Apun said quietly, "Boatman want five taels when he come back."

Richard settled in the stern, felt for his revolver, and then left his jacket unbuttoned so that the Chinese crew could see its handgrip. With this insurance against piracy on the open water, the trip to the *Cumfae* went smoothly.

At one point, a Russell shuttle steamer passed them filled with frightened American women fleeing to safety. Mrs. Williams, who had once sniffed about wonderfully efficient servants, clutched her billowing dress, fleeing from the Chinese that had once waited so nicely on her. Lokker and the drunken sailors splashed along singing lustily, "Away-aye, blow the man down," and tried to keep the river current from carrying them farther away from the *Sea Serpent.*

The empty sampan swiftly sculled back to the landing and Richard disembarked and handed the boatman Chinese coins, as Apun had suggested. It seemed a small sum, but Richard supposed that Apun had also paid the man. The boatman left without protest.

Arriving back at the godown, Richard spoke with Apun about their accomplishment. Without the comprador's loyal abilities, the job could not have succeeded. "Well done, Apun. We got the treasure to the *Cumfae.*" That was fortunate, for certain. "Your wonderful idea with the coal worked." Apun lowered his head, as if unfamiliar with compliments.

Richard asked, "By the way, what did you pay the boatman to get him to help us."

"No pay." The Chinaman showed a sly smile. "He pay me."

"Paid you?" Richard's jaw dropped. He'd seen Sunchong take a kickback, too. These men were cheating the firm that employed them. He thought it right to report them, but if he did, no comprador would work for him again when he needed help. The small payback was insignificant to what Apun had accomplished. Again he decided not to report what he'd seen.

A thunderclap reverberated over the waterfront. The two men looked up. The little steam gunboat *Nimrod* had fired over the settlement toward the rebel army.

25

RICHARD CHANGED HIS soiled and wet clothes, and walked over to the partner's offices where he reported to Cunningham and Grew, who praised him for successfully having protected the firm's treasure.

"I am tired and must do sentry duty tonight. I'd like to rest."

"Good. The attack may come tomorrow."

He awoke two hours later, stretched, yawned, and dressed for his shift as nighttime sentry. He stopped at Olyphant & Co. to relax with Augustus for some gossip, food, wine, and billiards before they spent the night on the ramparts. They had not talked to each other since their visit to the joss house.

"What have you been doing since we dunked a redcoat in the river?" Augustus asked as they entered the billiard room in a good mood, each well filled with wine, Augustus carrying a half-empty bottle.

"I'll tell you as we play."

Richard regaled Augustus with the adventures of the arms sale, of the drunken sailor, and the fight with thieves. The friends fumbled shots repeatedly when Augustus laughed at the way he told the stories.

"Whatever became of the stolen statue and your houseboy?" Augustus suddenly asked.

Richard sipped some wine and sighted on the five ball. "Oh, that's another long story." He told about his boy's beheading, the puzzling comprador, and then the baby's rescue and the old woman's fear that Whipple would eat it. He tried to be funny to avoid stirring up his nightmares. "Missed. It's your turn. Try the six-ball."

"You're mad," Augustus said. He stood straight up; his eyes sparked, and his grin spread. "You cheated boatmen, double-dealt in arms, and then added kidnapping to your litany of crime."

Richard raised the heavy butt end of his cue and aimed a blow at Augustus. He meant to jest, but he nearly swung. He had sinned as his friend said—he'd lied, hid crimes against the company, and broken his word. Augustus had hit a guilt nerve.

"Hey, I'm joking," Augustus said quickly, raising his cue.

"I know. En garde!" Soon they were chasing each other around the billiard table, fencing, whacking cue sticks, laughing heartily, and releasing taut nerves. They had rounded the table three times, when a stick cracked when Augustus parried Richard's thrust to his belly. Augustus rolled the eight ball into a corner pocket with his hand.

"Come on," Augustus said. "This game is over. Enough wine."

"Let's eat."

At dinner, they had their brandy replenished one last time. Augustus said, "A bit more Dutch courage can't hurt. Our British friends at the joss house will need our help," he said.

Dusk came under a cloudy sky. The two friends, each packing rifle, pistol, and ammunition, walked out to the volunteer positions. Through the tenements they walked, frightened women gathered clothing, utensils, mats, bags of rice, and children in blankets. Their men collected planks, sticks, shovels—anything that could be used as a weapon. Bricks and rocks lay in piles near doorways. Richard felt able to hold with bare hands the tension rampant in the Chinese communities.

Richard carried the unused, unfamiliar gift rifle from the Taotai. Why hadn't he asked for his own hunting rifle sooner? The revolver hung heavy under his jacket. The two friends looked over the field between them and the Taiping positions.

"How did we end up allied with the Imperial Army when we're fighting against it in Peking?" Richard said to the air. Augustus didn't respond. A light rain began to fall.

The two Americans set up their posts in line with other American, French, and British civilian volunteers on a newly-built rampart. A small stream had made a ditch in the field before them that split around the British settlement and flowed into Soochow Creek and the Wangpoo river and a wide stone arch bridged across its four-foot-high rocky banks. To their left, city wall battlements held cannons and a handful of British and French soldiers that had stayed to help the Chinese riflemen fire and aim the cannons. The Imperial Army guarded the city's gates. The foreign sentries spread to positions on the newly built rampart about twenty yards from each other along the length of the foreign concession from the Imperial Army's right flank to Soochow creek. Augustus stationed himself to Richard's right and disappeared into the dark. A Frenchman, also invisible, lodged himself to Richard's left. Rebel campfires began to appear one by one in the woods across the field. Distant shadowy figures made tiny silhouettes against the fiery glow.

In the night, deserters from the settlements might run to the enemy, or rebel spies might probe the defenses. The air grew quiet. Blackness settled around the sentries, the city sounds of bustling and conversation hushed and dying campfires blinked in the distance like predators' eyes.

RICHARD LAY ON sloping ground, propped against a rock so he could watch the field. He cradled the rifle across his lap, and for comfort took off the holster with his loaded revolver and laid it beside him. He listened to the night—insects chirped, a frog harrumphed, and something skittered— until gradually he heard nothing at all, and the field was so dark he could not even see it. His eyes grew heavy.

Suddenly, his head snapped up. He looked around, frightened. Had he been asleep? How long had he slept? He could not see Augustus or anyone else. His jacket was wet—a light rain was falling. Silence prevailed.

He thought he heard something. A splash in the creek? A frog? It was a frog. He leaned back onto his rock. He fought sleep, again. He could not stay awake sitting on the ground with his feet up, with too much brandy in him, in the dark night, at the late hour, in the eerie quiet. He got up, stretched his arms, rubbed his eyes, shook his head, and walked in circles. In a few moments he picked up the rifle and set off to find Augustus. They could keep each other awake.

"Augustus!" he whispered, "It's me."

"Richard, over here." His friend was awake. They talked quietly; neither had seen any activity. For hours they jostled each other to stir the blood and hold off the relentless desire to sleep, until a faint glow began in the eastern sky. "Better go back. You don't want to add to your crimes by deserting your post, my friend." Richard left his cousin and returned to his post.

The rising sun soon cast long shadows before him. The drizzle had stopped. He scanned the contours and colors of the shallow ridges in the field before him as the shadows created outlines in them. Imperial troops under the city walls far to his left slowly stirred from their slumbers.

It felt good to stand, and he yawned long and hard, stretching overhead. He gazed over the field, feeling the rush of air. The sun silhouetted two dark rocks in the tributary stream bank under the arch bridge. He did not remember seeing rocks there before. He looked again. He suddenly dropped his stretch, jolted awake, now alert. One of the two rocks had disappeared. He was sure.

Richard stared. He fixed his eyes intently on the remaining rock, waiting for the sun to brighten. The rock moved. Someone was not thirty yards in front of him, hidden in the ditch. How many others were there? At least two men had snuck up near his position. He looked for Augustus. No sign of any soldier, no other volunteer.

"Who's there?" The heart in his throat made his words tremble. He tried again. "Stand and show yourself." He leveled his rifle at the place the rocks had been. The rifle shook so much, he understood so little, he could not have hit any target. Soon two figures crawled forward toward him. The closest man stood. His shaggy black hair jutted from under a red rag, which shadowed his face in sinister darkness. Another man crept up too, hatless, wearing deep blue clothes. He carried a bamboo pole with a knife tied to it. The morning sun glinted off its blade.

"Stand and show yourselves!" Richard said again.

He put his finger on the trigger and pointed the rifle toward them, first one, then the other. "Stop! No closer!" His meaning could not have been missed. Would other sentries hear him?

The last time he faced an enemy with a gun, Fookie Tom in the Min River, his nerves twitched his trigger finger and that resulted in a beating. He fought to prevent that again. *Stay calm. Think.* If he had not called these men out, they might have gone away. He prayed they were spies and would not attack, just assess his position. If he pulled the trigger, he could alert others and might cause them to shoot. Best not to shoot, not to risk provoking a battle. Gunshots would reveal other defensive positions. These rebels had no guns. Richard's revolver lay on the ground behind him. The sword was in his room. He suddenly remembered that he had not loaded the rifle.

The soldier extended his pole forward so that the blade reached halfway along the rifle's muzzle and pointed directly at Richard. Will a threat with the rifle be enough to halt them? Richard swung his rifle toward the spear to knock away the threat. The rebel stood firm, recovered from the knock, swung his spear back, and struck Richard with the blade before pulling it back. Richard refused to react to the sharp pain in his arm but stepped back. The rebel returned to his position—withdrew as if he had not intended to wound Richard. Richard struggled to maintain the threat. *Don't shoot.* He held the rifle steady, could not let them see that he was hurt, even as blood began to ooze through his jacket. Forcing his voice to be steady, he waved his rifle to the side. "*Ting!*" He remembered the Chinese word for "stop." "Go back to where you came from. *Ting. Zou!* Go now."

The taller scout spoke to the spearman in a sharp whisper. He held his arm out over the spear, forcing the soldier to lower it. The two exchanged unintelligible remarks. Then as silently as they had come, they turned about and headed back across the field, ducking into hollows and ditches until they could not be seen again. Richard collapsed onto the ground. He sat there clutching his arm. The pain had subsided into to a dull ache. He took off his jacket, unbuttoned his bloody shirt, and opened it enough to slip the damaged arm out of the sleeve. A thin slice about four inches long cut cleanly across his triceps. Hoping it was only skin-deep, with his teeth and free hand he tied his kerchief tight over the slice.

He stood, picked up his rifle and revolver, and walked with care over to join Augustus, breathing hard when he collapsed next to Augustus's position. "Rebel scouts came up to my position. I stopped them," he panted. "I almost pulled the trigger."

"I thought I heard something. What happened to your arm?"

"It's nothing," Richard lied.

Early sunlight began to light the field.

26

THE ATTACK DID not come with the dawn. Richard had gone to bed and slept soundly. After dressing, cleaning, and drying his spear cut, his arm no longer pained unless he moved it overhead. He recuperated on the roof where he could rest his wounded arm and observe the distant action, at times sharing a ship's telescope with other Russells. The attack was sure to come. With it would come more bloodshed, more death, more disembodied heads. The field soon would become a killing ground.

Gunshots and yells, distant but unmistakable, reached the men on the roof. An imperial squad had jumped from its position under the city wall's west gate and was running toward the rebel line waving flags, banging gongs, yelling, and firing indiscriminately. Before reaching the Taiping positions, the troops paused. Rebels, perhaps twice as many as the Imperials, charged into the field. The Imperials immediately turned and ran back to the gate. The gate opened to let them in. The Taiping rushed toward the city gate. Rifle fire and an explosive cannon volley from the city walls blew holes in the Taiping charge. Dozens fell. Leaving behind wounded comrades, the remaining rebels quickly fled back across the field and out of range.

"The Imps lured them close and into cannon range," Grew said to Richard.

"Nearly sucked them all the way through the gate," said Doyle.

"They won't try to assault near the city again."

"You know what that means," Richard said. "With success like that against the walls, General Li will attack directly across the field tomorrow."

"We're next," Grew said.

THE FOREIGN SETTLEMENT slept little through the night. Though the Chinese would not likely attack at night, the city prepared. Wu Taotai ordered the slums outside the west and south gates set aflame to destroy cover for any spies and troops in the city. The burning hovels outlined the imperial troops' positions without intending to, letting the Taiping assess the defense.

Richard again armed himself with rifle and revolver. He strapped on a military sword that he had found in a small arms shop. He ran out of the house and joined the volunteers rushing to the defensive stations in front of the settlements. Before the light would return, Richard, Doyle, Augustus, and young volunteers from each of the American houses set up positions the on the rampart along the excavated ditch before the settlements. Other foreign volunteers worked into positions alongside the Americans and the Imperials. To the Americans' right, British civilians and the joss house soldiers guarded their settlement. Swords, muskets, and equipment rattled as they all scurried to secure rifles and dig shallow holes to protect themselves. There were no rock walls, no balustrades, no trees to give added protection. Chinese residents who had not joined the defenders on the rampart fled toward the Yangtze waterfront or stayed in their hovels.

Augustus, digging next to Richard, pointed over to the British regiment. Their Brit friends, some in their splendid red, some in dark uniform, formed into ranks. "There's our redcoat sailor, Jack."

"We'd best rely on our own strength to hold up our flank," Richard said, remembering the joss house debauchery. "Where is the Loodiniah Regiment?" The rebels would charge before the Indian troops appeared.

In the long shadows of morning, the Taiping army of thousands advanced on the Chinese city, walking as they came, slowly speeding to a trot, then to a full-speed charge concentrated on the west city gate. The British, French, and Chinese defenders on the wall met them with devastating musket, rifle, and cannon volleys. Hundreds fell, but they continued the charge up to the Imperial Army's defenses.

The volunteers crouched in their holes. Richard clutched his rifle and glanced over at Augustus, tense and also looking toward the battle to their left. The battle line seemed to ebb and flow. Firing from the city walls continued. Then the rebel army deliberately turned away from the walled city and moved parallel to the defense lines. Mounted warriors joined the ground troops, and, in terrifying ranks, the Taiping army thundered toward the foreign settlements, shrieking like banshees, banners flying, hooves pounding.

As the Taiping turned from direct assault on the city, imperial troops charged out to follow the Taiping rear and attack them from behind. A rebel rear guard met the imperials. Richard watched and waited. Mounted riders slashed swords at foot soldiers, pounded heavy leather jackets and knocked soldiers off balance where the enemies stabbed and slashed, splattering each other in blood. A horse shrieked as a spear pierced its flank and it fell to its knees. Spears flew in both directions. Blood squirted when a soldier yanked his spear from a body to face another. A rebel horse stumbled over a body and crashed headfirst, hooves flailing, its rider crushed when it rolled over, and a soldier severed his head for good measure. But the Taiping army kept coming, with nothing but a small stream, a ditch, a low rampart, and the foreign volunteers between it and the European settlements.

"Get ready!" Cries went along the foreign defenses as the front rebel ranks neared the stream. Richard hunched into his hole and lifted to look at the coming army just beyond rifle range. An occasional spear flew toward the rampart but fell short. Soon they would be close. When the rebels had reached the open field in front of the foreigners, the British dispatch boat, *Nimrod,* fired exploding shells from the Yangtze River over the settlement into the fields. Too small to go with the British navy, the little gunboat *Pioneer* had moved into Soochow Creek, and it lobbed thirteen-inch shells into the rebels. Exploding shells flattened entire squads in bloody splatterings of body parts. Imperial cannons on the city wall shifted to reaim their fire to track the Taiping. The British regiment that Richard and Augustus had met stood in ordered ranks and delivered gunfire and rockets in volley after volley. Deafening explosions, rockets, and flying debris broke up and disorganized the rebel ranks. Shrieking Chinese soldiers and cries of horses pierced the din of explosions and gunfire. The imperial troops continued to attack the rebel rear. Stench of gun smoke and death rose over swinging, stabbing, shooting, falling, running, blood-spattered armies.

The volunteers waited. Richard waited. At any moment could come a charge of yelling savages, gunfire, swords, and spears. His hands ached from keeping an iron grip on his rifle. He could not tell who out on the field was attacking who. His sword lay by his side, the revolver ready and loaded in its holster.

Over thirty Taiping rushed toward the stone arch over the tributary, their staves, swords, and guns brandished forward. Volunteers waiting fifty yards from the bridge tensed. Richard drew his sword from its scabbard and then leveled his rifle. Running forward, the joss house Brits rushed to the bridge.

The enemy squads met. A rebel soldier in the lead fired a blunderbuss filled with shrapnel toward the Brits, then turned the empty gun around ready to swing it at the first one he met. Another rebel fired his blunderbuss, and smoke enveloped their attack. The first rank of redcoats fired, and then dropped to their knees to reload. Rebels fell and ducked; their padded jackets no protection from bullets. The second redcoat rank stepped forward and fired another barrage. A rebel toppled into the stream, oozing red into the water. Two others fell. A rebel kicked a wounded soldier off the bridge and started up the arch. Black smoke engulfed the mayhem, and the reek of gunpowder reached the volunteer line. Then the Brits charged up the other side with bayonets and swords. The Chinese drove ahead with staves, pikes, and swords. Metal and wood rang and knocked. Men shouted and yelled. A redcoat, a pike stuck in his chest, fell from the bridge with a cry. The singer from the joss house swung his bayonet at a rebel's ankle, toppling him, then, off balance, the singer stumbled off the bridge into the ditch, recovered, climbed up the bank, and returned to the fight. A broad rebel sword chopped a Brit. Jack, the joss house swimmer, swung his blade, cut the rebel's neck and shoved him off the bridge. Jack led the redcoats up the bridge's arch. A rebel sword, already blooded, flashed and caught Jack in the abdomen. He dropped his weapon; the rebel swung again, shoved him, and Jack tumbled into the stream.

"We have to help," shouted Richard, trying to find a target in the smoke.

Augustus yelled, "Don't hit a Brit."

Richard ordered, "Shoot at the rebel rear." Volunteers shot and reloaded.

Another rebel toppled off the bridge, blood gushed from his severed arm. Determined British soldiers, battle-trained in India and Pakistan, kept charging. They ran over their own fallen comrades, their lethal bayonets and swords blooded and unyielding.

Before the American volunteers could join the fight, the Taiping retreated off the bridge, leaving their dead and moaning wounded. Two dead English soldiers lay on the bridge. Jack lay where he had fallen, in the creek with the Chinese corpses. The redcoats continued to fire at the rebels, protecting the bridge from another crossing attempt.

"Come on," someone shouted. Richard, Augustus, Doyle, and several British volunteers ran to the bridge. They helped the soldiers pull their dead off the bridge back to their lines. Richard and Augustus climbed down to help Jack in the bloody creek. They shoved away a dead rebel, rolled Jack over to his back, and saw that he was dead. They raised his body by the shoulders, and a British volunteer seized the legs. They carried him back to the remaining troops.

"Thank all of you," Richard managed, "Jack and our friends ..." After a moment, he added, "You have saved us." There was no time to mourn Jack.

Richard ran back to his position and checked his ammunition. He made sure his pistol was clear of dirt, his rifle reloaded and clean. Then he rolled back to look at the battlefield. The Shanghai volunteers had stiffened. All along the line, imperial troops, European soldiers, mercenary units, civilian volunteers and the wall-top cannons and ships' guns' crossfire pounded the Taiping. No more rebels tried to cross the ditch. Richard, like others, fired shots without aiming. The Imperial Army squads ran onto the field screaming. They fired a few shots and retreated, rested, reloaded, and raided again. Rebels with empty rifles and old single-shot muskets, medieval pikes, and swords now cowered on the open field, trying to hide behind fallen horses and soldiers. Crazed horses stomped on fallen men. Some rebels rose and ran out of range. Dead bodies cluttered the field, and wounded men moaned and shrieked in pain, writhing on the wet, bloody ground like so many maggots. Rebels still carrying ammunition peeked out of craters or from behind bodies, fired, and dropped down again to reload.

The rebels endured for another fifteen minutes. The Indian Loodiniah regiment finally appeared. The explosions and gunfire stopped. Richard surveyed the field through the smoke. All along the front, Taiping rebels crept out from among the corpses and mutilated bodies on the tortured earth and left the dead to their heavenly peace.

The blood-covered Taiping army limped away, slowly retreating beyond cannon range. Behind the retreat, imperial troops jumped out of their holes to look for wounded rebels still struggling on the field. Richard looked away when he saw a blood-spattered soldier lift a dripping head high and throw it at a fleeing rebel. Imperial troops, Taotai's troops, Chinese ships' crews, and individual natives climbed about the battlefield, scavenging for weapons, clothing, boots, anything useful. Any rebel found still alive or twitching in death throes was skewered, chopped into pieces, beheaded, disemboweled, or castrated, as he lay. The victorious Chinese stuck heads and limbs on pikes and placards and, boasting to their fellows, carried the heads into the city.

Later hundreds of dead would be shoveled into mass graves.

27

TAIPING GENERAL LI withdrew from Shanghai. He would be back, he threatened, and he would bring foreign help next time. His army remained in the vicinity, threatening nearby towns and the possibility of cutting Shanghai off from everything but the sea. In the days following its successful defense, Shanghai fielded a steady stream of fortune seekers, mercenaries, and putative deal-makers, trying to take advantage of the unsettled business atmosphere and opportunities to join a fight that promised loot.

For the time being, all residents in the foreign settlements relaxed a little, and business at Russell & Co. stopped altogether. Richard took time to catch up on sleep, to fully heal his arm, to relax with friends bonded anew by the combat, and to enjoy mild exercise, food, wine, piano, and billiards. He tried unsuccessfully to ignore the unforgettable slaughter and bloodshed and death. The Taiping were still nearby, and more fighting seemed likely. Thoughts about going home recurred when the horror of combat surfaced in his mind. The lack of business also worried him, and he missed his girls—missed any girls.

As he relaxed and the battle receded in time, he remembered that before leaving for China he had told Annie that he was going for the adventure of it. He had certainly had adventures— escaping pirates, rescuing silver, delivering arms to the terrible

Taiping, surprising rebel scouts, and defending the settlements. He had survived in these adventures, felt the electricity in their challenges and threats, and learned that he could stand up to them. The partners praised him in each case. Go home to escape or stay here to recover? He had no quick answer. The excitement he'd felt stirred something in him. He had quickly fallen back into normal business routines and needed variety, and yet the gnawing thought about returning home would not go away.

The latest letter from Meto had said that South Carolina's threats to secede from the Union were increasing and that secession seemed certain if Abraham Lincoln was nominated a presidential candidate. She worried that his aunt Mary had married a New Orleans businessman who was now an ardent advocate for secession. There could be excitement at home, too.

ONE DAY ABOUT a week after the Taiping attack, he thought of Hop Tzu's baby, and decided to visit the Baptist Mission. Knowing that he could never care for a baby, he had told the baby's old caretaker that Hop Tzu wanted him to care for this newborn infant, and he had entrusted the baby to the missionaries, hoping that they would take her in or find her a home. Concerned about keeping his word and still nagged by guilt, he decided to visit the mission. Near many charred ruins, the stone mission house still bore below its entry a yellow banner signifying that the Taipings were not to attack it. He stood in the entry hall, its bare beige walls without cheer or decoration, the only furnishings a line of straight chairs around bare walls, the only person a small Chinese in Western clothing. Richard was comforted to see no images of the Savior with blood seeping from him like those in his home church. He didn't need to be reminded of bloodshed. The young Chinese in Western clothing ducked through a door, and a moment later, Reverend Whipple emerged.

"Hello, Reverend. I came to see you and to find out how the baby Chinese girl you took in is doing."

Whipple shook his hand and welcomed him to the mission. "She is here and doing well. I will get her for you."

Whipple's assurance satisfied him that she was safe. "No need," he said. He had expected this offer, but he wasn't sure he really wanted to see a month-old Chinese baby. "If it's any trouble? If she's sleeping … don't wake her just for me."

Whipple departed for a moment and soon returned followed by a middle-aged Chinese matron carrying a scrunched, wrinkled infant with yellow skin, half-closed eyes, and thin black hair swaddled in a pink blanket.

"Your little girl will grow into a Christian beauty," the cleric said proudly.

"Have you named her?"

"Her name is Grace, for God gives grace to the humble."

"I like the name. It's appropriate. What name do you suppose her parents gave her?"

"Praise the Lord, she has escaped that. We have saved the child from a poverty-stricken and heathen life."

The mission matron cooed at the baby, fussed with her blanket, and showed the scrunched little face to Richard. He gently tickled the baby's small chin, causing the eyes to blink open. Grace smiled, then closed her eyes again to express a large yawn and settled back to sleep. Richard expected that she would grow up knowing the Ten Commandments and about Jesus, and he felt relieved that she was alive, clean, well fed, and clothed. She had no parents, but she was being cared for.

"Thank you, Reverend. I can see that she is comfortable and happy as can be."

Grace and the matron retreated back into the mission.

Richard also was curious about Simon Brown, who was living at the mission. The last time they talked, his one-time cabinmate had been unhappy in China when he thought of leaving for home. Nevertheless, he asked, "Is Simon Brown still here?"

Simon soon entered the room. "Simon, how have you fared? We didn't see you during the recent fighting."

"I'm okay. Everyone here said they trusted God, not weapons. They were scared witless. How was it for you all?"

Richard stepped toward the door. "Thank you for helping save the orphan baby. Let's walk outside for fresh air."

Brown recounted how fires had come close to the mission, how he and mission Chinese had worked with water buckets to keep flames away. Brown's skin was pale and his red hair was unkempt, even though days had passed since the enemy withdrew. "Still smells like charcoal out here," Brown said without a smile.

Richard said he had seen the fighting close up when the rebels attacked. Brown seemed unimpressed; instead, he looked depressed about something. Richard wondered whether business problems still bothered him. When they had walked several yards through the sooty slum toward the waterfront, Richard said, "I have been thinking about our lack of business, Simon," he said. "What have you heard?"

"Is money all you think about?" Brown shot back.

That silenced Richard. Not what he expected. He stopped walking.

Brown huffed, "Nuthin' … I dunno." They reached the waterfront lined with the swarming sampans. "Richard, I've had enough of this place," Brown said. "I'm goin' home."

"Really? Business can only get better."

"It's not the business. This place is a hellhole. It's impossible. Chinamen kill everyone; everyone kills Chinamen. The mission is swamped with rabble looking for protection and food. The missionaries want to make Christians out of every slant-eye, rebel or no. They blame traders for the troubles. That includes me and y'all. I'm needed at home. I won't live here any longer."

The torrent momentarily left Richard with nothing to say. Even though Brown's company dismayed him, Richard tried to assuage Brown's emotional concern. Fighting will probably continue, he thought, but he said, "I hardly think that the Taipings will attempt to take this city for the present. The British will soon whip the Chinese into shape, and things will return to normal."

"Yeah," Brown agreed. "Normal is hell … I've decided." He looked over the water as if in a trance. "Chinamen will fight each other forever. If there is fightin' to be done, I'll do it at home, fightin' niggers and Yankees."

There seemed no point in arguing with the big redhead. For Brown, bigotry proved powerful, Richard saw. "Normal" might still be hell for him in this place.

"Simon, I wish you a safe return."

Both men looked over the expanse, past the junks and sampans, past the steam shuttles, past the distant masts, down the river toward the far ocean. "Home is over there," Simon said and pointed.

On the way back from the water, they talked amicably about the cooling weather and Simon's lengthy voyage home. Reaching the mission, they parted. Richard promised to see him off when the time came. "Good luck to you, Simon."

Richard slowly walked back to the American compound. On the way his thoughts wandered from Hop Tzu's tragedy to mysteries of life and death. The heathen Chinese, he had seen, killed people and let people drown. They were unconcerned about death. Did they believe in life after death? Christians promised life after death. The godless Chinese thought torture was punishment and death merciful. Christians glorified suffering and abhorred death. Why did Christians honor, protect, and save lives if life was better after death? Perhaps life after death only means people remain alive in descendants' memories. Chinese honor their ancestors. Christians remember them. No one knows the answer, of course, but Richard would not easily forget the punishing deaths or the tiny life in the mission.

SHANGHAI WAS NOW isolated. Taiping armies withdrew to nearby Soochow and Wu-Chiang and occupied other cities on the broad peninsula and surrounded the big port city. The rebels controlled traffic on the roads and waterways, where they could stop traffic and trade at will. The Emperor against whom rebels and foreigners fought was not so successful. During the Shanghai attack, British and French regular armies had flattened the Tagu forts, besieged Peking, and looted and burned the Imperial Summer Palace to the ground. The Emperor had fled into the countryside. Diplomats worked to extract as many concessions from the government as they wanted.

The Imperial Army, no longer divided to defend both Peking and Shanghai, was now free to turn full attention to the rebels. To help them, Frederick Townsend Ward, a thin young American, commanded the Foreign Arms Corps, a military unit of Chinese and foreign mercenaries. Latest news reported that Ward's Corps had captured a city from the Taiping and looted it, raising glimmers of hope that the Taiping could ultimately be defeated. But the Taiping rebels still controlled the Yangtze River.

"The Brits think that buttoned-up Ward is a freeloader," said Augustus to Richard. "They claim that a Chinese banker named Yang Fang paid Ward seventy-five thousand *taels* to plunder and repay him with loot. The Brits call him 'Takee.'"

Richard took care not to reveal his reaction to this. Yang Fang? Chinese banker? Kung Loong's friend? "Takee sounds like an appropriate name," he said, tucking into memory another reason to beware of Kung's ideas.

Sleep, good food, games, and occasional trades occupied Richard, Augustus, and the other civilians who had risen to the defense. Richard scrambled for business among his British contacts for shipments to book on the *Sancho Panza*, an American hull just arrived en route to San Francisco from Manila. He had some success, earning small commissions for the partners. Exercising with dumbbells, long walks, occasional horseback rides, and frequent rows on the creek occupied his empty time over the hot summer, often leaving his mind unoccupied with Russell & Co. business matters.

Richard thought again about Kung Loong as a source of money for personal investments. Be sure to remember that 'Takee' could be behind Kung's dealing, he told himself. He sent a note by courier to Kung's weighing house suggesting that he wanted to talk about another loan. He asked for an office address or other place to meet. He had nothing specific in mind but knew no other way to reach Kung.

Shortly after he sent this note, Augustus happened to tell Richard that he had an opportunity to go on the *Hartford* to the recently opened Japanese port of Nagasaki. "If you get the chance," Richard proposed, "let's together buy a small cargo of Japanese porcelain or silk or other curiosities that we can ship back home. I'll contribute. We can share the profits."

Augustus agreed. "Will you let me select the products?"

"Of course," Richard said, "I'll give you $100 to invest. Our first joint venture.

Two days later, at the same restaurant at which they had previously met, Richard hoped to surprise Kung with a new Chinese expression he had learned for the occasion: "*Zenme yang,*—How's everything."

Kung, smiled, raised his eyebrows, and replied, "*Hen Hao xiexie!*—Well, thank you."

"*Wo e le*—I'm hungry," said Richard, "and that's all my Chinese."

Kung laughed. "Yes. What you want eat?" He ordered, and the waiter brought spring rolls and a meal of sesame chicken, and disappeared.

Richard thought that Kung understood English well enough for a simple transaction. No one had come to translate. For a preliminary, Richard said, "Before we talk business ... We have known each other for months, and I want to ask you something. There has been so much killing and violence around us that has made me wonder."

Kung sat back, smiling slightly. "What wonder?"

"I wonder, do the Chinese believe in life after death?"

"Why want know?"

"Christian people believe it. Are the Chinese the same?"

"Chinese and barbarian no same. Barbarian worship money; no worship ancestors."

Richard started to argue, then realized that Kung usually avoided a direct answer to anything. Maybe Chinese beliefs could not be expressed in English terms that Kung knew.

Richard changed the subject and told him that he had an opportunity to buy some Japanese goods through an agent in Japan and wanted to borrow $100. I will repay, as before, when I have sold the goods and have the money."

Kung acted deeply thoughtful, frowned and looked away, munched a spring roll, twirled his mole hair, and proposed, "Bank lend money. We need deposit in bank first."

He was adding terms again, likely remembering the tiny interest on the loan Richard paid immediately. "If I had money for a deposit, I would not need to borrow it," Richard said. "You took my word before. Take it now."

"Yang Fang partner set terms. You no pay interest before."

"I hear Yang Fang takes loot from the Foreign Arms Corps. He does not need a deposit from me."

At this, Kung's sly expression told Richard that their bank did indeed finance Ward's army. It also confirmed that he needed to stand firm. Richard stood and said, "Thank you for lunch. I'll get my loan somewhere else."

"Sit. Sit," Kung barked.

"I'll talk with Kung. Not Yang."

They negotiated the repayment terms, including a token deposit. The insignificant sum did not matter, but the precedent that Kung and a man called 'Take-ee' held his money mattered greatly.

28

ON HIS RETURN to the office, a pile of papers from the mail boat lay on his desk. He flipped through the dispatches, until his eye caught a newspaper headline about Abraham Lincoln's election as president. He had heard talk about the election but paused to read the lead article. It described the nation's reaction, including likely secession by southern states because they saw Lincoln an abolitionist, slave liberator, and destroyer of their way of life. Richard's own thoughts repeated in his mind. He favored an end to slavery but had regretted the abolitionists stirring up belligerency. He feared that the states' union would break apart, that brother Willie would be forced to fight his own countrymen, and that his Meto would be separated from her sister Mary, perhaps now a secessionist. There was nothing he could do except worry for his Meto's well-being. Thoughts of returning home recurred. Should he return home to help his family if secession causes trouble?

He turned to sort the rest of the mail. A letter from home stood out. The date it bore showed that it had been written soon after he had first arrived in Shanghai over a year ago. Its edge was singed on one side, and the outside writing was smudged as if water had touched it. Somewhere on its way to China, a storm or collision must have delayed it.

He slit it open, skimmed through the routine greetings and wishes and recital of letters sent and received, then read.

I do hope with all my heart that you are not as serious about that Delano girl as your letter sounded, and that you will have nothing more to do with her beyond the requirements of your position with the company. You have no need to associate with any of the sort of girl that frequents heathen cities. Any girl who sails around the world in uncouth conditions to live however short a time in that country cannot have the place in polite society that you deserve.

He laughed. There were no girls now. Meeting an attractive young American girl in Shanghai was surely impossible. Meto need not worry. Even the thought of a Chinese concubine had disappeared when he had heard about an American sailor who had once loved a Chinese girl, and was murdered by her Chinese lover. The Delano girls were long gone from his life, and he had seen nothing that endeared him in Chinese girls or married women since. In any event, would that there was an attractive girl in China of any society, any race.

The mail ship would soon carry mail for New York. He wrote to Meto, expressing his thoughts and chagrin at events at home due to Lincoln's election and hoped that Meto would be well. He avoided any suggestion that he had thought about coming home. What could he write Meto about this deadly, violent place that would remove any added worry about him? He assured her that he would not marry anyone he met in China. She would certainly read about the attack on Shanghai, and he wrote, as if he was not alarmed, "Large bodies of insurgents are still in our vicinity and keep the Chinese in a state of constant alarm." Then, as he often did, he commented on his prospects with Russell & Co. and added, "There is little or no business doing on account of the current trouble, but I try to be contented here."

EDWARD CUNNINGHAM'S NEW wife, Constance, had recently arrived from America, and social duty required a call. While Augustus was in Japan, Richard knocked on the Cunningham home's paneled door. A houseboy took his card, turned, and left him standing in the entry hall, where he braced for another awkward visit with an unpleasant married woman. He fidgeted with his gloves, finally pulled off the one on his right hand, and placed his hat on a lacquer table.

"Richard Starr. Hello." A smiling lady in a verdant silk walking dress extended her hand to him. He took it, looking into deep-blue eyes that bewitched him immediately. Sandy hair neatly bound up revealed a necklace of pearls against her alabaster skin. "Edward has told me much about you," she said as she led him into a small sitting room. She immediately sat down on a knobby velvet Victorian settee and patted the seat beside her for him to sit. A crack of sunlight shone on the smooth silk of her bodice, outlined in lace. She nodded to a boy, who soon brought a tray with tea and cookies.

"Richard, you must tell me what you have been doing." She poured boiling water through the small strainer filled with tea leaves. Richard, hoping that his face was not as red as it felt, pulled at his other glove and squeezed his knees together to avoid touching her leg.

"Just working as I hope the partners desire," Richard replied when she had filled two teacups. She had been in Shanghai a week after stopping in Hong Kong. "How do you find living in China?" he asked her.

"Oh, it is too new to me. I expect I will acclimate." She conversed easily, smiled often, and admired his bravery. She had heard "marvelous things" about his confrontations with pirates and rebels. He protested that the stories were not true. When he minimized a story, she praised his modesty. Time and conversation passed quickly and easily. This was her first visit to the Orient, and she hoped to go to Japan.

He could have talked for hours with this attractive, pleasant lady, but the second rule of calling was not to overstay one's time. He stood. "I am sorry, but I should get back to work. I do not want to keep you."

"That's all right," she said. "Edward has not come home yet."

She walked him out of the parlor. He lingered in the doorway. "Thank you for the tea, Mrs. Cunningham." He replaced his gloves and held his hat in both hands. "I hope I may have the pleasure of calling again."

"You are welcome any time," she promised. "Oh ... please call me Constance."

He stepped out the front door and into a fresh autumn breeze.

29

THE MAIL STEAMER from Hong Kong brought a rare letter for Richard. He slit the letter open and unfolded thin paper to face his father's tiny cramped handwriting. A winter storm beat a continuous tattoo on his window. Little light entered, so Richard lit his oil lamp and tossed the match away. Correspondence from the father he admired but hardly knew usually concerned formally delivered advice.

"My Dear Richard," it began.

This letter comes to you with warmest greetings. I write from the Don Quixote, on which I am bound for Liverpool. After a several months' stay, I plan to sail on to New York. There I intend to rejoin your mother and to pursue my commercial activities at home. I hear that you are well thought of at Russell & Co., and I am proud of your progress. If you continue doing well at the assignments given, you might expect to be invited to join the partnership in several years. At that time you will need to contribute your capital share.

Partnership was the ultimate goal at Russell & Co., but in Richard's present circumstances, the idea of paying the firm even more was an investment burden he could not meet. He had a small amount saved, and Kung's bank to repay. The report about his progress was encouraging, but the idea of going home did not go far from his thoughts. He read on.

The small Baltimore clipper Coquette is expected to arrive in Shanghai in November if the weather holds steady. She carries a cargo of Malwa opium. I have acquired fifty chests from Kessressung and consigned them out of Portuguese Damaun through Augustine Heard to you. The fifty chests, freight, and brokerage have been paid. You may sell these chests for your own account. If placed well, and you invest the proceeds safely, you should profit sufficiently to cover somewhat more than your eventual capital contribution. I do not anticipate that you should have any trouble with Cunningham or Delano about this.

Richard laid the letter down and stared unseeing across the room. *Opium?* Richard shook his head. *I'm grateful, Father, but ... opium?* Father had never hinted that he had been trading opium. Opium trade had been illegal for many years while father traded in China and India. Richard was stunned. *Why had he kept it from us?* The man he placed on a pedestal, the man who wrote kind and loving letters to Meto, the man whose advice he accepted without question, that man had been supporting his family with contraband. The money, the gifts, the shipments for them to sell in New York, all bought with illicit profits. He would not believe that his father was a charlatan who left his family for money.

Richard stood and strode to the window. He stared out at the water. He'd seen the opium ship in the Pearl River, another one was out there close by now. He could not imagine his father selling drugs to smugglers. He walked around his table and sat heavily. He read the letter again.

Questions troubled his mind. Shouldn't Father be admired for trying to help his son in a way that he knew, not disrespected? The fortune that Meto enjoyed, the horses, the Berkshire farm,

college, the society life, the fine home, all provided for them by
Father working hard. But he helped destroy lives, too. Delano had
once said that it did not matter what people did once opium was
sold. Was that also Father's attitude, that if the Chinese abused
opium, it was their own fault? Did Meto know what Father really
did overseas?

The more he had thought about opium, the more his conscience had told him not to have anything to do with it. Opium
led to hallucinations and addiction, then stupor and insatiable
longing for more until dying a miserable death, adding more misery to this miserable land. Richard wanted to support his family
too, but not by illegal and immoral trafficking. What to do with
fifty chests of opium?

Over the next several days he began to understand how the
profits in teas, silks, and porcelains paled when compared to
that from opium. The Russells never talked about the trade, but
Delano had acknowledged that they engaged in it when it was
legal. Clearly, the great fortunes that had been brought back to
Boston and New York had been made in the opium trade. The
treaty signed after the Canton opium battles legalized the trade,
but the Chinese resisted carrying out the treaty until the recent
negotiations. Thanks to the British, the opium trade was legal
again. When he thought about the future, a question persisted:
would he be able to build his nest egg without opium?

He decided to learn more about the unpleasant business. He
took the shuttle steamer out to Woosong, then arranged to borrow a small sailing vessel that he could handle alone in choppy
seas, and soon he approached the stern of Russell's opium storeship, *Ann Melot*, anchored in the lee of a small uninhabited island
near Woosong. Eight closed gun ports hid her guns. The watch
officer made a show of his rifle and hailed the little boat. Richard
called, identified himself, turned his boat into the wind, and came

alongside. The officer allowed him aboard, where a mate forced him to wait for half an hour before he was summoned into the captain's cabin.

The cabin was luxurious. A red and blue oriental carpet covered the deck, and brass fittings decorated the windows, cabinets, and lamps. Clipper ship art hung in available wall space. On the captain's desk sat a detailed scale model sloop made of whalebone inside a bottle. A tray of liquors topped a shelf within reach of the captain's easy chair.

Captain Eli Barrows looked familiar. Richard had seen his large nose and graying black beard about the company compound. His ruffled shirt lay open in front, exposing a hairy chest.

"I'm Richard Starr of Russell & Co.," he began. "I am expecting a shipment of opium. I want to arrange to store it here until I decide what to do with it."

"For whose account?" Barrows asked without any ceremony while remaining slouched behind his ornate desk.

"Mine. And I want to learn about how to sell it."

"You and everybody else, it seems." Barrows's surly tone betrayed the depressing effects of living most of the time on a ship without going anywhere. "How much?"

"Fifty chests."

"When?"

"It's supposed to arrive soon on the *Coquette*."

"The *Coquette*, eh?" Barrows sat up. "Haven't ya heard?"

"Heard what?"

"The *Coquette* was lost in a typhoon near Amoy. She ain't gonna arrive."

Richard was speechless for a few moments. He looked around the luxurious cabin. Mixed relief and disappointment surged in him. Relieved to be rid of the drug problem, but from somewhere inside that he did not like, he felt discouraged. There seemed nothing more to say to Barrows about the *Coquette* cargo.

"It's time for food," Barrows said. "I want company. Stay here." He poured two glasses from a bottle on his shelf, and once glasses were emptied, they partook of a full-course meal prepared by the ship's cook, who must have trained in New York's best restaurant. Russell & Co. well compensated this man who stores and sells its partners' opium.

"What do ya want with opium anyway?" Barrows asked.

Richard did not know. He didn't really want it. "To make money," he said. Barrows would understand that. "Why else does anyone want it?"

Barrows's tongue loosened with wine, and he regaled Richard with stories of sea fights, of the days when the trade was illegal, and of smugglers escaping imperial enforcers.

"Did Russell & Co. trade the drug then?" Richard asked.

Barrows put on a smile that revealed the truth, when he said, "Now ... I'm not to say, ya know."

Questioning Barrows further, he learned what he could about opium prices, which were usually negotiated in advance, and that Barrows's account for Russell & Co. earned a sizable percentage. Barrows delivered to legitimate importers as well as smugglers who avoided the import duties.

Richard sailed back a little wiser about opium trading but oddly disappointed that he had none to trade, thinking about what he would have done with it, and relieved that he need not be concerned about the moral questions. Without a foundation for his fortune handed to him, he would just have to work that much harder to earn his savings. He recalled Uncle Sam's advice nearly three years ago that he would have to make his own opportunities. For over two years, events in China had conspired against his saving—nepotism, expenses, then war, rebellion, and now shipwreck. Back to work or go home?

Augustus returned from Japan with a shipment of $200 worth of Japanese silks and porcelain. Richard arranged to load the shipment onto the *Sancho Panza* consigned to Goodhue & Co., his family's bankers in New York. The cousins would share the profits equally when Goodhue sold the goods. Although the opium gift did not work out, his father's report that the partners thought well of him decided him to keep working for now.

China was not what he had imagined when he had told Meto that he'd be back in a year or two with enough to sustain them all. His small personal ventures in rifles, porcelain, and Japanese silks had been modestly profitable. Kung Loong's willingness to help him was encouraging. The Chinese Emperor had recently died; his successor was six years old, and the imperial government was weaker than ever. The Brits have forced open more treaty ports. The situation was improving. He held on.

30

I F THE PAVILION'S sweeping, upturned roof had been made of goatskin instead of exquisite wood and tile, it would have resembled a Mongol warrior's tent with polished teak poles. Near the elegant house, water flowed peacefully under an arched bridge, its bright red railings dulled by an overcast sky. Each end of the bridge rested on a pile of pocked rocks. Two men dressed in silken robes crossed the bridge. Embroidered serpents slithered on their robes as they walked.

"Yang Fang, your garden most auspicious, as always," said the bigger man, speaking in his Cantonese dialect. He had a black beard, a mouth of bad teeth, and a mole on his cheek. The two looked out over the water to overhanging pine branches hung with paper lanterns.

"Yes, place for most careful planning," replied thin Yang Fang.

"Young American repay loan fast." Kung Loong was pleased. "He make deposit now."

"Decent profits, for he pay shipping cost," said Yang. "He pay high price we no get anywhere else."

They paused in the center of the bridge. Kung said, "Wise to use Kee Chong barbarian new to China. Young Starr will come to me again. If not, I go to him." Kung placed his hands on the railing and looked over the water, searching the lily fronds and fish for some portent. "Kee Chong's young Starr want more business himself," said Kung Loong. "He link to barbarian buyer. I make easy loan for him. Next add more interest. Next add deposit. He agree all. He trust me now. Foolish barbarian no take squeeze."

Laughter never came from Yang. He smiled broadly. "Barbarian big source for prosperity."

"Barbarian call you 'Takee' in English language for good reason."

The two merchant bankers reached the end of the bridge and stepped into the tent-like pavilion. Awaiting them were two elaborate and bulky chairs carved from heavy burled hardwood into fantastic shapes looking like a nest of entwined snakes. They sat cupped in the snakes while servants brought three plates of *cha nau* appetizers and two painted drinking cups. A petite girl in a silk robe poured clear *shao xing jiu*. They raised their cups and sipped the sharp rice wine.

While they sampled the plate of delicacies and sipped the wine, they talked of anticipated business and of ways to avoid customs duties that the foreigners now collected for the imperial government. Kung raised his cup to his lips. "We want Yangtze business, no?"

"Yes, good friend," said Yang, with a broad smile that narrowed his eyes unnaturally. "To save regime, Imperial Prince Kung give barbarian what they ask. Ports on Yangtze soon open for barbarian now."

"Yangtze," Kung said. "Again great river of life."

"Certainly. We must be ready." Yang barked an order at a boy, who scurried out, and the serving girl immediately shuffled back with another pot of *shao xing jiu*.

The fall season on opium from India was nearly over, so many merchants deposited the drug aboard storage ships near the anchorages while opium dealers waited for prices to rise again in spring and summer when fresh opium again became scarce.

"Barbarian no need pay *likin* fee to city when send opium from Shanghai inland. Chinese need pay," Yang said, selecting a piece of cold pickled eel. He savored the treat in thoughtful silence.

"Opium storeships full now," said Kung Loong, as he lowered his cup. "I have idea for Starr. Starr know Kee Chong barbarian business way."

31

"You want to trade in the Yangtze River ports? Go. Go trade in them," Prince Kung had said, in effect, to Western diplomats. Prince Kung had persuaded the Emperor's council to appease the *fanqui*. He had argued that imperial armies could turn full attention to the rebels, who threatened to overthrow the empire, and the barbarians also would fight the rebels to force their shipping rights. The empire would be saved.

No Western negotiator could imagine a more untrustworthy visage than that of the dominant member of the child Emperor's ruling council. Taiping rebels controlled the Yangtze below Hankow, so river trade would be difficult for the foreigners. Prince Kung's permanent frown pulled on his narrow eyes, and his mouth protruded when he had told the Europeans firmly, through translators, "Make no mistake. Do not expect help if rebels interfere with you. Imperial government will not be responsible if harm comes to you."

British envoy Lord Elgin ordered his admiral, Sir James Hope, to lead a fleet of gunboats the six hundred miles up the Yangtze to Hankow in a show of power. Admiral Hope did so, and persuaded the Taiping to agree not to interfere with British shipping; the provincial governor of Hupeh Province around Hankow welcomed the foreigners, and Hope declared the Yangtze open.

Chinese rules and agreements negotiated by the British applied to Americans under the most-favored-nation treaty provisions, so American Admiral Cornelius Stribling promptly led the warships *Hartford, Dakotah,* and *Saginaw* to Hankow and demanded safe shipping as well. When he returned, he declared the river open for Americans and stood ready to protect American shipping with the three powerful warships.

When the big warships anchored back at Shanghai, the news had come that civil war had begun in the United States. The *Hartford, Dakotah,* and *Saginaw* were ordered home at once, and Admiral Stribling, a South Carolinian, was relieved of his command. There would be no military support for American commercial shipping.

ONE MORNING LATE in June, the managing partner asked Richard to come to an important meeting. As he strode toward the godown on the way to meet, Richard noticed a blooming pink lotus flower in Soochow creek that had not flowered the day before. A pristine white egret rose to spread its wings and glide over the water. The soaring beauty made him smile, and he hoped, as the Chinese believed, that the lotus and egret were favorable omens.

As Richard entered the office, the three Shanghai partners, Cunningham, Grew, and recently arrived David Clark, stood up to greet him. Cunningham gestured to an empty wicker chair across the room. This unusual reception puzzled Richard, and he stood before the chair, waiting for the others to sit, wondering what was next. The former Russell & Co. partners, a somber white-bearded Samuel Russell and a frowning John Murray Forbes, seemed to intently study Richard from their heavy gold frames that hung over the chairs. As the partners sat, they looked as serious as the painted old gentlemen. The wicker creaked under Richard. His smile had flown away along with the white egret's auspicious omen. He perched on the edge of his chair and clasped his hands tightly.

Cunningham began, "Richard, as you know, the military has gone up the Yangtze as far as is navigable. Over six hundred miles. If we buy tea in Hankow near the mountains where it grows, and we use our own steamships, we can get it to Shanghai for almost nothing. No duties or entry fees are charged when foreigners ship from one Chinese port to another. We'd also eliminate the fees and squeeze of Chinese boatmen."

The partners looked expectant, as if waiting for Richard's reaction. To end the pause, Richard said, "I heard that the governor general welcomed foreigners. Why would he do that?"

"The Emperor told him to," said Grew, sounding cynical.

By the time Cunningham spoke again, Richard knew the answer to his own question—money, of course. "He knows we will bring money."

Cunningham stood up, stepped to the lacquered cabinet, opened a brandy bottle, filled a glass half-full, handed it to Richard, and sat again, his own full brandy glass in hand. Grew and Clark sipped theirs. *Why brandy at a business meeting?*

"All the larger houses, European and American, will soon start running steamers up the river," Cunningham said. "We can beat the Brits to Hankow if we send a steamer immediately."

Richard swallowed a mouthful of brandy.

Cunningham looked Richard in the eye, his expression filled with the fire of competition. "I have engaged the *Scotland* to leave in two days. I will have her loaded with provisions and supplies and a sizable amount of treasure."

The steamer's great side paddle wheels would churn the shallow hull built for river travel like those on the Mississippi. Below the hull, twin screws could be used for added control and speed. The *Scotland* promised a quick journey upriver.

The others turned their eyes on their experienced clerk. "We want you to go with *Scotland*. We want you to set up the trading business for us in Hankow."

Richard swallowed another mouthful of brandy.

32

"I REALLY HAVE NO idea what's going on when Chinese are involved," said Richard to his cousin that afternoon as they found shade on the veranda.

Augustus, dressed casually in an open-collared shirt, flopped into a veranda chair. "It's a chance to really see China up close. You've always wanted to confirm your fantasies about it." A boy brought two gin and tonic glasses.

Richard caressed the drink, his middle finger circled the rim, trying without success to make it sing, as he pondered the partners' plan. "I have wondered if it was time to go home. In nearly three years here, I have very little saved."

"Are you worried about the rebels getting to Hankow?" Augustus probed.

"I sometimes wonder if I should be home in case it is necessary to face down our own rebels." He stared over the water.

"If there is to be fighting at home, the affair will be over by the time you'd get there," Augustus said. "You could be stuck with a bayonet or shot at home as well as in Shanghai or Hankow."

Richard still stared over the river. "I think the Russell partners do like my work." He paused before continuing to muse aloud. "I've progressed by doing what the partners asked. This is not the time to refuse them."

"You are not a quitter. I know that." Augustus put his arm on Richard's shoulder. "You can handle yourself," he said. "And the Chinese."

The next day, Richard met with the partners for a final briefing. Excitement about this new venture bright in his face, Cunningham outlined the need to find property and a storage godown, to secure the treasure they'd send, and to establish relations with the local tea brokers. "Be sure to report to me often." Richard nodded. Cunningham went on. "Apun has agreed to go to Hankow as your comprador."

Apun, whose parents had been killed in the British attack on Canton twenty years before, hated the British from childhood. At the same time, he envied the foreign merchants' power, wealth, and comforts. He had learned English, sweated as a coolie heaving goods in and out of foreign godowns, studied foreign techniques and expectations, absorbed the intricate Chinese bureaucracy, knew brokers, earned trust, and implemented local trading methods in Canton. He had been a comprador in the American factory for seven years and moved to Shanghai when Canton natives burned the foreign waterfront. Though he preferred to hide his despised queue, a sign of subservience to the Manchu government, coiled under a cap, he could let it hang it down his back when an imperial loyalty mattered to the job at hand, and he developed skills to manipulate the imperial bureaucracies like a ship captain manipulates his sails, knowing the expected manners and when to fawn, to be firm, to prevaricate, or to argue. At Russell & Co., Apun had become a valuable liaison, translator, and facilitator, and a vital connection to Chinese merchants and mandarin officials.

Cunningham assured Richard, "He has proved loyal to Russell, and I want him with you. You and he worked well together protecting our treasure. Apun will help you with business translation and contacts in Hankow." Richard liked Apun in spite of his sly smile that sometimes suggested secrets.

THE NIGHT BEFORE he was to leave, Constance Cunningham invited Richard to dinner with her, Edward, Henry Grew and David Clark. A Chinese barber razor-trimmed Richard's thick black hair and shaved his cheeks, and a boy helped him into his best dinner jacket. Over an *au jus* rib roast of beef, Yorkshire pudding, roast potatoes, creamed onions, and a warming French claret, Constance's gracious smile, her polite conversation, and the lilt in her voice enlivened the dinner. "Do stay with us whenever you come to Shanghai," she said, placing her hand on Richard's when the meal was done.

"Thank you. I most certainly will," Richard said, blushing at her touch. "If it is convenient for you."

"It's always convenient," she said with her own sly smile.

Following after-dinner liqueur, Richard said his thank-yous and good-byes to his bosses, feeling awkward as he did so because he'd see his bosses the following day to say good-bye again. The partners remained in the drawing room with their cigars while Constance walked him to the door. A pang of upcoming loneliness grabbed him. "Thank you for a special dinner," he said.

Constance put her hand on his shoulder and kissed him lightly on the cheek. "Take care of yourself." Her kiss roused him. He blushed again. "I know that you will do a wonderful job for Edward," she said. "We will miss you." She was indeed the definition of beauty.

THE FIRM HAD released a house *sous-chef* to be his cook, plus servants and a house comprador, Ma-Wei, who knew English well enough to translate and would lead the house servants. Apun had recruited eight Cantonese coolies, tough-looking and muscular, to handle goods, load and unload steamers and junks, and supervise any necessary work by locals. Several of these men had helped Richard protect the silver. Richard scurried from dock to ferry and ferry to *Scotland*, supervised loading the hold, repeatedly checked a list of goods, and spoke in nervous tones. Apun gave orders to the workers.

An initial cargo of matting, iron tools and implements, and cotton textiles filled the hold. In went cartons of rice, salted meat, flour, some New England furniture, bedding, enough utensils to stock a house for twenty people, and lumber and tools. Deep under the bow, hidden behind water barrels, went several crates of gold, silver, and copper coins and ingots.

Richard's personal articles, his luggage, and a barrel of bedding went to the cabin deck. He secreted aboard six Sharp's rifles, two revolvers, a Toledo sword Meto sent him, and the hunting rifle that had finally arrived from home. Captain and Mrs. Percy Dundas, Ephraim and Abigail St. John, an American missionary couple, and six native passengers, plus Apun, Ma-Wei, and all the coolies, would board once the steamboat was ready.

Richard regarded the *Scotland* at anchor in the harbor as the final barrels on the dock waited for a sampan to ferry them out. Augustus and Cunningham stood beside him. To Cunningham he remarked, "This quick a start will surely beat the British to Hankow."

"On the way upriver, you are in charge of the steamer's progress. Keep Captain Dundas moving."

Richard turned from Cunningham and said, half-seriously, to Augustus, "Unless we run aground."

"You've got Admiral Stribling's pilot," said Augustus. "You won't."

"I'll come to Shanghai as often as I can, my friend." His eyes drifted to Constance, standing a few yards away.

"Good luck," Augustus said.

"Thanks. I'll need it."

As they shook hands, Augustus said with a grin, "I'll not ask you to get me a job in Hankow."

Richard looked at him sideways. "Tell old Olyphant to send you!"

He turned and climbed into the *Scotland's* small tender. As the boat pulled away, he looked back at Augustus, Cunningham, Constance, Grew, Clark, and several clerks who had come to see him off to beat the British to Hankow. He waved confidently, firmly, even though his nerves tingled. Everything now aboard, Captain Dundas wasted no time launching his first voyage up the Yangtze. The screws and paddle wheels turned, her stacks belched, and the *Scotland* moved out into the great river's main stream, high from the spring's rains and snow melt from a thousand miles away.

UNNOTICED ON ONE of several sampans passing off *Scotland's* stern, a figure in a drab mandarin robe watched. A smile crept across Kung Loong's gnarled face.

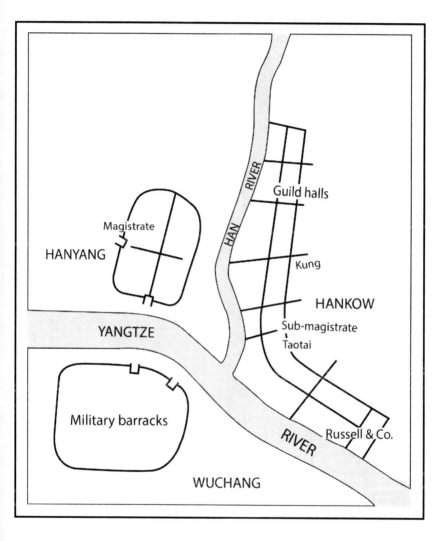

HANKOW CITIES

PART 3

Hankow

July 1861 to August 1863

It is not the person who has too little,
But the person who always craves more, that is poor.
Chinese fortune cookie

33

STUCK FAST IN the mud. The *Scotland* had barely entered the Yangtze proper when the steamer shuddered and plowed to a stop. Captain Dundas cursed his Chinese pilot with every sailor's invective known from Bombay to New York. He reversed the paddle wheels to back off, the crew moved cargo aft, all hands pushed poles to lift the hull, brown froth splashed all around, and the *Scotland* settled deeper into the mud.

"There is no place to unload weight. Send a boat back to Shanghai and return with another to take weight," Richard urged, and Dundas promptly dispatched a junior officer in the steamer's cutter. Ship, passengers, crew, and cargo sat and waited for the British to steam past.

In three days the fast-steaming Russell shuttle from Shanghai sidled up to take passengers and much of the cargo off the stuck steamer. A huge redheaded crewman of enormous strength heaved cargo as if it were filled with chicken feathers. The lightened *Scotland* lifted a bit, Captain Dundas shouted over the engines, the screws and paddles churned, the water boiled, the coolies poled and cursed, and slowly the *Scotland* backed off the mud.

Richard, having heard the big crewman's accent as he worked, later asked him his name. "How does it happen that a Scotsman works on a boat named *Scotland* in China?"

"It's a wee bit o' home under me feet," said Sean McShefferty, flashing yellow teeth. He ran his hand through the red bush on his head.

We all could use a wee bit of home, Richard thought.

FOR AN AGONIZING week, the steamer chugged up the Yangtze against the current under Richard's demands to make up lost time, but Dundas and the pilot, fearful of running aground again, slowed to under eight knots and centered *Scotland* in the river even when the water's color suggested that the deep channel ran to one side or the other.

While they traveled upriver, Richard planned for Hankow. Ma-Wei, the clean-shaven steward, would organize the six domestic servants and, with Apun's men, protect the house and cargoes. The cook would buy food. Apun would find residence and warehouse for Richard to approve. He and Apun, working together, would have to find business leads. Richard wanted to roam the city shops, warehouses, and manufacturers for bargains and quality. Since he would be out of sight of the partners, some personal ventures were also on his agenda once he had settled in.

Apun spent several hours each day trying to force some useful Chinese phrases into Richard's head but could not make Richard's tongue, lips, or mouth come up with the necessary sounds, and he constantly said something completely different from what was intended. Apun laughed heartily at the occasional obscene or sexual mispronunciations. Richard hoped to learn something in time but resigned himself to reliance on Apun and Ma-Wei for translation.

For many miles they could see little of the distant shores. But for a few junks and sampans hugging the shore, little traffic plied the river. Coolies and crew slopped about the *Scotland's* deck, slept, played gambling games, told tales, laughed, and argued.

On the third day of steaming, they entered a more narrow section of river. Piles of rubble and charred sticks that once were human shelters poked unsteadily into the air, and the ashen smell of burned debris drifted from them. Small groups of homeless natives wandered around the ruins. Richard and Abigail St. John stood on the second deck rail to watch the passing scenery. "The rebels have been here," said Richard.

Abigail's blue eyes watered as she spoke. "Those poor people." She shook her head.

Forests of firs ideal for spars and staves and scattered dwellings began to appear, and small sampans sometimes lined the shore. A four-story pagoda perched on a rock island, no one near it. The shore rose up slightly, breaking the flatness that had been the only view.

"What in God-rotting hell is that stink?" said Captain Dundas on the fifth day.

"Chinkiang. Makee vinegar," the pilot answered.

Acidic odors of fermenting sticky rice and secret herbs forced Abigail to hold her lace handkerchief to her face.

The *Scotland* puffed on, through floating logs, old barrels, pieces of mysterious debris, on through the river's dull water mixed with brown swirls and yellow streaks from the Grand Canal. Chinese vessels sailed and floated across the Yangtze from behind a low hill on the Grand Canal. On shore, burned buildings and earthen rubble surrounded Chinkiang's stone walls, and people climbed among the ruins looking for things to salvage.

"Oh, dear God," cried Abigail. She crossed herself and turned away from the rail. A partially clothed dead man drifted by face down. Remembering his initial shock at a floating baby, Richard turned away with her and sought words to ease her anguish. It was inappropriate to comment, "It happens," or "Chinese have no respect for death," or "You can expect to see lots of bodies," and he said nothing. He hesitatingly put his arm around her shoulders until she went inside to find her husband. In Shanghai, Richard had seen enough of this form of Chinese flotsam to no longer give it a second look.

When the *Scotland* steamed free of vinegar smells and the canal's cross-traffic, the Chinese shipping volume, inhibited by the Taiping, remained light; the shores rolled into rounded hills; the steamer spewed its ash-laden smoke, and they pressed on.

"Look!" Abigail pointed into the water. Two unusual arching white backs slipped slowly in and out of the water, speeding along as if racing the *Scotland*. "White dolphins," she cried. "Aren't they beautiful? Almost haunting. I've heard of them but never expected to see one. There are two ... three ... four ..."

"God's creations exist everywhere. Even in heathen China," said her husband, Ephraim. The three watched the dolphins arch out of the water and marveled at their sleek white shapes until they passed out of sight in the steamer's wake. *Scotland* steamed uneventfully until the river narrowed, and cliffs pinched the water into rapids.

On a shore trail under Mirror Mountain, laborers pulled lines tied to a junk, hauling it against the roiling current, step by step up the rapids. Oarsmen on board synchronized their strokes with the efforts of the shore laborers. Stroke by stroke, heave by heave, the junk lurched up the rapids. The *Scotland* spewed a cloud of coal soot onto the struggling Chinamen and smoothly steamed past them.

"Ephraim aspires to rescue the heathens from such a difficult life," Abigail said.

"Steamers on the river will do even more to rescue them," Richard said. He saw steam moving cargo for the Chinese someday as well as for foreign merchants.

Seeing more of the run-down, ruined, and dirty land that he was headed into, Richard could not imagine what he could do to build a business. He was not even halfway to Hankow.

Past the narrows, the river widened again toward Nanking, the Taiping capitol and main river port. The *Scotland* had passed around rebel General Li's armies that had surrounded Shanghai, and now the Taiping controlled the shores. At Nanking, however, imperial troops besieged the city, and reinforcements freed from French and British pressure at Peking had moved south to help with the siege. From here on, although the Taiping rebel armies held the land, both rebel and imperial forces shared the Yangtze with the natives and the foreigners.

More shipping appeared on the river now—junks, sampans, and homemade square-bowed, flat-bottomed boats propelled by wind and sculling with single stern oars. Far ahead, the men and women on the *Scotland* could see the stacks and masts of an English warship anchored off shore near Nanking.

"That ironclad is supposed to protect us," Captain Dundas said.

The pilot suddenly pointed toward Nanking. "Someone's coming!" he said. Fast closing on their starboard side, a steam gunship neared. Its bow gun was aimed squarely at the *Scotland*. It carried no identifying marks or flags; at least a dozen dirty men jammed the gunship's forward deck. Some of the crew carried rifles.

"Who is it?" Richard asked Dundas.

"Maybe pirates. Maybe rebels. Maybe Imps." They were still far from the British gunboat's protection. "Maybe just wants to know who we are."

"Find our damned crew," Dundas called to his mate. "Quick."

The mate descended to the lower deck, where he quickly alerted his officers. The crew on watch eyed the approaching vessel. Richard expected someone on the gunboat to hail the captain, but no one there said anything.

The Chinese coming close had matted hair, varicolored shirts and headbands, and looked like they had not bathed or changed clothes for months. They carried too many weapons for a peaceable purpose. The anchored European ironclad was over a mile away.

"Where's Apun?" Richard ran to find his comprador. He felt *Scotland* slowing. When he and Apun returned to the upper deck, the gunship had pulled alongside, and they stood on the upper rail of the paddle wheel guards, where they could see their crew gather. The intimidating Scottish giant, McShefferty, in a white shirt too small for his brawn, his huge arms bare, stood on the deck, his flaming red head above the rugged international crew around him.

"Everything we need in Hankow is aboard," Richard said to Apun. "See that our coolies guard the hold and our cabins. Especially the treasure."

Without saying a word, Apun went below. Abigail and Ephraim joined Richard. The missionary couple held hands and mumbled prayers. Ephraim clutched his ever-present Bible in one hand as hard as he clutched his wife's hand with the other. "We are surely in God's hands now," Ephraim said.

Richard scanned the armed men facing them. "They resemble the rebel soldiers I saw at Shanghai."

Abigail shut her eyes and turned to Ephriam. She squeezed her husband's hand harder. She gazed imploringly from one man to the other as if they could do something if God didn't. The Chinese among *Scotland's* crew jabbered among themselves. The three Americans understood nothing. The potential invaders were trying to lash the ships together.

Apun returned to the guards. "Taiping. They want search ship. Captain say no."

Abigail shrieked and fainted at their feet. Ephraim fell to his knees to tend to her. Turning, Richard and Apun glimpsed the motionless girl for a second. Then they saw what she had seen.

"Help her, Richard!" Ephraim apparently thought Richard could be God's agent. "Help Abigail!" he screamed. Richard looked back at the fallen, pale girl.

Another gunboat had come up on the other side of the *Scotland*. Like the first, its deck was crowded with armed men prepared to board. A banner on its fantail unmistakably identified the vessel. "Imperial gunboat!" Apun said.

Richard yelled, "My God! These Chinamen have been fighting each other for years. We'll have a donnybrook on deck."

"Keep them separated. Don't let them board," Dundas barked. A beefy Italian sailor handed pistols to the officers, who promptly raced to the imperial threat.

Richard fingered his revolver. "I have to protect my goods. Everything for Hankow could be lost," he shouted. The Hankow mission would be over. His priority was to stay alive and reach Hankow. Ephraim's plea and the thought of what heathen soldiers could do to Abigail stopped him. *I'll need to trust Apun in Hankow. I must trust him now to save our goods.*

He came back to crouch beside Abigail while Ephraim ministered to her. Richard held her head and shoulders up for comfort. He could only watch the melee on the lower deck.

The armed enemy crews faced each other from their ships with the *Scotland* crew between them. The pilot translated demands. Chinese invective vaulted back and forth. Rival militiamen made faces at each other and shouted taunts. Only the *Scotland's* armed and uniformed crew prevented the enemies from charging across the deck at each other.

Suddenly, two Taiping ruffians leapt aboard. One rushed the first mate, who stopped him with a swift fist in the face. The other ruffian swung his stick at the mate, who stepped back to avoid him. This started the rest of the rebels crossing the small gap between ships. When the Imperials saw the rebels boarding, they, too, advanced onto the deck.

Apun joined the three Americans.

"The government promised no protection." Richard said. "Will the Imperials drive the rebels off?"

"Probably try," Apun said. "Then steal something."

Dundas and his officers exhorted the crew. "Keep them on their own ships. Break up any that threaten a fight. Keep them apart."

Apun shouted in Chinese to his head coolie, "Help *Scotland* men. Keep three men at gangway with stave!"

Richard did not understand Apun's command, but he saw his coolies run to the gangway. Richard left the missionaries and ran to the rail.

A rebel, larger than most, gnashed his black teeth, shoved his greasy, shaggy beard into the captain's face, and drew a knife. A second man pushed into Dundas. As he pushed, the sticky ends of his shaggy black hair slapped Dundas. Both men loudly threatened Chinese obscenities. The captain recoiled at the slap and spat a hair out of his mouth. This enraged the two rebels.

"Gentlemen! That be no way to treat me captain." The crew knew the booming voice. McShefferty, his face as red as his hair, stepped up behind the two insulting rebels. He quickly grabbed their long hair, tied the two men together with a twist, and with a yank on the joined hair, marched both rebels backward and off balance toward their gunship. They squawked and sputtered. The knife dropped. McShefferty kicked it into the water. He gave the hair a harder yank and, with a lion's roar, propelled them over the water gap and onto their knees aboard their gunboat.

The skirmish quickly quieted. The *Scotland's* crew took the offensive and pushed the rebels back toward their boat. The boarders resisted but retreated to their ship. When they had all left the deck, Dundas, with McShefferty standing at his side and the pilot to translate, let two apparent leaders on board to state their demands, and he steadfastly refused them. Two more pairs tried to make demands, and Dundas refused each. The Taiping soon tired of the game. They cast off, and their gunboat steamed back toward the capital city.

With the Taiping gone, the Imperials retreated to their ship and soon steamed away.

The Taipings wanted rice in return for passage on the river, Apun reported later. Dundas had refused the blatant extortion. He had lied that he had no rice.

Dundas then ordered full steam ahead back to the river's channel. "I'll not stay around here," he said to Richard. "The damned Nanking officials may have agreed to open the river to us, but those rebels didn't get the word."

They heard a single bang of a ship's gun in the distance. A puff of black smoke blew from the imperial gunboat, and a splash rose about thirty yards from the Taiping gunboat. Several more futile shots, and the two rival gunboats abandoned their token fight and soon disappeared into the shoreline swamps.

Abigail had revived, and with Ephraim had retired to their cabin. Richard and Apun stayed on deck watching the final derisive shot splash harmlessly into the Yangtze. The *Scotland*, its boilers blowing hard, reached the channel, left Nanking behind, and headed upriver again. Richard said, "It seems that both the Imperials and the Taipings ignore their agreements like the Emperor does."

"*She de*—Yes. And their governments. Now far from Peking," Apun said. "Hankow also far from Peking."

Richard reflected, "Far from Shanghai … and New York."

34

ALL ALONG THE waterfront, one- and two-story gray wooden buildings tottered over the water, most on stilts. At intervals between them, narrow wharves wobbled into the water like thin long-legged bugs. Between the ship and the shore floated thousands of sampans, houseboats, and cargo carriers—long and narrow, flat-bottomed, roofed with matting, masts poking into the heavy summer sky, pulsing with men and women and children building, cooking, gambling, arguing, playing, and working. Vessels of all descriptions sailed, sculled, and rowed, crisscrossing the river, traveling up and down with the current and wind.

Hankow was built on a marshland where the Han River met the Yangtze. The water and marsh had been an effective defense until the Taiping had attacked and burned much of the city. Two-thirds of a mile across the Yangtze, the defensive walls of the regional city and military post of Wuchang could be seen. The third city at this river junction, small Hanyang, the local government seat, lay across the narrow Han from Hankow.

Richard said to Abigail, "Father Huc wrote that there must have been four million people at this tricity river intersection. Looks like a lot less now." Abigail shook her head. Was she impressed or depressed at the reality around her? Nothing they had passed approached the three sprawling waterfront cities in space or population.

This great commercial center in central China had for centuries been a focal point for shipping all manner of goods hundreds of miles following the Yangtze, Han, Yuan, and Hsiang rivers and their tributaries to and from Hankow, linking Tibet and the deserts and mountains with the more fertile central and coastal provinces. These rivers carried produce, manufactures, minerals, crafts, and raw goods that sustained the nation. Here in the city Richard approached, Chinese freight was traded, sold, bought, and transshipped, and Russell & Co. wanted its share of the business.

No protective wall surrounded Hankow. Half the city lay in ruins. Seen from the Yangtze, red rafters among the brown roofs highlighted more substantial buildings. Clay brick single-story structures—no telling what they held—no doubt the myriad clutter of any crowded Chinese city. Rubble and blackened remnants of Taiping devastation remained visible everywhere. Heavy smoke like that from furnaces darkened the air at the western edge of the city.

As a steady four-mile-an-hour current held the *Scotland* taut against its anchor chain, an enormous fleet of sampans quickly surrounded the steamer.

Richard called Apun, Ma-Wei, the firm's Canton coolies, and the household staff into the crew's mess cabin. Only Chinese eyes focused on their American employer. He could talk to no one on shore without a translator. He did not know who or where the local authorities were. He did not know the government offices, guild halls, commercial streets, and trading areas of the city. He had already given Apun money, discussed facilities they would need, and instructed him to locate places where they would do business.

"I want Apun and his pick among coolies to go ashore now. The first order of business is to find a place for all of us to live and a safe place to store our supplies and goods that we need to trade," Richard told them. "When we start business, we will have to carry goods from ships through the sampan swarm to a warehouse near water. The house also must be near the waterfront." He paused while Apun translated to the others, then continued, "We will need local help. Try to identify reliable workers. I will remain on the *Scotland* for now. Please report every day on your progress."

He dismissed the men, and within an hour, the ship's rope ladder dropped. A bare-chested and sweat-soaked boatman slid a bamboo taxi up to the ladder after having shoved away several competitors for the spot alongside the *Scotland*. While McShefferty steadied his bulk, Apun in his ankle-length robe managed to climb down the six rungs of the flapping ladder and dropped into the taxi. There he sat, immobile, clutching the bamboo gunwales, and the taxi carried him and his coolies all the way to shore.

Abigail and Ephraim left the ship on a later taxi, to start to the little country village to which they had been sent to minister. "I wish you all the best," Richard said. Her fair face did not belong in a small country village, he thought. Country life would be far more daunting for her than Hankow life for him. "If you ever come into Hankow, please find me for some American company. I will need it, too," he said.

Captain Dundas kept the *Scotland* at anchor to refuel, to store supplies, and to house Richard and his staff until they settled in and had found a return cargo to Shanghai. The ship's manifest lay before him: rice, household supplies, cotton goods, furniture, and more stowed aboard. "Now I have to sell some cotton," he said to the empty cabin. From the deck he had regarded the demolished buildings in Hankow, worn-out looking Chinese, dilapidated houseboats, unsteady buildings, and the unknown place he would live.

With all his household staff gone ashore, Richard sat alone at a small table. He scratched an itch on his forehead with the end of his pen, and then wrote to Meto, telling about the voyage, omitting the soldiers' confrontation near Nanking. "I am now in the middle of this godforsaken country," he wrote. "This miserable place looks like any other Chinese city. People hear of luxurious living in China, but any such impression as to life in Hankow will for a long time be most erroneous."

Next he wrote his report to Cunningham to send back with Captain Dundas. Being the first merchant intending to stay in Hankow, he had beaten the British agent to the new treaty port. "If the rebels do not trouble us, and the surrounding country ever becomes quiet," he scratched on the paper, "this will doubtless again become a great commercial depot." Cunningham will be pleased, he judged with satisfaction as he sealed his report with soft wax.

When one had to use a word like "doubtless," he thought, the matter was certainly not without doubt.

35

E IGHT CANTON COOLIES gathered around Apun at the end of
the dock. The comprador reminded them that most Chinese
inland of the Pacific Coast had never seen a barbarian devil. They
probably would think the foreigners ugly and hairy and armed,
he said. "The Hankow natives will be curious … and afraid." He
advised his men not to reveal their barbarian employer until he
comes ashore. For now, Apun dispatched his men to investigate
both Yangtze and Han riverfronts, to note the activities, the
buildings, and the numbers of soldiers and officials they might
see, and to try to identify competent boatmen and efficient gangs
of stevedores. Apun, himself, could learn the local dialect and
government structure quickly. Now, away from Russell & Co.,
this was an opportunity to personally profit from his considerable
skills with the Chinese. A sly smile appeared.

Apun walked into the city along a dirt lane lined with unoccupied reed-and-mud hovels and piles of debris. Gradually
the street became more crowded, and structures became more
substantial. When he reached a wide street paved with stone,
he joined the foot traffic and let it carry him along while he
savored the local bustle. Pots, pans, tin cups, strings of vegetables, and small animals hung from racks on stalls lining the
street. Tradesmen hawked their wares. Men perspired under loads
of reeds, lumber, bamboo, and stones headed for construction

projects. Acrobats, magicians, and peddlers entertained. Red, yellow, and green banners and signs advertised an endless variety of wares, including some Western manufactures, all sold in the open-air shops lining the street. Everyone moved with a purpose. He strode the streets, relishing the spices and the smells of working men, mentally mapping the shops, offices, and warehouses. Three wide stone-paved avenues ran parallel to the Yangtze and then turned to parallel the Han. Lanes and alleys that crossed the streets led to the rivers' wharves, where stevedores loaded and unloaded vessels with goods, materials, and crops.

Apun planned to act as a textile merchant to hide his foreign association. After the long journey, he wanted to enjoy good Chinese food and surrounding comforts. He sent a messenger to the *Scotland* to say that he would spend several days in town before he returned. He hired a room at a nearby inn, purchased a silk robe suitable for the wealthiest of merchants, and ate an excellent meal of *tángcù yú*—sweet and sour fish—savoring the conflicting flavors and his happy mood. To learn the city, Apun wanted to visit tea houses, guild halls, and government offices, asking questions and eavesdropping on conversations. On the first morning out, odors of cooking sauces near the inn enticed him to an eating and wine house trimmed with hanging paper lanterns. He pushed aside a bead curtain and stepped into a dining room crowded with wooden tables and chairs. Through the smoke he spied a vacant seat across from a bearded fellow in a merchant's robe. A large jade stone on his smooth middle finger marked him as a man of some wealth.

The bearded fellow's eyes turned to the stranger. "You from coast?"

Apun sat in the vacant chair at the merchant's table and signaled a waiter. "Shanghai," he answered.

Smooth, narrow fingers combed the beard. "Come on barbarian steamer?"

Apun wanted answers, not questions. "Yes. I maybe open shop here. Tell about this place."

Apun played the newcomer from down the Yangtze, a potential business owner. The merchant readily shared his knowledge of the city. The Hanyang Prefect, headquartered in the wrecked village across the Han, officially governed the three cities. The prefect mostly left Hankow to locals, the man said. Business was returning since the Taiping scourge had passed. In a few minutes, this naturally talkative man taught Apun the shops that predominated on the larger streets and the locations of important guild warehouses and local government offices.

Deep into the crowded city, wood and brick buildings lined the streets. Apun found the multicolored tile facades that identified the two-story stone and brick complexes of the cotton, tea, salt, hemp, and silk guilds, each of which controlled trade in one of those commodities most valuable to Russell & Co. Inside the guilds' protective walls, he glimpsed factories, warehouses, temples, and meeting rooms in various stages of construction.

Apun found the city's administrative offices. No bell tower, drum tower, or city-god temple rose above the plastered one-story brick buildings. This told him that the higher-level mandarins were officed elsewhere. He paused to read notices posted on a wall. One announced the arrival in Hankow of a newly appointed Taotai, Chen Lan, to be responsible for diplomatic and customs affairs. Apun noted that Starr would need to know this man. Another elaborate official order announced: "European barbarians come to Hankow in next weeks. The Emperor order that no one interfere with the barbarians or their business."

Apun weighed what Richard might do during the first days he would spend in the city. Hankow's people had had no experience with the barbarians, but the population had heard stories that they carried firearms, that they demanded privileges that no one else had, that they had repulsive big noses, that they were covered with disgusting body hair, that they refused to speak Chinese, and that the foreigners were very, very rich. All that was true. The Emperor's law enforcement mandarins and soldiers were across the rivers, and Hankow police matters were settled by Hankow officials, so Apun expected that people might ignore or resist the Emperor's order not to interfere with the barbarians.

The submagistrates and clerks thought Apun to be a prosperous broker from Shanghai who readily gave bribes for information. By the end of his surveys, he had located a respectable two-story house behind eight-foot walls with a wing that from the outside looked suitable for housing Richard, rooms for the compradors and Chinese staff, and space for storing goods. On the eastern end of the city, the house fronted on dirt-packed Tsen Kai, a street that in less than a mile reached the major commercial blocks on Chung Lu thoroughfare. The banks of the Yangtze lay a hundred yards away along a narrow alley bordering a weed-strewn property holding a number of dilapidated wooden sheds.

Apun smiled and gave four of Russell's copper coins to a low-level clerk in the magistrate's office who taught him that a Manchu merchant named Ching Ka owned this house and several other properties.

The following morning, Apun stood before Ching Ka's gate dressed in his new robe embroidered with two red and blue herons. The hated queue fell down his back. He stepped past a houseboy without a word and entered a dirt courtyard. He strode rapidly to the entrance door and pushed into the house while the boy scurried behind him muttering ineffectual protests.

Once an upper-class house, Apun saw, as he perused faded crimson paint above the rafters, the darkly soiled floor. The walls were solidly constructed, the courtyard sparsely landscaped, and the rooms simple, colorful.

"What you want?" Apun turned to confront a thin man wearing a plain blue merchant's robe. The man scowled at the intruder.

"I respectfully beg pardon for intruding, Ching Ka, my friend," Apun said with a broad smile and slight bow. "Your servant, Apun. We become friends."

The stunned Ching Ka frowned and stared back in silence. Apun, by now fluid in the dialect, spoke in a conversational tone, his hands politely clasped together inside his great sleeves. "I agent for American who arrive on steamer *Scotland* now in Yangtze-Kiang."

Ching Ka squeaked, "What barbarian want? How you know name?"

"American want place near river where establish trading house. He bring new business and profit to Hankow. He bring Ching Ka great profit, if reason and opportunity." The landowner lifted a brow. Apun continued, "You own property. You help find suitable house."

"No house for a barb ..."

Apun would not let him utter the pejorative. "Ching Ka, you know Emperor open this port to barbarian."

"Why me? I am poor man."

Apun had noticed his earlier reaction to the word "profit." "More foreigner come. I graciously offer you opportunity to profit from first to arrive. American spend money." Apun paused to let Ching Ka absorb this. "I see Chen Lan Taotai tomorrow. He be sure treat foreign merchant correctly. It well for you I tell Taotai you own place with wall to confine American."

Apun sensed that Ching Ka was thinking over the possibilities and needed to say no more. "You interrupt business. Go," said Ching Ka.

He dismissed Apun with a wave of his hand and looked to the boy to show Apun out.

Apun turned and walked toward the door. He would come back.

"Come back two days," Ching Ka said.

WHEN APUN HAD left, Ching Ka summoned his boy to bring him a writing brush, ink, and paper. He wrote: "To honorable Chen Lan Taotai: American send comprador today. American want occupy old house with wall on Tsen Kai in area that esteemed governor general suggest for barbarians. Expect comprador tomorrow. Tell him house for sale, but agree nothing. I finish bargain. Then something for you. This first barbarian come under plan that we devise."

The next day, to impress the mandarin official, Apun again let his queue fall down, dressed in his merchant's robe and boxlike cap, and visited the Taotai. A clerk announced him, and he stepped into an undecorated office and stood before the immaculately dressed middle-aged official. A small pointed beard grew beneath his small mouth. Everything about the official was clean, from his tiny button cap, green silk robe, and neatly trimmed mustache.

Apun began. "I represent American trader name Richard Starr of Kee Chong, Shanghai. He desire property for warehouse and residence."

Chen-Lan absently rolled some scrolled documents on his teak table. "Ah … so it starts," he mumbled under his breath. "*Fanqui* gunboats scare Emperor's weak-knee minister. Now they come here."

Standing before the teak table, Apun bowed respectfully, though the man continued rolling his scroll. "Honorable sir, I not familiar with your city …"

The Taotai looked up. "Hankow no *my* city. I no authority over city or land in city." He spat the words. He gestured to the door to dismiss Apun.

Apun did not move. Unperturbed, he said, "Your Excellency please suggest suitable official for land and property?"

"Nothing can be done for property here. Seek property for your *fanqui* elsewhere."

Apun reached into his sleeve and produced three silver coins. "Perhaps, Excellency, in your place as diplomatic affair Taotai, not as land official, you consider give me information so that I approach proper authority?"

Chen Lan took the coins. He said with a huff, "Emperor order me cooperate with foreigner."

Chen Lan motioned that Apun sit in a straight-backed chair near the door.

With judicious questioning and more coins, Apun learned that the Taotai had arrived in Hankow a little over a week earlier, appointed by the imperial government to handle trade affairs. He still knew little about the men that the Hanyang Prefect had appointed in Hankow—the local magistrates and subprefects mostly concerned themselves with safety and law enforcement. Everyone in Hankow bought and sold everything without official participation, Chen Lan said. He suggested land might be available in eastern part of city. Apun should buy or rent his land from any owner he could find. The magistrate's office would record the transaction.

Upon hearing Apun's report the following day, Richard said, "That sounds good, Apun. Before we commit to it, I'd like to see the house."

36

A TALL MAN DRESSED in black and wearing a hat that looked like an inverted cooking pot rode to the city standing in a sampan taxi. McShefferty and two of *Scotland's* crew accompanied him. A crowd gathered on the riverbank to see the first barbarians in their city. Curious Chinese pushed and shoved to get near them as they climbed to a wooden dock. The crowd backed away from McShefferty, who towered over everyone; his size and flaming red hair drew looks of fright, awe, and revulsion, and stirred up finger pointing, shrieks, and lots of conversation.

House coolies joined them, and they formed a wedge around Richard, and all marched to the street, the crowd opening before them. A tall ragamuffin with crooked teeth grabbed at Richard's hat. He ducked aside, kept the hat, and swept his arm as McShefferty shoved the man away. Another tried to touch McShefferty's red hair but couldn't reach it and jumped away from the Scotsman's glare. The barbarians continued down the narrow street lined with mud and wooden buildings.

Time and again, the Chinese tried to touch Richard or McShefferty, knock the top hat off, feel clothes, beg for money, or yell at them. To Richard, the unintelligible voices sounded rude and insulting. At times, a whiff of body stench from summer sweat made him squinch his face. The blur of bodies, the blue drabness, and the dirty arms and faces seemed much like other crowds he had encountered, but the excessive curiosity bothered him. He stood a few inches taller than most Chinese, stayed surrounded by the coolies, near giant McShefferty for protection, and tried not to react. They finally reached the walls surrounding the new house and entered the compound. The coolies barred the gate behind them; Apun greeted Richard, and the crowd lingered outside.

Richard looked around the compound. The Yangtze could be glimpsed down the side alley. Apun told him that the Hankow business center was about a mile away. The strong walls, the size, and the floor layout pleased Richard. Bare wood floors and garish colors decorated this building. Chinese houses were never built for comfort; even the upper-class homes he had seen lacked beds, sofas, or easy chairs. Light came through small pieces of semitransparent mica covering a window in each room. A few stiff, straight, wooden chairs and tables were the only furnishings. They would need to buy furniture right away and paint. They also needed to build a stronger gate.

"Let's get it." Richard told Apun. "There seems no need to search further. You think the owner will sell it. When you have the set the terms, confirm with me." Richard hoped to tell Cunningham he'd found a bargain.

After Richard and the crewmen returned to the *Scotland*, Apun returned to Ching Ka. The two Chinamen agreed on a price for the Tsen Kai property. Ching Ka demanded additional money to "register agreement with the Magistrate," more cash to cover his "costs," and a payment for moving out. Apun objected to these extra payments, but when Ching Ka agreed to pay Apun a fee for bringing a buyer, Apun agreed without argument to the squeeze arrangements and the high purchase price. Russell & Co. would pay it all.

In two days of arduous work, the *Scotland* discharged into the house all the cargo, supplies, furniture, treasure, and a vault.

The day following move-in, Richard set out with his house comprador, Ma-Wei, to find more furniture and to get to know the city. He decided to leave his top hat behind. Too often for his comfort the Chinese crowds had tried to knock it off. The two turned onto Tsen Kai, the through street that ran to the city center, and in a few blocks local pedestrians began walking along beside them. Dirty in appearance, pockmarked skins, baggy trousers, bare feet, the heathens followed close behind Richard. One fellow grabbed at his arm. Others called monosyllabic noises that Ma-Wei refused to translate. The pursuers grew as they walked along. Abusive-sounding hoots and hurtful pokes frustrated their progress. Richard soon recognized "*fanqui*" among the hoots and knew it meant him. Once he was tripped and nearly fell. Ma-Wei and Richard shouted in Chinese, "*Zou. Zou*—Go away." The abuse continued.

Richard could not do any business or learn his surroundings if this continued. "We've got to go back to our compound," he said. "In time, they may get used to barbarian devils."

The next day, Richard tried again to walk in the city, this time with Apun at his side. Richard taking a stout and wieldy stave to double as a walking stick and weapon, they set out. A group of curiosity seekers again followed them as they strode into the commercial streets. Hankow seemed like all China—unwashed, unhappy people jammed into overcrowded slums. Half-naked laborers sweated in loincloths, scurried up and down, carrying loads, pushing, and pulling loaded and rickety carts. Richard winced, not at savory sauces, but at the smells of acidic spices, frying fat, and feces in the street. Morose people in faded, wrinkled, and loose dirty blue clothing were everywhere, apparently their only entertainment involved following or hooting at a stranger. Instead of a rousing commerce, Richard saw vendors selling caged birds and dead rats and fish, and shabby groups of men gambling and gaming. Richard blinked, and generally fixed his gaze in the direction ahead to avoid noticing the intrusive stares and the squalor around him. Apun again admired the busy activity and hardworking men, and savored aromatic flavors.

Laughter and shouting up ahead signaled a commotion that blocked their way. A man staggered into the street wearing a four-foot-square wooden platform around his neck. In obvious distress from its weight, the man could not control his legs. Children ran up to throw rocks or rotten vegetables at him. Adults jeered when a missile struck well.

"Punish man in *canque*," Apun told Richard.

One skinny man handed the miscreant a wet rag. Someone is merciful, Richard thought, and then realized that the *canque* prevented him from reaching his mouth or head. Passersby teased him with food and drink held out of reach. The man struck the opposite wall, his exhausted legs buckled under him, and he collapsed under the *canque's* weight. His eyes closed, and sweat and dirt sent rivulets down his body.

Richard pulled out his handkerchief, soaked it in a nearby animal watering trough, and ran to the man. He knelt beside him and carefully straightened out the man's legs. The man opened his eyes, first in obvious relief, but stared blankly at Richard. Richard then rung out the wet cloth above the man's head so the water ran on his face, then held it at his mouth. The parched lips sucked the refreshing coolness until the cloth was nearly dry. Richard resoaked it and left it tucked into the *canque* where the man could feel and suck from it.

"We should move on, "said Apun, "Man is criminal. Many object to what you did."

"How long will he wear the *canque*?"

"Depend on crime. Maybe die fast."

The poor souls in Shanghai whose heads looked down from pikes probably suffered less. Beheading was merciful compared to the likely slow and lengthy suffering Richard had just seen. He thought of the crucified Christ saying, "Forgive them for they know not what they do." With long strides Richard walked fast, hoping distance would let him push the images out of his mind.

He and Apun avoided serious annoyance for a time, until Richard felt a tap on his shoulder. He turned to see a tanned young man in a soldier's uniform carrying a sword and a fan, and grinning mischievously. He pointed to Richard's finger ring, then, getting no reaction, indicated Richard's watch chain and watch. Richard shook his head vigorously. "No. *Zou*. You no take."

He walked on. The soldier followed. Soon Richard felt another tap, stronger than the first. He turned on the man and raised his stave to threaten. He was in no mood to tolerate Chinese incivility. The man reached for his sword. Without waiting to see if he would draw it, Richard swung the stave, hitting him in the midsection just above the scabbard. The soldier doubled over and then retreated into the crowd, which parted to let him fall back. The rabble seemed to enjoy the man's shame. Richard walked on in the streets where anyone's discomfort amused the heathens.

He returned to his house without reaching the rest of the commercial areas on Chung-Lu thoroughfare, which he must explore later. He was too clearly unwelcome, even though the government had authorized his presence. He could not move freely about the city. His frustration had let him swing a stave without thinking. Trouble often followed an unthinking reaction like that. What if the soldier had drawn his sword? Not long ago he had not reacted so dangerously and had recognized the consequences of shooting the Taiping scout. He must keep calm when confronted now, think before reacting, and consider the consequences. Why did he react so quickly now? He leaned on his table; pushed aside the empty ledger books and blank invoice forms, closed his eyes, leaned on his elbows, and held his head. *Am I going to be a prisoner in my own house?*

HE WOULD NOT isolate himself. He decided to show his revolver on his next trip into the city. Becoming the first to personally meet Hankow's tea brokers and wholesale dealers would give him a strong start over the competition. Apun took along four of his Canton coolies armed with staves.

Soon enough, the little army arrived at the tiled entrance to the walled Black Tea Hong Guild compound. A guild representative met them at the entrance near a small temple guarded by lion statues and escorted them into the compound, where he introduced a tea broker. The two Chinese seemed nervous being with the barbarians but evidently were prepared to work with them. With Apun translating and helping negotiate, Richard purchased a chop of fresh, fragrant tea. He gave the broker a note drawn on Russell & Co. for payment in sixty days. Apun talked with the broker to have it delivered to the *Scotland* and promised future purchases, thus concluding their first Hankow transaction and beginning a relationship with a local guild through which most trades occurred.

At night alone, Richard fought for sleep. He made mental lists of things the house needed and tried to plan business. How could he go about more freely? Wear Chinese clothing? *I refuse to dress like a woman.* Ride hidden in a covered sedan chair? No, he concluded, he could not tell porters where to go. There seemed no immediate solution other than taking his own men for protection. In the morning Richard told Apun: "Give the men extra money if they have to fight in my protection. Use your discretion in the amount."

"Excellent idea," Apun readily agreed.

Richard preferred to be less dependent on others and to avoid that uncontrollable expense. Show the revolver at all times, he concluded, but never fire it. As he imagined scenes in which he might pull out his revolver, none of which were entirely satisfactorily resolved, an idea popped to mind.

"This idea just might work," he said to Meto's picture on his wall. Then Richard stretched his shoulder, picked up his pen, and wrote a dispatch to Shanghai.

> *My dear Augustus, I am writing to ask you to do something for me. I need some means to quiet crowds of ragamuffins that follow and pester me while walking about town. Can you find and send two nasty dogs that I can take on my walks? They should be large and ugly. I'd like to intimidate an aggressive rascal without resorting to use of a revolver. If I were to shoot a Chinaman the local authorities would give me all sorts of trouble.*

He closed with some friendly words, promised to visit Shanghai at the next opportunity, sealed the dispatch, and delivered it to the *Fire Dart*, which had arrived from Shanghai ten days after the now departed *Scotland* had anchored in Hankow.

The *Fire Dart* had brought the first two Englishmen, agents of Jardine Matheson. They had found houses in the area the Chen Lan Taotai had planned for the barbarians, downstream of the Russells' house and farther away from the guild halls and commercial areas. Richard visited the Brits one afternoon, found them typically aloof, and, except to speak English with someone, could imagine little reason to befriend the competition. During the ensuing weeks, two or three more steamers arrived with European agents to fight for Hankow's business. The scramble was on.

Richard and Apun's initial contacts with Hankow's merchants and brokers resulted in orders for Chinese and Western trade goods, and the purchases were shipped down the river when an occasional steamer appeared. Richard worked stocking the storerooms, filling out shipping documents, and confirming credit arrangements that Apun had made and guaranteed. He reported to Cunningham, sending a dispatch with each downstream steamer, arranged his household with Ma-Wei, met with steamer officers, and accompanied Apun to guilds.

One day, Richard was bending over his writing desk when excited Chinese shouts burst from the courtyard. Startled, he dropped his pen, spattering ink onto his papers, and knocked over the blotting sand bowl.

"Damnation." He grabbed for the blotter. "What in Sam Hill is going on?"

A house coolie banged on Richard's door. "Ma-Wei need you come." Fright plainly showed on the man's face. "Chop chop. Bad man here."

The shouts and banging increased. He ran to the open window overlooking the courtyard. Eight or ten undisciplined soldiers on time off from training at the Wuchang Imperial Army garrison across the Yangtze yelled, rattled, and banged on the gate attempting to force their way in. The gate's hinges almost gave way to a sudden surge.

Richard had stored loaded rifles in the corner. He left the rifles, seized his revolver and ran down stairs to find Ma-Wei. "Let them in," he shouted. "Tell them they are to behave well. Say that we have many weapons and will use them."

Ma-Wei started to deliver the message, but before he could finish, the gate flew open, and the soldiers burst into the courtyard. There were eight of them. Several carried sheathed swords. Richard arrived in the yard, his hand on the revolver and his heart in his throat. One of the soldiers shouted something. Ma-Wei backed away from the onslaught. "They want money and valuables," he said. He shouted to the house coolies to oppose this mob. They rushed into the courtyard brandishing staves.

"Tell them they will have nothing," Richard ordered. "Tell them if they are quiet and leave their weapons, they can look around. If they do not keep order, there will be trouble." Ma-Wei translated. His voice may have betrayed his fear to the intruders. One rumpled soldier laughed insolently and drew a sword.

"Quick. Tell the coolies to do as I do." If the coolies became frightened he'd have to fire his revolver. Richard grabbed a bamboo stave from the nearest coolie, clenched his teeth, and whacked the soldier's arm holding the sword. Again he whacked. The sword dropped. The soldier's insolent grin went away.

The coolies followed Richard's lead. Those with staves fell upon the gate-crashers; their white servants' jackets belied their ferocity. The soldiers fought back, but the coolies had startled them. A soldier tripped trying to unsheathe his sword and dove into the dirt. Soon coolies had cut off any retreat out the gate. They swung staves at anyone trying to get away. One coolie took a sword's blow on the arm and fell to his knees clutching a red stain beginning to drip into the yard. A coolie rammed one aggressive soldier in the gut with the stave's butt, sending him reeling backward, his wind gone. In a few moments half the soldiers lay on the ground amid blood and torn uniforms, broken staves, dropped swords, and bamboo splinters.

"Enough," Richard shouted.

Ma-Wei commanded the men to stop fighting.

Soldiers still standing helped their beaten comrades out the gate. Three or four soldiers were so badly hurt that Richard thought they would not recover. He tied a soldier's torn shirt tight around his wounded coolie's arm. Ma-Wei's housemen set about cleaning up the debris and helped their bloody comrade inside. The trouble was over.

Richard feverishly tried to think what to say to his household help and looked for Ma-Wei to translate. Ma-Wei returned from helping the wounded man and gathered the remaining men. Richard praised them for the stout resistance they made. The soldiers might come back another day, but now they knew what to expect. He instructed Apun to give the men a cash reward. Then he returned to his room and rubbed his ribs where a wild bamboo stave had hit him.

37

Li-Chih, the magistrate responsible for law and order in the city, sat at his black lacquer desk smiling a polite but meaningless smile, and listened as Richard described his concern. Street crowds inevitably followed and molested his unarmed employees who, being Canton men, were universally disliked, Richard said. Unable to understand the local dialect, his coolies had to use staves to protect themselves. Frequent fisticuffs, fights, and injuries interfered with business, although the Emperor had ordered that Chinese not interfere with foreign business.

Apun translated calmly, not showing the frustration that Richard had expressed in English. Richard was sure that Apun added proper words of introduction and respect. Apun told Richard later that he had said, "Foreigner want friendly relation with natives. Cannot be friendly when people attack his workers."

The magistrate pulled at his graying mustache. Richard was about to start another plea, when the smiling magistrate recited expressionless Chinese. Apun translated Li's words, "If you seize leader of attack, magistrate Li will punish. Leader go in front of house on toes with head in *canque*."

Li-Chih sat back, his smug expression reflecting confidence that the barbarian would be satisfied and that he had promised everything he was empowered to do.

The prospect of a man with his head in the medieval *canque* chained to his gate moaning for days was not the relief Richard wanted. Nor would he risk subjecting anyone to the treatment that Hop Tzu received in Shanghai. He could not predict what might happen if he detained a local ruffian. Sunchong had once said, "Punish to prevent punishment." His conscience rebelled at the draconian deterrence policies in Chinese justice. Extreme measures did not deter anything. Richard said, "Thanks anyway, but no. I don't want that." Apun translated politely, and they left, smiling as if they were satisfied with Li-Chih's solution.

When they had returned to the street, Apun turned to Richard. "If you apply to authorities in Wuchang," he said, "you probably get soldiers as guards. You must give food and lodging."

Richard had just seen imperial troops in action. He imagined that they would turn useless when he most needed them. "Food and lodging? I'm not running an inn. They would be a bloody nuisance."

"Possibly."

"No." He looked sternly at Apun. "Our own people are strong," he said. "They are capable. They are becoming confident in their own abilities."

When the pair reached the compound, Richard called Ma-Wei, the coolies, and household staff. Speaking through Ma-Wei, he said that there was no help from the Hankow officials and that they would have to continue to defend themselves. "Do not attack first. You are learning to handle your staves very well. Practice fighting exercises. Whenever and wherever you are attacked, do not hesitate to make stout resistance. Strike hard and effectively."

Richard next selected four men to teach the house staff how to shoot rifles. He brought two rifles to the yard and set up a target. Richard demonstrated how to load bullet and powder, and how to aim and pull the trigger. A nervous Ma-Wei gingerly balanced a rifle at arm's length. Then Ma-Wei passed it to a man who volunteered to be first. The man took the rifle and swung it around; the muzzle waved out of control. Richard leapt aside and ducked. The rifle went off. Flame flew out the barrel. Black smoke engulfed the terrified coolie. A mica window in the kitchen shattered. A clatter of broken pottery came through the break.

"Aiieeeee! Yaaaa!" Inside cook's unique oaths burned the ears.

The marksman dropped the gun. His eyes popped wide. Ma-Wei and the selected men fled inside.

Richard could not stifle a chuckle. "Now you know what the rifle does," he called after them. "Thanks for listening."

Any further training would have endangered his household more than any ruffians would. The Russells would have to rely on these men and their staves.

By mid-September steamers were arriving from Shanghai at irregular intervals. None kept to a schedule. More Europeans—French, Dutch, Russian, Swedish, Indian, and others—steamed in. Merchants from the British firms Dent & Co. and Jardine Matheson, and the American Augustine Heard & Co., now competed with vigor for good tea prices. For the most part, they stayed to themselves in business and entertainment. Richard and Apun managed to sell goods brought from Shanghai and to send back modest shipments of tea, porcelain, or silk fabric on each return trip.

Richard could foresee competitive complications. To win full tea cargoes, the foreign merchants constantly tried to outbid each other. Europeans, as well as Richard, would not cooperate with each other against Chinese sellers who drove hard bargains. Prices rose. Demand for tea brought out the charlatans. Sellers had their own definitions of weights and measures, so cheating was rampant. Chinese brokers and compradors demanded commissions from foreign buyers, who eagerly paid any price and any commission to get a buy.

Foreigners outbid Chinese buyers, and thereby stole shipments from local merchants. Prompted by complaints from merchants, and to steady the markets for the Chinese, the Provincial Government Agency met with the Chinese tea brokers and compradors. To protect the Chinese buyers and sellers, the parties agreed that all teas for foreign export would be sold through the *Hsieh-hsing Hung*—Black Tea Guild. They agreed that all weights and measures used in Chinese trades with each other become standard. They were free to squeeze, levy fees, charge commissions, and use other devices with foreigners, all to be divided among the Black Tea Hong members and compradors conducting tea trades for foreigners. Under this agreement, Apun would receive a small percentage to add to his commissions from Richard. The Provincial agent directed the compradors, "No need tell your employers that you agree to this. Barbarians will devour themselves."

In early September, the creaking old British steamer *Governor General* had brought newspapers from home. The states' fights about slavery and secession had broken into war. The South had ordered an embargo on cotton, hoping to force Britain to support the South to maintain a cotton supply. A disrupted cotton trade would have worldwide effects. President Lincoln had imposed virtual martial law on the Union states and was organizing an army. The latest news reported that in July an overconfident and untrained Union army had been routed at a place called Bull Run between Washington and Richmond.

Richard rose from his chair and circled the room and talked to the walls. "There is serious fighting at home now, too ... Lincoln will keep the Union together ... I hope." He gazed out the window while he sorted out thoughts about war, family, and work. "Must not fret about home," he said aloud. "With our warship support gone, the celestials won't respect us. The Brits have no reason to protect our river shipping." He looked at Meto's picture. The walls did not react. Neither did Meto.

He suddenly felt silly and sat back down. "Damn, I'm talking to myself." He began expressing these thoughts to Meto in a letter he would send on the next ship. "The fighting won't last long," Richard mumbled aloud trying to reassure her as well as himself, talking as he wrote. "Lincoln will make short order of the rebellion. The South will be no match for Union boys." Then he finished his letter. "It is hardly right when our country is in difficulty for young Americans to be scraping for dollars out here."

Writing and releasing words aloud relieved for a few moments the stifling boredom of being unable to speak to any American. He took a deep breath, then dipped his pen again and began his report to Cunningham. After he had described in detail the shipments and cargoes of the past three weeks, he turned to the state of the Hankow operation.

"The Chinese bureaucracy and the guilds and multiple agencies here require more and more forms and contracts that I cannot read." He rubbed his eyes. *How much to explain?* "Negotiable prices, taxes, fees, commissions, schemes, kickbacks, bribes, and squeeze lubricate trades at every change of hand," he scribbled. His thoughts ran wild. Scraping for dollars required navigating this wild system. Chinese and Europeans. Everyone was unscrupulous, while soldiers and a populace of ragamuffins violently harassed him.

He said aloud, "I can't trust anyone's word. Is there any point in being honest anymore? There is no order or standard practice. Every deal has to be written down." Then he pressed on to Cunningham: "I must write out contracts, responses to guild demands, and forms. Apun translates so the Chinese clerks can make

Chinese renderings. I have no idea what they are scratching on the paper." In a burst of exasperation, he blew away the blotting sand, and continued writing.

"I cannot go outside without staves, firearms, or bodyguards. I must do all the papers for shipping, instructions, orders, and reports. The paperwork here has become all-consuming. All this in three copies or more." He nearly threw the pen into the wall as if to spear a mandarin merchant with it. "And I don't know what the Chinese say to each other. Or what the papers say to them."

Three months of the daily strain had exploded onto the paper in exasperation. He took a deep breath. He rubbed his tired eyes. He shook out his hands.

"No." *Leave the complaining for Meto's letters.* He tore up his report. Then took up the pen and dipped it again. Nothing suitable came to mind.

That night, befuddled by a half bottle of wine, he cared nothing about Cunningham. What was he doing this for? What did Russell & Co. matter? The world was at war. Chinese bribed and cheated and lied, and he didn't understand them. He worked hard for four years to be honest among thieves, but all he had to show for it was dirty looks and a sore body from stave blows. He didn't know what made sense any more. *Violence does not deceive. Maybe violence is the ultimate honesty.*

38

H E AWOKE SLOWLY, rolled onto his back, looked around his bedroom, and stretched to ease out the creases of a long deep sleep. He relieved himself in the chamber pot and then stepped to the open window. Cold air awoke him. Sunlight blasted onto his red walls advertising a bright, clear day. In the distance the Yangtze water sparkled in the morning light. The day rose bright, the sky clear and promising.

A good sleep and his rant the day before had cleared his head. Look out there, Richard, he told himself, the day is clear and sunny and the river is shining. A good day in any place. He looked at Meto's picture highlighted in the sun and he promised her, "I'll help the family from here. It's a good day to begin changing things." There was war at home; if he were there he'd join the army and help his family.

The first task was to finish his report to Cunningham in time to catch the steamer that left in an hour. This time he was brief. Business was growing so well that he needed help, he wrote, stretching the truth a bit about the true state of his business. "I am reluctant to ask, but would you be able to send me a clerk to help with the office work, so that I can spend more time buying and shipping? Please let him be someone who speaks good American English." Content with his report, he sent it off.

Another idea brewed in Richard's new resolve to make changes. His house godown was nearly filled with his own people, as well as with Russells' and clients' valuables. Thieves, soldiers, and gangs had tried to break into the compound several times. He needed more secure storage and better protection from potential thieves.

He summoned his comprador. "Apun, I want to buy the property between this house and the water. Money is available."

Apun listened respectfully. Confident as always, Apun said, "He sell. For price."

"Negotiate it the best you can. Use the usual means of persuasion. Assure that it happens."

The 'usual means of persuasion' included a price high enough to kickback to Apun, and to cover a bribe. Apun readied for the task. Not wanting to appear too wealthy, he put on a faded blue robe without adornment, visited the office responsible for property rights and land disputes, slipped a judicious bribe to a clerk, and learned that the land owner had not paid fees because last winter's flood had damaged several of his properties.

Apun let down his queue to show deference to Manchu officials, changed to a fresh robe, and visited Chen Lan, Taotai for diplomatic affairs. With silver coins, Apun convinced the bureaucrat that American ownership of the waterfront property would bring good American relations with the Emperor's government, as well as important benefits to Hankow and, not incidentally, to Chen Lan.

Apun then found the landowner, a bearded man who lived in a modest house in town, and, armed with knowledge about his damaged properties and financial defaults, spoke to him about the waterfront property. The landowner wrinkled his brow, blinked his dark eyes, and clasped his hands inside his sleeves.

"Family great financial need. Sell for twelve hundred *taels* silver," the owner said. His beard trembled with the motions of his mouth.

"With utmost respect to your need, my principal prepared to pay for property, and very wish to help your family. But superior in Shanghai control how much pay for help your family."

"Barbarians pay much money. The price twelve hundred *taels*." He hid nervous hands while his dark eyes fixed on Apun.

"Relationship with his superiors no good if he no complete task assigned. You escape debt. Principal pay for land, not your fee and tax."

If the bearded man was confident, the hands would be calm and exposed. His eyes would be serene. Apun judged his man desperate to get the money. He leaned forward and spoke softly. "I must account for barbarian money earned from land. If you accept nine hundred *taels,* barbarian will agree." Then he waited to give the calculating landowner time to compare the offer with his obligations.

"My family great debt for tax."

"Nine hundred taels. And barbarian pay one hundered for tax."

"*Fanqui* make plague on Hankow," the landowner said, then relented. "I must agree."

Apun reported back to Richard. "Discount from original price of twelve hundred *taels*." Richard waited to hear the final price. "Price one thousand *taels*." The big Chinaman's cheeks battled each other trying to stifle the sly smile. Richard saw that. He expected that his comprador had added a squeeze of at least fifty *taels* to the price the landowner would get. No matter, the total was acceptable; he needed the land, and Apun was doing good work.

After Apun registered the land purchase, his Chinese buyers acquired bricks from the Hankow furnaces, brought lumber and bamboo scaffolding from Parrot Island, and then supervised local construction coolies recruited from the rebuilding crews. Tough skilled men drove pilings into the newly acquired ground, scrambled over rickety scaffolding, and in a few weeks a godown with storage rooms, offices for the Chinese staff, and a vault room, rose a block from the shore. Another smaller warehouse extended over the riverbank on stilts.

IN EARLY FALL the Yangtze reached its lowest and muddiest level. The water ran thirty feet below its high mark as the weather cooled before the wet clouds of winter swept in. Richard and Ma-Wei stood atop the bank watching stevedores struggle on the forty-five-degree slope of mud and rocks and makeshift steps, slip and stagger weighted down with loads for the ships at anchor in the river. Boatmen slowly pushed and sculled long sampan oars ferrying goods and people out to the large junks and steamers and back. Richard pondered this inefficient, laborious, and time-consuming work. *There must be a better way.*

Coming from the latest steamer to arrive, a British paddle wheeler, an officer in dress whites left a river taxi at the muddy shore and awkwardly climbed the riverbank, mud splattering his white uniform. He lurched and jerked trying to control two large English bulldogs that grunted and snuffled, their feet caked with mud, their jaws dripping goo.

"Good old Augustus!" Richard laughed as the bulldogs reached the top, and they pulled the officer up.

"Are you Starr? Take these bloody beasts." The officer almost threw the leashes to Richard. Happy to feel solid land, the dogs scurried about.

"These bulls are magnificent. They look like those ugly lions that are all over China."

"They're all yours. My captain's delighted to loose these things. Ate us out of good meat!" The Brit turned, shook his head at the mud on his white trousers and shoes, and started back down the slope. Richard chuckled that his feet could slip from under him and dirty another part of his trousers.

One muddy white bulldog sniffed the ground, his flat face searching for things dogs search for in a new place. The other bulldog, tawny and streaked with tiger-like black stripes, ran back and forth as if looking for a Chinaman to bite. Two sharp lower teeth protruded above his lips. Nearby coolie stevedores backed well away.

Richard bent to hold his hand to the white bulldog. A low growl greeted his outstretched hand.

"They will guard our house. Take good care of them," Richard told the frightened Ma-Wei, who ducked behind him to keep away from the dogs.

Richard led the dogs back to the compound. He had not heard from Augustus, and nothing had been done to prepare for the dogs. Ma-Wei kept his distance, hurrying ahead to arrange a small but strong kennel and dog run for them. Richard instructed Ma-Wei, "Be sure to feed and water them every day. Have a boy take them for a walk outside the compound on days that I do not take them out."

The otherwise strong Ma-Wei said, "Lion dog great bad. White dog mean someone die."

Ma-Wei shut the kennel gate on the two excited beasts that indeed looked like the sacred temple guards.

Over the next few days, Richard conceived of building a floating dock large enough for steamships to land at any water level. Apun hired local coolie laborers and set them to work driving pilings into the bank and moving dirt to create a series of terraces and lumber steps up the riverbanks. They fashioned a floating raft half as wide as a typical river steamer was long. When the river changed levels, the dock would be lashed to a terrace step.

The construction nearly finished, Richard, pleased with the result, thought a new suit would make a nice present for himself. His old business suit had sprouted threads at the seams. He looked at the bright day ahead and remembered passing a tailor shop on one of his walks down Chung Lu. He gathered the old suit to show the tailor what he wanted and set out to find the shop.

At the shop he remembered, two finished garments hung in the door—one a fine robe, the other a Western suit that advertised that this shop could make him a satisfactory suit. Rolls of fabric leaned against one wall, and clothing segments covered a table. The tailor bent over a job with his needle.

"I need a new suit," Richard said to the shop's sole inhabitant. The middle-aged, heavy-lidded man seemed to understand what he had said.

More importantly, the tailor recognized a customer, a foreigner who would be able to pay well. He stood, said something, and smiled. Richard fingered a fabric and compared his old suit next to it. The tailor understood when Richard displayed the old suit. Without a word, and with a nod, the tailor looked over his shoulder and called something.

Presently a raven-haired girl of extraordinary beauty entered. She wore a form-fitting dress, no doubt handmade, and moved sensuously, catlike, as she took the suit from Richard and laid it on the table. She looked Richard up and down as if she were measuring him. He could not take his eyes off her. With points, nods, shakes, and signs Richard picked out a fabric, slightly less black than the old. "I like," he grinned.

The girl spread out his gabardine and began to let out the seams on his old trousers to use them as a pattern. He eyed her—watched her chest as she bent over her work. He tried vainly to stifle the heat in his groin.

Trading finger indications, he negotiated a price with the tailor. More finger negotiation, and Richard understood that he should return in a week for a fitting.

WHEN THE NEW dock was done a week later, American low-draft steamers and many other vessels could dock directly at the shore, thus avoiding the cumbersome and more costly process of anchoring in the river and loading and unloading small ferries. Stevedores could carry goods up and down steps in the terraces, avoiding the steep muddy hills elsewhere.

The dock infuriated the boatmen's guild when they saw that the *fanqui* would longer need their services or pay the extorted fees for ferry and taxi jobs. Within a week, a boatman refused to carry a French merchant's cargo by whacking him with blows with his oar. One day, Richard had to threaten a boatman with his revolver to persuade a taxi to row him back across the Yangtze from Wuchang. He was not too concerned about it; the resistance was typically Chinese. He had other things occupying his thoughts.

Richard stood in his shirt and underwear at the tailor's. The beautiful helper handed him his trousers, her eyes, onyx-black, almond shaped, raised to his. Flawless dark skin, tight to her round arms, moved without a wrinkle. As she moved, her feline form's exquisite curves rippled from neck to tiny, well-formed feet. He could not pull his new trousers on fast enough to cover himself. He watched her ready his jacket while the tailor fussed with the trousers. Richard flinched when the tailor tested the fit at the crotch. The man surely felt what was happening to him. "Likee?"

The trousers or the girl? He remembered the word, "*She de*—yes."

Excitement rose when she held the jacket out for his arms and brushed against the back of his shoulder. The suit fit well on this first fitting, but he needed to take it off for a few adjustments. He did not want to reveal himself again. "I come back for you finish," he said. The tailor spoke to the girl. She nodded and smiled at Richard. She reached out and took his hand in hers.

A tingle went up his arm. He managed, "*Ni Hao*—hello," but the words sounded as if they came from someone else. She pulled him to the back, out of the shop, and up a narrow stair. Strong hands, firm, but sensitive. The tailor massaged his own hands.

The upstairs room was bare of decoration. She closed the door. On the floor, a mattress of sorts, and laying on it, a pile of exotic pillows in reds, yellows, and greens, and decorated with geometric shapes. One pillow such as Richard had never seen before stood out, a pillow of patterns, of smooth silk, indescribably blending colors and brightness that spoke a message of soft comfort. She must have made it herself from scrap fabrics. Cleanliness and softness surrounded him as she lifted his jacket off, then undid his trousers, careful not to prick him with the marking pins. He expected her to leave and let him rest while they finished the suit.

Holding both his hands, she eased him onto the pillows. She sat beside him, her arm resting on his thigh. He could not control the swelling tightness.

Richard pointed to his chest, found the words to say, in English, "My name Richard."

"Lei ... Cha," she said, repeating.

"No. Ri ... chard."

She laughed and put her palm on his chest where he had pointed. Her eyes sparkled. "Lei-Cha."

He laughed too. "Lei-cha it is, then. *She de.*" A natural happiness touched them. "Your name?" He pointed to her chest—smooth, round, lovely under her tight dress.

"Mei-li," she said. Her lips puckered sensuously as she spoke.

"Mei-li?"

"*She de,*" and she laughed.

They fell back onto the pillows. Her hand touched his cheek and stroked the stubble. She made purring noises. His hand touched her pure face, caressed the high cheeks, and traced the sumptuous lips. She leaned toward him, and he kissed her. She responded to the kiss; pulsing with passion, her fingers slid down and started unbuttoning his shirt. He threw off the shirt so she could run her fingers through the hairs on his chest. She slipped out of her dress; her sensual wriggling drove him to a new level of passion. He hesitated, not having seen human nipples so near at hand, but couldn't stop and caressed the perfect breasts. The silken pillow's colors blended perfectly with the tones in her skin. He felt warm; the air was hot. He was bursting with passion for this girl he could not talk to. He discovered that he could play tickling games with her and laugh. Each game led to more kisses, more caresses, their legs entangled.

His conscience tumbled in confusion. She was of heathen race. If anybody, he should be with Annie Wiley or even Dora Delano. Meto had taught that lying with a girl without marriage is a sin. *I've never been with a girl like this. Stop!* he told himself. He couldn't stop.

Mei-li knew what to do.

An hour later, Richard descended to the shop, Mei-li right behind, holding his hand. Embarrassed before her father, he dropped her hand like it burned. He picked up his finished suit and paid the tailor. Silently, Richard looked back at Mei-li and said mentally, *I will come back.* He had never experienced a girl in that way. Never had an afternoon satisfied him like her laughter, those indescribable hugs and jerks and writhing. Mei-li saw his smile, smiled too, and then turned and disappeared upstairs. She left him tired, yet oddly relaxed, and perfectly happy.

The tailor held out his hand again and screeched something. He rubbed his fingers, the universal sign that he wanted more money. Richard said, "Why? We agreed. I paid you."

As soon as he said that, he realized. This charlatan had sold his daughter's body. Does she want this? What her father was doing was despicable. Memory of the sinning in the Hong Kong brothel flashed into his head. What Mei-li had just done on her pillows was beautiful compared to that. God had made such incredible beauty, how could something so grand be sinful? God let Adam and Eve love each other, why should loving be a sin? Mei-li had exhilarated, relaxed, inspired, energized him so much that he easily paid what the father wanted.

Richard knew he would come back to this exquisite Mei-li.

THE NEW DOCK was ready for the first steamer to land. The *Fire Dart* soon arrived again from Shanghai. Richard, in his shirt-sleeves, took the two bulldogs for exercise to watch the first loads come out from the paddle wheeler. Apun's coolies and the *Fire Dart's* crew stepped up the terrace's stairs, dropped their loads in wagons for the short carry to the new godown and returned for more. At the new dockside warehouse, coolies lifted off the goods and in a few steps had them stored inside. For a lengthy storage and better security, they would move them to the larger godown. The dock and dockside storage were working well, he thought. European and Chinese shipping would pay a fine fee to use this dock. Anyone can easily store goods for transshipping, too.

"Mr. Starr?" A young man, impeccably dressed in business black, carrying a large envelope, and sporting a stovepipe hat much like Richard's, strode purposely toward him. He had lifted his round body up the staircase from the *Fire Dart* without puffing for breath. "Mr. Cunningham sends his compliments to you. I am Webb," the man said. "I am to be your clerk."

"I am delighted to meet you." Richard could hardly contain his pleasure. An English-speaking companion would be a daily comfort. "Please, call me Richard. What's your first name?"

"I have always been called 'Webb.' I will be happy to have you address me as 'Webb.'"

While they walked back to the house, Richard outlined the duties he had in mind for the new man, alerted him to likely annoyance from natives and soldiers, and probed to learn about his character and qualifications. He showed Webb around the facilities, introduced him to Apun and Ma-Wei, fixed him a temporary bunk in his red-walled room and a work table in an office, and then let him familiarize himself with the books and records he would work with. "Tomorrow we will walk into the city."

As he departed the *Fire Dart* speaking English freely, having seen his new warehouse fill, having seen his new dock work efficiently, and having loved Mei-li, Richard confirmed, *If life doesn't suit you, change it. Whoever said that was right.*

Meanwhile, the *Fire Dart* continued discharging passengers. A familiar figure in a splendid indigo robe embroidered with a snake stepped ashore and melded into Hankow's Chinese crowd.

39

I N THE MORNING, they did not take the bulldogs, Jack and
Butch, or coolies. Instead, as usual now, Richard carried his
revolver. He wanted Webb to experience the streets. A typical
group of beggars confronted them, crowded close, and impeded
their tour. They kept walking. Richard used the word he had
learned for "go away," "*Zou. Zou,*" but no one went away.

"A British friend told me to try this," Webb said. He pulled
out a box of pink pills and offered it to the most forward tormen-
tor. Webb popped two or three pills into the man's mouth. Two
more wanted pills, seemed pleased, and others crowded in, open-
mouthed and eager. Soon the pills were gone. "Cockle's pills,"
Webb said. "Preferable to showing a revolver, though a little slow
in operation. Wait a minute."

One by one, each Chinese beggar who had taken a pill soon
hurried away. Men heaved into the gutter. Others purged on
the roadside or against buildings. Webb and Richard burst out
laughing.

Farther on, a ragtag squad of inebriated soldiers obstructed
their way. They would not take Cockle's pills, and their weapons
prevented a full response with the revolver. Shouts and harass-
ment flew at the Americans as they walked. Richard pulled out
his revolver. "This won't really work," he said. "Soldiers know
we won't use weapons."

Webb showed his personal revolver. "See that water carrier across the street?"

With a prominent swing of his weapon, Webb fired. The water carrier paid no attention to the gunshot, but when he saw water squirt through a hole in his pail, he shrieked, "Aiiiieeee." Unbalanced, his pails clanged and spilled into the street. The astounded soldiers stopped mocking and let the two go on. Webb satisfied Richard on all accounts.

Richard decided on another idea for a change in business. Foreign merchants were exempt from the *likin,* the local fee for shipping. If Russell & Co. bought tea at the mountain fields themselves before it got to Hankow, they could lower the costs of getting it to Shanghai for export. This idea would violate local practices, but the prospect of undercutting both the British and the Chinese brokers was too tempting. This was not breaking laws; it was avoiding them.

"We will save costs and avoid middlemen," he told Apun. "The tea could go on a Russell ship from the fields to Hankow, then on to Shanghai, perhaps on the same ship."

Apun nodded. "My men do it. I go first time. Make owner appoint Russell & Co. or Kee Chong agent to ship and sell tea."

"Okay. Let's do it."

FOLLOWING A ROAD that paralleled the river, Apun and four coolies carried provisions for a three-day hike to the tea-growing hills. Each man strapped to his waist a hidden sack of silver coins. The caravan strode with purpose for two days, then the road turned into the mountains where woodland trees surrounded them and the trail began to rise. They pulled into a clearing, set out a camp, kindled a fire for warmth, and settled down for the night. The fire cooled to embers, then snuffed itself out. A thin early moon shone meekly through gossamer spaces in the overcast sky.

Apun woke, crept away from his sleeping men, and sought a tree to relieve himself. When he finished his business, he heard a soft horse's snort. Walking slowly, shapes in the dark moved on the opposite side of the camp. One rider was on horseback; others were on foot. The horseman turned his mount toward the sleeping coolies, his arm lifted to signal silence until five others crept forward to surround the sleepers. One of the coolies cried out as a man tried to search his body.

Apun had no weapon. He could not help his surprised, barely awake, and outnumbered men. He crouched behind a tree to hide. One of his coolies tripped trying to run. A bandit swung a stick overhead and down onto him. Men wrestled, arms and legs flew, swung, kicked, as the bandits tried to steal anything useful. Darkness hid details from Apun. It was impossible to tell a coolie from a bandit. The horse stepped through the melee, its rider bending over to slam targets. The bandits picked through the unconscious coolies on the ground, rolled them over, searched for valuables, stripped and took everything: shoes, knives, the hidden silver. The raid ended in a moment. The bandits left as quietly as they had come. Apun's four coolies lay on the ground.

He hurried to his men. He stared at the mess around the bodies. Would he have to report a total failure of his mission?

"Apun?" One stirred on the ground and lifted his head.

"You hurt?" Apun asked

"You hurt?" his man asked.

"Where you hurt?"

"Everywhere."

In a few more moments, all four recovered consciousness. Two lay down, two sat up. Apun scraped together twigs and grass and rekindled the fire. Every man bled somewhere—bloody nose, cut arm, raw scrape, or bruised head. One man had a hoof-shaped bruise on his thigh, another coolie a similar one on his back. No one claimed a broken bone, but all needed recovery time.

When daylight came, everyone ached and nursed bruises, crusted cuts, and black eyes. All the silver sacks had been stolen. Several men would have to walk barefooted. Clothing was torn or missing and no food remained.

Apun determined to complete this mission and did not want to return having failed.

"I go find food. I think tea farms one day walk. Food there."

The men agreed that he should go, while they helped each other recover.

"Stay here. Stay together," Apun instructed.

Apun hiked along the trail that led through scrub woods until he glimpsed orchards of tea plants covering the hills to his right. A cottage and shed soon were outlined against the hills. In a clearing near them, tea leaves dried in the sun on open-air tables and farmers packed dried leaves into bags. A horse in traces stood nearby ready to haul a full wagon down to a tributary that eventually flowed into the Han River. Apun hoped that his appearance advertised only that he had traveled for several days.

A well-dressed farmer, his rugged features sculpted from a lifetime of outdoor work suitable as the farm's owner, emerged from the cottage. Apun stepped toward him. "I seek owner."

The farmer bowed to the robed merchant. "Wou Sang."

Apun returned a shallow bow then told Wou that he wanted to buy a shipment of tea to be sent to Hankow. Wou was willing to sell but would not ship anything without being paid in full first.

Apun understood that Wou would not give credit to a stranger out of the woods. He said he was agent for an American company called Russell & Company, called Kee Chong in Shanghai. "Credit good."

Wou said, "Howqua own this land. Howqua sell Russell tea. Russell credit good. Not know you."

After more clarifying questions and assurances that Apun was indeed the agent for Russell & Co., Apun said. "Please to make me agent to sell tea from this farm? Good for business. You make profit."

They retired to the cottage and wrote an agreement. They discussed quantities available this season and expected prices, and the deal was done. Apun wrote a note drawn on Russell as payment for the agreement. The farmer would cash in the note to confirm Apun's honesty. Wou agreed to sell his season's crop to Russell & Co.

Apun said, "Kee Chong men return with order and payment."

The battered tea caravan arrived back at the house empty-handed. While Ma-Wei tended to the wounded men, Apun explained to Richard what had happened. Apun carefully copied the agreement for his own file and translated for Richard the formal-looking original. Richard nodded at the acceptable terms, ignorant of untranslated terms that gave Apun a 2 percent commission on every shipment.

Russell now enjoyed a source of inland tea that avoided the river taxes, any middlemen, and the Black Tea Hong's guild fees, as hoped. Richard and Apun decided not to carry silver into the mountains without armed guards, and, thereafter, coolies disguised as traveling farmers trekked to the tea hills carrying only Russell's paper notes for payments. They returned floating down the Han River at night with loads of black tea from Wou Sang's farm—dried, crushed, and bagged for shipment and quickly unloaded into the Russell godown. The new godown now held a sizable shipment for the next steamer to Shanghai.

"The docking fees are earning well," Webb said to Richard several weeks after the new dock began operating. "Chinese merchants like it, too."

"We have stolen a march on the Brits for a while. How long do you suppose it will be before they quit hauling up the bank and copy our dock?" Richard also wondered how long it would be before the tea guild did something to prevent the tea farmers from selling directly to the *fanqui*.

"We'll take the business in the meantime."

Richard trusted Apun and Webb implicitly. Apun had proved his loyalty, and no one could match his business-making contacts with the Hong. His understanding of Chinese business methods and sly smile sometimes caused Richard to suspect that those methods involved squeeze for Apun, but he never questioned his comprador's production for Russell & Co. Webb had proved his loyalty with accurate reports and bookkeeping as well as his mettle in the streets. The three Hankow Russells worked well together, and the partners praised the results of their endeavors.

An imposing tile-decorated gate on the Black Tea Hong Guild walls admitted Richard, Apun, and Webb. Jack and Butch had stretched Webb's arms during the long walk, and he flexed and rubbed them after securing the dogs to a stake meant for tethering horses. Two bulldogs face-to-face with two lions forged a perfect metaphor for the British versus Chinese tussles over trade rights. Two Chinese-style lions guarded a nearby temple entrance keeping evil spirits way. To their right, the magnificent godown cast the fresh fragrance of mixed teas over the grounds. They entered and met two guild brokers.

The trio's request for an agreement to commit the Hong to sell a percentage of all its foreign tea sales to Russell instead of to other Western companies met with typical Chinese intransigence—indirect answers, pleas to consult higher levels, complaints about difficult procedures, and inconsistent and ambiguous comments.

"Our request is clear," Richard said for Apun to translate to the two Hong agents. "Your responses are not clear. What we ask will be profitable for both of us." Apun added proper courtesies to his translation.

One of the two brokers said. "Why we give you advantage, when you get tea from farmer and no pay guild fee?

"You will always have a sale to us," Richard said. "No need to compete among foreigners. Each sale will always be decided on a fair price each sale. And always, you can sell to Chinese before Kee Chong. We want a decision. I have no patience for time-consuming talk."

Apun looked the highest ranking of the two brokers directly in the eye as he translated Richard's words, crammed into polite Chinese business talk.

The official spoke a few words, for him a change in tactic. Apun translated to Richard, "He want to know if you will pay transaction fee."

Richard looked at Webb. Webb looked at Richard. "Is he suggesting a bribe?" Richard asked Apun.

Apun nodded. "Bribe often Chinese business way."

Richard knew that, but every moral instinct in Richard cried, "Don't do this. You are going down a dangerous path." The agreement was advantageous to Russell, and with it he could make it difficult for the Brits to buy from the Guild. Paying a bribe was not as sinful as taking a bribe, Richard persuaded himself. No agreement was likely to happen unless this man got his "transaction fee."

"Okay," Richard said to Apun. "Offer him one hundred Spanish dollars."

The two Chinese settled on a fee of two hundred dollars. Now that he was actually paying a bribe, Richard still hesitated with his hand in his pocket. Then he handed over the two hundred dollars. The Hong agents agreed that Russell & Co. would have the first right to buy a tea shipment before it was sold to any other barbarian merchant.

IN QUIET MOMENTS when Apun was busy, Richard's thoughts turned to the temptations of the tailor shop. Soon the weather would be turning cold. He decided he needed to repair a jacket that had torn on a sharp split log used to build the godown.

When the tailor finished measuring him, Richard pointed to the upstairs room, smiling with the obvious question. The man smiled and called. Mei-li came trotting down the stairs to greet him with open arms and promptly took Richard by the hand.

Her glorious shape and golden skin choked his words. "So lovely to see you again."

"Lei-cha."

She wore the same form-fitting dress as before. He hadn't remembered its color; now it was a seductive green that enhanced her flawless skin. Her lucious hips swung smoothly back and forth as he followed her up the stairs. Calves shaped by constant stair climbing flexed and pulsed, step by step. In a few moments, his shirt and trousers lay on the floor; she dropped her dress, and the seduction was complete. They stroked and tickled and giggled and loved. They rested awhile on the silken pillow, splayed naked. No talk was needed. Then they rolled together in another torrid embrace.

The visit was worth every coin the pandering father demanded.

RICHARD REVIEWED BUSINESS and the string of changes he had made after his resolve one sunny morning several weeks earlier. He was in a good mood after the visit to Mei-li. Stunning beauty was available to him for a few coins anytime he wanted. He did not let the fact that she lay with other lovers bother him.

He didn't want to tell Webb about Mei-li.

Instead, he said, "The new dock and godown have made storage and shipping efficient for a change."

"In the process we have angered local laborers and boatmen."

"Maybe we have. But more importantly, we have given Russell a big jump ahead of the competition in teas."

He appreciated Webb's presence. Someone he could talk to. Yes, the changes were working. And since getting the dogs, the local rabble bothered him less. "With more foreigners here now, the Chinese seem to be more used to seeing us around town."

Webb, always good-natured, smiled when he said, "Doesn't mean they like us any better."

40

W HEN STEAMER ARRIVALS pressured their own coolies and
godown workers, Richard needed to hire local laborers
who were willing to work at the lowest rates. Tramp stevedore
bosses, angry that foreigners had stolen their business, threatened
that the locals would not work unless Richard paid a much higher
wage. Richard had always resisted the bosses' demands when men
were willing to work for less. Meanwhile, a new steamer at the
dock whistled a demand to start loading.

Two local hired men lifted the first load in the godown, bales
of hemp suspended under a pole slung to their shoulders. A second
pair followed, and they carried their loads out of the godown.
A block away, eight men dressed in loose, dirty clothes, two of
them carrying a stave each and a third an oar, stood directly across
their path. The burdened workers stopped. The armed hoodlums
shouted abuse and demands. The leading pair set down the crates.
Apun's largest coolie, See Kwan, a man of fierce visage and pulsing muscle, shouted from behind, "Ignore them. Go on."

Apun reported to Richard. The first men bent to pick up their
carrying pole. Instantly the boatman wielding an oar faced them,
shouted, and struck the first man on the shoulder, causing him
to drop his pole again. The man rubbed his shoulder, looked the
hoodlum in the face and, mumbling a curse, picked up his pole.
Pokes with the staves and whacks with the oar drove the working

local coolies back through the main godown cargo door with their loads. One coolie ducked a blow, stumbled just outside the door, and dropped his bales. Two of the godown's Canton coolies dashed forward and rescued the bales and the man.

The hoodlums remained outside, restless and shouting unintelligible obscenities. Richard understood nothing they said, but he knew they intended to force his hired workers to refuse to work. He immediately sent a messenger out the godown's back door to ask the magistrate for help controlling the mob. Then he and Webb, carrying revolvers, ventured out to talk to the troublemakers, with Ma-Wei to translate.

"The governor order that no one molest foreigners," Richard said through Ma-Wei. "Let men work. No bother you if you no bother cargo."

As they talked, more stevedores, boatmen, and laborers angry at the *fanqui* who had destroyed their jobs crowded down the side alleys and joined the first eight. A number of them carried heavy oars, and spears once held by Taiping raiders. The reasonable approach, "don't bother us, we won't bother you," accomplished nothing. Of course, the *fanqui's* very presence bothered them.

The leading hoodlum, one as large as See Kwan, flexed his bare muscular arms and stared Richard directly in the face. He spoke stern words through broken teeth.

"He say Hankow coolies no move unless we pay full wage. If move cargo, mob attack," said Ma-Wei. *Very likely, higher union wages would not do much for our hired day workers*, Richard thought; the additional pay would only line some boss's pocket. Besieged inside the godown, Richard's people and his local hires could move nothing.

Richard retreated inside. "We cannot give in to this threat," he said. "Wages now, what next? Business will stop unless we stop threats now."

"It looks like a case for firearms as well as staves and dogs," said Webb, taking out his revolver.

The messenger returned promptly, and Apun translated: "The magistrate says he do all he can to protect our men."

Richard added, "This means the magistrate is no help."

He said to Webb, "This is a new one for us all. Our coolies have had many successful scrimmages with mobs. House coolies have defended the house from army soldiers. Our men are not easily intimidated." A roundhouse swing with one of the poles would clear a space in front. Everyone knew that a stave butt end could disable an opponent, take his breath, break a rib, or a joint. A solid hit to the head caused blackout. Richard had every confidence in all his coolies to protect the cargo caravan. Would the local hired men continue to work? Richard saw clearly that any force he could muster would be badly outnumbered in a fight.

Apun advised, "Canton men no respect locals. They fight if needed. They confident in revolver."

"We can take the dogs out, too," said Webb.

Richard decided. "Get ready to carry the hemp again." He directed Apun to organize his Canton coolies to act as escort, with house and godown coolies to support them. "Carry staves. Local workers carry the cargo. Apun, tell them they will be protected. They always will have jobs." Apun turned his persuasions on them. The locals lined up, staged their loads, and stood ready to go.

Richard turned to Webb. "We should carry our revolvers in plain sight, fully loaded. Use them only as a very last resort. The sight of bulldogs and firearms had silenced most Chinese street crowds. Ma-Wei and See Kwan will take Jack and Butch on long leashes."

Richard then ordered Apun, "Tell the crowd that we are about to move some goods to the wharf. Say that anyone who interferes with coolies carrying goods will be treated as robbers." The hoodlums would know the punishment for robbers. Hop Tzu's severed head flashed into his mind but disappeared quickly. "Tell them we intend to use our revolvers."

Apun passed some more instructions to his men. When he nodded "ready," Richard opened the door. The local coolies slung loaded poles onto their shoulders. The Canton coolies flanked the cargo, each man with a stave held at the ready. Would the bluster work?

The gang reacted immediately. The Canton coolie guards responded in earnest. Blows answered blows. All along the line of cargo carriers every coolie prodded or swung at a hoodlum. A bloody nose splattered one attacker. Another attacker tripped and crawled out of harm's way. The crowd yelled Chinese curses and retaliated with blows. Coolies parried blows, shoved, and kept open the path. When all the loads were out and on the road, Richard and Webb stepped out, revolvers drawn. Ma-Wei and See Kwan followed with the dogs, drooling and looking like they wanted someone to bite.

From behind a building, a lanky stevedore loosed a spear at Richard, who saw it coming in time and ducked, and it flew by and stuck in a bale of hemp. When he turned to see where the spear had gone, a hard thrust with a stave caught him in the stomach, momentarily taking his breath. He quickly straightened and continued on with the caravan. More brutes rushed into the fray. Another spear arched into the caravan, narrowly missing a carrier. The man set down his load, pulled the spear out and heaved it back. This angered the crowd, and it surged forward. A house coolie stepped back, lost balance, and a thug kicked at him. The defensive line weakened under heavy blows. A sword flashed; blood splattered a Canton man. He seized the swordsman, wrested the sword away, and hacked back. The swordsman cried, fell, and was overrun by the next raider, who fell on the Canton man and raised a sword up to chop. Webb shot him.

The spears and swords had to stop. Richard fired into the air. For a moment, the two sudden gunshots quieted the fight. No one expected firearms. The Canton men rallied while the hoodlums stalled. Jack clutched a hoodlum's leg, shook it, and growled through the man's yells. Butch snapped and barked.

"Shoot at their feet," Webb called to Richard. He fired at a foot; the bullet ricocheted and hit another in the leg. He cried out and limped away.

One by one, the hoodlums backed off. They were no match for firearms. They retreated down the side alleys. Canton men followed with their staves to make sure they stayed away. Barking loud, Butch and Jack ran after them as far as Ma-Wei let them.

The cargos reached the dock, where stevedores took them onto the steamer. A second and third trip to the wharf met sporadic heckling but no violence, no mob. Richard clutched his aching stomach, his souvenir of a stiff stave poke.

After the goods were safely aboard, and all the Russells and their hires had relaxed, nursed their bruises and cuts, and thanked and praised each other for their individual acts, a scrubby Chinese official and two armed thugs from the magistrate's office arrived at the godown. Apun reported that they had come to see that our goods had been loaded and were happy to see that the job had been completed.

"Where were they when we really needed them?" Richard asked Apun.

"They say much trouble in city and not enough force."

After the official left, Richard muttered to Webb as they returned to the house, "Expected that. Very polite. And profuse with the excuses. Chinese officials always promise everything and do nothing."

41

R ICHARD AND WEBB rehashed the events of the previous day. Richard had been toying with an idea of his own. He had always loved horses, rode well, and knew how to drive them pulling a carriage or wagon. "I have an idea that may solve several problems for us."

"What's that?"

"Horses. If we had horses, we could load cargo into a wagon and carry it to town and to the ships much more easily and quickly. We could ride faster than walk to the commercial areas."

"Of course," Webb wholeheartedly agreed. "I like to ride."

"Why didn't I think of that sooner?" He had missed his horses. Another positive change to make right away. "I'll probably have to teach Apun and Ma-Wei to ride."

Richard called Apun. "We need to build a stable for four horses. I'll plan the materials and design. There is space beside the new godown. Hire what you need for workers and start right away."

In less than two weeks, a stable for four horses stood on the property, two stout wagons were stored nearby, and four husky Mongolian horses munched away at oats in their stalls. Richard rode each one in turn, sensing its character, finding each one accustomed to riding and hauling, and responsive to commands of rider and driver. He was surprised to find that Ma-Wei rode well and understood the animals. Apun could learn to drive a wagon.

"Webb, we have made another useful improvement in our lives in this miserable place," Richard said.

"What else can we do to improve things? It seems as good as it will get," Webb said.

"All these changes have helped Russell & Co. We need to do something to help ourselves. Private ventures on our own."

42

"WHY IS CAPTAIN Barrows writing?" Richard said, opening the letter just dropped from the mail boat.

I am bound to tell you that the shipment of opium we discussed some time ago has arrived, in part. The Coquette had wrecked, and for a time, it was thought that all was lost. However, a portion of her cargo has been salvaged in good condition. Your shipment has arrived. There are twenty-six chests. I await your soonest instructions.

Richard reread it and told Webb that opium was available to them for the asking.

"Why would we want any?" Webb said. "You don't secretly smoke, do you?"

Richard laughed. "Of course not. It's a well-meaning gift from my father."

Both instantly realized possible uses for the drug. Distribute the drug. Sell it direct. Trade for tea, porcelains ... bribes ... anything.

"Do we really want to get into that shameful trade?" asked Webb. Most Americans felt that the opium trade was odious, causing addiction, laziness, hallucinations, ruin, and, eventually, a miserable death. The imperial government had tried to prevent foreigners from importing it, which had caused war and some

Chinese to grow domestic opium. Opium dens populated every Chinese city.

"I don't really want to get into it," said Richard, "but importing is legal now. The firm does import and distribute it when there is opportunity. I've been to the storeship off Woosong."

Webb looked surprised. "No one mentions opium at the firm."

"Whoever makes money on it keeps it private," Richard said. His conscience once had nagged him about what to do with his father's opium. Richard's reservations had faltered when he found out that his father had supported the family on opium. Opium was the family business. Should he succeed his father in it? Offensive as the drug was, if duties and fees were paid, everything about trading it was legal. Russell partner Delano had once proclaimed to the effect that there was no law for foreigners but self-interest. There certainly were personal profits in opium. Especially when it had no cost.

One evening soon after the news from Barrows, Apun read to Richard a message in Chinese characters and sealed with maroon wax. "A new bank open in Hsin-an area, near guild hall," he read.

"Name Hankow Merchants Bank."

Richard knew that the Hsin-an area was near luxury homes and high-rent shops selling luxury silks, jewelry, and jade.

"It seems a new Chinese bank opens every week," Richard said. "Toss it out."

"Read more before toss out."

"What more is there?"

"Bank want business from foreigner. Deposit, make loan, help with trade."

"That's the banking business. Toss it."

"It say Kung Loong owner."

"Kung Loong?"

His Shanghai acquaintance. What is he doing in Hankow? Richard's sometime suspicions about Kung returned, but he was curious. Kung certainly wants to make money from the commerce foreigners bring. *Could Kung help do something about Father's opium?* Maybe he would buy it. If he bought it all, Richard would have a fund to finance his own ventures. He sent an answer to Barrows: "Please await instructions."

Kung Loong, robed in royal blue, greeted Richard with a smile that spread his newly trimmed beard and flashed the gold tooth. Chinese bankers in the lobby of the single-story recently built and plastered Hankow Merchants Bank turned to watch them shake hands, bow to each other, go into a back room, and shut the door. Kung and Richard sat in square wooden chairs around a round table. A painting of two thin cranes, one bending down, the other reaching for a bug, hung on the bare wall.

"New bank for Hankow business," Kung began before Richard spoke. "Lend money for make better trade." Kung and his partner Yang Fang, he explained, wanted to take advantage of the expanding business on the Yangtze by financing Chinese merchants who were congregating in Hankow to exploit the foreign-generated business there. The bank expected to draw, in addition to Chinese merchants, at least a few trustworthy barbarians to help fund the capital.

"I am surprised to see you in Hankow," Richard said. *Why am I not surprised?*

"You want money, no?"

"Yes, I do. But I do not want to borrow it from you."

Kung widened his oriental eyes, put on a practiced expression of disappointment, and immediately shut down any enthusiasm. No smile showed.

Kung did not resort to being unscrupulous when it came to talking about money. Acquiring money was another matter.

He would not buy something from a barbarian if he could find it himself, Richard thought, but Kung's greed would ultimately take over. Richard gambled that in any transaction, Kung would avoid duties, the *likin,* and trouble from government agents. He decided to be direct now. "Opium season is beginning. I might be able to import some through Kee Chong," he lied. "I will sell it to you for a good price."

Kung thanked Richard in flowery oriental fashion, then as casually as he could manage, asked, "Where you get opium?"

"Kee Chong policy is not to reveal sources," Richard said. He did not know whether there was such a policy or not, but he thought it believable. Kee Chung had nothing to do with this opium. If he told Kung honestly where he got it, Kung would know that it cost nothing and might be damaged. For now, let Kung assume that Russell & Co. imports high-quality, expensive Indian opium. "I can say that any drug I sell will be good quality," Richard said. "When I have it, I will tell you." Kung's craggy jowls fought to dull his eagerness. "I will confirm and return with a price and quantity," said Richard.

A few days later, Richard told Kung that he could get ten opium packages of Indian Malwa. They negotiated a price 15 percent below the average Shanghai high season price and shook hands, as they had done over tea contracts and previous loans. The gold tooth sparkled in the corner of Kung's smile.

"I make sure opium good before I pay," Kung said.

"You do not trust me?" Richard said, feigning shock. He had noticed Kung's mole hair tug. "I have always done as agreed. You know my word is good. I expect full payment now."

"I no pay until receipt from resale."

Richard had bargained with Kung using the same tactic. "Not acceptable. You own a bank. You have money. If you want opium, pay me your cash."

"I must sell opium first. I no cash in bank now."

Kung is lying, Richard thought. Chinese bargaining. "I bought the opium. I need to cover my cost," Richard lied again. As they negotiated their lies, Richard several times threatened not to sell at all.

Finally Kung proposed, "I pay half now. I deposit the other half to new account for Kee Chong in Hankow Merchants Bank."

The agreement was not entirely complete. Richard now did what the Chinese so often did. After an agreement, additional conditions were raised, to take advantage of an increased bargaining position. Richard said, "The opium is in Shanghai. To get it here I have to pay duty. I have agreed to give you a discount, but we have not agreed on shipping and duty. You must pay those costs."

Kung's fury knew no bounds. He roared, gnashed his gold tooth, and pounded the table. Richard had seen this before and let him rant. The fit finally passed. Kung calmed, then smiled and turned charming.

"Instead of pay shipping, I send man to pick up opium in Shanghai. You no ship."

That meant that Kung intended to smuggle past customs and to sneak up the Yangtze without paying *liken*. That didn't matter to Richard. After a sale, it didn't matter what the buyer did with it, Delano had said. It would be Kung's problem if his man got caught.

"I agree. You can do shipping," Richard said.

After more negotiating, Richard agreed that Kung would pay one-half the price now, Richard to return this cash if the opium was not delivered. The other one-half Kung would credit to Kee Chong in a new personal bank account. Richard said that he did not want to risk Kee Chong's money in this new bank and demanded that it be deposited in his own name.

Kung prepared a document appointing Kung's man as agent authorized to take delivery of ten cases of opium. What did it really say? Why hadn't Richard brought Apun to translate? Should he stall and come back with Apun? *It is too good a bargain for Kung*, Richard judged, *and I've gotten cases sold already for cash. I'll go ahead with the Chinese contract and translate it later.* He signed the paper. To identify Kung's shipper, they tore the document in half, Kung to send one half to his man, Richard the other half to Captain Barrows with full translation. Kung returned from his vault with a bag of gold coins. Richard counted the correct amount, and Kung created a new account at Hankow Merchants Bank in Richard's name.

They shook hands again, and Richard returned to the house, in firm possession of a profit and, confirming his new account, a document that proved, on translation, to be correct. He wrote instructions to Barrows about the delivery, included the torn half paper, and asked that his remaining sixteen cases be sent to him via Russell & Co. steamer as soon as possible.

As soon as Richard had left, Kung brought out his paper and brush to write to Yang Fang. "Hankow Merchants Bank grow," Kung wrote. "Kee Chong's Starr sell opium. We have money for buy opium. He sell for less than other barbarian ask. As we discuss, I plan dilute these drugs, package for resale. Make ten or twelve times what I pay." He sealed the report with his maroon wax and called for a messenger.

In due course Captain Barrows did as he was instructed, and the opium was on its way to Hankow with Kung's smuggler.

43

Dear Father, I am writing to thank you for the delivery of opium from India to help me reach partnership with Russell & Co. You may know that the Coquette wrecked on the way here and that all was thought lost. However, some of the opium you sent has arrived here. I have sold much of it and will make good use of the remainder. By arrangement with Jardine, Matheson, the proceeds of the sale are being sent to Barkley's Bank in London and deposited there to a new account in my name.

H E SIGNED OFF the letter with expressions of concern about the family's welfare now that war had struck the United States, and made no comment on the morality of what they'd done, since he'd settled any problems over opium trading. He signed the letter with the usual complimentary and polite remarks, sealed and sent it out for the next mail to Bombay.

Then he stood and stretched. Dealing with Kung was done for the time being. There was time to see Mei-li. Before he set out to the tailor shop, he asked Ma-Wei to teach him some Chinese phrases.

"Why you want know? We translate for you."

"I ... I'm curious. I'd like to learn. I know *Ni Hao*, and a few others, *Ting*, and *Zou*."

"You say greeting, 'How are you? And 'stop' and 'go.' New words. When leave someone after dinner you say, *Jinwan hen yukuai*. That say, 'This very nice evening.'"

"Perfect." Now he could tell Mei-li how he felt. Ma-Wei had no better luck teaching Richard pronunciation than Apun had had on the *Scotland* but managed to get him to repeat, "Zee one hen you kay."

"That close. Try again." More tries. "Close … Again."

Richard rushed the words, frustrated, but anxious to see Mei-li. "Good enough," he said, after more impatient tries. "Thank you. We'll learn more later."

He rode to the tailor shop on his favorite horse, a tan mare with a heavy mane, named Brutus. Richard tied Brutus to a post outside the shop, entered and dug out silver coins as he had on his two previous occasions. When the tailor saw that the customer carried no clothing samples, he peered over his shoulder and barked, "Mei-li!"

Mei-li entered the room slowly, hesitated, then saw Richard and said, "*Lei-cha*." She smiled, held out her hand.

He said, "Mei-li."

They did not need further conversation to make their way up the stairs to the room with the colorful pillows. They sat on the pillows together, as if to know each other better in conversation. Richard remembered one phrase. "*Ni hao ma?*"

Mei-li's eyes flew open, and she grinned that mesmerizing grin. "*Wo zai fand an menkou dang ni hen gaoxing renshi ni xiding yao kan women ni xiang yiqui qu ma.*"

He swept her up into his arms and looked into her startled eyes. "I'm happy, too. You look lovely." He spun her around with a waltz in his head. "We can be happy together any time you want. Time with you is what I want. Your smile thrills me."

The grin gone, and serious in her manner, she put her finger to his lips. He felt her pull him down onto the pillows. His shirt slipped off. He opened her wrap, closed his eyes and felt her firm, warm body against his chest. With no further talk he fondled and entered her. Her usual combination of softness and physicality that he loved had hardened, turned into almost routine motions, and he knew she was troubled.

He lay naked with her and cast his gaze over her golden breasts, smooth shoulders, and shapely arms. A dark bruise marred the smoothness of her upper arm. "What happened here?" He whispered as he stroked the spot with care. She said something and shook her head and rolled away. His survey continued on down her rounded thighs. They made love again, but she seemed unusually passive.

He rose from the pillows and dressed without speaking, concerned about the lack of the enthusiasm that she had shown him, so different from the previous times they had been together. He tried to remember the phrase Ma-Wei taught him. She lay snuggled into the pillows, under her head the soft, silk colors emphasizing her beauty. She looked sad.

"Zee one hen you kay."

That brought a weak smile to her lips but a quizzical frown to her forehead. She shook her head. He bent down, kissed her. "I had a very nice evening. Wonderful as always," he said, but it was only nice, not wonderful. "I'll come see you again soon." He descended to the shop and left, pondering the sadness in her and the dark bruise.

A WEEK LATER Webb, Apun, and Richard opened several of the sixteen wooden opium chests they'd kept. Split panels and watermarks evidenced the shipwreck. Virtually all the chests showed some kind of damage. Richard's heart sank. Had Kung's man selected all the undamaged chests? Did Kung get damaged opium?

If he got damaged goods, he wouldn't pay the rest of the money he owed. Richard had already received good money that he hadn't expected, but this could ruin his plans with Kung.

Watermarks discolored the packages of raw opium inside the first chest they opened. Webb asked, "Do you suppose the opium is ruined?"

"I don't know. Would a wetting really matter?"

Apun opined that the brown stains reduced value regardless of the effect on the drug itself. "Priest at Taoist Monastery say for smoke, opium must cook in water. Priest say cook opium. Water and brown go away. No ruin drug."

The practical Webb asked, "How do we cook it?"

Deep in the city, Apun located an unsavory back alley factory that prepared opium for a price. The place cooked ten of the sixteen chests, reducing the weight and leaving them with twelve chests full of one-pound packages ready to smoke, sell, or trade.

"You know that Apun is certain to have received some squeeze from that opium factory," said Webb over a dinner of chopped Chinese-style chicken and vegetables.

"I'm sure of it," Richard said. "That was my opium; I should share in some of that squeeze, in all fairness." Sunchong had secretly taken squeeze from the Taiping weapons trade; Apun had squeezed the boatman who ferried silver out, and many other compradors squeezed regularly. Of the three Russells in Hankow, only Apun currently collected money by taking advantage of Chinese methods considered unethical by the Americans. The partners evidently let it happen for the sake of a trade or did not know about it at all. Why not use Chinese methods too?

Webb had a different concern. "Apun gets Russell money to use for bribes and expenses. He does not account for what he does with that money. He could keep some himself and we'd not know."

"Shanghai seems satisfied with the profits we send, and has not questioned our accounting," Richard said. "We need to discuss this with Apun. I'm thinking, why not take some opportunities ourselves?" said Richard. If he was ever to get home with savings, he had to change to some different ideas.

The two Americans told Apun that they knew he took squeeze, expenses, bribes, and kickbacks regularly when he conducted Russell business. Richard, trying a subtle threat, suggested to Apun that the extra money Apun earned, such as keeping part of his expense money, ought to be accounted for in their reports to Shanghai. Webb supported Richard's implications by describing the financial effect of the practices.

The implications were clear, but Apun remained typically expressionless, except that his sly smile betrayed the truth of what they had said. Nevertheless, under the threat, Apun agreed to account for all his expense money, including bribes paid and received. After further persuasion, he acknowledged that he added squeeze for himself by bargaining without translating and that his salary, without squeeze, paid him well for translating.

Richard agreed to let Apun keep the Chinese methods of squeeze on business he found or negotiated without reporting to the company but insisted that in business he had nothing to do with, as when he translated only, the opportunities should belong to Richard and Webb. Between themselves, Richard and Webb agreed to share equally a percentage of all squeeze, fees, and payments other than prices, services, and expenses from customers that came to either of them. When their lengthy conversation concluded, the three Russell employees had developed a veritable partnership.

Turning to Webb, Richard said, "We are six hundred miles from the Russells, and I expect that we can report finances without revealing our arrangements. From now on, let's not be afraid of Chinese methods."

Richard had heard nothing regarding the opium shipment Kung Loong had received. Possible water damage concerned him, and he wanted to collect the second half of his payment.

"Did your opium shipment arrive?" he asked Kung.

Kung glared at him. "Opium come from shipwreck, no?"

He got the opium, Richard thought, *but he has kept my deposit.* Richard wanted to deny that, but a small voice said that Kung knows already. "Yes," he said, a morsel of morality left in him.

"Fookie tell me. You try cheat with damaged opium."

Richard tensed for argument. *Be steady. This is not a tea negotiation.* He turned on his angry face. "Go to hell, you scoundrel. Fookie took the best cases. You'll dilute it anyway and sell for ten times what it's cost you."

Kung stared deeply into Richard's eyes and held his own angry face for a long moment. Then he pushed back from the desk and laughed heartily and long, and then stopped, suddenly serious. "Fookie inspect before take. Fookie bring all dry opium from *Ann Melot.*"

Richard knew Kung's games, so the deposit account still worried him. He breathed a deep sigh. "Good. Pay me the rest of the price."

Kung registered displeasure. "You no keep account to buy goods?"

"Another time I will make deposits to save money I earn. Now, you owe me for opium. Time to pay."

Kung refused. Richard stood up. Red-faced, he glared back at Kung. "Damn you. You owe me that money. We agreed. I trusted you to make two payments. Never again." He pounded the desk hard so that it jumped.

"I keep payment until you do something for me."

Richard had already decided to deposit any extra earnings with Kung's bank when placing money in his Russell account might raise questions. "I've already done something for you. Pay me."

The experts in faked anger argued. Kung agreed finally to pay Richard, in exchange for Richard's agreement to borrow with cash or opium collateral when he needed a loan to make a purchase. They shook hands and parted amicably as they had done so often before. Richard immediately shipped his money to his family's bank in London.

OVER THE NEXT few months, Richard accumulated extra savings by accepting commissions or kickbacks for arranging shipping and storage for Chinese buyers, and, true to his word, he deposited his take with Hankow Merchants Bank.

One morning, Kung invited Richard to his elegant home. Richard rode Brutus to the address Kung gave him, entered, and looked about for a moment before Kung met him.

Without formality Kung said, "I want you do something for me."

"What is that?"

"Steamer at Russell dock leave this afternoon. I need fast ship to Shanghai."

"That steamer is full. No more spaces for cargo," Richard said.

"This important. Not take much space."

"I would have to unload something a customer has already paid for. I cannot do that to other customers."

Kung reached into his desk. "What cost to move other cargo?"

"Need to pay back a customer, maybe hire a stevedore. But no can do."

Kung pulled out a bag of coins. "Take these. Enough for ship and fee for you."

The Chinese way to trade, Richard judged. He might be shipping treasure. Richard judged the bag's weight, took out the coins and counted the silver.

"Get your goods to the dock in two hours," Richard said, pocketing the bribe.

RICHARD HAD NOTICED a fine porcelain shop on Chung Lu. He arranged with the owner to buy for six months his entire production of English-style teacups with handles, saucers, dinner plates, and serving dishes, painted in bright blue and white Chinese designs. For this, the owner would kick back 5 percent of each shipment. Easy profits swamped Richard's earlier qualms about selling ballast, and he never thought again about supporting a human cargo of poverty-stricken Chinese.

"I want to borrow money to buy porcelain," he told Kung. They arranged a loan with interest and required deposit. Richard made the deposit and made the sale promptly. In three weeks he was free of debt to Kung. Plus, he was richer after kickbacks and squeezed profits.

Conflicted transactions no longer bothered his conscience, except once, when he paid such a large bribe that he lost money trying to steal a contract from a rival Chinese. This reminded him of what he had done to Simon Brown, and a prick of conscience jabbed, but it soon passed. Chinese tactics violated American and European ethical scruples, but Richard figured that if he acted in one way with exclusively Chinese transactions and differently with Europeans, he could maintain his reputation for honesty. Chinese traders viewed his lucrative moves as clever and expected.

Richard had not written to his mother for several months, and the evening before the mail boat was to leave, he sat in his colorful home, grinned with his success, wondered about the war at home, took out his pen, paper, and blotting sand, and scratched with energy.

"My very dear Meto, How sorry I am that I was obliged to miss a mail and not write to you. I never was so busy in my life since coming to Hankow." He followed with the usual about family, friends, and his health.

"It's a pity that Massachusetts and S. Carolina cannot do their own fighting without getting the rest of us by the ears. I am more anxious than I can express that the Union Army may be successful so that the union be preserved. I am glad to hear that General McClellan is capable and popular. Do not be discouraged, for all will doubtless come out well in the end.

"Russell & Co. have expressed themselves pleased with my management of their business thus far, and if I can give entire satisfaction for one year more, I hope to receive my appointment as a partner. I can tell you that I am learning the business methods in this miserable place and have improved my production." He told her no details about the business methods.

Remembering her response to his note about Dora Delano, he also added, "I do not like any of the ladies I have met in China except Mrs. Ed Cunningham. I do not see much ladies' society." The letter, like his father's, hid what he was really doing and went off with the mail boat in the morning.

44

Throughout the winter and into the next year, Richard bought and sold to Chinese commodities that Russell & Co. disdained, such as salt, lumber, foods, and Chinese-grown opium. Opium served him to resell, to use in bribes, and to trade. His modest personal saving he diversified among the historically sound financial firms, Russell & Co.; Baring Bros., London; and Uncle Samuel's firm. By the river's rise in the spring, his Hankow Merchants Bank account held over $20,000 US.

He occasionally relieved the pressures of business by riding Brutus into the countryside. The route took him past the wall being constructed for Hankow's defense, a stone and mud-plaster barrier about twelve feet tall. They rode through the marshes and fields, where Brutus picked his way along irrigation ditches and among bent women picking vegetables. Several times Richard noticed a wall-worker urinating into the irrigation water, disturbing the insects and polluting the ditches. He rode quickly past the smells and finally into open land and woods that in time became as familiar as those in the green Massachusetts hills. The fresh air rushed over him as Brutus trotted and galloped more smoothly than he had expected from a horse descended from the rough Mongolian war horses of Genghis Kahn. As the hooves pounded under him, the ground flashed by and the breezes whipped through his hair, Brutus's shaggy mane waved, and it all refreshed his spirit.

All this time he did not forget the luscious Mei-li and her pillows above the tailor shop. Liaisons with Mei-li from time to time all fall and into the winter kindled his energy, cured any tiredness, and got him laughing again. Even when his bowels pained him, her caresses settled any problem.

It had been over a month into the new year since he'd seen her. He pushed into the shop as usual. This time he found her arguing with her father. Over some sewing job, he supposed. When they saw him, the argument stopped immediately. The tailor rushed forward to greet him. Mei-li backed into the doorway to the stairs. Richard paid and stepped toward her with a broad smile.

She did not return his smile this time. Unusual with her—she had always been happy to see him. He followed her upstairs as usual, savoring the undulations of her body. The pillows lay in disarray. Mei-li dug for her silk patchwork pillow, hugged it, and flopped onto the other bigger ones. He saw no sign of her usual cheer.

"What is wrong? I have come now. I'm sorry it has been so long. Business has kept me away. Let me hug you. That will feel good again."

She did not understand but she held out one arm to him. The other held the pillow against her cheek. She wasn't rising to him, as if she did not care to be with him. He did not wait for her to come to him. He disrobed quickly without her help and knelt on the bed. She lay passive while he undid her clothing. He lay next to her and began kissing her smooth golden shoulders, up to her neck, around the neck. The pillow interfered, so he pulled it away. Then he saw it, a dark, fresh welt on her cheek. Mei-li moaned and turned away from him.

"What happened? I heard you arguing with your father. Did he hit you?" He raised a fist to help her understand his question. She misunderstood. She flinched and shut her eyes. She did not try to talk, but when he put his arm down, she hesitated, then wrapped both her arms around him and squeezed. A slight trembling made him realize that she was crying.

He held her until she stopped crying. She wiped her eyes on a pillow, then reached for Richard and pulled him into the pillows with her. They made love, not with giggles and tickles, but with a gentle passion, a relief, a tenderness.

When they had done and rested, Richard said tenderly, "I must go now. I know you can't tell me what's happened. I hope you understand my feeling for you. I want to believe you do. You are sad. I care for you even more when you are sad. But I want you to feel happy. I pray that you will. When I come back, we'll have fun again. Get some rest. Tomorrow will be a better day."

She said nothing, but tears welled up again as he kissed her good-bye.

45

" THE GOOD WORK in Hankow that you have built can continue," Richard read in Cunningham's dispatch. He
thought of the secret squeeze he and Webb had received, and an
inward snicker overcame guilt that they had gotten away with it.
"Business shipping to the East Coast is difficult because of the
war," Cunningham wrote, "but California business holds promise. Mr. Grew and I want you to consider finding goods to ship
to California, particularly San Francisco."

San Francisco. As reported in the occasional city newspapers,
Americans were not fighting in California, but making money
there, digging gold and silver mines, building new cities. That
night, Richard dropped into bed, tired and ready to dream about
American cities in peaceful California, a bustling land of cattle
and gold. Suddenly, he jumped from the bed. Pain tore through
his bowels. By a hair's breadth he made it to the chamber pot before his insides exploded. He staggered back to bed, bent over to
relieve the sting of the diarrhea. An acidic stench followed him.
In a few hours he was feeling normal again. He slept a little, and
in the morning got back to work.

On the second day after the diarrhea attack, while working
in the godown, he felt uneasy again. He raced out to the alley
behind the godown, where he relieved himself as the Chinese
did—in the gutter. Over the next few days, the diarrhea struck

again and again, day and night. He got weaker, and could only put in a few hours at his desk. After a particularly sleepless night, he was feverish, huddled in bed, and decided to stay there. He could not focus on Meto's picture or anything else.

"You need some help. Something is seriously wrong," Webb said. "I hope it is not the dysentery. Did you eat something polluted?" Webb found some laudanum in Richard's chests and served him two spoons full. The opium tincture did no good. Richard could hardly speak. He ate nothing and drank little.

He whispered to Webb, "Need ... doctor."

"There are no doctors here. I'll send a messenger to Shanghai," Webb said. "It may take several weeks."

"Quickly ..."

The invalid's yellowish skin and dull eyes worried the entire household. Ma-Wei tried to sooth him with wet cloths to chew on. Apun found a tub and filled it with cold water, and Ma-Wei bathed him to cool the fever. The diarrhea continued. With little to eat, Richard endured dry spasms and cramps all day.

The next morning, Richard opened his eyes enough to see Apun and Webb but said nothing. A small Chinese man in a wrinkled ankle-length cream-colored robe followed the two into the room. The man's eyes lidded, his mouth pouted, and thin black hair circled his lips. A second Chinese man, apparently an assistant to the first, carried into the room a large red lacquer box covered with Chinese characters.

"Yung Yuan," Apun introduced the man. "Doctor from temple. He help you."

Richard protested a feeble, "How ...?"

He tried to sit up but fell onto his side with a groan.

"This is the only available help in Hankow," Webb said. "We got good recommendations about this man. He is a Taoist healer. He can help you."

The healer said nothing as he stroked the sides of his mustache. He studied the patient, pulled out Richard's tongue to observe a thick yellow coating, smelled Richard's sour breath, felt the pulse on Richard's wrists and neck, and mumbled something. He then lifted from his bag a cloth package and unrolled it.

"Stay on back," Apun translated the healer's words. With Ma-Wei's hand on his shoulder, Richard stayed on his back. He tried to lift his head but could barely glimpse what was happening. The healer pulled up Richard's nightshirt to reveal his legs. Offended, Richard tried to push it back down but couldn't.

The healer moved ceremoniously, smoothly. He opened the cloth package and set it on the table. His back to Richard, he said something, then slowly turned to face Richard, holding an eight-inch-long needle between the ends of his thumb and index finger and stepped to Richard's left leg. Then Richard saw the needle.

"No ... no ... what?" he said weakly.

"*Zusan-li,*" the healer said, apparently explaining the treatment. His voice was calm. He held the needle over Richard's left leg. Richard twitched to avoid the jab.

"Lie still," said Apun and Ma-Wei together. "Relax."

Ma-Wei put a hand on his leg. Richard braced for the pain. He tensed as the healer slowly, easily injected the needle just below his kneecap. And left it there. *That didn't hurt.*

Yung Yuan then inserted more needles into both legs. "*Lan wei xue,*" he said as he pushed a six-inch needle four inches into the right knee and spun it between his fingers, maneuvering it slightly in and out. Richard felt tired. The healer inserted needles in Richard's feet, left hand, and right ear. A mild electric sensation flashed up his thigh. His leg twitched, flopped like a fish, and stilled.

The healer spoke to Apun, who translated to Richard, "Lie quiet. No move thirty minutes. He make medicine."

He tried to pray. *At least they are killing me mercifully.* He closed his eyes. *Our Father* ... His friends were quiet. He fell asleep. Sleep lasted a few moments.

A murmur half-woke Richard; he wanted to sleep but heard the healer slowly, deliberately speak to the assistant, and open the lacquer box, revealing a series of small drawers. Yung Yuan opened a drawer and took out a root, which the assistant then ground with a stone mortar and pestle. Next, Yung pointed to more drawers, and the assistant piled into the mortar flakes that looked like dried leaves, some powder, some chopped substance, and ground them thoroughly. He gave the mixture to Yung Yuan, said something, and left the room. The healer waited silently while Richard slept again.

When Richard opened his eyes, Yung painlessly pulled the needles out of his legs. The assistant returned with a warm pot of tea brewed from the herbal mixture, which Yung poured into a cup. Apun translated, "Sit up to drink."

"*Huang Lian,*" said Yung Yuan, offering the cup. Richard sat up feeling not like he had just been awakened but strangely relaxed, and found it awkward to move. He sipped a dark, sharp liquid from the cup. He had never tasted a tea as bitter but was too weak or relaxed or sick to spit it out or resist the cup and swallowed all that the healer offered. When he finished the last of it, he dropped back on the bed and soon fell asleep again.

WEBB SAT IN Richard's room reading a paper.

"We ... bb?" Richard had woken up in a cold sweat.

"Good morning, sleepyhead," said Webb. "How do you feel?"

"I don't know. What happened? I was treated like a pin cushion, and then drank something awful."

Webb described the healer, the acupuncture needles, the assistant, and brewing the bitter tea. "You slept for about three hours.

We could see that you were perspiring heavily, but he said that was the brew working. The healer has gone."

Shortly the healer's assistant returned. He looked at Richard's tongue, felt his pulse, and studied his skin and eyes. Having no language to tell Richard anything, he left. What were they going to do next? "I hope he says something to Ma-Wei," Richard said to Webb.

Yung Yuan came again and repeated his treatment with the needles and herbal brew. After a worrying thought that needle would hurt this time, he relaxed after the first painless pierce. The herbal brew tasted no better. He slept and again woke up perspiring heavily.

Yung Yuan handed to Ma-Wei a silk bundle that was the size of his fist and looked like it was wrapped around a batch of leaves. Ma-Wei translated, "Boil bundle in water. Drink one cup every day." They exchanged a few words, and then Apun slipped a different package out of his sleeve and passed it to the healer.

Richard asked, "What did you ... give him?"

"Opium."

Richard had not had diarrhea since the first needle injections. The fever had gone. Soon he felt able to work at his desk for several hours a day, not much more. He was weak and felt like eating only a little bland food. He avoided any semblance of Chinese food. The healer's brew tasted so toxic that he tended to forget to drink it.

Ten days later, Dr. Ralph Porter, the American doctor recommended by Cunningham, arrived on the *Scotland* and immediately examined Richard. His white mustache wiggled as he looked in Richard's mouth and poked his body with his stethoscope.

Richard told him about the diarrhea. "I'm no longer feeling cramps or pain. What got into me?"

"What did that Chinaman do to you?"

"He stuck me with needles. In my legs. And ear."

"I've heard of that needle trick. Sheer poppycock. A shaman's fraud on unbelieving Chinamen."

"He also gave me a drink that tasted vile enough to kill anything."

"Including you, no doubt. You should have waited for me. You should have been bled to get rid of any infestation. I think you may have passed through a bout of dysentery."

"You mean a bout of dysentery passed through me," Richard said.

"It may only have been too much bad Chinese food. It would be best if you left this unhealthy place for a while," Dr. Porter said. "Some time in Shanghai with wholesome food and rest will be good for you now."

46

EDWARD AND CONSTANCE Cunningham had invited Richard to recuperate in their finely furnished home in the American settlement. Living with his boss, he shied away from attending their meals or teas, but Constance nursed him well. She made sure tea and biscuits were available any time he wanted; meals were plentiful, and as he strengthened, he joined them more and more often at dinner. She greeted him every morning with a smile and a tray of his favorite pancakes and syrup.

"How's my patient?" Her company cheered him, but he looked forward to the day he felt like dining with Augustus or in the firm's dining hall combating the clerks' jeers for scratching the boss's back or polishing his apples.

Richard and Constance often conversed for hours, and they walked together around the American compound for exercise. The attention embarrassed him, but Constance was so gracious and attractive that he wanted to stay in their house as long as possible. Once, she confessed that she had married Edward hurriedly a little over three years before and come to China without time to adjust to married life. She was only four years older than Richard.

"Now Edward spends all his time working, and I see little of him," she said. "It is an enjoyable diversion to have you here."

Soon after he had arrived in Shanghai, still feeling weak and resting in a silk robe in the Cunningham's parlor, Augustus and

Richard talked, delighted to meet again. "We could have used you here this winter," Augustus said. "The rebel armies have stayed near Shanghai, taken a few small cities, but haven't come close to the city. Remember Frederick Ward's troops on the barricade? They have won some battles, and the Chinese are starting to call them the 'Ever Victorious Army.'"

"I've read of the skirmishes."

"Rumors have it that Shanghai's Wu Taotai and banker Takee finance Ward."

"Takee's cohort Kung Loong has formed a new bank in Hankow," Richard said.

"Sounds like these Chinese scoundrels are getting rich while we *fanqui* fight their battles."

"Yes, they do. I've seen how they do it."

"Interesting when you think if it, but the graft is unthinkable for us, isn't it?"

"Indeed," said Richard.

AFTER THEY HAD returned from a walk one day, Richard asked Constance, "Tomorrow, will you come with me to visit the American Baptist Mission near the walled city?" They stood on the lower step of her front door, covered from a light drizzle.

"Why do you want to go there?"

"I want to visit someone." He told her about Hop Tzu, his deceased wife, and the baby girl. She listened intently while he told her of the old woman and how he and the missionary took the baby. As he talked, she shook her head at each improbable event—the theft, the beheading, the wife's death, the woman's shrieks, and how she thought missionaries ate babies.

"I want to see her, to see what she might look like as a toddler."

"What an unusual thing for you to do." Constance looked at him with questions on her face. "I'll go with you," she said, after a moment's thought. "I'd love to meet her."

He began to sense pressure in his groin, backed away from their closeness, and opened the door for her to go inside.

That afternoon, Richard sent a boy to the mission to tell Rev. Whipple of the upcoming visit. He bought a small doll dressed in a red silken robe to give Grace. In the morning, Constance and Richard rode a shuttle to the landing near the French Consulate and walked in the dirt streets through the mud-brick huts, laughing as they jumped hand-in-hand over scattered puddles. They were still laughing when Rev. Whipple met them at the mission door. Constance immediately stopped laughing, apparently remembering why they had come.

"Mr. Starr. It's been nearly a year." Whipple's voice seemed cold.

"I've been in Hankow." Then he introduced Constance.

"Charmed, I'm sure," said the Reverend. "Wait in the lounge," Whipple said before he stepped out. "You can see Grace. I'll fetch her."

Richard and Constance looked at each other, Richard wondering what Rev. Whipple had done with the child and what Constance would think about her. Constance looked nervous, as if she felt she should not be there.

A moment later, an elderly Chinese woman in a black robe entered, holding the hand of a little girl walking unsteadily beside her. The child was no longer wrinkled and ugly; her oriental eyes had become cute, her skin smooth. Grace's long, straight, raven hair was pulled away from her face in two side braids, making amusing pigtails. A yellow ribbon held each. She wore a loose red jacket over white pants. She moved toward him in a way that lived up to her name. She looked apprehensive as Richard knelt down to her level. He hoped she wasn't scared. He held out the colorful doll. After encouragement from the elderly Chinese woman, she took it. A broad smile spread across her face, dimpling her round cheeks.

"She's adorable!" Constance said.

Richard looked up to the caretaker. "Will she speak English?"

"She no speak. Little girl."

"Hello," he said. "I'm Richard." He had not talked with a child for years. "How old are you?" The caretaker spoke to her in Chinese, and Grace shyly held up one finger.

Constance came to his side and knelt before little Grace. "What pretty bows. You are a beautiful little girl." The nun translated for Grace. Her little nose wrinkled again, and she modestly turned her chin to her shoulder and smiled.

They visited for a half hour. Richard played a finger game folding his hands together to form a church, forefingers raised to a steeple, then opened the thumb doors to show her all the people inside. When the people wiggled, Grace giggled, and Richard's heart warmed. She and Constance played with the doll in the simple way that girls know.

Then it was time to leave. Richard pulled Whipple aside to talk with him before leaving. "Grace is growing into a very pretty little girl. Thank you for giving her a home and proper care." Whipple said that the old woman from whom they had taken the baby had visited several times and seemed content. "We have two additional orphaned children now. This is the beginning of an opportunity to further God's work among the heathens."

They walked back through the slum and charred remains not yet rebuilt, chatting about Grace and the visit. They passed by the burned-out areas and took a different route through the hovels. The dirt passages closed in on them, and slovenly people lounged against walls and in corners. They looked for a way out.

"Let's head back this way," Richard said.

Constance turned with him, and pointed to a woman sleeping in a corner, shaggy black hair covering her face. The woman clutched a pillow. "Look at those beautiful colors," said Constance. "I've never seen such patterns in patchwork."

"I don't believe it," Richard cried. No other pillow was like that. He ran to the woman and knelt beside her. He shook her shoulder gently. She looked up, hollow-eyed. "Mei-li!" he cried.

She rose onto an elbow. " … Lei Cha?"

He brushed the hair out of her eyes. "Mei-li, Mei-li. Why are you like this? Sleeping in the street. How did you get here? You cannot stay in the street. I will help you."

Mei-li stood slowly, stared at him, then wrapped her arms around his neck, and hung there. She began crying. He was afraid she would fall if he let go. He held her close.

"Constance, I must get her to the mission. They can feed her. Someone can translate."

Constance watched, dumbfounded.

Richard supported Mei-li with his arm around her waist. They shuffled back toward the mission. Mei-li reached back toward her pillow, the cloth that had covered her, and a small bundle of belongings.

"Constance, please bring the pillow and her other things."

Constance said, "You know her? A Chinese street woman?"

"We must get her to the mission."

"Certainly not. She's filthy … and heathen. Her rags are filled with lice and lord knows what else."

"Please Constance, do as I say."

"Get them yourself. If she can cling to you like that, she can carry them."

In spite of her remark, Constance relented, took off her wrap, piled the rags and pillow into it, rolled it up to cover them, and keep herself as clean as possible. She would have held her nose if she didn't need both hands to pick up the dirty, rumpled, odorous covers.

"Thank you. We're doing a good thing for this poor girl."

At the mission, Constance immediately dropped the rag bundle. Whipple and a Chinese youth named Peter Liu took them inside the mission's residential area. Their expressions showed that Whipple saw Mei-li as another convert to Christianity and that the youth saw a beautiful face under the black, sticky hair.

"Please help her clean up and rest. I'm sure she's hungry," Richard said.

Whipple assured him that they would help her. Peter led her slowly back to the bedroom area while Richard followed with his eyes. Whipple said, "She is a poor sinner that needs the care of Christ Jesus."

"I'd like to come back tomorrow and speak with her," Richard said. "Can someone here translate?"

"Peter speaks English quite well."

"Good. Thank you. This means a lot to me. I'll come back tomorrow."

Constance stared and said nothing while she listened and watched. Richard said to her, "We can do no more here now." He reached for her hand. "Thank you for helping."

She yanked her hand away from him without a word, turned toward the door, and strode out. Once outside, Constance headed straight to the shuttle dock.

Richard followed, taking long strides to keep up. "Constance, what's wrong?"

"That woman's been all over you. You are covered with filth."

"She needed help."

"You obviously know her."

"I can explain."

"I suppose. Are you going to rescue any more homeless tonight?"

The sarcasm was uncalled for. "Please."

They pressed on without speaking. She had seemed a more charitable person than to refuse help to a homeless girl, he thought. When they reached the dock, the shuttle was yards away. They had to wait. Richard sat on the bench. Constance stood motionless and stared out over the water.

"All right. Explain."

He could not hide the affair with Mei-li, but he was too afraid of losing Constance's friendship to admit that she was a concubine on call when he wanted her. She had become something more than that.

"She is the daughter of a merchant that I have done business with in Hankow. He introduced us."

She did not look at him. "'Introduced?'"

"She is a beautiful girl … really … and delightful company. A friend."

Constance remained distant. "How did she end up here?"

"I don't know. I recognized the silk pillow. It was a favorite in her father's … place of business."

The shuttle arrived and took them back to the compound.

The next morning, he wondered whether he would have to forage in her kitchen for his own breakfast, but Constance brought him his pancakes as usual. He had not slept much; his mind spun tales, lies, and confessions most of the night. In front of Constance, Mei-li had simply let him help her up, he told himself. He had not been able to understand Constance's attitude. Was it jealousy, revulsion, disbelief? Why the silent treatment?

He said the safe thing, "Good morning." After a moment, he ventured more, "It's good to see you."

"Richard, I have thought a lot about yesterday."

"I have, too."

"You did a charitable deed yesterday. I was wrong to act so insolent."

A welcome relief swept over him. "Thank you for help with her. Your acts were charitable as well."

"There were fine, expensive fabrics in that bundle of rags. She comes from some wealth, doesn't she?"

Richard hesitated. Mei-li had little or no wealth. "At her father's, her company gave me moments of relief from the stress of business in Hankow."

Constance said, "I know how stressed Edward can get. I foolishly thought you might have met her in one of those singsong houses."

"No. I would never go to those."

"Will you see her again?"

"I do want to find out how she ended up on the street in Shanghai." Should he ask Constance to come with him to the mission again? Clean and brushed, Mei-li's beauty will raise suspicions about his relationship. He was not ready to admit that he had a concubine. Mei-li might say more than he wanted Constance to hear. No, he thought, he wouldn't ask her. "I'll visit myself later today."

"Please tell me what she says."

Mei-li met him, her hair combed, wearing clean tunic and trousers, and a smile again on her face. The suffering she must have endured did not show in her face. Through Peter's faltering English translation she told them her story. After her mother died she lived with her father while a child. He abused her for refusing to allow him to bind her feet. Peter added that high-class men would think her less desirable with big feet. She worked hard for her father and became strong, but she feared him. When she became a woman, he sold her services to customers who came into his tailor shop. Some of these men were friendly, and she was content to lie with them. Others, however, were rough, abusive, and physical.

One day she refused to lie with a man her father had brought. He threatened to sell her to the man for money. She had a terrible fight with her father. The following night, she gathered her pillow, a small bag of rice, some cloth for blankets, and a little clothing, and ran away into the streets. To break away completely, she left Hankow by succumbing to the favors of a captain who let her sleep on his junk to Shanghai. She lived in the Shanghai streets, lost, lonely, and looking for a job using her skills in tailoring, but in spite of her normal feet, men showed interest only in her beauty, not her work experience. For food she made a little money using the hated skill she could sell.

Her beauty still entranced Richard as he listened, but his heart hurt when she talked of abuse. He felt guilty at having been part of it. His heart beat faster when she escaped, and hurt again when she became lost. She had taken a brave course, and now she will return to health. "Mei-li," he said, "I have missed you. Missed the happy hours we had together. Now it will be different."

Peter translated his words. Mei-li said, "Thank you, Lei cha, for bringing me here. I feel safe now." Peter continued translating for Richard too.

"Men will no longer abuse you for money. This makes me very happy for you."

"I happy," Mei-li said in English.

"I will go back to Hankow and may not ever see you again. I'm sorry." Her tears welled up. Richard caught the emotion. "You will be well cared for here. I hope lessons from Reverend Whipple will give you support from now on. Good bye." They embraced, and he kissed her on the cheek. She returned the platonic kiss. Peter seemed to smile as he heard Richard's farewell.

RICHARD CONVALESCED AT the Cunningham's for another four days, taking walks by himself and with Constance, meeting with Augustus. The eggshells over which he had navigated with Constance had ground away, and conversation with her became comfortable again. She did not question him about Mei-li any more. They both seemed to treat the subject as if the past no longer need affect them. Whipple sent a message that Mei-li was progressing toward conversion already and was learning that God and Jesus had rescued her. She and Peter had become good friends, he said.

Richard sat in the bedroom while Dr. Porter, black bag opened on the floor, examined him. Constance left them alone while the doctor poked, felt, listened, and looked into Richard's mouth. "Everything looks normal," he said. "You need to regain the weight you have lost and build your strength."

"Can I go back to Hankow?"

"Your best road to full strength is to get good food and be in a healthy climate. I do not think you can get that in Hankow."

"I guess I can stay at the coast a while longer." Webb and Apun certainly could tend to all that was needed to keep the business moving awhile longer. Augustus always amused him, and he hoped that he could maintain his friendship with Constance.

Dr. Porter said, "For that matter, Shanghai's climate is not the best for you either."

"I don't think Mr. Cunningham will let me go home to New York."

"Three months on the water and eating ship's food to get there? No, I'm sorry. The voyage could cause a relapse. Sea motion can upset the stomach." Dr. Porter had another suggestion. "Many who have been to Japan say that its climate is cooler and drier. You should do well there. The voyage is much shorter than going to America, and the food is fairly easy on the stomach."

Richard told the managing partner what Dr. Porter had said. "I can be more efficient if I am back to full strength. Will it be all right if I stay here a bit longer?"

"Of course," Cunningham said.

"Thank you. Thank you, too, for all the care and food you and Mrs. Cunningham have given me. I can move to an empty clerk's room now."

Cunningham stood, apparently to excuse Richard, and then he paused for a moment. "Constance is planning a visit to Japan soon. I would be most comforted if she had a trustworthy male escort. Would you escort her? You would please me and carry out Dr. Porter's advice at the same time."

47

THE *ST. LOUIS* steamed slowly up the long inlet to Nagasaki on the sixth day out of Shanghai. Constance and Richard stood by the rail together. "Edward said that the bungalow rented for us is on a hill above the city," Constance said. She put her hand on his, and they admired the first sights of Japan. They looked up at the steep green hills, dotted with small low buildings, and in the harbor floated fishing boats, potbellied cargo craft, and junks, some decorated with black and blue drapes. She turned from the view to face him. "It's sure to have a magical view down to the sea."

They entered the harbor and anchored a short ferry ride off the stone breakwater surrounding Dejima, the island entry where early Portuguese and Dutch traders had once been restricted. Leafy and flowering trees softened hills terraced with rice paddies. The water rippled clear except for mud surrounding the island; the air was crisp. Dejima's white warehouses and residences looked neat and clean. Topknots on inspectors' shaved heads bobbed as they poked through the opened luggage, looking for forbidden Christian books. Richard had ignored his Bible for over a year and had not brought it. After the inspectors waved them on, a former Russell partner, Thomas Walsh, now the American commercial agent in Japan, met them in his office a block from the landing.

Richard and Cunningham had planned to do business in the port, recently opened to American trading, and, relieved from the pressures and risks of doing business in both the American and the Chinese ways, Richard also planned to share trade opportunities with Augustus. Walsh arranged an escort to their lodging, and he agreed to meet Richard the next day.

Leaving the fishy smells in the harbor, Richard and Constance walked uphill to a small bungalow where they had views of the hills and the harbor. Paper walls and sliding panels separated the four rooms in which they would spend the next two weeks. Constance selected a bedroom with an outside door overlooking the harbor. Richard's room faced cherry blossoms in full bloom. Two chairs, a table with a single lotus flower, and a Western-style bed furnished each bedroom. A pink flower in a ceramic vase atop a low cabinet decorated a third room, where a low square table waited for them to eat their next meal.

Over the next days, Walsh introduced Richard to Japanese and European trading houses and helped arrange trades for Russell & Co. in cotton and grass cloths, silks, porcelains, and black and scarlet lacquer ware. For acquisitions to share with Augustus, Richard found good bargains in fans, silks, brightly painted vases, and some decorated lacquer boxes of various sizes. The clean, scenic city let Richard forget the squalor and dirt in China.

When alone, Constance enjoyed the quiet beauty, the company of American missionaries Jacob and Maria Griswell, tried to converse with the bungalow servants, and walked about the city.

Richard began to worry that he had been away from Hankow too long. Although confident that business was in the capable hands of Apun and Webb, he missed important squeeze opportunities and feared that someone in Shanghai would learn what he'd been doing. He made personal trades in Nagasaki, however, enjoyed outdoor air with Constance, did exercises to strengthen, and toured the city. Walsh often guided his two guests to intriguing sites such as the vermillion Sofu Kuji temple, other decorated Buddhist temples, and gardens of rock and raked sand.

Japanese servant girls on clog sandals gingerly served them clear soup with noodles, tiny quail eggs, sponge cake, red or black roe, and spiced beef and fish. Soft, smooth white fish slipped down, but Richard avoided squid and some rubbery foods. He could consume delicately flavored salads, sticky rice and raw fish, even cones of seaweed filled with unknown raw seafood. Between meals, they ate bite-sized and unusual but pleasing snacks. Hot baths, the changed climate, and clean diet restored his energy.

Constance's care, her beauty, and his own laughter lifted his spirits to levels he had not known with Annie, Dora, or any other American girls. His joy with Mei-li had had no bounds, but only lasted a few hours. Happy times with Constance had lasted for weeks. He felt strong again. At night, through the thin walls, he listened to Constance's soft noises as she washed and readied for bed. She rustled off her long dress in his fantasy, splashed her fair face, dropped a shoe, slid under her futon, and he imagined her naked, like Mei-li, lying on her back, her hair loose and flowing.

When two days remained of their stay amid spring flowers and filled with fresh, light food, Constance and Richard stood outside their bungalow admiring a black sky that shimmered with stars. A sliver of moon highlighted a night of ten thousand twinkling lights.

"A heavenly light above," Constance said.

"Hard to believe how bright the stars are," Richard said. *Why does a starry night next to an earthly beauty make my heart flutter?*

Constance squeezed his hand and laid her head against his shoulder. Richard tensed; the tingle that made him walk awkwardly returned. He pointed at the Orion constellation shining above up to his right. They looked up without speaking. He said the only thing that he dared, "Have you heard the legend of Orion, the hunter who chased beautiful maidens through the forests for seven years?"

"Chasing love?"

"Orion never caught his nymph." He put his arm loosely around her waist. He let his arm drop from her waist and pointed skyward again. "See that constellation? Seven stars—the Pleiades—Orion's seven nymphs now in heaven. Where Orion chases the heavenly girls for eternity with no hope. Seems futile to chase single girls."

She slipped her arm around his waist.

He tensed. "See that very bright star?" he said, pointing higher. "It's Venus. The goddess of love and beauty."

She turned her face to him. "This night sky shines on love." His heart fluttered. Her eyes reflected the light of the goddess of beauty. Like Orion, he was doomed for eternity never to have her. She was the wife of another.

"We must go in now," she said.

Alone in his room, Richard changed into his nightshirt and sat in the candlelight, trying to read a book on accounting principles. He could not concentrate. Standing with Constance under the stars replayed in his mind. She had touched him, looked as if she would kiss him. He had resisted temptation but by romancing the stars with a love story had encouraged her. By holding hands, putting his arm around another man's wife, he had violated every serious rule of proper social behavior he had ever learned. He listened to her night noises a while and tried not to think of Mei-li.

The sliding panel slid quietly open. Constance stepped into the room, carrying a tray of little rice cakes. "I thought these would taste good," she said. Her hair fell loose down her back and draped away from her face. Wrapped in a Japanese silken kimono, she smiled at him. A yellow sash around her small waist accentuated her hips and bosom. Her tray held a pink rose, two small decanters and two tiny cups.

Richard moved his legs aside as she set the tray on his table and sat next to him on the bed. She poured two cups of *sake*— clear rice wine—and held one out to him. He took it. She raised hers. He raised his. Then he downed it in one gulp. Immediately his throat was on fire. He coughed, spit air, tried to generate saliva to wash it down, and coughed again. Constance burst out laughing.

He gained control of his breathing, his face flushed. He saw her laughing, and he burst into laughter too. Together they giggled, as they tasted the rice cakes. "Soaks up the *sake*," Richard said. She giggled again. He refilled his cup and took a sip. Constance sipped her cup, and chewed another rice cake. Her lovely lips moved in an entrancing pucker.

"Sticky stuff," she said. Richard thought she said 'icky' and laughed. "Here, try this." She fed him a bite dipped in *sake*. He munched and poured her another *sake*.

"This sash is most uncomfortable." Constance took it off. Richard helped her unwind it. The sash caught under her. He reached around her; her kimono slipped open. A bare leg showed. Richard pulled the silk back to cover her shapely thigh. She opened it again and put her arms around him. Her lips found his mouth, and they kissed long and hard. Together they fell back on the bed. He felt her tongue search his mouth. His nightshirt twisted, and he pulled it off. He hugged her soft breasts against his chest. Nipples hard. Skin soft, smooth, white. Richard hard. He rolled onto his back. She played with the little hairs on his chest and stomach. When her leg wrapped across him, he felt he would burst.

Her hand guided him …

Edward Cunningham met them at the wharf when the shuttle from the steamer *Hu-Quang* landed, still leaking its boiler smoke. The married Cunninghams embraced; Constance seemed happy to see Edward as if nothing other than sightseeing had happened in Nagasaki. Richard blushed inwardly. He shook Cunningham's hand. "Good to be back, sir." Then he thanked Constance for her hospitality. They had done improper things, and he had liked them very much.

Russell held mail for Richard. The edges of a letter from home were singed as if it had been rescued from a fire. Had there been a fire on the mail ship? Did Meto get it too close to a candle? He read quickly, anxiously. "The government is taxing everything," he read. "William is at the Naval Academy. Things are difficult for the family." She had seen no fighting and thought General McClellan was capable and popular, but the war was not over.

He wished that Massachusetts and South Carolina had fought their own battles without getting all the rest in the abolitionist fight. It seemed to him that the South must soon be defeated. He hoped that the money he sent had reached home. Richard had been able to send Meto larger sums through Uncle Samuel than ever before, but he had found it taxing to write anything of interest to her about Hankow. For some time he had not written home, so he described for Meto his illness and recovery in Japan. "Mrs. Cunningham has been very kind to me," he wrote, not mentioning their unchaperoned behavior, "and I like her very much."

Edward Cunningham wanted to see Richard the morning after he and Constance returned. "Thank you for looking after Constance in Japan. Constance says she had a delightful time. Loved the sights and food. Walsh reports that you were able to make some trades, too. Good work."

Cunningham's familiar voice sounded like a far-away echo. *Thanking me for making you a cuckold?* "Thank you for letting me go with Mrs. Cunningham. I'm glad I could help."

Conversation with Cunningham at meals and parties often tied Richard's tongue. Guilt nearly swallowed him. He lay awake at night brooding. He had committed adultery. He tried to avoid Constance, although he longed to go to her. She ignored him at times, too. Once, he thought that maybe she was practiced at covering unfaithful liaisons. At gatherings, when put together with others, they politely reminisced about the sights and food of Nagasaki, but they found no private time. He wouldn't know what to say if they did. She once stunned him by telling him in the company of others, "I saw the Pleiades on the last night— Orion has not caught them yet."

He had briefly stared at her, then said, "Really?"

The sooner he got to Hankow, the better.

48

I N A LITTLE over a week, Richard stepped ashore onto the dock
where Apun and Webb waited to welcome him. "Good to
have you back," said Webb. The Russell & Co. trading post had
performed well in his absence. Webb peppered him with questions about his health, his trip to Nagasaki, events in Shanghai,
and rebel activities. Richard had questions too.

American traders representing Augustine Heard had opened a
two-agent American house, and they imported expensive Malwa
opium shipments. Steam and sailing ships docked more often than
they had before he had left, and goods moved quickly within
China on foreign-registered ships. Chinese shippers used the
Russell dock to transship cargoes, earning a steady stream of
docking and storage fees for Russell & Co. and squeeze for the
Hankow Russells.

Webb had sent gold and silver to Shanghai hidden in crates
or barrels of water, tea, silks, or matting. A sizable treasure also
rested in the Hankow godown, securely locked in the ironclad
vault. The Hankow post's growth would draw careful scrutiny
in Shanghai. Did all ship landings match docking charges? Did
all cargo quantities match the prices? Had any unnecessary fees
been paid? Richard saw many more entries based on records of
Chinese shippers, captains, and junks than before. Chinese numbers seemed correctly recorded in Apun's records and Webb's

books, and numbers balanced where they should. Webb managed the finances so that their personal and separate accounts steadily grew and remained untraceable. Richard's personal saving also grew. The extracurricular collections by the three men seemed well hidden from any review in Shanghai offices. Richard's and Webb's balances, added together, in Kung Loong's Hankow Merchants Bank swelled to nearly $45,000.

Spring greenery had begun sprouting in the nearby woods and fields. The river shone in the sun, bright warming air fanned gently and blew away any concerns about the moral cost to the three partners' hidden business methods. Trading continued well all summer, and in the fall the weather began to cool, and the water level dropped.

As DUSK FELL on one of the coolest fall evenings, Richard decided to make a quick inventory of recent additions to the warehouse in preparation for a morning steamer arrival. He left for the godown while Webb read Melville's new book, *Moby Dick*. The wind turned icy near the water, making Richard shudder and hug his jacket close as he fumbled with the godown's locks. In the warehouse, a lantern he held before him lit the way between crates and cartons, making it easy to read markings, names, and logos of Western shippers or steamers. The stack of recently landed Chinese goods he was looking for stood near the vault, so he set the lantern down on a crate to examine them. He thought he saw some broken boards on the outside wall about twenty feet away. He stepped around the iron vault in which ingots and coins had been locked and stopped still. He heard a rustle, a scurrying footstep. Movement flashed behind some crates. On the wall was a shadow outline. A man crouched.

"*Ting!* Don't move! *Ting!*" Richard called.

A Chinese vagrant stood up. A dirty tunic hung on his bones, and the man said nothing. Richard stepped toward him. The lantern's light flashed on a knife in the man's hand. Richard had no weapon. Thinking to let the man escape as long as he took nothing, Richard moved toward the door to the back alley and, keeping an eye on the thief, managed to open the door. Cold air rushed in. He stood aside, faced the thief, and waved him out. "*Zou*—Go!" he shouted. The thief held the knife as if to attack. Richard snatched a stave leaning against the wall, and stepped away from the door. "You can go. *Zou*," he said. The thief did not move. Richard motioned with the stave. "*Zou. Zou.* Go."

The thief jumped toward his escape, then turned abruptly. "*Aiee-Yaaah*! He lunged at Richard, thrusting the knife ahead. Desperation and fear sucked at his hollow cheeks. Richard swung the stave. It struck against the man's bony shoulder. The thief staggered, slipped off the threshold, and fell into the street. A sickening crack. His head snapped on the stone step.

The thief did not move. Rivulets of blood seeped from under him, flowing red between the stones. Kneeling beside the man, Richard tried to staunch the blood, his hands and handkerchief soaked red as he pulled the knife from under the body. Helpless, Richard watched life leave the man.

"Help! Help! Someone!" he called.

Devastated, Richard knelt over the limp body and the blood. He had killed a man, not a warring soldier or a rodent. His body shook even as he inhaled the cold to get his breath. He didn't mean to hurt the man.

Richard could not stand. He rocked onto his haunches, still holding the man's bloody knife. Did the thief take anything? He felt in the man's pockets. He saw the stave lying on the floor.

Without warning, two imperial soldiers appeared. Before Richard could react, one soldier grabbed his arm and pulled him up onto his feet. The second knelt by the bloody body and spoke to the other. Two more soldiers joined them, jabbering and laughing, apparently drunk. The four soldiers surrounded Richard and addressed him in Chinese. This caused more jabber and laughs among the drunks, who poked at the hapless foreigner. The men bound Richard's wrists behind his back and marched him away from the scene. The dead thief lay behind on the ground.

Richard struggled in vain. "It was an accident! He was a thief. He fell."

The soldiers laughed at his efforts and seemed to joke to each other as they yanked on his bound wrists, sending pain into his shoulders. He only understood the word "*fanqui*," and succumbed to his helplessness. They marched him to the water, Richard barely aware of his whereabouts, and with pulls and shoves, forced him down into a sampan, knocking him off his feet. He sat on the wet floor, thankful not to be in the river, but his arms useless, while the soldiers rowed. The sampan landed; the soldiers pulled him out and hauled him stumbling through streets now in total and frigid darkness. Everything passed in a blur. Along the way, two Chinese uniformed officers confronted the drunken party. These new officers acted like police and sternly spoke to the soldiers. The police walked them all into a plastered building. Humiliated, bruised, shivering, and bewildered, Richard was dragged into a rude hallway and left there with a guard carrying a stick.

In minutes that seemed like hours, a robed official opened a nearby door and led Richard inside, where he and one of his captors lined up before a high desk guarded by an angry green dragon hanging over it. Three guards flanked Richard and the relatively sober soldier—one guard armed with a club like a bowling pin, another with a stick, and the third a whip. The guards stepped to the side when a magistrate climbed behind the desk.

The mustached mandarin yawned and then frowned down on him. The official gestured and grunted something. In apparent response, the soldier knelt before the magistrate. Richard saw what he was supposed to do, but, unsure of his balance, he hesitated. He was too slow. A guard whacked him behind the knees with the stick. Richard dropped onto his knees. The guard shoved him on the back, and his head banged forward onto the floor, a forced kowtow.

One of the guards said something to the magistrate and handed him the knife caked with blood. Then the soldier delivered a speech from his knees, apparently telling how he and his companions had found Richard with a dead man. Richard watched the magistrate lift his eyebrows at times during the speech, scowl over at Richard, ask questions, and peer at the knife, and when the two had stopped the grunting and squeaking, the magistrate dismissed the soldier. Then he looked directly into Richard's eyes and delivered a gruff unintelligible diatribe.

Richard started to explain, "It was an accident ..."

Another lecture from the magistrate interrupted. The dragon on the wall bared his teeth and glared over the magistrate's shoulder. Two guards jerked Richard to his feet, and the magistrate unrolled a parchment and added a row of authoritative scratching to record one more nighttime crime processed.

Richard was marched out, led past stone walls. A torch lit the way to another building, where he was shoved into a rough ten-foot-square cell. The stout wooden door slammed shut. Light from the torch went away with the door slam, and he collapsed into a corner.

49

DURING A BREAKFAST of fruit, fish and toast, Webb asked Apun and Ma-Wei if they had seen Richard. When they had looked at each other and both said no, Webb said, "I suspect that he might have spent the night with a local girl."

Apun also thought that Richard had found a girl. "Why not?" he said. "He always come back."

"When he gets here we can tease him and find out." Webb finished his meal and went to his office to work on the books. By noon no one had seen Richard. Webb remembered that he had gone to the godown in the late afternoon.

"You see him go?" said Apun.

"Yes, but I was reading. Barely noticed."

"Say where go?"

"No. He was on foot. We'll go to the godown," Webb said. A light snow was falling.

All four horses stood in the stable. As usual when a ship was not tethered at the dock, the godown was quiet. The three rummaged through the business rooms, then searched the warehouse between stacks of crates and rows of bales.

"There. This lantern is empty," Webb said, shaking it. "He had it when he left last evening."

They made a search near the back door. "Here," Apun called. On the floor, in a rarely inspected area of loaded Chinese goods, lay a broken board and Richard's inventory book, its pages splayed in disorder.

"The back door is open," Ma-Wei said. A stave lay on the floor near the door, bloody handprints on it. Just outside the door, more blood clotted on the cobblestones.

"That's a lot of blood," Webb said, now scared. His imagination conjured worries about an accident, or mob attack. "What happened here? If he were unhurt, he would have come back."

They stepped outdoors, saying nothing. The others, fixed on the bloodstains, remained quiet too, each in his own thoughts. "He could be badly hurt. Richard is in trouble."

According to the treaties, foreigners in trouble were supposed to be controlled by their own authorities, and Richard was the only American authority in Hankow. A consul had not yet arrived. Here, the Chinese city authorities may not know of the treaty. There were no doctors. Where would Richard have gone?

Webb said, "I'll go to the British house and ask if they've seen him or heard of anything."

He told Apun, "Go to Chen Lan Taotai. He knows Richard." The Emperor's liaison with Hankow foreigners, Chen Lan was supposed to know what foreigners were doing.

"It late. Office close." Apun said. "I go in morning."

"Pray that he is safe," said Webb to Apun and Ma-Wei, as he left for the nearest British house.

A LITTLE WINDOW high in the wall let cold air and wisps of snow into the stone jail. Richard awoke nearly frozen after a fitful, mostly sleepless night, curled in the corner. Surprised that his bonds had been taken off, he stretched his arms, flapped them to get blood flowing, rubbed his wrists, and splayed his legs out in front of him. A dirt floor, a wood ceiling, four stone and chipped plaster walls with only one little window confined him. He held onto a protruding stone and pulled himself up to let the sleep unfold. Numb with cold, utterly confused, stiff and sore, especially behind his left knee, he walked around the small cell. His head began to clear. He needed to urinate.

The cell remained in deep wintry shadow. Lichen and mold spread in ancient smudges on the rough walls. A line of ants marched across the packed dirt floor following leaders into an invisible crack in the stones. In a corner was a hole that looked like mice had bored into the earth, so he relieved himself into it. He paced the room again and began talking to himself, wondering what Chinese justice would do to him.

"Am I going to be suspended by the neck in a cage standing on tiptoe while my head stretches off? Maybe it would be easier to die if they did behead me." His head wasn't clear yet. "No. Don't think that way … Not yet."

This day, he thought, he will find out what they are going to do. They weren't supposed to interfere with foreigners, and that is certainly what the soldiers had done. He would be released soon.

He lay on a narrow board he saw on the floor and stared at the planks in the ceiling. A spider crawled slowly along as if it searched for something to eat. Soon the spider reached the window, and there it began spinning a web in the corner to catch any bugs entering from outside.

Richard rolled to his side so he could examine the far wall. Stone and mud mortar punctuated with holes and cracks. A pattern of cracks among the moldy smudges looked like the oak tree outside the barn at "The Pines," his family's Massachusetts farm. He blinked, and the picture in the cracks disappeared. He tired of the stony view, rolled to the near wall, and fell asleep again.

When he woke up it was still daylight, still cloudy out the little window, but the snow had stopped. He stood and walked around the cell. In a few moments, he used the mouse hole again, then had a bowel movement, which he scraped into the hole. It didn't fit, so he enlarged the hole with his foot, covered it with dirt, and tamped it down. The odor filled the room. The board served to push dirt into a pile to cover any more foulness he might need to bury later. He paced the room in circles, then the opposite direction, then around again. The pacing dispersed the cold for a while, but it returned when he stopped. Unable to do anything, he stood by the door and listened. It was time they brought him some food and water. He heard nothing.

"I'm hungry!" he called, and banged his fists on the thick, wooden door.

He heard nothing from anybody for hours. No guards, no visitor. No one knew where he was. He didn't know where he was. Once he thought he heard someone beyond the door moan quietly. The shadows deepened. Richard itched. He scratched his head, and the more he scratched the more it itched. The night came. He lay down in his corner and huddled with himself for warmth and sleep.

He looked around as he woke up for the second day. Dim daylight had replaced the blackness. He smelled must and urine and heard silence. He looked for food, maybe slipped under the door, but found nothing. No water either. They must be going to release him.

He rolled his head left and right to ease out kinks, ran his fingers through his hair, and scratched. He lay on the floor with his eyes closed. Disturbing thoughts crept into his head. *Apun and Webb don't know where I am.* "God, give me enough faith. Please God, bring help, get me out of here," he prayed aloud for the first time in over a year. The walls did not answer. He rested his head on his curled arms and tried to sleep again to keep his mind from racing through futile ideas to get a message out—send a paper airplane out the window, but he had no paper; catch a mouse, tie a handkerchief to it and put it out the window, but he had plugged the mouse hole; yell out the window, but he saw no one. How long will he be kept here?

He stood and paced. He dropped onto the floor and forced twenty-five push-ups. He stood, swung and stretched his arms, pumped deep knee bends. No sounds reached him. How fast could he run ten times around the room? Caught his breath and did it again. The frenetic activity warmed the room.

He had once read a novel in which the imprisoned hero had kept track of time to keep his sanity. As night fell again, he scratched a mark on the wall with a stone. "Should I mark two days or three nights?" he asked himself.

BACK IN HANKOW, Webb, riding on Caesar, galloped eight blocks to the British Concession and burst past a doorman into the house's parlor. "Please, where is the head agent here now? Was there anyone on watch last night?"

The doorman said nothing but managed a formal, "Wait here."

When William Bailey, a merchant for Jardine, appeared, Webb did not wait for introductions. "Richard Starr has not been seen since last night," he told Bailey. "Have you or anyone here seen him? Have you heard any stories about foul play or ruckus last night?

"Sorry, old fellow." said the Brit, as he motioned Webb into a chair and called for tea. "We haven't heard of anything of the sort. Bet he's found some doxy and is having a downright good time. He'll turn up, tail between his legs."

Webb fidgeted, his left leg bouncing rapidly, unfolding and folding his hands, trying not to blurt out, "Damn it ... someone take this seriously." A young man with a sharp nose dropped his paper and looked up.

"Pardon me, but I may have heard something. I overheard laughter some distance from our house. Most unusual at night."

Webb perked up at this news. "We saw blood in the street near our godown," he said.

"Laughter rarely leads to bloodshed," said Bailey, a broad grim spreading across his wine-pink face. "The doxy probably poked Starr with her elbow while he got overly fresh with her."

These people aren't going to help at all, thought Webb, but the story was a clue that someone may have been out in the streets at night. Webb rose from his chair and left without further word.

Apun remembered well the previous empty promises that had come from law and order magistrate Li-Chih's office when Chinese gangs had obstructed their workers, and he did not expect much help this time. Nevertheless, the office clerk readily took Apun's coins to let him look through the records of the night's activities. He rapidly scanned through reports—a theft of firewood, a fight over a gambling debt, a steering oar missing from a sampan, a collision between rickshaws. Then one report caught his attention—a complaint that drunken young soldiers from Wuchang had come to Hankow the afternoon before and harassed several merchants.

He walked briskly to the Chen Lan Taotai's foreign liaison offices. Without looking up from papers on his desk, a slovenly clerk told Apun that he could see the Taotai, but that he was not in, and he would be back the following day. Apun jingled the coins in his sleeve. "I have important business for his honorable personage Chen Lan. In your position, you no want Chen Lan official rage now." The clerk, at these words, looked up from filling out his papers, and Apun said, "The Taotai will be available for me. You will tell him I represent the American merchant of Russell & Co. on a matter of urgency that may be rewarding for him."

The clerk held out his hand, as he said, "Taotai be back in morning."

"He will know you obstruct official duty." Apun held out a silver coin and said, "The Taotai will see me now."

The clerk took the coin. "Go. Enter office."

The Chen Lan Taotai was not there.

RICHARD STOOD ON his board the third morning, shook his head to rid the effects of a frightening dream he could not remember, stretched overhead, touched his toes, did ten jumping jacks, and began walking.

"God must be punishing me," he said aloud. He raised his hands. "God forgive me." His head hung. "Help me. This miserable country has made me the worst kind of sinner. Now I have killed."

At each turn around the cell he replayed the deadly sins in his mind—lust for Mei-li and Constance, gluttonous living in foreign compounds, greed in his quest for money, pride at impressing partners, coveted luxury he'd seen, and stolen squeeze. He'd lied to Constance, to Cunningham, to Kung, to Brown, even to Meto, white lies, big lies, selfish lies, prideful lies. His Bible lay deep in a trunk unread since his early days, prayers rarely used except in times of danger. He confessed, "I forgot family and God, I killed, I stole, I lied, and I coveted another man's wife. I felt excited, not revolted. I've become a sick person. I don't want to be what I've become."

The room stank. He heard only silence.

"They say life passes before you before you die," he muttered. "Is that what's happening?"

A rat crept out onto the floor, grinned at him, and snickered. He threw a shoe at it. The rat peered up at him, as if to say, "Bet you can't hit me." Richard retrieved the shoe and threw it again. The rat stepped aside. "Damn you. Get out of here." He rushed at the rat, which scurried to one side. It bared its teeth; Richard heard a hiss, then stepped toward it and kicked. The blow sent the rat splat against the stones. It fell stunned. Richard picked up a loose rock and crushed its skull.

He walked away and tried to peer out the little window at a darkening sky. Storm clouds covered the sun. He put his shoe back on and thrust the dead rat into the corner. With his toe he shoved it aside and drilled with his toe to dig an opening in the dirt deep enough to bury it. The rat had to be tamped in. He scuffed up more dirt from the pile he had made for shit, covered the animal, then stamped it. Again and again and again.

"I have become a killer," he confessed out loud some more. He sat down on the floor, in a corner diagonally across as far as he could, but not far enough, from the dead rat in its grave. He held his head in his hands. Heathen death that had once horrified him now meant nothing. He cried, "What has this hell-bound land done to me? Why did I stay in this miserable country?" He closed his eyes. "Why?"

FIRST THING IN the next morning, Apun watched the Chen Lan Taotai sling a scowl at his clerk, a scowl he had come to bestow on anyone who bothered him, and then he regarded Apun with the same scowl.

Apun ignored the customary formalities of respect. "Honorable Chen Lan, you know employer, American Richard Starr. He help Chen Lan Taotai with new revenue with dock and business."

"Why interrupt? What hurry?"

"Emperor order that barbarian not be interfered with."

"Yes, yes, I know all that. Why you here?"

"No see Richard Starr for three days. Taotai responsible for foreigners might know what detain Starr. If Starr in criminal activity, I want know."

"Know nothing about Starr."

"If Chinese official capture Starr, must turn over to foreign authority. Starr only American authority in Hankow. You know foreigner must go to foreign official. Local magistrate maybe not know this. You help free him. He return to make money for Taotai."

"Where is Starr? Tell me what happen before I help."

Apun produced from his magic sleeve a half package of opium and set it on the Taotai's desk. Chen Lan pretended to ignore it. Apun said, exaggerating, "I have report that army recruit from Wuchang in Hankow, make trouble," and, having no evidence of it, he gratuitously added, "Soldiers look for harass barbarians."

Apun caught the Taotai's longing look at the package, a look suggesting a habit, perhaps induced by his official position. "Soldiers harass Starr before," Apun said, his expression calm but firm.

The Taotai glanced at the opium again and said, "I no authority. Hangyan Prefect across Yan River have authority over army men that break law in Hankow."

Apun thought that word from the Taotai would help persuade any official. "Please sign official chop to introduce me. Say Emperor order no one interfere with foreigner. Say to release Starr."

The Taotai wrote the chop with official flourishes everything that Apun had asked for and sealed it with an imperial seal. Apun pushed the opium across the desk. Chen Lan stifled a smile, took the half-package, pulled out a drawer, and placed the chop he had just written inside it. Apun started, reached out. "Wait, need scroll now."

"I must first have permission from Peking. I seek instruction in the morning."

RICHARD BROODED ALL the morning of day four. His stomach growled, and he could only manage twenty push-ups. He walked and walked and replayed. When he had entered the Tiger's Mouth, he had wanted to go to China. In three years, China, like a ravenous tiger, had devoured his morals.

"Now I want out," he shouted. "Out of jail. Out of Hankow. Out of China. Home before I go out of my mind." Enough with heathen people he couldn't understand. Enough with the partners. He sat again. *Money, lies, squeeze, bribes—no more! What have they done for me?*

He jumped up and yelled, "A damned dark dirt prison."

If he ever got out, he would not stay in China. Apun and Webb didn't need his help. They didn't even know where he was. He was dependent on the merciless Chinese to let him out, and they'd rather put his head on a pike. They didn't care whether he lived or died. They only wanted money from him. So did the partners. If he ever became a partner he'd still share most of his work with the others, and he'd remain a greedy, immoral person for no good purpose. "I will leave this miserable place." That was a promise.

Replaying and reaffirming his promise consumed the day. As soon as he finished a good meal, he would hand Cunningham his resignation. At night he tried to blank his mind so he could sleep and repeated the prayer, "God, forgive me my sins," over and over and over until sleep came.

APUN'S MAGIC SLEEVE had produced the other half of the opium package, and the opium produced the scroll, and armed with the chop from the Emperor's official responsible for treatment of foreigners, Apun returned to the house. Webb had had no luck finding any clue to where Richard might be.

"A report in magistrate's file. Soldiers harass merchants in Hankow that night," Apun told Webb and Ma-Wei as they sat before a small meal of Chinese finger food. None of them felt much like eating.

"If soldiers had come over from Wuchang," Webb said, "we must go there to look for him. As soon as we can tomorrow."

In the morning, Apun and Webb dressed to impress the military leaders they would have to find and strode to the dock to hail a water taxi to take them across the Yangtze. No boatmen were waiting for a fare. Webb walked in circles and then stood shifting from one foot to another for fifteen minutes while no sampan came within hailing distance, so they walked, almost trotting, along a lane paralleling the Yangtze to a landing used by the Chinese. By the time they had stepped onto a sampan with a surly but well-paid boatman, nearly the entire morning had been wasted. They crossed the river, climbed the bank, hurried several blocks in the direction of a bored sentry, and at last entered the military gates.

Apun asked a few questions that Webb did not understand and led the way to an office that Webb supposed was an officer of the day. Apun spoke to the man, a clean-shaven, heavy-set man, sitting at a desk. After a few words to Apun and a scowl to Webb, he rose to usher them out of his office.

"He say he know nothing. Soldiers go to Hankow all time."

"So what now?"

"We go to general."

The general, obviously perturbed by the interruption of something far more important than a demanding merchant and a *fanqui*, looked up when the orderly, a silver coin richer, opened his door. More Chinese talk, then they were again ushered out of the frowning, angry presence.

"Well?" Webb's impatience showed.

"He say he hear some time soldiers make trouble for civilian. But no punish unless come back late. Civilian people afraid of soldier. He say that good."

"What about Richard?"

"He not know about Starr."

"Is there someone else who might know? A military policeman?"

"We look more."

By the time the sun began to set and the light grew darker, they had walked the entire base, tried to recognize any soldiers they had seen before, bribed for information, showed the official chop, talked to more officers, and learned nothing. More coins hired a boatman back to their Hankow dock.

CHINESE MURMURING OUTSIDE his door on day five. He sat up sharply and yelled, "Who's there? What's going on? Help me. I'm hungry."

Noises at the door. He looked at it. A dirty hand reached around the door, placed a small bowl of rice on the dirt floor and retreated. The hand returned with a cup of water, spilled a dark spot in the dirt, and set it down. He leapt up to stick his foot in the opening but wobbled and had to put a hand on the wall to steady himself. Richard had not reacted fast enough. The door slammed shut. He might have knocked over the water or stepped into the rice if he had lunged to get his foot in the door. He seized the bowl. His fingers stuffed the dry, dusty, sticky rice into his mouth, and he savored it as if it was the finest dinner in New York City. It was gone in an instant, consumed by his frantic chewing and washed down with the brown water.

Nourished, he walked around the cell, then broke into a jog, lapping the space several times, then the other direction, again and again until boredom set in. Back in his corner, he sat with nothing to do. No rat, no spider today, only the gray sky out the window. He wanted to cry, but Meto believed men do not cry. His head dropped onto his knees; he clutched his legs, choked a sob, and tried to relax.

Then he remembered to mark the wall, now with four marks—fourth day now, five nights passed. That done, he sat again and stretched his legs out. Another whole day to pass. He exercised, he paced, and he tried to sleep. "This is it. This is going to be my last home on earth." After an eternity, night fell again and with it the agonizing effort to fall asleep.

50

DAY FIVE BEGAN with a scratch on the wall and silence around Richard. The morsel in his stomach the day before made him even hungrier. He stared back at the door that seemed to hold hope for another feeding, sat on his board bed for a while, and then lay on his back, staring at the ceiling, his thoughts numb. The overhead boards held nothing interesting to break the torpor.

Presently, a centipede crept into his stare. A hundred stubby legs carried its heavy body slowly trudging, navigating the splinters, determined on a mission to somewhere. He followed it with his eyes all the way to the stone wall, and there, fixed to a stone, mission apparently accomplished, the bug stopped. *Was this his own destiny, too,* Richard thought, *trudging an inhospitable road to nowhere?*

"Good luck, little centipede. I know what you feel, trudging too long. Time comes to stop."

He closed his eyes, hoping to sleep, knowing he would not. The day wore on. Should he bother to keep exercising? Yes. For now. He started around the room. "Will Webb and Apun ever find me?" Around again. He only could do half as many push-ups as yesterday. Back around the other way. Lay back down. The board was beginning to be comfortable. He closed his eyes. *I'm hallucinating. Talking to bugs.*

He heard voices, Chinese voices, louder than before.

"Food! Rice! I'm hungry," he shouted and jumped up. A chain rattled, scraping and clinking of keys, and the door swung open.

A burly Chinaman in a dark blue merchant's robe stood in the doorway smiling a sly smile.

Apun carried a bowl of rice. Speechless, Richard took it with both hands, swallowing it all in big mouthfuls. Apun spoke to the jailer and guard behind him. Webb stood in the hall outside the cell and greeted Richard with a hearty handshake and a broad smile. Richard grinned, said "Webb!" and stifled tears of relief.

They led Richard to the magistrate, the same man Richard had faced six nights before. More Chinese talk, papers passed hands, the magistrate signed, and Richard and Apun walked out onto the street. Richard squinted in the sunlight. "Thank you. Thank you. I was not sure I'd ever see you again. Never so pleased. Where are we?"

"Hangyan."

"How did you find me? How did you get me out? Why did they hold me?"

"Later we tell. Now home and good food."

Richard sat at the dining table set with roast beef, noodles, turnips, and wine. Apun and Webb watched him gorge, and Ma-Wei made sure the servants kept the plates full.

"We guessed that you might have run into soldiers that recognized you from earlier tussles with them," Webb said. Apun then told about their search in Wuchang, how he and Webb crossed the Han to the prefecture in Hangyan, sought one magistrate after another, worked their way, dispensing silver and opium as necessary, using the Taotai's imperial chop, and finally discovered the official who had ordered Richard jailed. The offense had been murder, and the magistrate intended to leave Richard there, feeding him occasionally. The magistrate claimed that not interfering with foreigners meant not to torture them, but to leave them alone, as he had done. Apun and his bribes convinced the magistrate that the Emperor's wrath would hold him responsible for violating the imperial order, and persuaded him that Americans would punish the prisoner severely. The official had pardoned all offenses, looked satisfied to be rid of the problem, and was happy with the opium.

Richard told them his story, cleaned up, changed into his casual blue trousers and white shirt, and relaxed. He soon fell asleep, stomach full, and free among friends.

"How can I thank you?" Richard asked them often for several days thereafter.

WHEN A PACKAGE of dispatches and reports from Russell & Co. arrived, he took it and returned to his desk. His heart leapt when he read the first sentence in a letter addressed to him from Cunningham. "I am pleased to inform you that the partners of Russell & Co. have proposed to offer you a partnership, effective January 1, 1864."

He blinked and shook his head. He read Cunningham's letter again. Yes, it was there. He was to be a partner.

Cunningham wanted him to go to San Francisco to promote the firm's business. He suggested that he then should travel to New York and Boston, where he could meet partners and sign the partnership agreement. He could go home for a deserved vacation. The letter included an invitation from Mr. and Mrs. Cunningham to stay with them in Shanghai as soon as he could arrange to be away from Hankow.

IN THE JAIL, Richard had decided to leave China at the soonest opportunity and forget about the partnership he had chased for nearly four years. He did not want to return to the business that had transformed him for the worse. He had planned to leave Hankow and China as soon as he could with the Russells' steamer, *Huquong,* expected to leave for Shanghai a week after his release, but he had not told anyone this plan. He now revealed his thoughts to Webb and Apun and absorbed their surprise and their questions.

When he had persuaded them of his resolve, he pointed out the risks he would leave them with, and the possible reactions the partners may have to methods they had used that partners might view as cheating or even criminal.

Apun admitted that for years he had been doing everything for himself. "Russell & Co. know I squeeze trades. Let me squeeze to get business." He was not concerned.

Webb responded. "I knew the risks when I took them. If Cunningham finds out, I may be fired. I wouldn't mind going home either."

"I am being allowed to go home," Richard said. "I might well decline to accept the partnership and not return to China at all." He had no debt now. He had available savings.

Richard wrote Meto to anticipate when he'd arrive. She would be delighted that he was to be a partner, so he said nothing about his thought not to return to China. He then wrote Cunningham that he appreciated the partnership offer and a vacation at home. He hesitated about the invitation to stay with them. Then, it struck him—it must have been Constance's idea to invite him. Repeating his resolve to sin no more, he accepted the invitation.

Before leaving he had to withdraw his savings from Kung's bank. He trotted on Brutus to the Merchants Bank, saddlebags draped over the horse's shoulders ready to carry ingots and coins.

As they rounded the corner to the bank, he heard voices shouting. A crowd filled the street, pushing, yelling, and shoving each other; some raised angry fists, and some threw rocks at the bank. Window glass broke. He recalled a similar scene in New York four years ago.

"A raid on the bank? It looks like the bank has failed!" Richard said aloud.

Kung would flee at the first sign of trouble, he thought. Where was Kung? He galloped back to the house.

Expecting that Kung would resist his claim for a large withdrawal, he loaded and strapped on his revolver and secured Webb to help and to get his own deposit. He took Ma-Wei to translate and handle bulldog Jack. He called a muscular coolie, See Kwan, to intimidate Kung if necessary and to help carry heavy coins and ingots.

Immediately, the four raced the horses to the house Richard had seen once when he delivered opium to Kung. They soon pulled up before Kung's walled compound. They dismounted, tied the horses, ran to the heavy gate, and pounded. Inside, a horse whinnied, Richard heard Chinese voices and bumping and scraping sounds—no way to see over the walls. Webb took out his revolver. See Kwan found a stave and banged hard. No one inside responded.

As See Kwan backed away to ram at the gate, it opened slowly. A coolie slipped out, shut it behind him, and stepped aside to relieve himself. See Kwan immediately pushed through a small opening, and they all slipped inside the gate and shut it behind them. See Kwan replaced the bar.

Inside Kung's compound, relays of coolies hurried as they loaded three timbered wagons with Kung's belongings. Horses in the wagons' stays snorted and pawed the ground. Furniture was stacked on one wagon; bales, bags, boxes, and trunks filled another. Nearest the gate, the third wagon remained partially filled with boxes, trunks, furniture, and rolled rugs. A coolie held a tarpaulin covering half the wagon, ready to pull it over all.

Where was the money? In which wagon? Maybe it had been loaded first, and disguised in the furniture? In the boxes and trunks? Richard thought Kung would stay with the money.

Richard walked past the partially loaded wagon nearest the gate as he scanned the yard looking for Kung. Two workers seemed to strain with the weight of a wooden box as they lifted it onto the wagon and drew the tarpaulin over it. That's silver or gold, Richard surmised.

A stocky thug stepped in front of him. He said something stern in Chinese. Richard demanded Kung Loong.

"Kung no here." The man spoke Pidgin.

Webb leveled his revolver. To Ma-Wei, he said, "Tell him to lead us to his master now."

Ma-Wei spoke firmly, See Kuan shoved the man, and, under threat of the revolver, the thug led them into the house. Keeping the man with them, Richard, Webb, and Ma-Wei searched empty ground-floor rooms.

Webb said, "Let's take the money. Why do we need Kung?"

"I want him," Richard said. "He deserves a lesson."

Silks and hangings no longer decorated Kung's walls. Furniture was gone. Richard opened doors and slammed them on empty rooms until he reached the back of the house. *Find Kung somehow.* He opened the back room door.

Kung looked up from stuffing a trunk and glared wide-eyed at Richard. He was dressed in rumpled, dirty blue trousers and a jacket, like a common worker. A flat coolie's hat lay nearby.

"Why you here?" Panic or fright fought with anger across Kung's face. He slammed the trunk lid and glared at Richard. It was not an act.

"Don't let Kung talk or signal his servants," Richard said. Apun relayed the order to Ma-Wei and See Kwan, who made sure Kung's thug understood that the command applied to him too. Staring back at Kung, Richard scowled, "I have come for my deposit. Gold and coin now."

"Impossible. No money."

"You have money. Your bank was full of it." Richard's voice barked.

"Bank no open," Kung said. "Money not here."

"If you do not return my money to me, I will take you to my house, and you will stay there. If you call for help, I will shoot you … in self-defense."

Kung barked. "*Zou.* Leave now. *Zou.*"

"You will not leave Hankow until you pay me." Ma-Wei translated to be sure Kung understood. See Kwan grabbed Kung's arm, twisted, and turned him around to face Richard's revolver.

They marched outside pushing Kung and the brute before them. The brute carried Kung's trunk. See Kwan steered Kung by jerking his arm. Richard and Webb followed with pistols drawn, Ma-Wei held the leash, and Jack nipped at Chinese heels. Servants in the yard stopped their work and gaped at the procession.

Kung shouted something in Chinese. Instantly See Kwan turned and hit Kung in the mouth. The blow silenced the seething banker except for a curse. "He say keep working," said Ma-Wei, but his expression suggested that Kung had really said, "Kill them." The servants stood still, their eyes on the revolvers. Four workmen stepped forward, one holding a sword. Others crowded behind them.

Richard raised his revolver and, at Richard's prompt, Ma-Wei shouted in Chinese, "Your master go with us. Stop or *fanqui* shoot you."

Richard fired into the air. Kung's workers backed away. Richard and See Kwan guarded Kung, and Richard ordered, "Tell this thug to put the trunk in the wagon." Ma-Wei told the thug. Jack growled. The thug did as he was told.

See Kwan forced Kung into the wagon, bound Kung's hands behind his back, and tied his legs to cleats next to the driver's seat with sailor's knots that Richard had taught him would tighten when pulled. Ma-Wei leashed Jack in the back, where he stood growling at Kung. Webb opened the gate, and stood by their four horses. Richard seized the reins and climbed up to drive the two horses.

Richard shouted and slapped hard with the reins. The horses jumped, and in lurching steps Richard, See Kwan, and Kung raced out the gate in the loaded wagon. Webb and Ma-Wei gathered their four horses, mounted two, led Brutus and Cicero, and followed the wagon toward the Russell house.

Avoiding busy streets, they had driven eight blocks in silence, when Kung said, "You kidnap me?"

"Yes. You'll stay in Hankow until I have my money. I trusted you. I should have known better." Richard scolded Kung. "You have cheated and ruined people. You planned to steal my money from the beginning." Kung's expression showed only fury.

They rode for about ten more minutes, when Kung turned and confronted Richard. Richard kept his distance, eyes focused on the road.

"You have my money now," Kung growled. "In wagon. Take me back."

Richard halted the horses. "We stay right here."

Webb and Ma-Wei rode up. Richard pulled back the tarpaulin, uncovering Kung's trunk and several small boxes. Webb opened one of the boxes. Richard beheld lead weights for a scale. Kung had lied. Richard glared at him, his expression saying, "Don't lie to me."

Had they taken the wrong wagon? "Open another box," Richard ordered Webb. His worry showed in his voice, and he tensed, sick that they had missed money but for Kung's trunk.

A second box gleamed with gold ingots. Relief surged through Richard. His savings were nicely packed for him. Webb inspected the contents and counted the ingots, estimating the value. A third box, filled with silver coins, added to the rest and satisfied Richard and Webb that they had all their money. Kung's trunk also held more gold and silver, and perhaps more stayed on the wagon. Ma-Wei and Richard put their money boxes into the saddlebags on Brutus.

"Now take me back," growled Kung, still steaming and angry. He must have been worrying that his workers were looting his goods. Richard swung the wagon around while See Kwan and Webb's revolver guarded Kung. The horses turned slowly. Richard let them rest, while Kung blew off curses in a tirade half in English and half in Chinese. Webb, on Brutus with the money, and Ma-Wei on Cicero leading the two empty horses, rode a little way toward the Russells' house and stopped. The wagon headed back toward Kung's house with the remainder of the bank's money, and Kung quieted, still well tied.

Two blocks later, Richard, the horses walking slowly, turned the wagon off the street and away from Kung's house.

"Where you take me?" Kung said, surprise and horror in his voice.

"Back where you belong."

Richard drove the wagon toward the Hankow Merchants Bank, and Kung began to squirm. Soon he yanked, he pulled, he hollered Chinese invectives. He screamed, "*Bu Shi! Bu Shi!*— No. No." Jack barked at him. See Kwan unleashed Jack but held him away from Kung. The rioters at the bank came into view. The wagon neared the bank. Kung hunched down to hide, and reached for the tarpaulin as if he wanted to crawl under it.

Richard whipped the horses and shouted to excite them. They picked up the pace and ran until they galloped hard toward the fiery crowd. The distance closed. The wagon's momentum was unstoppable.

Ten yards from the mob, Richard called, "Jump!"

Richard and See Kwan hit the ground and rolled. Jack dove away, and the wagon, money, and Kung charged into the mob. The crowd parted when the charge hit. The horses slowed, the crowd swarmed the wagon, and men climbed onto it. It rocked. Wrathful men tore at the tarpaulin. Kung flailed while they cut his bonds; the wagon tipped over, and Kung tumbled into the mob.

51

RICHARD PASSED OUT bonuses to Webb, Ma-Wei, and See Kwan, and a steak for Jack. Apun greeted them with smiles at their success, and they told him the tale of Kung's bank. Over the next few days, Richard picked out some books, the photo of Meto, his Bible, writing material, and clothes to go into his luggage. The Bible his mother had given him lay in the bottom of a drawer, covered with clothes. He decided to pack it where he could easily read it again on his journey home. His houseboy finished packing the trunks and boxes with more clothes, souvenirs, and articles such as a small statue of a tiger and a jade incense burner. Richard's cash savings were packed in tea and hidden in square wooden boxes with shipping labels.

Apun and Webb continued business as usual. "Take care of the account books, Webb," said Richard. "You and Apun can carry on as you wish until Cunningham has other ideas."

Richard treated his staff and the Canton coolies to bonuses from Kung's money and a farewell meal beginning with wontons and fried vegetable rolls, followed by roast beef and local duck, Chinese style. Everyone fished with chopsticks and forks in bowls filled with smoked fish, peppers, noodles, and squashes, and washed everything down with as much French wine and *sake* as they could hold.

At a closing toast with the last of the *sake*, Richard said, "Thank you all for helping me in Hankow." He turned to each. "I wish you success in the future."

He embarked for Shanghai and California the next morning.

RICHARD STOPPED AT Cunningham's office in Shanghai to say that he had arrived, that he appreciated everything, and that he was ready to help where he could. Cunningham congratulated him on making partner.

"Thank you. I'm pleased. I will contact the partners when I get home."

He stored his luggage and then headed out to the Cunninghams' house with his duffel bag.

Constance said, "So good to see you. Do come in. Your trip was uneventful, I hope? Do you have any more luggage? I'll show you to the room we have arranged for you."

Constance chattered on and took his arm to walk together up the stairs. She did not let him talk at all, it seemed. The boy unpacked his duffel and then left the room.

"Close the door," Constance said.

She sat on the four-poster bed while Richard changed his travel clothes in the washroom.

"I need to get a shirt from the bureau," he called.

"Come on out," Constance said, "I don't mind." She remained sitting on the bed.

He emerged wearing only trousers and a tight undershirt that outlined his lean muscles. She had pulled up her skirts and revealed a beautifully curved calf hung over her knee. Patting next to her on the bed, she said, "Our time in Nagasaki was very special, wasn't it?"

"It certainly was," he said, joining her on the bed.

"Edward won't be back until five o'clock," she said. She placed her smooth hand on his thigh.

They kissed on full lips, embraced, and fell back onto the bed. "I can't do this!" Richard said.

She fondled him and stroked his thigh. "Yes, you can. How about Nagasaki?"

Richard stood up from the bed, his groin tight. "No. I promised myself after Nagasaki. You are married. That was wrong. This is wrong."

"You scoundrel!" she said with a smile, her eyes laughing. "That Chinese girl was too good for you." She reached toward him. "Come back to me."

She was right about Mei-li. In Nagasaki he had found Constance soft, not firm; pasty white, not as enticing as the golden skin; passionate, but not physical. It was wrong to be with her, wrong to cuckold his boss, wrong to risk being caught, wrong to sin, and wrong to explain to her any more. He shook his head and left her sitting on the bed.

When Edward returned, Constance's charm and perfect hospitality continued as usual. That evening at dinner, she acted as if time had obscured his rejection of her as well as their Nagasaki dalliance. Constance was so natural with him in public and her private aggression was so hidden that the formalities once gripping him with proper Annie and Dora seemed ridiculous now. Constance's perfect act as a dutiful and obedient wife left him convinced that Edward would never know what he had done. He only felt the pleasure of her beauty and charm. And missed Mei-li.

The next morning, he returned to the Baptist Mission for another visit. Little Grace, now a precocious and adorable toddler, approached with her matron. Grace shied away from his effort to reach to her. "She has no idea who I am," he said to Rev. Whipple.

"No, I expect she doesn't remember."

"No, and I'm sad about that, but she is well. It's probably best." Richard gave her a spinning top, and showed her how it worked, but she just watched it slow, topple over, and lay on the floor. Richard stood and regarded her a few moments, and when she cautiously picked it up, he turned to Whipple. He thanked the Reverend again for taking her in and promised that he would send money to help Grace and the orphanage. Whipple smiled.

"I want to see Mei-li."

Accompanied by Peter Liu, Mei-li came to see him, looking as beautiful as ever, but dressed modestly in bright slacks, and a loose red blouse, a high collar covering her neck. Rev. Whipple stepped away from them.

"Mei-li, it is good to see you looking well," Richard said. "Are you happy here?" Peter translated for her.

"*Gaoxing.* Happy. *She de,*" she said, and her eyes met Peter's. She said in a proud tone, "Yes."

Richard told her that he would be leaving China and would miss her. When Peter had translated, she wrapped her arms around Richard, kissed him, held him, and said, "Good-bye, Lei-cha." A tear ran down her smooth cheek.

"Good-bye, Mei-li."

He could say no more. He watched her look back at him as she walked from the room.

Whipple stepped to him. "Thank you for the gift you promised. Your help will further God's work with Grace and others." Richard parted from the mission and his two Chinese girls.

He spent time with Augustus, who updated him about imperial and foreign mercenary troop victories over the Taiping rebels, and they settled accounts over their joint ventures in trades. Augustus also hoped to leave China the next year, and they celebrated each other's successes and prospects. Cunningham and Grew gave him instructions, suggestions, and letters of introduction for business in California. Cunningham said he was busy with the Shanghai Steam Navigation Company and for the time being would leave operations in Hankow with Webb and Apun.

After Constance's formal farewell kiss on his cheek, good wishes, good-byes from the partners, and Augustus's hearty handshake, Richard left for San Francisco.

FIFTY DAYS OUT of Shanghai, tide and wind slipped the *Emily Banning* past the high and rocky Fort Point, where soldiers could be seen drilling, and on into the narrow strait that led into beautiful San Francisco Bay. The *Emily Banning* soon anchored among a fleet of international vessels loading riches and unloading passengers, immigrants, and supplies. Richard saw his trunks to the four-story Occidental Hotel. Shops, homes, hotels, railroads, and ships, were being built everywhere in the city. The only currency was gold or silver, and everything was expensive. "A fine and thriving city," he wrote Meto.

An earthquake, a saloon fire, a bowie knife killing, a riot among Irish and Chinese laborers, watered stock in railroad and mining companies, and a departing steam clipper to Baltimore carrying $2 million worth of gold showed Richard that lucrative mayhem prevailed in California. Late news of Union victories over the Confederacy at Vicksburg and Gettysburg reminded him that the war was still going on in the East.

For the next two weeks, Richard rode with Frederick Macondray, whose father he had met in Shanghai, to Marin Sulphur Springs, Almaden quicksilver mines, and several large ranches to discuss exporting hides and minerals. Along the way, they partied and danced with Mexican girls and bought fans, shawls, textiles, leather belts, holsters, and shoes for resale. Richard could have stayed in California longer, but home pulled him East, and he sent a final report to Cunningham. He soon strode up the gangway onto the three-masted clipper *Golden Age* and began the voyage to Panama, where he would take the railroad to the Atlantic and board another ship to New York.

52

New York had changed from the city he left—just as crowded and hot, but commercial buildings and upper-class homes had expanded northward. He stepped from the cab in front of his home on Twelfth Street and stood still, aghast, his mouth open. The driver had to jar him to remember his fare. The front door was unlocked and hung angled off its hinges. A smashed window was open to the street. Richard entered a broken and ravaged house, filthy, with discolored and marred places on the wall. Inside, he saw an upside-down table, ripped rugs, curtains torn, and drawers opened and dumped. The place looked unlivable. He pushed aside hands full of stuffing, sat down on a torn chair and stared blankly.

Neighbors told him that Irish and other immigrants rioting over armed Negroes and Lincoln's draft had vandalized the area, and they had ended up raging at upper-class privilege. Nothing Richard could do about their home now, except board up the windows and get the door repaired and locked. Meto must be staying at her sister Sarah Lee's home in Massachusetts, as she often did when she left the city for the summer. Perhaps she had gone there for the duration of the war. Traveling by railroad up beside the Hudson River and by stage over the Berkshire Hills, Richard reached Lenox village, alighted on the main street, and walked to Aunt Lee's house.

Meto immediately burst into tears. She and Sarah Lee stared and stared at Richard.

During the first week of his visit, Meto repeated for the umpteenth time, "You have changed. You look well. It is good to have you home. We need you." Richard reciprocated compliments. She said that she had not been in New York during the draft riots. She looked tired, and he saw gray in her hair. Yes, she's aged, he thought.

Over the following days they talked often of his success at Russell & Co., and of the war difficulties at home. "Oh, Richard, this war is doing frightful things," she told him. "The city is too dangerous for us. Everyone has left the city. Our house is ruined. We had to sell The Pines ... our farm is no longer ours." Tears welled up as she listed her troubles, reaching for Sarah's hand to hold her own. "Etta's fiancé was killed at Gettysburg. She is still in mourning. William has left Newport, and I worry much about him in the navy," she said. "He has just been assigned to the *Hartford*."

"I'm here to help with anything that I can," Richard said.

"I'm sure you want to see some old friends," Meto said during the third week. "Now that you have been home awhile, I have arranged a dinner for you and invited the Schemerhorns and De Peysters of New York. Planning a party seemed to boost her spirits. "You will enjoy it. Ann Schemerhorn will be a delightful dinner companion for you."

Miss Ann Schemerhorn, prim, with a long nose and the posture of a beanpole, conversed in platitudes, and Richard enjoyed talking across her to his college friend, Ed De Peyster, who had married his old "dear," Annie Wiley. Annie could not dine with them, Ed said, as she was with child and resting. Richard learned that Will Forbes had married Dora Delano, but Ed said that the frail Dora had died last winter from an ague caused when Will insisted on leaving the window open at night. When Richard asked about war service, Ed boasted with a proud smile that he had avoided army conscription by paying the $300 commutation fee.

Following another arranged dinner and visits to friends now married, he realized how little he had in common with former friends. They had moved on with husbands and wives, fought, or helped in the war. Some were strong Union patriots, like Richard, and some, like Ed, were not. All seemed to have comfortable lives and continual social obligations.

Richard tried to identify ways to help his mother. The New York house could be sold or repaired when the war was over. Meto did live well in Lenox with her society friends. Now full-grown, Willie and Etta had left home, but her regret when children leave couldn't be helped. The war had caused her worries, but she had excellent food and shelter. He might continue living with her, but that would not help end the war. Nor could he bring Willie and Etta to her, or make additional money.

One day, Richard happened to mention to Meto that he had arranged that money be sent regularly to the Baptist Mission in Shanghai.

Her eyes popped open. "Baptist?"

"Yes,"

"Why?"

"I feel obliged."

"Obliged? How? Are you not obliged to keep money here for the family?"

"I saved the life of a young baby girl who lives there now."

Horror showed all over her face. "Richard Starr! What have you done? Is this your child?"

"No! How could you think that?" He had not expected that reaction. "She faced a life in poverty, so I made sure she'd be cared for. She'll get a Christian upbringing as well. It was the only orphanage."

"The heathens have changed you. You're like them." Voice raised, tears coming. "How could you?"

"Mother, I won't argue. I am determined to help support the mission. Your scruples won't stop me." He had been "like them," and came home to leave them. Now he realized that in other ways he was a changed person at home, too. Richard thought that she'd never understand.

She burst into tears and could say no more.

A few more days produced another strong argument. He wanted to begin gently, but it was impossible. "Meto. I know you have been pleased that I have been offered a partnership in Russell & Co. I have to tell you that I am thinking about not accepting that offer."

Shock mixed with disappointment spread over her whole being. "You do not want it?"

"No, I do. But I don't want to go back to China."

"You cannot mean that. You have worked hard for the partnership. Everyone at the club expects you to be a partner next year."

He expected this argument. "I really do not care what everyone at the club thinks."

"What will your father think?"

"He will understand. The China trade is not what it used to be. Only opium makes money, and I do not choose to trade it, like father did." He spoke in haste.

She turned sharply to him and spoke vehemently, "Your father did not trade in opium."

She didn't know. His father had not only profited from the odious drug but had lied to hide it from his wife. The concern that surfaced when Richard received the first letter about opium now returned, further ruining his reverence for the man he had once admired from afar. *Father had become a man that I do not want to be.*

"Well, opium's about the best way to make money now. New banking practices and Chinese competition have changed everything."

"You deserve to be a partner. Don't give that up. Think of your future. You should not be anything less."

"I am thinking of my future. I am not the kind of person to do that work."

"You should finish what you started."

"I am finished with China."

Giving her time to adjust to the idea, he explained in successive conversations. "You are right that I have become like the heathens in some ways. I do not like myself when I'm living among them—the constant fighting and cheating and death. China is nothing like the colorful, romantic place I once imagined. Plus, the luxury at Russell & Co. is unnecessary and corrupting. I promised myself not to return, and I will keep my word."

Her entreaties reaffirmed his resolve. China had ruined his moral sense. He needed his integrity back. One day he pulled a chair up to the writing desk. He sat forward, ramrod straight, arms on the table, and took a deep breath. Then he reached forward, found stationary, picked up the pen, opened the ink, and wrote "Dear Messrs. Forbes, et al ..." He included customary polite preliminaries, expressed appreciation for their invitation, and concluded, "I choose not to become a partner. Thank you all very much."

That night, he said to Meto, "I have done it."

Resignation in her voice, she said, "The decision must be yours. I'm glad you will be in America, at least."

"Our civil war will eventually end with or without the rebel southern states in the Union," Richard said. "Then new business opportunities will open here, in the West, and in California. Railroads will spread over the country. Promoters are raising money for a railroad over the mountains to California; others are selling shares in a mining company in the Nevada Territory. There will be many business and real estate opportunities here.

"Meto, I know it will take time to rebuild a career, to find a New York home, and, as President Lincoln said, to build a new nation. You are comfortable here; you have friends; there is natural beauty here and society for you. The social life you live is not for me. Some of my friends are married. They are living quiet lives. I feel restless. I was busy and tested in China. I did like the challenges and being busy. I have energy and want more action now.

"Meto, the troubles you feel, I understand. In the end, they are all caused by the war. The best way I can help you and our family is to do what I can to help end the war."

At the end of August, Richard left Lenox, rode to Springfield, and enlisted in the Fourth Massachusetts Cavalry. Meto dabbed at her eyes and asked for her tea.

Afterword

INTO THE TIGER'S *Mouth* is a work of fiction based on details from the letters and reminiscences of Richard Starr Dana. Some comments from his letters have made their way into Richard's conversations and inner thoughts. Events and anecdotes have been fictionalized and embellished. Following is a brief summary of the more prominent true events and people described in the novel.

On his way to China, Dana's ship met a storm at sea, a sailor was lost overboard, and Malay natives boarded at Anjer. He attended a Fourth of July party that the Delano sisters arranged on the American ship *Hankow* off Hong Kong in 1865, not 1857. He became infatuated with Dora Delano, but her character is fictional. The Forbes and Delano families were important to Russell & Co., although the descriptions of the individuals are fictitious.

In Shanghai, Dana lived luxuriously and became a primary tea trader. Edward Cunningham was the head partner of Russell & Co., Shanghai, but his character is fiction. Although Dana once attended a singsong show with a Chinese merchant, Kung Loong, Kung's character and Richard's relationship with Kung are fictional. Dana once kidnapped an unnamed Chinese buyer to force him to pay. Hop Tzu is a fictional character, but servants to foreigners were known to spy for information on their employers, and beheading was a Chinese punishment for traitors.

The description of the Taiping rebels, imperial troops and government, British military, and American navy, and their activities in China at the time of the novel, are embellished. The Taiping attack on Shanghai and the English-French attacks at

Tagu and Peking occurred while Dana was in Shanghai. At this time he joined the volunteer corps and helped defend Shanghai and the foreign concessions against the Taiping attack. He also moved his firm's treasure to a ship and visited a joss house with Augustus Hayes, his cousin and friend also working in China.

Dana was the first Western businessman to open a trading post in the newly opened treaty port of Hankow (although some British historians dispute that Americans were first). On the Yangtze River trip to his new post on the steamboat *Scotland*, both rebel and imperial troops boarded at the same time.

The harassing attacks by soldiers, street mobs, and individuals in Hankow are related in Dana's reminiscences. He confronted thieves in his warehouse and flogged several, but did not kill anyone. He was generally healthy, though he did contract dysentery in Hankow. He recovered, not with acupuncture, but with rest in Shanghai and Nagasaki, where he stayed in a bungalow with Mrs. Edward Cunningham. Although there was a real Mrs. Edward Cunningham, her character, the affair, and the name Constance, are entirely fictitious.

Dana's writings included general remarks about Chinese people but never named any specific individuals except the one mention of Kung Loong. All Chinese characters in the book are fictitious, except that Apun, Sunchong, Ahyue, and Takee are real names. The first three were Russell & Co. compradors, while Takee (Yang Fang) was a banker. Apun was with Dana in Hankow. After Dana left, Apun was fired for embezzlement. Mei-li is entirely fictional.

Other real people in the book are treated as fictional characters. These include: Warren Delano, P. S. Forbes, Henry Grew, Webb, Captain Barrows, , and several Chinese officials and Russell employees. Simon Brown, John Blake, Rev. Whipple, Dr. Porter, Fookie Tom, and some Chinese are fictional. All references to trading opium are entirely fictitious except the general Russell & Co. and Chinese policies on opium.

Except during visits home, the Civil War was over by the time Dana returned to America.

In China, the Taiping armies were defeated by the "Ever Victorious Army" and imperial troops, and the rebellion collapsed in 1864. The imperial government remained weak under the regent Empress Dowager Cixi, who appeased the foreigners and resisted modern ideas. By 1898 antiforeign sentiment led to the Boxer rebellion, wars, and eventually to the collapse of the Manchu Qing dynasty.

After the visit home after Hankow, Dana returned to China, where he became a Russell & Co. partner and head of the rebuilt Canton house until 1868. He spent a total of ten years in China, and returned to New York weakened by intestinal problems incurred in China and continued in financial business in New York. He married Florine Turner of Connecticut, built a home and farm in Lenox, Massachusetts, and had two sons, Richard and David. He died in 1904.

Acknowledgments

I N ADDITION TO the letters and reminiscences of Richard Starr Dana, much research and many friends and professionals supported and helped me write this book.

Journals and letters about China at the time, documents of Russell & Co., and diplomatic dispatches were found in the National Archives, Laguna Nigel; the Baker Library, Harvard Business School; the Franklin Delano Roosevelt Museum & Library; the Massachusetts Historical Society; and the Peabody Essex Museum and Phillips Library. Information on the history and persons involved was found at the San Francisco Maritime Museum Library, the New York Public Library, the Columbia University Library, the Massachusetts Historical Genealogical Society, and the University of California, Irvine, Library. The courteous and helpful staffs at each of these libraries helped me track down relevant documents.

Many British and American interpretations of the complex historical events of the time have been published. Among them, William T. Rowe's two-volume *Hankow,* Yen-P'ing Hao's, *The Comprador in Nineteenth Century China,* Jacques C. Downs's *The Golden Ghetto,* and Jonathan D. Spence's *God's Chinese Son* were particularly helpful. Articles and books about opening the Yangtze to foreign trade, the Taiping rebellion, and the opium wars abound.

Nan C. Shu and the late Timothy Chang helped me with the Chinese language. Some Chinese words and phrases are from a modern tourist phrase book and dictionary. I have used the transliterations of Chinese place names that Richard Starr Dana used if they are still familiar (e.g., Peking not Beijing, Canton not Guangzhou). The late Cathleen Channing transcribed Richard Starr Dana's *Recollections and Reminiscences*, and my wife, Marcie, transcribed all his handwritten letters as I read them to her. Tim Carlsen drafted the maps.

Relatives of families in the China trade in the 1850s and 1860s graciously took the time for interviews and to send papers from their collections: Phyllis Forbes Kerr, Crosby Forbes, the late Constance (Pix) Hsia, and Bayard King. Professor Yong Chen of the University of California and Scott Lieth, acupuncturist, each shared specialized knowledge.

Philip Dana Kopper helped me to learn the book publishing business and provided some family lore and encouragement. Readers Cliff Lange, Phyllis Forbes Kerr, Rosamond Putsch, and Yong Chen added support and suggestions to the language and story. Editors Mike Sirota, Susan Wolf, and Bryna Kranzler had many suggestions, ideas, and methods to improve the final product, giving invaluable advice, constructive criticisms, and corrections. To them, and to all these friends and professionals who spent their time and used their skills to help, I am ever grateful. Especially important was my late wife Marcie's constant support, helpful comments, love, and companionship throughout.

CPSIA information can be obtained at www.ICGtesting.com
Printed in the USA
BVOW01s1341250414

351722BV00001B/1/P